THE TROUBLE WITH TWEEDLE

The Curious Case of Mary Ann, Book II

by JENN THORSON

Waterhouse Press

PITTSBURGH, PENNSYLVANIA

Published by Waterhouse Press. Pittsburgh, Pennsylvania, U.S.A.

ISBN: 979-8-9865056-0-2

Cover photography and cover design by Dave White.

Printed in the United States of America

Dedicated to anyone who's had that creative idea
in their minds but wasn't sure they should try it.
Do it. Do the idea. Try the creative thing.
Explore. Fail. Learn. Try again.
Go forth and be frabjous.

Other Books by Jenn Thorson

THE CURIOUS CASE OF MARY ANN (Book One)

THERE GOES THE GALAXY (*TGTG*, Book One)

THE PURLOINED NUMBER (*TGTG*, Book Two)

TRYFLING MATTERS (*TGTG*, Book Three)

"Tweedledum and Tweedledee
Agreed to have a battle;
For Tweedledum said Tweedledee
Had spoiled his nice new rattle.

Just then flew down a monstrous crow,
As black as a tar-barrel;
Which frightened both the heroes so,
They quite forgot their quarrel."

—Lewis Carroll,
Through the Looking-Glass and What Alice Found There (1871)

ACKNOWLEDGMENTS

It's been a few years since *The Curious Case of Mary Ann, Book One* led us all through the looking-glass to Turvy. A second tale of Mary Ann's adventures was always in my mind, if not as swiftly put to paper, and I appreciate my readers' continued support and patience as this book came to life.

I'd particularly like to thank my friend Dave White, for his photographic and design skills as applied to the frabjous *The Trouble with Tweedle* cover art. It is truly commendable the way he rallies when I show him a bag of weird, disparate items related to the story, give him a giant checkerboard background, and tell him, "Here ya go, bud! Use whatever strikes your fancy!" Everyone should have the kind of amazing creative friend who goes boldly forward when faced with a Victorian rattle, a miniature rowboat and a giant bird feather.

I also want to thank my beta readers for offering their honest perspectives on the story, taking my questions about their experience seriously, and sharing their moments of delight throughout the reading process. As a writer, the honesty is invaluable to create the best possible reading experience. And it's also unbelievable fun getting random texts from readers as they chuckle over various lines, become surprised by turn-of-events, or muse over clues. That I sometimes get to follow along in this manner is worth its weight in Burgeonboosh.

MAP OF TURVY
(FLEETINGLY)
FOR THE PURPOSES OF THIS STORY

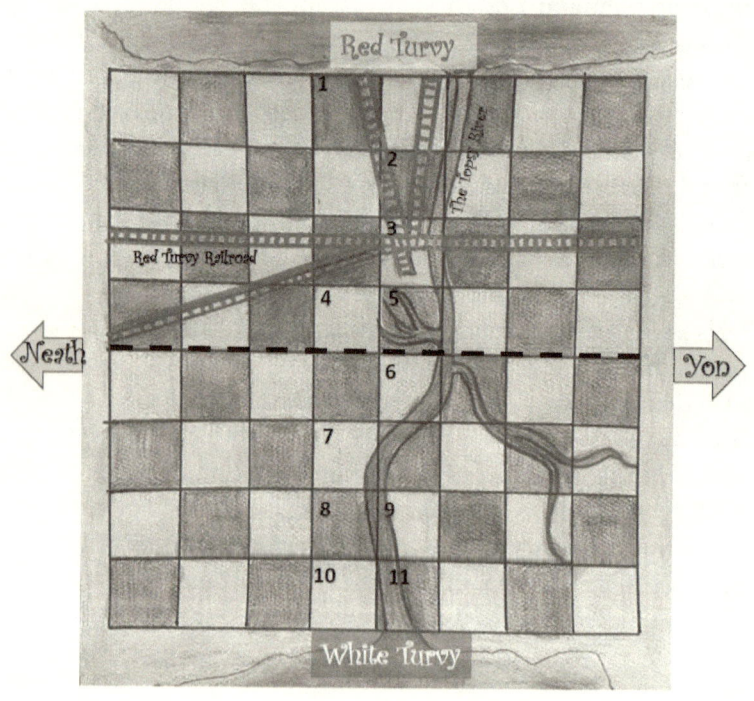

"GREAT GRYPHONS, GIRL, WHAT IS UP WITH THAT MAP?"

Chess enthusiast readers have asked me about the layout of Turvy and its Squares, trying to picture the paths the characters take on the realm's chessboard.

Here I must start by admitting an embarrassing truth: I don't know chess. Like, at all. So, from the beginning of the *Mary Ann* series, I based my topography on the literal moves the Red Queen explains to Alice in Lewis Carroll's *Through the Looking-Glass and What Alice Found There*. This means Square Three had the railway, Square Four had the Tweedles' cottage, Square Five had the store Alice visited and the river, Square Six was home to Humpty Dumpty, etc. But these are obviously not the way chess squares are actually gridded out.

Also, I did some research, and it seems that while Lewis Carroll himself claimed he had mapped Alice's journey to an actual game and included a map of this in *Looking-Glass*, people who know chess indicate it's a little dodgy. It seems that his game only works if one player takes too many sequential turns, and does that multiple times. (Sorry, Mr. Carroll, I'm only reporting what I read.)

Additionally, the plays Carroll cites in his book aren't listed the way today's chess players name the squares (in 1-8, a-h vectors). So that convention wasn't one I could follow, either.

Which is a long-winded way to say: this is Turvy and it does what it wants. Carmine Manor will always be in Square Four, but where Square Four ends up in five minutes, tomorrow or next week is anyone's guess. Following Mary Ann's very good advice, we can only embrace the madness and let it carry us along where it will. May all of your adventures be frabjous!

—Jenn Thorson

1

Mary Ann Carpenter could still feel the grip of the looking-glass on her skin, a strange suction, a gelatinous sensation that oozed and rippled down her neck, arms, and legs, well-after she'd stepped through its field into the land of Thither.

If this is what traveling by mirror is like, she thought, trying to brush the feeling from her limbs, *the system is not assured to catch on.*

She turned toward the device, hoping to catch a glimpse of the aftermath she left behind in Neath. To see Sir Rufus riding off to safety, far from the angry mob of Queen Valentina's supporters—the people Mary Ann had failed in some way.

There was Celeste, the errant Lady's Maid who had lost her position with Lady Carmine and blamed Mary Ann's influence. There was the guard Mary Ann had cold-cocked with a fire poker (twice for good measure!) to free Sir Rufus from Queen Valentina's dungeon. There was Mr. Milliner, the hatmaker, whose perpetual tea-time was inconvenienced when Mary Ann fled his employment as serving girl. And there were people Mary Ann didn't even know, swept up in the exhilarating drama of a good chase scene.

She had to admit, there was variety.

She told herself quite sensibly that, by remaining on horseback, Sir Rufus was in an excellent position to escape home to Turvy as planned. And Turvy's Red Queen, Rosamund, with her no-nonsense manner, would likely support her citizens, whether Queen Valentina of Neath liked it or not. Rufus' parents, Lord and Lady Carmine, might return home to Turvy with a somewhat tarnished reputation for their son's role in the day's events. But surely they could polish that up without facing any dangerous reprisals—couldn't they?

Mary Ann's thoughts were interrupted as a figure began to emerge from the mirror. She dodged to the side, expecting to see Rufus had made some impetuous decision to join her, his metal shoulder plates shining and ginger curls all askew. But instead, a middle-aged man in a charcoal grey suit brushed past her. He was off to work in Thither as any other day, unaware of inter-realm conflicts, the aftermath of Royal betrayals, and a series of murders solved by a housemaid very few people noticed.

Mary Ann sighed. It was just as well that Rufus carry on as planned. He needed to quest for the Vorpal sword and wrap-up his prophecy, as foretold by the epic poem that Sir Loral Clew penned so long ago. With that task done, he would finally be liberated from this burdensome obligation—one that had been set upon his shoulders before his very birth. He deserved this new freedom. She hoped that he got it.

Mary Ann decided to follow-up on Rufus' family's situation as soon as possible. If there were the slightest hint she had caused any of them problems, she would return to Turvy and make it right. But for now…

She finally got a moment to appreciate where she had arrived. Thither's foliage was awash in warm colors — deep oranges, yellows, cranberry reds, and purples. The road before her was made up of large, black rectangular tiles with white pips on them—she believed the bricks were called "dominoes." The pips were set in various numerical configurations, with the pattern on one end of the tile matching the first pattern on the next domino, and so forth, brick-by-brick. It made a rather dizzying street view, but it did give a sense of progression to the place, like following the road would ultimately reach somewhere wonderful. So, follow the road, she did.

The buildings, too, she noticed, were made up of dominoes in various colors. Her eyes fell on a new construction project that seemed to be humming along quite well, until one of the bricklayers mismatched the pips on his bricks, and a wall crumbled, dominoes tumbling onto the street below. Mary Ann made a quick note to always cross the street rather than walk under any new construction in Thither; as she hit the bricks to Cornelius Clashammer's, there was no guarantee that the bricks wouldn't hit back.

And, as for that matter, where *was* Cornelius Clashammer's school? Because he was such a renowned trainer of knights, she'd naively expected his business to be instantly prominent. But now that she'd finally gotten to Thither, she recognized that there was a whole realm before her, and there was no likelihood his operations were anywhere near the looking-glass portal she'd used.

Mary Ann wondered: what if she couldn't find the place? There was a certain amount of hurry-upishness involved in getting training from Mr. Clashhammer. Following her birthplace's fine tradition, anything done right in Turvy was done backwards—and Mary Ann's sword capabilities were no exception. While it was all very exciting to discover one was suddenly highly-skilled at sword-fighting, it was also critical to reinforce that talent straightaway with the requisite training. Failure to do so meant the ability would vanish as quickly as it arrived. In Turvy, rigorous follow-through was key!

Besides, quite a lot had already transpired that heavily depended on Mary Ann's vast sword knowledge — the successful slaying of a monster, the Jabberwock, the most central. So, as she strode down the main street in Thither, it was both anxiety and feet that propelled her forward.

Soon, she came upon a barber standing next to his striped pole. The pole's stripes were moving upward, powered by the steam pumping through them. It shot through the top of the pole like feverish breath.

What luck! she thought. *Through shear connections alone, this barber should know the school!* So she paused to address him. "Excuse me, sir? Could you tell me where Cornelius Clashammer lives?"

But alas! Silently, the barber's head swiveled on his neck in a firm, horizontal "no," as if he were steam-powered, as well. She didn't wait for him to erupt, however; she simply thanked him, her hopes vanishing like the water vapor, and moved on.

Ahead of her on the street was a well-dressed mother beagle with a row of tiny puppies trailing after her. There must have been six of them, all saucer eyes and wiggles, sniffing their way down the path. "Pardon me, madam...Could you—?"

But the lady dog looked Mary Ann up and down with a snuffle of her nose and flipped a coin at her. "That should do you, girl. Don't ask me again, mind you!"

"Oh no, madam, I—" Mary Ann smoothed the dirty pink skirt of the ill-fitting uniform she'd stolen from one of the Queen of Hearts' maids. "I was just wondering if I could talk to you about Cornelius Clashammer?"

But the answer came by way of a newspaper swat to Mary Ann's nose. "Heel! No more money! And no proselytizing!" the beagle said. "Bad girl — shoo!"

Mary Ann shooed.

It was only after two hours and a dozen inquiries that Mary Ann was rewarded for her efforts. A duck in a duckcloth suit had information that fit the bill. "You see right down there, by that lamp pole, left side?" The duck extended a wing. "It's there. Six-hundred-and-a-quarter's the address."

"Oh, thank you, sir! Thank you!" she said, starting off in the direction indicated.

"But you won't get in to see him," called the duck. "No one ever does."

"Thank you!" she shouted over her shoulder. After coming all this way, she refused to be daunted now; she was impervious to daunt. She moved as swiftly as she could, just shy of running, to the 600 block of the Thitherian city.

"Let's see ... 596 ... 598 ... 600!"

The sign said it was a tailor's.

"Perhaps next door then." She read the number on the door. Six-hundred-and-two. "Peculiar!"

Was there a door between the spaces and perhaps the place was upstairs? She surveyed the structure. No. She folded her arms and stepped back, standing on her tip-toes trying to peer in the second floor window of 600. Was that all tailoring then?

A tinny voice projected from somewhere around her. It had the echoing, distant crackle of a recording on a gramophone. "How unhumble!"

"I beg your pardon?" She looked around to determine from where this voice was emanating. She stared hard at a top-hatted man passing on the sidewalk. Possibly too hard because he blinked, flustered, and picked up his pace, like he thought she might jump him.

"Unhumble," repeated the voice. "If you want the attentions of Cornelius Clashammer, you must humble yourself before you can rise to greatness."

For the second time today, Mary Ann looked down at her oversized and rumpled uniform. She patted her half-unraveled plait and felt something crinkly in it. She came away with a leaf. She couldn't imagine how much more humble she could appear. So, she did the only thing she could think to do. She curtseyed. "I apologize to Mr. Clashammer for my arrogance," Mary Ann said.

And that is when she noticed a very small door, no bigger than a wrought iron heating grate, marked with a ¼ over the transom, with an even smaller brass plate fixed next to it. She leaned down and squinted at it. It read:

CORNELIUS CLASHAMMER
Trainer of Noble Knights
FULFILLER OF DREAMS

The Wanderlands' Premier Questing Beast Combat Expert
Including, but not Limited to: Boojums, Cyclops, Jabberwocks,
Glurbwoppels, Griffopotami, Minotaurs, Snarks, Wyverns,
and Felinus Catus
Mentor to the Tolerable
Notary Public, Chooseday and Whensday, 10am to 2pm,
by appointment

There was a tiny button to the right of the door and, underneath, another smaller metal plate with holes in it. She pressed the button. "Hello?"

"Found it, did you?" The tinny voice projected from the holey metal bit. "So, what do you want?"

"Sir, I have come all the way from Neath to see Cornelius Clashammer for sword and Jabberwock training."

"Ah, then more's the pity. Because the class is full-up. No room! No room!" said the voice.

"Oh, but sir, I clearly need to complete backwards training! I'm a housemaid who's strangely good at swordwork with no fighting experience whatsoever," said Mary Ann. "I taught Jabberwock defense to Sir Rufus, a Red Knight of Turvy, who slayed the Jabberwock as prophesized. And if don't get my backwards training all pinned down — and soon! — then how could I have trained Sir Rufus? And how could he have slayed the Jabberwock? And his prophecy will unravel, and the Jabberwock will rampage over Turvy and …"

"Did you say Jabberwock?" There was interest in the tinny voice now.

She clasped her hands before her and eyed the door hopefully. "I did."

There was a long pause. Then: "And who did you say you were?"

"I hadn't." It wasn't as if her name were exactly one to open doors. "But it's Mary Ann Carpenter."

The door opened. "Mary Ann Carpenter?" A grasshopper in a blue suit and a yellow silk waistcoat emerged through the door. He was speaking to her through a megaphone. "Is it that time in Turvy? We've been expecting you for ages now. We'd given up all hope."

She blinked. "Ages?"

"Oh yes, Thither's ahead of its time, you understand."

"I'm afraid I *don't* understand."

"No need to be afraid," he said. "A lack of understanding isn't going to pull a blade on you in a dark alley and steal your coin purse, is it?"

Mary Ann frowned. "Depending on the context, I could see where a lack of understanding might very well lead to—"

"You are a bit loud, and more than a bit over-tall," the grasshopper said. He had disappeared back into the darkness past the door, but his voice called, "So what I need from you right now is for you to be a more appropriate size. I don't suppose you have any Dwindleade on you?"

She had not. She usually kept a bottle of that shrinking beverage on her, and a bit of the growing cake, Burgeonboosh, as well. But she had used her last in Neath. She said so.

The grasshopper emerged with a silver tray, and upon it was a thimble-sized cup. "Fine, fine. We keep it on hand for just such poor planning." And he extended the tray to her.

She carefully picked up the little cup and drank from it. The shrinking sensation always made her lightheaded, but in a moment it passed, and she was at eye-level with the insect.

"Ah, that's better," said the doorman, setting both the tray and megaphone on a side table. "I am Mr. Springer. I'm Mr. Clashammer's household administrator. Follow me. I will announce you."

They entered a room with no furniture and approximately twenty people. Well, "people," of the beastie, reptile, insect, and human variety, anyway. Some of them were sparring. Some were performing exercises. And at a podium, surveying the group and occasionally shouting instruction, was a plump, brightly-colored caterpillar. Mr. Springer cleared his throat. "Mr. Clashammer, Miss Mary Ann Carpenter has arrived."

Everyone grew silent.

Clashammer pointed to a mantis in a training uniform. "Mrs. Hedgepeth, please take over class instruction for a few moments, will you?" And he stepped from the podium.

The crowd parted to let him pass, which the caterpillar did in such a fluid motion, it appeared he was gliding. Mary Ann didn't believe in stereotyping, but clearly she still needed to work on her own predjudices, for she'd never once pictured the renowned trainer of knights as larva.

"Ah, Miss Carpenter, you have found us!" He looped one of his many arms through hers and led her to the door. "Let us go where we might talk," he said.

And, momentarily, he brought her into a space with two toadstool chairs, a desk made of fungus, and a spongy lichen rug. Mary Ann thought, *This must be the facility's MushRoom.*

"Have a seat."

She sat. The toadstool was comfortable enough but a bit damp.

"I am assuming, since you are here, that the Jabberwock-slaying was successful?"

Mary Ann said, "That depends on one's perspective, sir. From Turvy's, yes. From the Jabberwock's, less so. And the slayer still has some ethical reservations about the lot of it."

Clashammer shrugged this away with several sets of shoulders. "With these old prophecy poems, that can hardly be avoided. They tend to be too black and white. No room for the grey areas. But the boy, the slayer—he remained uninjured?"

"Sir Rufus is alive and well. He plans to quest for the Vorpal sword next to put this whole backwards deed to rest." At least, she *hoped* he was alive and well. She'd been so busy trying to find Clashammer, she hadn't been able to verify the Rufus situation. She made up her mind to find a Turvian or Neathan newspaper as soon as possible and see.

Clashammer tapped the fingers of five sets of hands together. "Fine. That's all fine, then!" He leaned over the desk between them, "And how are you at cleaning?"

Her eye twitched. She was trying to find words and any coming to mind at the moment were certainly not clean.

"Cleaning?" he said again. "Light dusting? Doing the wash?"

A cold disappointment was washing over Mary Ann right now. Had it been a mistake to come here wearing maid's clothes? Had they only admitted her because they needed a housekeeper? Was this all for naught? "I—I'm sorry?"

"You do look sorry, true enough," said Clashammer, assessing her. "And sad. Your hair and garments are a fright. It suggests you're not good at cleaning at all, really." He scratched his chin. Or at least where a chin would be if caterpillars had them.

"Much has gone on today," Mary Ann heard herself say. "I'm normally more presentable."

"So 'yes' on the cleaning?"

She fought to say the words: "Are you, Mr. Clashammer, offering me a maid's position?" This seemed right somehow, didn't it, in a terrible, horribly wrong way? Of all the things... Here Mary Ann was, thinking she'd seized an opportunity to do something fresh and new—everything within her grasp—and now she was right back to grasping a feather duster. She sighed. "I happen to be rather good at cleaning, yes."

"And cooking, too? You can cook?"

The position was, regrettably, expanding by the moment. "Enough to get by," she admitted.

"Excellent!" said Clashammer. "Because, you see, all the students pitch in here. If you can clean and cook and do a bit of gardening with the rest, that'll take care of your room and board. And of course, the value of your training."

"So, there *is* training? You'll train me? Really?" She could almost see the rays of hope!

Actually, no, it was daylight reflecting off the gong Mr. Clashammer just rang. "Springer, please take Miss Carpenter to her quarters."

Mr. Springer appeared at the door before the gong stopped reverberating. "If you'll follow me, miss..." He bowed to Mr. Clashammer and then vanished through the door.

Mary Ann scrambled to her feet. "Thank you, Mr. Clashammer," she managed. "Thank you so very much! I will pull my own weight with the cooking and cleaning, I assure you." And Mary Ann darted out the door on the trail of Mr. Springer.

The student quarters were very utilitarian, but heated and well-lit. It was one large room with perhaps twenty single cots, generously spaced from each other.

"This shall be your cot, Carpenter," Mr. Springer said, indicating a little bed the second row in from the entrance. "At each end of the room you'll find a wash basin and soap, and changing screens for privacy. There is a tub next door. It features a rather ingenious water-pumping system, so water does not have to be fetched. We keep a strict schedule each day. I have taken the liberty of making a copy of it for you here." He handed her a sheet of paper.

"In that chest of drawers," he pointed to a high dresser in one corner, "are training clothes. Find a set that fits and change into them. Everyone wears the same thing, but each student has their own training plan. Everyone works together but each will accomplish training in their own time. Mr. Clashammer has you down for a backwards accelerated course to knighthood, with a major in Jabberwock defense. Does that sound correct to you?"

"Yes, I would assume so," she said. "But pardon me: why is it accelerated?"

"You've worked as a housemaid for a number of years, correct?"

"Since I was ten, sir."

"And you ran errands, fetched, cleaned, and otherwise served your employers?"

"Yes, sir."

"That's quite comparable to page work, and a bit more. And you supported Sir Rufus in a squire capacity, as well? Do we have that information correct?"

"I did only briefly." She had stepped in as squire the day of the Jabberwock quest, but only because Rufus' actual squires had gotten themselves hopelessly lost on their way to squire practice. It was hardly much actual squiring.

"Mr. Clashammer feels you can skip the page training, with time served, and we can knock off a bit of the squiring, as well. We call it 'advanced placement.' Now," he said, "get dressed in your training gear. Review the schedule. And Mr. Clashammer will see you in the workroom."

Clashammer saw her in the workroom, all right. It all started with a test of skill, and Mary Ann was surprised to discover her debut combat would be against Cornelius Clashammer himself. To look at him, one wouldn't expect a caterpillar capable of any feats of athleticism — at least not beyond the turning-to-goo-and-cocooning type. But the fellow's technique with a blade was startlingly swift, nimble and relentless.

CLANG! She savored the familiar sound of metal-on-metal, as her sword met the blade in her teacher's uppermost left hand! As she saw a lower right hand was on the move, Mary Ann struck with a second clang, then broke the block with a sudden side-step. Things had escalated quickly, and weapons of varying types seemed to appear out of the ether into Clashammer's deft, many-armed grasp.

Despite this, Mary Ann felt she was holding up well so far, meeting blow-for-blow with real focus. And this! This was why she was here! And it was not an opportunity she took lightly.

He circled around her, bending in such a way that no human opponent could manage, and with many more hands at his disposal. It was an odd advantage.

And that's when she felt the flat of a blade strike her shoulder, a solid whack, punishment for her failure to block it, but merciful by its edgeless impact. It forced her to scuttle backward in a quick shuffle, and again it seemed he was both before her and behind her, and on the attack.

CHING! She met the blade this time. And then next time, as well! She was onto his strategy now and answered each blow, swords clanking. This went on for what felt like days, but it was surely only a moment or two, until Clashammer's many arms sank to his sides at once and the teacher said, "Well, I've seen all I need to see."

Mary Ann waited for the verdict, afraid to move, to breathe.

He said, "Your form is admirable. Your strikes are controlled and intuitive. You make use of your small stature and center of gravity well, even against a larger opponent. And you adjust your tactics to match your challenger's with ease."

She exhaled.

Then the worm turned. "It's horrible. Which is why we have a long, long, *very long* way to go with your training. Why, I'd no idea it would be this problematic! Yes," he sighed, "this is going to take some time."

"You're disappointed?" She blinked, unable to believe her ears. She was sure she'd done quite well, all told.

"I admit, I *was* hoping this would be an easy case. But now I see I have this horrendous mess of competence before me." He eyed her carefully. "You do understand how this works, don't you, Carpenter? In forwards training, you don't start out knowing anything. You learn over time. You get better and better. But in backwards training, you begin knowing everything you'll ever know, and grow worse and worse. You devolve. Your head empties. And when all's said and done, you know nothing, and you graduate. It's that simple!"

It sounded anything but simple.

"Oh yes, you're a challenge all right, Carpenter," he said. "But Cornelius Clashammer does not flee from a challenge." He pointed to a clock. "It's time to prepare dinner now. Go wash up and join the others in the kitchen."

Mary Ann nodded and left him, silently. It was all a bit hard to wrap the brain around, really; here she was with a head full of knowledge — all the good Jabberwock-fighting techniques she'd imparted to Sir Rufus — yet this was also the peak of failure.

Living backwards was certainly not for the faint of heart.

Spirits in the kitchen were high, and burners on medium, as Cornelius Clashammer's pupils finished boiling the potatoes, chopping veg, and preparing meat for the evening meal. Their chatter was of boastful rematches, technique suggestions, and candied carrots. All the while, hot water poured straight from the copper spigots, proving Thither really *was* ahead of its time.

After dinner and dishes was an hour's free time, according to Mr. Springer's schedule. So, Mary Ann took the opportunity to acclimate herself to her neighborhood and locate a newsstand. She still had the coin that beagle had tossed her— enough to buy a paper, surely. She'd supplied herself appropriately from the school's stash of Burgeonboosh and Dwindleade and swiftly emerged, full-sized, into the city.

It wasn't very long before she came upon a newsstand, just three blocks north of Clashammer's. "Do you carry *Neath Undercover* or *The Turvy Mirror*?" she asked the proprietor, as she scanned the unfamiliar mastheads.

The newspaper salesman laughed. "Why, naturally we only have Thither news, miss. Thither's where we is, and the other realms can only wish they was here!"

Mary Ann frowned at this unexpected expression of nationalism. "Nothing from the rest of the Wanderlands? At all? When I lived in Neath, I could still get the Turvy papers. Are they ... banned here?"

"Not banned, miss. Hardly illegal. Just ..." he pushed back his cap, and considered it, "no point to get outside news. Not the way Thither works. It could never get here in a timely fashion. Talk about your 'ancient history!'" And he laughed again, elbowing her congenially, like he'd made some marvelous joke.

"I'm afraid I don't quite follow," she said. "If I wanted to find out how a friend in Turvy was doing while I'm here, how would I do it?"

"Well, we got a very nice postal system that's tubes and shoots." He indicated a brass and copper pipe set-up that ran up walls and along the rooflines. "Tubes and shoots, shoots and tubes, very efficient! All air-compression, all across the realm. Does your friend have tubes and shoots in Turvy? You could shoot 'em a tube!"

"No," she said flatly. "He's got winged messenger insects and postmen."

"Bugs and bags…What a shame," said the newspaper salesman, though there was a tinge of smugness in his voice.

"Do you know where I could hire a rocking-horsefly then?" She thought her single coin might pay for that.

"Not indigenous to Thither, I'm afraid. Read of them in books, I have, but never seen one here."

"Then thank you for your time," she said. She was disappointed, of course, but she reminded herself that all was not lost. Upon parting with Sir Rufus, she'd suggested he meet her here in Thither — *after* collecting the Vorpal sword and finishing off his prophecy, of course. At the time, it had been a bold move for her, and she'd surprised herself by even proposing it. But their adventures had created this delightful affinity between them, and it had felt quite right in the moment. Her concerns certainly would be allayed if he showed up on her doorstep in a week or two. She figured, at least, she could look forward to that.

She turned to go.

But the newspaper salesman wasn't finished. "Perhaps I could interest you in a copy of *The Thither Gazette*? Or I've some classic books here. How does The House of the Seven Mabels grab you? Or The Count of Outgrabing Wabe? I've some spicy novels of the heaving bosoms and flickering gaslight genre, too, if you're so inclined?" he called as she started away.

"Not today, thank you." She couldn't quite care about reading by gaslight or heaving bosoms right now; she simply had too much on her mind. She walked the three blocks back to Clashammer's, sipped her Dwindleade, dwindled, and rang the bell.

The evening wrapped up for Clashammer's students with some light chores — largely, a bit of mending; several pairs of the teacher's stockings were in a terrible state, and when you're a caterpillar you go through quite a lot of stockings at once. Mary Ann borrowed a needle, thread, and some scissors and began altering the maid's uniform she'd arrived in, removing the heart-shaped appliques down the front, and taking it in, so now it could only accommodate one Mary Ann at a time. The results were ... (she held it up, frowning) ... hardly high-fashion but it would have to do.

She had only just squared that away, when a gong reververated through the school, signalling bedtime for all the students. Unlike the others, Mary Ann had no nightdress — in fact, she'd no belongings with her whatsoever besides that altered maid's uniform. So, she slept in the grey tunic and trousers she trained in for the day, and borrowed someone's tooth powder, using it on her finger as she had no toothbrush.

It wasn't ideal, but Mary Ann Carpenter was used to Not Ideal. Life had always been a series of making-dos and tonight was no exception.

2

Her first full day at Cornelius Clashammer's began at five a.m., with the ringing of that gong. As warm sunlight crept through the far window, Mary Ann bounded from her cot, eager to begin turning this day to knight.

But the schedule showed there were household chores to slay first, so from scrubbing to scouring, and washing to watering the garden, Mary Ann and her colleagues did their duty, giving it big energy for 1/24 their usual size.

The afternoon was solidly devoted to training. Mary Ann learned there was an extensive library of books on questing beasts at her disposal, and stacks of detailed information about Jabberwocks to review. She appreciated the opportunity to learn jousting and, while riding on the back of a garden beetle wasn't *quite* the same experience as on horseback, she adjusted to it with aplomb. They tackled traditional knighting tactics — which included a strange amount of purposefully falling off one's horse (er, beetle) — and the modern ones, which thankfully didn't.

Then, for her hour's free time after dinner, she took a walk to Thither's mirror portal, and quizzed the incoming travelers for news of Sir Rufus, his parents, and Turvy. When one needed fresh Wanderlands information on a pauper's budget, this enterprise was well worth the effort. These questions weren't always met with the most welcome response, she noted, but visitors indulged her queries at a ratio of about two to one.

Alas, no new information was forthcoming this day but, Mary Ann retained hope, as each new day held new possibility. One man even gave her a small coin, just to get rid of her. So, technically, she was up on the deal. Besides, it was likely that before the month was out, she'd see Sir Rufus in person and get the details straight from the knight himself. And that was really the best of all possible outcomes.

So one week passed in this manner. Then two weeks. And still, Sir Rufus Carmine didn't make his grand entrance. As the weeks turned to months, each day followed the same routine: chores, knightly studies, and a trip to the mirror for news. The strict routine made her feel productive and more focused, and being small 98% of the time suddenly felt quite big enough.

She learned from her daily mirror-side visits that Queen Valentina was holding a second Unbirthday fete to make up for the last one. That the Red Turvy Hog Hoopers were in the realm's croquet finals. And that the White Queen, Crystal, stuck herself with her brooch pin again and needed minor medical attention. There were no indications the Jabberwock had returned to terrorize Turvy. There was no sign of any dangerous aftermath involving the Carmine family, or anyone else, for that matter. Neath and Turvy seemed peaceful.

Rufus remained conspicuously absent.

As for her backwards training, a whole year had passed and then another before her growing frustrations reached their peak. When she began, she'd sparred against Mrs. Hedgepeth, Clashammer's star pupil. And in these early days, Clashammer's advice rang true in Mary Ann's mind, echoing the backwards knowledge already lurking there.

But increasingly, his teachings grew muddled to her ears. She frequently missed contact with her opponent's blade. She got backed into corners. Ultimately, Mary Ann was assigned to spar with Mr. Soandso, a nice enough fellow, but as green in his sword-play as he was in complexion, what with being the newest pupil and also a lizard.

When even Soandso bested her, knocking her sword straight from her hand, Mary Ann's vexation finally overflowed its banks, forming a river of tears streaming down her face. "Oh, stuff and nonsense!" she said and kicked her sword in a way that was very unlike herself. But perhaps she wasn't herself anymore, was she? She had grown into something else, some galumphing oaf with two left feet and a holey brain.

"There, there, what is it, child?" Mr. Clashammer's voice came from above her ear, a few arms curling kindly around her shoulders.

"I'm giving it my best every day, sir, I can only assure you, and I hate that nothing I do is right! I'm clumsy, I'm confused, I'm not remembering the names of the moves you suggest…All that frabjously helpful information about Jabberwocks has vanished! I even fell off my beetle yesterday—accidentally!" She took the handkerchief he offered her and wiped her eyes. "Everyone else is improving, I see it, and here I am, losing any skill I had. It's been two years I've been here, as of last Whensday. Did you know? Two years! And this backwards training is just so ruddy infuriating now, I make myself sick."

And to her surprise, she heard him *laugh*, low and warm. She turned and stared at him agape. "Meaning no disrespect, sir, but how can you laugh?"

"Carpenter, pull yourself together!" he said. "You should be so pleased with your efforts. *Finally* you're getting *good*."

She sniffed. "Good?!"

"Which is to say absolutely terrible! You can take some pride in that. Yes, backwards training is much harder than forwards training due to the demotivation that students experience. Very few people have the fortitude to make it through backwards, and as a result, their whole enterprise comes crashing down. But the way you're failing, in no time you'll be so inept, you'll earn your certificate."

She dabbed her eyes. "Really?"

He went on, "Think about how long some knights must study for this going forwards. Like your friend the Jabberwock slayer. He likely started as a page at six, squired at 14, became a knight at 20, if he was lucky. If you manage it backwards between two and three years, as it looks like you will, that's a real feather in your cap."

"Thank you, sir," she said solemnly. She looked at the soggy handkerchief. "I shall launder this and return it to you."

"Never mind that now, Carpenter: pick up that sword and get back to failing!"

"Yes, sir."

The pep talk did, indeed, help. And for the rest of the day's training, Mary Ann told herself she could carry on, knowing her ineptitude had an end point. She reminded herself of this when she was unbeetled out in the backyard and ended up in the mud. She considered it when she completely forgot the word Jabberwock (her brain came up with "reptile-ragey-bat") and had to go look it up. And she made note of the idea once more when her jousting dummy swung round, caught her hair, and yanked her off her feet.

Performing so poorly, however, only seemed to return her concerns to the second thing that had been weighing on her mind for some time now: Sir Rufus had never shown up in Thither. That meant either something terrible had happened to him or, simply, he did not wish to come.

Thinking it through logically, no one arriving through the mirror portal had indicated any additional violence across the Wanderlands; if anything, the news was fairly mundane. Surely, if the prophesied Jabberwock slayer had come to a gorrible end, that would make the papers, and word would spread like, well, Jabberwock's fire. In this way, no news was likely frabjous news, because the alternative was simply unbearable.

But if Rufus were back home in Turvy, alive and well with the Vorpal sword in his possession, then, he simply decided not to come to Thither at all. And that idea, too, was not without its pang to the soul. And the more she considered it, the more likely that outcome seemed. Yes, he had helped her solve the series of murders across Red Turvy. But wasn't that in Turvy's best interest? He was Lord Carmine's son, after all, and would be the Baron of Carmine himself someday. He was a knight for Queen Rosamund, and now the renowned Jabberwock slayer to boot. He had infinite possibilities ahead of him, and none of them had one thing to do with the welfare of his family's former housemaid.

Yes, it may have *seemed* like there was something there between them. Something warm and pleasant and hard to pin down, like a fragrance in the air. But one couldn't count on that lasting. Not after the wind turned and the thrill of adventure had passed. Not when he had so many beautiful things to consider, a whole realm of options. And likely a collection of duke's daughters, earl's offspring, and other young, vibrant nobles, all eager to capture his attention with their elegance and taste. She was foolish if she believed otherwise, she told herself. And Mary Ann Carpenter would not be made a fool. She could carry on with things perfectly fine on her own, thank you very much. She knew it because she always had.

The jousting dummy spun again at her distracted parry, this time swinging round and walloping her in the head with its ballast. "Oh, curse it all! Pull yourself together, Mary Ann! Grow worse if you must but do spare the concussion!" She saw a few of her colleagues exchange glances as if to say, "Carpenter has cracked."

But she had summoned her resolve. Over the next few weeks, Mary Ann threw herself into her backwards training with all the passion she could muster, as her skills continued to fade, her injuries increased, and her studies leaked out her ears.

3

One warm and stuffy day, as the students were exiting the training room from a particularly effervescent round of sparring, Mary Ann emerged to see Mr. Springer in the hall. He was leaning on what appeared to be a large posterboard. "Miss Carpenter?"

"Yes, Mr. Springer?" She wiped her brow with the back of her hand, her eyes falling on the posterboard. "Do you need help hanging that somewhere?"

"No, thank you, miss. A young man called for you during your session."

"A young man? For me?" It wasn't exactly like Mary Ann knew a lot of young men. Certainly not ones likely to call for her in Thither. And that's when her breath caught. *Oh, but it couldn't be. Not after all this time, surely!*

"He left you this." And Springer held out the posterboard.

It was, in fact, a calling card of the non-Dwindleaded variety. It read simply:

SIR RUFUS
CARMINE MANOR
CARMINE, SQUARE FOUR, RED TURVY

Her hand flew to her mouth. "Oh my! It's been two whole years!" She didn't know whether to be annoyed or thrilled, but thrilled seemed to be winning out, despite all good sense. She turned to Mr. Springer. "Did he look well? Did he seem sick or injured at all?" Mary Ann had visions of the knight spending the past two years languishing in Queen Valentina's dungeon, awaiting execution, only to have his sentence commuted, because no one recalled what he was in for anymore.

Mr. Springer reflected on it. "Not so as I noticed, Miss. A posh young gentleman. Very red. Nice boots."

Mary Ann realized the view from the school's doorway did feature visitors' footwear rather prominently. "That's him!"

"He said he would be taking supper at the Copper and Brass, that restaurant down the street at the corner. And that it would be most agreeable if you would meet him there."

"And when was this?"

"About twenty minutes ago."

"Oh dear!" She looked down at her training clothes, which were filthy and drenched in sweat. She patted her hair, which was sweaty around the temples and neck, and had come unraveled. "Um… I need to … I should really…Five minutes!" And she ran to the communal bedchamber.

At the wash basin, she cleaned up as quickly as she could, then unbound her yellow hair, brushed it, and tightly trussed it up again. Since childhood, she'd only ever worn it this one way, unless her maid's uniform dictated otherwise, and she'd gotten very good at putting it together swiftly.

She gave herself a cursory glance. Well, the face was clean, the only real expectation she had for it. Otherwise, it hadn't greatly improved in the past two years. With its round shape and slight overbite, she always felt conscious of her resemblance to a garden-variety chipmunk. A fine and noble creature to be sure, but not exactly beauty goals for a young female human.

Nothing to be done of it, she thought, *one mustn't dwell*, and moved to the wardrobe closet. She rummaged amongst the clothes there and shortly found the item she sought. It was the pink housemaid's dress she'd altered and de-hearted. She hadn't worn it since she'd gotten to Clashammer's—there had been no occasion — and it was no more stylish than when she first reconfigured it. But it was freshly-laundered (well, two years ago), and it was a dress, and it would have to do. She put it on and raced out of the room and down the hall.

Mr. Springer was by the front door now and while she was running out, she backed up suddenly and stopped before him. "Am I allowed do this? Is it against house rules at all?"

Mr. Springer shrugged. "Last I checked, it's a school not a prison."

"But it's also not proper convention, is it? Young women meeting men in restaurants?" Her mother had never been around to guide her in these matters, but she'd picked up certain ideas about it from listening to her former employer, the Duchess of Additch, gossip with her friends.

He shrugged again. "You're studying to be a knight, backwards. You sleep in a bedchamber with twenty strangers. You ride a beetle round the backyard. You're worrying about convention now?"

"Words of wisdom, Mr. Springer." She waved goodbye, and out the door she went.

Rufus was easy enough to spot in the restaurant, not simply because of his exuberant, flaming red hair, but because it was early for supper, so the place was practically empty.

"May I help you, miss?" A primly-dressed hostess mouse stepped into her path.

"Just meeting a friend," Mary Ann told her, "I see him there." And she dodged around the mouse unescorted.

Rufus was frowning at an unfamiliar object on his plate but when Mary Ann approached, his expression cleared. He stood. "Mary Ann!" He looked like he didn't know whether he should shake her hand or hug her. And really, what *was* the proper etiquette in a former employer-employee relationship that had grown into friendship where the two people had also spent a great deal of time nearly getting killed together? He settled on pulling out a chair. "Please," he motioned, "have a seat." A waitress was already bringing her a menu. "Wonderful to see you," he said warmly. (To Mary Ann, not the waitress.) "You look well!"

"As do you!" she said. His red shirt and trousers matched his curly hair. He wore a checkerboard silk waistcoat and a blue brocade jacket that matched his eyes. While always stylish, truth be told, Sir Rufus Carmine was not *precisely* a handsome young man. His features were a unique collection of unexpected angles and shapes that steadfastly defied the mathematical average. Still, he always *projected* this sense of handsomeness. She wasn't quite sure how he managed it; it was a remarkable illusion, and it fascinated her.

She said: "It seems you didn't land up in Queen Valentina's dungeon, after all!"

"Not twice, no." He flashed a smile. It was a very nice smile. "After you went through the looking-glass, Goodspeed and I took off for Tulgey Barrens and the angry villagers with torches gave up rather swiftly after that." Goodspeed was his hired horse. "My parents extracted themselves from the Unbirthday party, paid their respects, and made a surreptitious exit. Rumor has it that relations are still a bit icy between Queen Valentina and Queen Rosamund. But I imagine that will blow over in due time. We are, however, all banned from Neath."

"We who?"

"You. Me. My family. Possibly Rosamund, really not sure. But definitely you and I." He pointed to the object on his plate. "What do you think this is?"

She assessed it. It was blue, roughly elliptical with the occasional pimple on it. "I haven't the foggiest. Some kind of potato?"

He considered this. "I didn't order a potato."

"Another mystery to solve," she said. "Speaking of which, I'm curious what prompted you to come here now."

He blinked. "You asked me to, didn't you?" His face flushed under his collection of freckles. "Should I not have come?" He seemed genuinely concerned.

"No, but I asked you *two years* ago." She laughed. "Not that I'm not delighted to see you. I am. But after all this time, I stopped hoping. In fact, it was hard not to take it rather personally."

He squinted at her, like she'd just said something mad. "Two weeks, you mean."

"Two weeks since what?"

"Since the Unbirthday party and the mirror and the running." He shook his head and murmured, "So much running."

"Rufus, I've been here doing backwards training for over two years. I know Mr. Clashammer said it's an accelerated program but surely it's not *that* accelerated."

His eyes went wide. "Oh, I see! You don't know!" he said. "Didn't you learn about Thither in your geography lessons?"

"I never had geography lessons. My neighbor, Mrs. Nightwing, taught me to read. And my father taught me maths, but that was mainly so I could do his account books. That concludes the extent of my formalized education."

A pained expression. A nod. "Understood. Well, Thither is on a different time schedule than Turvy. It's compressed over here. I don't precisely know how it works, but they fit a lot more days into the day than the other realms of the Wanderlands. Two years' worth to two weeks, it would seem; I hadn't realized until now the ratio was that wide. Now I feel terrible you believed I'd forgotten you."

"But I saw the sun rise and set many, many times," she insisted.

"I'm sure you did. And that's just the way it is here. Thither is ahead of our time. In Turvy, it's been two weeks."

Thither is ahead of its time. Now it made sense! Mr. Springer wasn't saying that Thither was particularly innovative, though it was. Thither was *literally* ahead of Turvy's time. "No wonder I couldn't get the Turvian papers. They'd be considered dated here." Then another thought occurred to her. "So, wait a minute, I was 18 when I left. I'm 20 now. But if I go back to Turvy, I am I still 18?"

"My head hurts," Rufus said, looking down at his plate again. "And this is definitely not a potato."

"Are you ready to order, miss?" asked the waitress.

"Nothing for me, thank you." Mary Ann handed her the menu.

"Are you sure?" Rufus looked puzzled and the waitress paused. "I'd rather not sit here eating this fine…er, whatsit… alone."

"That's an indibobble, sir." The waitress' tone suggested he must be a bit dim to not recognize it, but that dealing with dim customers like this was her lot in life.

"Oh, I'm quite certain I'll not order, thank you very much," Mary Ann replied. And as the waitress left, Mary Ann explained, "I ate earlier, you see. I'm simply stuffed." Of course, this was a lie. She hadn't eaten since breakfast, and that was just a bit of scrambled egg. The truth was, she hadn't any money, and she didn't feel comfortable with the idea of Rufus paying for her. The inequity of a future baron socializing with a former housemaid was problematic enough. Being unable to pay one's own way seemed doubly wrong somehow. She decided it was best to change the subject, swiftly. "So you *must* tell me…Did you quest for the Vorpal sword, then? Is your prophesied epic complete?"

"Ah…" He cast his eyes ceilingward, turning them a very pale and wintry blue in the shift of light. His voice dropped to a low, grave tone. "About that…"

"Oh no, what happened?" Mary Ann leaned in. "The Puddlefae didn't tell you to hop it a second time, did she?" The first time they'd popped round to the sword-distributing mud-puddle fairy, it was solely for some non-Vorpal information. Nonetheless, the fae was quite saucy about Rufus potentially jumping the gun on his prophecy poem. Apparently, magic swords were not to be released prematurely. There were rules from the whole magic-implement-dispensing union, or something. Who knew?

"Alas…" he sighed, "the mud puddle was dried up when I got there. The fae is gone. My epic tale, vanished as vapor."

Mary Ann gasped. "Oh, how horrible! Does this undo everything? Is the Jabberwock alive again? Is Turvy now in danger? Is—"

"Kidding," he said, with a grin. "It's here." And he pulled a fierce and strange-looking sword in a scabbard out from under the dining table.

She swatted his arm. "And to think I helped you get your sense of humor back, for you to misuse it in such a fashion. And on *me*." She held back a laugh because she didn't want to give him the satisfaction of it.

"I couldn't help myself, I'm sorry," he said, though he didn't look a bit sorry. "But now it's your turn. Tell me all about this backwards training."

So, she told him about the school and how difficult it was to first locate, due to its scale. (Rufus agreed that, given Mr. Clashammer's reputation, he, too, was expecting it to be a somewhat larger operation.) And she told him about the shared chores, the schedule, the beetle jousting, and Mr. Springer. And then she got to the backwards training, and explained how if Rufus sparred with her today, he wouldn't find it at all a challenge. "No matter how hard I try, I'm dreadful," she said. "And I'm likely to only get worse in the coming weeks. Given my current state, I'm not sure how that's even possible."

"Ah, but you've a knack for the impossible, don't you? It's one of your strengths." He was finishing the last of his tea.

"I hate every minute of it," she admitted. "It goes completely against my general approach to quality work, failing like this. But it must be done."

"Indeed, it must. Which is why I was thinking …" He set down his empty teacup. "I might spend a few days here in Thither and have a bit of a holiday. All my life, I've been preparing for that day of battle with the Jabberwock. Now it's complete, and here's me shocked that I wasn't actually ripped to shreds in my armor like a tin of potted meat." He laughed, but it rang a bit hollow to Mary Ann's ears. She knew he'd been deeply depressed, but she hadn't realized he'd felt that faithless about his own prophecy poem. Especially since he'd braved the situation without much hesitation.

He went on: "I believe your contributions to that day are largely why I'm still in here one piece, and I don't think you've received enough credit for it. So, if I've not expressed it fully enough: thank you for everything. I am grateful." There was such sincerity in his expression, she didn't know what to do with it.

"No need to thank me," she mumbled. "It's nothing." And she felt her face go hot.

"After all that pressure, it's very strange to find myself unexpectedly alive and freed up." He looked at his hands clasped on the table. "I imagine it sounds silly, but I hadn't made any plans for this part of living."

The thought pierced her like a sword. "I'd no idea. And I'm very sorry." Her voice sounded small to her own ears.

But he shrugged it away. "I know you have your training and other obligations," he said, "and I don't want to distract from that. But as a part of my holiday, would you be amenable to sparing some time, as schedule permits, to get to know each other a bit better? You know, under non-murder-and-monster conditions?"

"I'd like that," she heard herself say. It felt very surreal that this conversation was not only taking place but involving her. It wasn't precisely that she didn't feel worthy of the attention. It was just that she'd never gotten much of it, and certainly not because someone's life wasn't snuffed out prematurely, and now they were excited to take time to get know her. "It's just… would your family approve of this?"

The waitress set down the bill. "How do you mean?" he said, examining it. "I told Mother where I was going."

"It's just …" Mary Ann wasn't sure how to say it. "I suspect it's not every Lord and Lady's dream for their son to spend time getting to know their former housemaid better."

"Oh." He laughed. "Well, I'll tell you. Mother has a saying: 'In the Wanderlands, no one is ever who they are for long.' I'm not the same person I was a month ago, or two months, or two years. Are you?"

She shook her head.

"See? And in Turvy, where one might wake up to discover they've grown too large to fit in their own house, or turned into a pig, or suddenly can go invisible now and again…" he grinned, "well, we can't dwell on fleeting appearances. At some point, it's out of our control. We must make our own path." He put money down, rose, and grabbed the Vorpal sword from under the table. "Are we ready?"

"Oh," she said, "yes. Certainly!" She was still absorbing the words of their conversation, and now she rose quickly, trying to play catch up with the information swirling about in her mind.

"May I walk you back to Clashammer's?" He held the door.

Without thinking, she waved a dismissive hand. "Oh, that's very kind, but it's really only a few blocks. I won't run into any trouble in that distance."

He made a funny little grumble at this. "Mary Ann …" His tone was firm, his expression half exasperation and half amusement. "I am aware it's unlikely you'll be attacked by rampaging marauders in the next three blocks. I asked to walk with you because I would enjoy talking to you a few minutes more."

"Ah." She could feel embarrassment and surprise burning her cheeks. "I see."

He laughed, but not unkindly. "You are really terrible at this, aren't you? Hopping hedgehogs, whatever did the world do to you, Miss Carpenter?"

"It's a long story," she said.

"Well, I hope you'll decide to share it with me sometime," he said. "In the meantime, I see I'm going to have to be very forthright with you about these things going forward."

She nodded. "That's probably best, yes." The idea even made her feel a little better. He was right. She was absolutely rubbish at ... well ... whatever this was. But still, she wouldn't have traded a moment of it.

It was when they got to Clashammer's and they stood outside working out the details of when they might meet again that the tiny door flew open. Mary Ann expected to see the antennae and large round eyes of Mr. Springer, but instead it was Cornelius Clashammer himself. He said something, but ...

"What was that? We can't hear you," Mary Ann told him.

He grabbed the megaphone. "I said, 'Is that the Jabberwock slayer you're with, Carpenter? If so, have him come in.'" And he disappeared into the building.

Rufus looked questioningly to Mary Ann. She shrugged. "You're to come in," she said and offered him her bottle of Dwindleade.

Clashammer was waiting inside. "All properly downsized now? Excellent!" He clapped two sets of hands together and turned to Rufus. "So. You're the one from the prophecy poem, eh? The one who slayed the Jabberwock?"

The knight extended a hand. "Sir Rufus Carmine of Turvy."

"Cornelius Clashammer," said Cornelius Clashammer. Mary Ann wasn't sure she'd mentioned that the renowned mentor of knights was a caterpillar, and she realized now she probably should have better prepared Rufus for that. "And this young lady trained you?"

"I had formalized knight training under the late Sir Corsen of Square Four, Turvy. Then, two years ago your time, Miss Carpenter helped me dispatch the Jabberwock, and guided me through the more specialized defense techniques as backwards training."

"So you've read the Jabberwock zoology books by Mills, Rainbucket, Flemhour and Biggles?"

"Er ... no." Rufus blinked.

"Did you study the Killhoff wing-disabling maneuver and mounted and unmounted assault techniques for long-necked beasties?"

His eyes darted to Mary Ann. "Can't say I recall it specifically...?"

"No, sir," she said.

"Surely you went over the Bimwhiffle Principle and the Blorechuckle Procedures?"

"Not as such …." Rufus shifted in his boots. He was growing very red and splotchy right along the cheekbones.

"Good gravy, Carpenter, what did you teach the boy?" Clashammer asked.

"We touched on all the basics," she said. "We got about ten days of work in. But then the Vorpal sword disappeared so we rather thought we were done."

"Bah! Newbie mistake!" said Clashammer. "And did you grow dreadful at it?" Before the knight could answer, Clashammer turned to Mary Ann. "How rubbish was he when you left off? On a scale of one to ten?"

"Not rubbish at all, sir. A one? If one represents the lowest rubbish level where ten represents the highest level of —"

"As I suspected! His general knighting may be sound, but his backwards Jabberwock training is shockingly insufficient." He sized Rufus up. "How are you at cleaning and cooking, my lad?"

Rufus said, "I polished armor and groomed horses as a squire, if that's what you mean?"

It was not what he meant. "And cooking?"

"Er … Cook is rather territorial about her kitchen. Try to make so much as a cup of tea and she'll chase you from the room like an angry swan."

Mary Ann knew this was true. She had witnessed Cook in swan-mode.

"So, no cooking or cleaning experience whatsoever. Right. We'll fix that soon enough. Springer? Get this fellow situated, show him around. I've signed him on for backwards Jabberwock training."

"Yes, Mr. Clashammer. As you wish." Mr. Springer motioned to Rufus. "This way. I'll show you to your quarters."

"My, holidays do go so quickly," Rufus muttered, as he followed Springer down the hall.

Mary Ann was in the kitchen, helping her colleagues prepare supper (by now, she was ravenous) when Sir Rufus entered. He'd been issued his training clothes, and Mary Ann noticed that somehow he managed to make those look dapper, as well. Presumably he'd seen the communal quarters and had been directed toward a cot. Now, his expression was wary.

Sir Rufus Carmine had experienced his 21 years of life with a rather lavish bedchamber all to himself back at Carmine Manor. (She knew this because she'd cleaned it.) He also enjoyed a splendid wardrobe featuring a favored collection of waistcoats that were not only in fine fabrics, they weren't untailored grey training clothes identical to everyone else's. As needed, he'd had squires to assist with the clanky/horsey tasks, and a modest number of staff for the remaining bits, neither clanky nor horsey.

Mary Ann suspected the knight's time at Clashammer's would involve a certain amount of growing pains.

But the next days and weeks went on quite well, all told. While occasionally, she would catch the knight scowling at a pile of laundry or curse their five a.m. wake-up, he generally approached the experience with a good-natured enthusiasm she hadn't foreseen. He enjoyed reading (there was always a book on his knightstand at home) so, he polished off the required Jabberwock texts in no time at all and seemed eager to discuss them. In the training class, he'd started out wanting to spar with her, wondering, "How bad could it possibly be?" But he only did so once before he agreed she had become entirely too rubbish to be any fun battling and was assigned to more competitive students.

"Just you wait, Rufus Carmine," she'd teased him. "Soon you'll forget all your Jabberwock lessons and drop the Vorpal sword on your big toe. Then we'll see who's smug!"

Her own work, admittedly, *had* become a serious slog by now, to the point she almost relished the household chores portion of things because they were familiar, and she had not lost her touch there.

But it wasn't long before Rufus, too, experienced the effects of backwards training on both his physical and mental state. His regular knighting skills remained intact, which was a noticeable difference between them. And that made sense in a Turvian sort of way. He'd put in the eight years of forwards page work, and four years squiring before being knighted, and that could not be taken away. But all the book learning and monster slaying techniques were gradually being forgotten and it made him irritable. She noticed the petulant and sarcastic side of him flare up now and again, reminiscent of when his sense of humor was missing. Like one morning, he woke up grumbling that if he ever figured out which roommate was snoring like a Bandersnatch all night, every night, he was going clothespin their nose shut. And Mary Ann knew it was best to just leave him alone until he'd had some tea and sorted himself out.

On the personal side, the student living arrangements made for possibly the strangest...well, what *was* it even? A courtship? Could one call it that? It seemed Mary Ann and Rufus spent so much time together working toward common goals around the school, that any unease Mary Ann felt about their disparate social positions and romantic overtures was swept away, despite herself. It was just all rather comfortable, equitable, and idyllic, and she found herself looking forward to every second of banter, passing playfulness, or too fleeting freetime that they might capture for themselves.

Each night, she would see him over there across the room, on a cot where his feet hung out over the edge, and she considered it was a very peculiar way to conclude the day with someone you'd grown to deeply care about ... Someone you had just tried to quickly kiss without being obnoxious about it in front of 18 sleepy, nightshirt-clad roommates.

But then, it never *had* been normal, had it? She'd first met Rufus when she was quite literally invisible (long story), cleaning his family's staircase and he'd tripped over her.

Looking back on that moment, it felt impossible, like a completely different book of her life. Yet, things had improved so much, she didn't want to question it, lest she awake to find it all melted away as a mere dream.

Ultimately, the day arrived when Cornelius Clashammer pulled Mary Ann and Rufus aside and said he was very proud of the work they had both accomplished. "I feel confident that your skills are so horrendous, and your heads so very empty of Jabberwock knowledge, that you can graduate from any further training with full honors."

Mary Ann told him it had been a pleasure; she even almost believed it.

Several of their classmates were notified of similar success in their forward studies, and Mr. Springer arranged a modest ceremony, where each of the graduates were presented with certificates. Mary Ann unrolled the lovely, pulpy scroll, admiring where her name was written in gold and Mr. Clashammer had signed the bottom. And that was the moment she felt all her knowledge and skill flood back to her. It was an enormous rush in her ears, and her vision swam as the thundering backwards education she'd acquired over the past two-and-a-half years stuck to her braincells for good.

As her vision cleared, she looked to Rufus, who was pale and unfocused himself, clearly getting a brainful of his own studies. "Good heavens, that was dramatic," he murmured after a moment, rubbing his temples. "Glad I was sitting down."

It was just as Mr. Clashammer announced the official promotion of Mrs. Hedgepeth to assistant teacher, which they'd all seen coming a mile off, that they were interrupted by the door chime, and Mr. Springer sprang to answer. He returned with a mangy, wild-eyed looking hare wearing a uniform that read "Royal Messenger Service."

Mr. Springer announced, "Mr. Harris March of Neath and Turvy to see you, sir?"

The hare held a scroll of his own in one hand, and a teacup in the other. He looked for somewhere to set the teacup. Not finding a convenient spot and missing the whole floor beneath his feet as an option, he unrolled the scroll whilst slopping tea all over it.

In a loud, clear voice, he read the dripping document. "Attention Sir Rufus Carmine and Miss Mary Ann Carpenter: Queen Rosamund of Red Turvy requests your presence immediately on a very important confidential matter. Please go with this messenger post haste and don't read the message aloud, Mr. March, remember to make sure you tell them this in private, write that down, are you writing it down foolish hare, good, don't forget!" The scroll curled up with a snap that, coincidentally, now matched the pleased enlightenment that was filling the messenger's eyes. "Ohhhhh, I get it now!" Then a second enlightenment, less pleased: "Bugger."

Mary Ann and Rufus rose and approached the messenger tensely. Had they done something wrong in the eyes of the Queen? Had circumstances spiraled out of control between Neath and Turvy and they were to blame for it? It was anyone's guess. The knight stepped forward. "Um, this is Miss Carpenter. I am Sir Rufus."

The hare blinked.

Rufus looked from the hare to Mary Ann, and back again. "We're the people mentioned in the scroll? The scroll you just read?"

"Oh! Right! Harris March," the hare said, shaking their hands with a zeal disproportionate to the occasion. "But my friends call me 'Haigha.'" (The way he pronounced it rhymed with "Mayor," but only if you said it in a posh Turvian accent.) "Right then, scroll people: let us be off! There's no time to waste."

"I'll grab my bag and the Vorpal sword," Rufus said. "Anything you need, Mary Ann?"

Mary Ann thought about the pink housemaid's dress she'd altered and stowed away in the wardrobe but shook her head.

He dashed down the hall.

"Would you mind telling us what this is about, Mr. March?" Mary Ann asked.

"Not at all," said the hare. And a long moment went by, with the hare absently biting a fingernail and finishing his cup of tea. He hadn't answered by the time Sir Rufus returned, and even then, the hare just got up and headed to the exit. Mary Ann and Rufus had only time to give Cornelius Clashammer a cursory wave and shout their thanks, before they were out the front door and down the walk, with the hare passing round Burgeonboosh cake like they were a troupe of ten.

It was nice to be one's proper size again for more than a few moments at a time, Mary Ann considered, but she was too concerned with their leader and their destination to relish in it for very long. Mr. March's pace was erratic, and he zigzagged on the sidewalk as if he might spin off in a new direction at any given moment.

"Mr. March?" Mary Ann pressed, summoning her patience. "Er, again—what is this about?"

"No idea!" he said with a bright, buck-toothed grin. "But if I knew, I wouldn't mind telling you! Not one bit! Please call me Haigha. All my friends call me Haigha."

Rufus' face was lit with amusement. "I do hope we get wherever it is that we don't know we're going."

"How would we know when we got there?" asked Mary Ann. "Or if we never got there?"

"Either way, what an adventure!" Rufus said.

Mr. March led them to a looking-glass in the middle of a park, which Mary Ann realized was a different mirror than the one that had brought her to Thither. The image inside the mirror was not a reflection of the park, but an overlooking view of a sitting room with a few overstuffed chairs, and a door to a garden.

"Okay, scroll people, this way! Through here," said March. "This is a departing mirror, you know. All mirrors in Thither are one-direction mirrors. Safety precaution, I understand. Otherwise, you get someone arriving and someone departing at the same time and ..." The messenger shuddered. "You'll need a lot of towels. So… follow me, but one at a time. And mind the drop."

"Drop?" asked Mary Ann.

Oh, there was a drop, all right! The other side of the mirror was located on top of a fireplace mantel, so Mary Ann emerged through the mirror's suction and plopped out with no footing at all until she landed on a rug at the hearth floor. Realizing Rufus was right behind her and similarly unprepared, she rolled out of the way before he dropped in, tugging his travel case through on the back-end, and the Vorpal sword sending a tableside chess set clattering. "Curse it! Are you all right, Mary Ann?" She said she was, and he helped her up, then moved to set the game table to rights.

Mary Ann noticed the mirror on this side was now a reflection of this room, not the park. But it was a duller room, a boring-er room. The room light in the looking-glass was much dimmer, the colors drab. She could see no one in the space but an unfamiliar cat with a boring-er face on the seat of an equally overstuffed but boring-er chair. The cat did not smile, and Mary Ann got the powerful sense that not only was it not smiling now, *it could not smile*, and so it had not smiled a day in its life. She suddenly felt very sad for it.

"Oh, I bet you don't levitate or apparate, either," she said aloud, thinking of her furry friend Chester the Cat, whose talents included both.

"Pardon?" said Rufus. He set the last chess piece in place.

But she didn't bother to elaborate, and there was no time, anyway. Harris March was pressuring them onward.

4

One step into the garden, and the flowers raised concerns about being trod on, then shared unwanted opinions about the aesthetics (or the lack thereof) of the travelers' "petals."

This is how Mary Ann knew they were back home in Turvy.

She had expected she and Rufus were being summoned to Queen Rosamund's castle, given their missive. Or perhaps Sir Rufus' home, Carmine Manor. And while completely wrong on both counts, that ended up quite advantageous. Because getting where you wanted to go in Turvy was never terribly easy, especially the more you wanted to get there. The land was notoriously dodgy and could change in the blink of an eye, so there were several methods to subvert these issues. The most effective was pretending you didn't care about getting to your destination at all and sneaking up on it. But another excellent way was genuinely believing you were going somewhere else.

This meant, Mary Ann and Rufus were quite surprised when they arrived at a long path leading to a cottage, where one sign read, "To D.M. Tweedle's House" and the other read, "To the House of D.I. Tweedle."

Even Mr. March seemed befuddled why they were at the Tweedle abode, but once he spied the figures waiting outside, he gained greater confidence and ran to speak to them.

It was quite a welcome committee, though the downcast expressions on the members' faces suggested it was not a happy one. As the travelers approached, Queen Rosamund stood resolute, her hands clasped before her with a flyswatter jutting out one of them. Lord Carmine was with her, bouncing nervously on his toes and chewing his ginger mustache. Two of Lord Carmine's guards stood protecting an area of the front lawn that had been cordoned off with rope and flags, the flags alternating between the Royal Rose symbol of Red Turvy and the backwards 4 symbol of the Square Four territory. A postman and a newspaper man stood among the group's ranks, as well. The latter's entire suit was made of newspaper and a masthead ran across his chest: THE TURVY MIRROR. (Of course, as it was a Turvian publication, this was all written backwards, as was proper.)

As Mary Ann, Rufus, and Mr. March stepped up the drive, the flash of the reporter's camera went off. A whiff of flash powder filled the air.

Queen Rosamund said, "Ah, well done, March! You found them."

The hare bowed low and deep, the tips of his ears brushing the ground, catching a bit of straw on the way back up. "Yes, Your Majesty! I brought the scroll people in good time. And you may call me 'Haigha;' all my friends do."

Her mouth twitched just slightly. "Forgive me if I continue to hold to the old formalities, Mr. March. I am set in my ways." And she waved the flyswatter grandly. "Thank you for your work; you're dismissed." As the messenger shook everyone's hands vigorously and scarpered, the Queen turned her gaze to the other two travelers. "Sir Rufus, Miss Carpenter, thank you for coming!"

As it was a Royal summons, what choice had there been? But Mary Ann appreciated the polite nod to pretense. She curtseyed.

Sir Rufus said, "Happy to assist in whatever way we can, Your Majesty."

And with this done, Lord Carmine greeted his son with a fatherly embrace. "Good to have you home, boy."

"I *am* sorry to have interrupted your studies at Cornelius Clashammer's," the Queen said, "but we're in a bit of a pickle at the moment. So, I said to Lord Carmine, given the way you both handled that series of murders a few weeks ago, we might consider applying your dual deductive skills to this, as well."

This was a surprise. Mary Ann had expected a reprimand at best, blame for an international incident at worst. Being handed a new job had never entered her calculations.

The Queen continued, "I was having a nice visit with Lord and Lady Carmine when we received a rocking-horsefly from this gentleman." She indicated the postman, using her flyswatter now like a pointer. "You, sir, stand up straight, chin up, toes out! Now, tell them what you told us. I want them to hear it straight from you."

"Yes, indeed," said Lord Carmine warmly. "Let 'er rip, old chap!"

"Well," said the postman, "I was coming down the walk as I normally does, bringing the post as is custom, when I noticed the outdoor furniture overturned. Then I saw one of the Tweedle twins lying on the ground out cold like this." He made a gesture of closed eyes, lolling tongue, and arms akimbo. Mary Ann noticed the position was echoed in a roughly Tweedle shape painted in the section of front lawn that had been cordoned off. "There was these tracks in the mud over there," the postman pointed, "and blood, and the giant feather. So, I ran over to the poor sod on the lawn and I saw it was Dorian who was hurt."

Rufus squinted at him. "Dorian?"

"Yes, Sir. Detective Inspector Dorian Tweedle, Sir. You can tell by the mustache. He wears it turned down, he does. Says it suits his face."

Which was funny, Mary Ann thought, because his brother's mustache always turned upward and he had the very same face.

The postman continued. "Now Dorian, he wasn't waking up, so I shouted for D.M. Tweedle."

"Dominic?" asked Rufus.

"Damian," supplied the postman. "And the title's Detective Major, if you was wondering."

Mary Ann, at least, was.

"T'was a huge point of contention that Damo was promoted a half-level up in the guards over his brother when they was first transferred here. Heard such a ruckus about it that week, I did. Battles and shouting, you'd've thought someone was being murdered." He flushed when he realized what he said, then cleared his throat. "But as I was saying, I called for D.M. Tweedle and he was nowheres to be found. So I went, quick-like, looking for two rocking-horseflies. One I sent to fetch the doctor and the other I sent to Lord Carmine about what transpired."

The newspaper man, Mary Ann noticed, was jotting this all down with a giant pencil on an enormous notepad.

Queen Rosamund explained, "D.I. Tweedle is in the house with the doctor right now. They should be done shortly. Once you investigate out here, you can interview him."

Mary Ann said, "So are we to take it that D.M. Tweedle is still missing?"

The postman said, "He is. And that's why I messaged Lord Carmine straight away. We haven't much time. If Ole Inky got him, as the evidence clearly proves, well, he'll be munched up by tea time and sadly well-past saving!"

"Ole Inky?" Rufus gave a short, sharp laugh. "Are you joking?"

"I'm quite serious, Sir," insisted the postman. "As they say in them Lenore Nightwing mysteries, 'Everything in the crime scene indicates it.'"

Mary Ann frowned. "Ole Inky? Who or what is that?"

Rufus said, "Don't you remember from childhood? The tales?" Mary Ann shook her head, so he went on: "Ole Inky is this rather eerie character in local folklore. A massive crow who arrives in a great black storm cloud to pluck liars from the fields—typically children, but the tale varies—and then dines on their bones like carrot sticks."

Mary Ann had never once heard this. Perhaps if she had, she would have thought twice about bending the truth as much as she did.

"But like I said," continued Rufus, "Ole Inky's a legend. He's not really flapping about the countryside. He's something your parents tell you to scare you into proper behavior." And at this, Rufus shot a narrow glance to Lord Carmine.

Lord Carmine's beard bristled. "You know very well *you* weren't the one I was trying to scare with those stories."

But Rufus just rolled his eyes.

Seeing an in, the reporter called: "Sir Rufus, do you have a moment to discuss how Lord Carmine traumatized you as a child?" But no one paid him any mind.

The postman said, "If Ole Inky's a fable, then how do you explain the feather? Eh? Eh?" The mail carrier had hooked his thumbs through his trouser braces — *very* like one of Lenore Nightwing's more self-important detectives.

"Yes," Rufus squinted at him, "what was that about a giant feather?"

The postman gave an impatient huff. "The giant crow feather here at the crime scene, Sir." And the witness indicated a muddy area, fully feather-free as far as Mary Ann could tell, where there were some deep grooves in the earth. There also seemed to be a few drying blood droplets. *Whose blood?* was the question. The postman's face reddened. "Well, the feather *was* here when I arrived…"

"All right, then. Perhaps the wind carried it away," Rufus said, giving it the benefit of the doubt, and he went off for a quick search of the lawn.

"How large was this 'giant' feather exactly?" Mary Ann asked the postman. "Six inches? A foot?" She chuckled. "Tall as me?"

"Tall as him," the postman said, indicating Rufus who was returning to the group now shrugging and featherless.

"How tall are you?" Mary Ann asked him.

"Little over six foot," said Rufus. "But, really, how big would a bird have to be, proportionately, for a six-foot-long feather? Crows don't get that large."

The Queen said, "Ravens look very like crows, don't they? And they're a *bit* larger."

"Jubjub birds get very large, don't they?" suggested Mary Ann. "And they certainly do attack. Do they ever have black feathers?"

"Why are you wasting valuable time?" demanded the postman. "I know what I ruddy-well saw! It was a crow feather. And I know it because I happen to be an amateur orthonolo—orlothol—Er, bird studier, and I pay attention! Which is a far cry more than you lot are doing!"

"Watch your tongue, sir," said the Queen. "Everyone is doing their best."

"I suppose," said Mary Ann, examining the grooves in the ground, "that these *could* be crow tracks. But … it would have to be a crow who got into the Burgeonboosh. Do you think Burgeonboosh is the key here?"

"Now there's an idea!" Rufus said.

"But we've got unicorns!" the postman shouted. "We got gryphons! We got giraffes! Are you aware that in some realms people don't believe in them, neither? So, who says there's no Ole Inky?"

Mary Ann could see the man was very stressed out and decided the least she could do is make him feel heard. "Perhaps you're right, sir," said Mary Ann gently. "Let's make note of it, Rufus, and we shall take it into our considerations. As investigators, we should be open to every avenue."

"Er, yes," agreed Rufus. "I suppose I am just a bit tired and off my game; most days I can believe as many as six impossible things before lunchtime."

"Not breakfast?" asked Lord Carmine.

"Not if I lie in," the knight said.

Here, the Queen said, "All right, then, let's move this thing along. I'm expected back at the castle shortly, so I suggest we go see the patient." She whirled dramatically on a heel. "To the patient!" The directive was supported by a determined point of her flyswatter.

At this, Mary Ann felt the subject could no longer be ignored. "Begging your pardon, Your Majesty, but what is the story with the flyswatter?"

"Oh, this?" As they crossed the lawn, the Queen regarded the implement like she'd forgotten it was in her hand. "My scepter's gone missing. I quite recall bringing it shopping in Square Five the other day, but then I must have laid it somewhere. Usually, I just make do with whatever I can get my hands on, until we find it again. You know how it is, don't you, child? Like when you need a bookmark, you just use whatever's near you in its place, like a postcard, a ticket stub, or a small dog? It's like that."

"A small dog, Your Majesty?"

"Yes, of course; that's how you get dog-eared pages," she explained and led the way into the Tweedles' cottage.

Inside, the ceilings were low, and there were many objects in pairs, from the portraits on the walls, to the chairs by the hearth, and the slippers beside them. The group—minus the reporter who'd been detained outside — marched straight through a sitting room into a back bedroom. There were two twin beds, but only one with a twin in it. It seemed D.I. Tweedle —(*Dorian,* Mary Ann reminded herself) — had gained consciousness, and the doctor was saying something to him.

The postman cut in, "You feeling any better, D.I. Tweedle?"

"How's our patient?" asked Lord Carmine.

The doctor said, "Our friend Mr. Tweedle here was struck quite hard with something." He indicated a bandage on the back of Tweedle's head. "There's a significant contusion on the cranium."

Propped up in bed, Tweedle had a notepad and seemed to be taking notes, as he might for a standard criminal case. "A contuberation on the geranium," he agreed, "got it!"

"As a result," continued the doctor, "Mr. Tweedle is experiencing fairly significant amnesia, though I suspect it will be short-lived."

"Not gonna live long," muttered Dorian Tweedle as he wrote, "too much namblesia."

"He doesn't seem to recall much, including his name," continued the doctor. "And I'm concerned about his written and oral expression. It's imprecise and jumbled. Perhaps the injury's affecting his verbal abilities."

"Injurification affecting burble capacities," Tweedle noted.

"Oh no, that part's fine," Lord Carmine assured the doctor. "He always talks like that."

Everyone nodded. Yes, yes, this was fine.

"Burble capacities righty-o," Tweedle scribbled, crossing out the previous line.

"D.I. Tweedle?" Mary Ann slipped the mechanical pencil from his hand now to gain his full attention and she asked softly, "Could you please tell us the last thing you remember?"

Tweedle indicated the doctor. "I remember that fellow poking me with things. Most bad-mannered, it was! Why, if my head hadn't been spinning dizzy, this fellow would have been in for *such* a fight, feeling up my personal self with pointy things!"

"And you don't remember how you got injured at all?" she asked.

"Cursed if I know." He checked his notes and pointed. "Says right here, my geranium's contubed."

"Do you know where your brother might be?" she asked. "Do you remember what happened to him?"

"I have a brother?" His round face lit up, and there seemed to be smile under the mustache, even with the ends so stylishly turned down. "Frabjous! I always wanted a brother! Maybe I'll invite him to live here. Coincididdly, I even got a spare bed for him! How's that for luck?"

"I see that," Mary Ann said, and patted his hand. "Most fortunate."

Rufus asked the doctor, "How long does it take for amnesia like this to clear up?"

The doctor exhaled as he considered the question. "Oh, it varies. I'd like to say it'll clear up in a few days."

"Right," said Rufus. "We'll come back then."

"I'd *like* to say it, but I won't," said the doctor, "because I don't know for sure. The brain heals itself in its own time. My concern right now is whether there's someone who can stay with him tonight, if only to make sure he'll be safe."

The Queen turned to Lord Carmine, "Can your guards stay?"

"Of course," said Lord Carmine, and he called the guards in. "Officer Wibbles, Officer Flamm, you'll stay here tonight to keep an eye on D.I. Tweedle. I'll check in again in the morning."

"Yes, My Lord," they said and marched out.

The rest of the visitors were on their way out, too, when something caught Mary Ann's attention. In the sitting room were several curio cabinets simply filled to capacity with noisemakers—more specifically, silver and wooden rattles. She had never seen so many, in so many different styles and types. There were ones shaped like animals. There were ones topped with Turvian fairy tale characters. There were geometric ones and some that looked like flowers. There were wooden ones used as party noisemakers, and the kind used by guards for crowd control purposes. There was even a shelf of ones with jutting angles that made them resemble a tool of battle, like a flail, and certainly not something you'd feel safe giving to an infant, unless you really, really hated children.

But it was in one display case, front and center, there stood a single display stand that was completely rattle-free.

"Did you notice whether this was missing when you came in?" Mary Ann asked the doctor, drawing him over.

"I don't know." The physician thought a moment. "Actually, you're right, I think it was empty when we brought the patient in."

The empty space was a good size, and so prominently located, that whatever had been there would have taken a pride of place. "Does anyone know what that rattle was? And I'm assuming it was a rattle."

"I've never been to the cottage before," said the doctor. "This is my first time meeting Mr. Tweedle, I'm afraid."

The postman said, "I don't generally come inside. But I do know the Tweedles is always getting packages of these things. Order 'em special from other collectors and catalogues, they do. Sometimes they open 'em up while I'm leaving the rest of the post. Mad collection for two grown men, if ya ask me. But I don't judge," he said, judging.

When they stepped outside, Mary Ann called to the guards, "While you're both here with D.I. Tweedle, if you spy a silver or wooden rattle somewhere outside the cabinets, could you please let us know?"

"Yes, miss," the guards said. "Gladly, miss."

Rufus said to her, "I'm curious what you think this means, this empty space. Do you think the missing item is connected to the attack? That Tweedle was, say, knocked out with a rattle?"

"I'm not certain," she told him. "It just feels a bit strange to my eyes, so I think it's worth noting."

The Queen smiled with satisfaction. "Now that's the kind of keen observational skills I like to see in my investigators! But," she turned to Mary Ann, "it just occurred to me, you don't officially work for me, do you, child?"

"Well...Not *as* such, Your Majesty," admitted Mary Ann. She wasn't sure any terms of employment were required in this situation. It seemed if the Queen asked you to investigate something, you investigated.

But the Queen was sizing her up. "You will be joining my knights once your training with Mr. Clashammer is complete, won't you? We always need good knights here in Red Turvy. 'A good knight brings a better day to our realm,' I always say. Or now. I've said it now ... YOU MAY QUOTE ME, MR. PENNWELL!" she shouted to the reporter, and he wrote it down.

Mary Ann said, "I have, in fact, just completed my knight training, Your Majesty. And Sir Rufus has finalized his Jabberwock training, as well." And because she had it with her, she unrolled her signed certificate. She'd never had the opportunity to present school papers with high marks on it to her mother, but she imagined with the right mother, it might feel something like this.

The Queen examined the scroll with a satisfied nod. "So, let us not waste time then, shall we? I have a full schedule and you have a missing persons case to solve. Give us a kneel, girl."

Mary Ann blinked. "Pardon?"

"Kneel, kneel! I can't very well do this thing with you just standing round, can I? There's a certain amount of pomp and circumstance this requires, you know. Standing isn't pomp in this circumstance. Or in *any* circumstance. And I should know, because I create the circumstances. Also, the pomp."

There in the middle of the Tweedles' front lawn, Mary Ann knelt, the ground still damp from a recent rain.

"MARY ANN CARPENTER…" Queen Rosamund said, in a voice designed to project across the Royal castle gathering hall, but here on the Tweedles' muddy lawn, it just rattled the windows. "I KNIGHT YOU … SIR MARY ANN OF TURVY … IN THE NAME OF ME, ROSAMUND, QUEEN OF RED TURVY. LONG LIVE THE ME!" And she tapped Mary Ann on the shoulder with the flyswatter.

This was followed by: "All right, get up, get up!" said the Queen. "Or, rather: YOU MAY RISE, SIR MARY ANN!"

And Mary Ann got to her feet, numb with shock and trying to absorb the remarkable thing that had just happened. Rufus dealt with the impromptu event in a more expressive way, completely forgetting himself, and sweeping her up in a loving embrace. "Congratulations! I'm so excited for you!" he said, and kissed her. And, as that action had a very effective way of making any numbness vanish, she kissed him back. It went on just a bit longer than they intended.

"Yes, yes …" The Queen struck them with the flyswatter several times. "Leave off that, please. You're both knights now and you have work to do that doesn't involve lips."

And that's when Mary Ann heard the camera flash go off again. Mr. Pennwell was saying, "Sir Mary Ann—how's it feel to be knighted? Are you and Sir Rufus official? How long have you been sneaking around in this tumultuous love affair?"

Oh dear. Blushing, Mary Ann turned, but didn't immediately see the newspaper man. What she noticed was the expression on Lord Carmine's face, which was very much the look of a father who had never been looped into his son's personal life. She wondered if she should say something. Like explain that while only a few days had passed here in Turvy, in Thither they'd been at Clashammer's together half a year. That nothing untoward had ever gone on between them while she was working for the Carmines, besides evidence-gathering, and dungeon-breaking, and Mary Ann whacking one fellow over the head with a fire-poker. She wanted to assure him that Sir Rufus wasn't in the habit of kissing housemaids, and that Mary Ann herself wasn't the type of maid to go round trying to gain the affections of the Lord of the Manor's son.

But before she could summon a word of it, the moment for explanations had passed because the Queen was already back to official realm business. "So, what's next in your investigation?"

Mary Ann forced herself to focus, for there was work to be done. And there *always* work to be done, wasn't there? Mary Ann Carpenter finally was at a point in her life where a lovely young man wanted to kiss her, and she wanted that, too, yet here they were again…Work To Be Done. It was a pity.

She thought quickly. "Well, I suppose first I'd like to talk to the trees. They've proven invaluable witnesses for me in the past. Then, I should like to interview the local crows. They might be able to shed some light on whether it's a chimera in their ranks prompting the legend of Ole Inky or just some crow with a passion for Burgeonboosh."

This plan sounded amenable to all involved.

"It's heading toward brillig," said Rufus, scanning the position of the sun in the late afternoon sky, "so I propose we gather a search party for D.M. Tweedle as soon as possible. I agree with our friend the postman here in that, if Tweedle really has been carried off by a giant crow, time is very much of the essence."

The Queen was nodding throughout this proposal. "Lord Carmine has kindly put some guards on this very task already.

But while you investigate here, I will summon any knights at my disposal to help search across Red Turvy, in the surrounding squares. We'll do what we can until nightfall and then pick it up again at first light." And she flagged down a passing rocking-horsefly to get the operations moving.

"I still need to finish me route," the postman sighed, grabbing his satchel from beside the cottage door and slinging it over his shoulder. As he trundled down the walk, he added, "Not looking forward to the outgrabe about today's late delivery, that's for certain."

"Would you care to give a statement about the outrageous delays the postal service has been experiencing lately?" asked Mr. Pennwell, pencil at the ready.

It seemed that was just one question too far. Queen Rosamund ran him off with the flyswatter.

5

"Excuse me, did anyone here see what happened to either of the Tweedle twins?" Mary Ann asked, as she and Rufus stood at the edge of the clearing around Tweedle cottage.

The trees creaked and groaned and then the voices began, an echoing rustle. "Oh, another day, another fight," sighed an Oak.

"There was a scuffle at that domicile once-a-day weekdays, twice-a-day weekends," confirmed a Maple.

"Weeks and weeks of it … Always the same," said an Elder. "The days blend into each other for us now and the cycle continues."

"Well, this would have happened today," Mary Ann said, hoping to tickle their memories.

If a tree could shrug, the Maple certainly would have. "Can't say we pay attention anymore to all the comings and goings…"

"The shoutings and shriekings…" sighed the Larch.

"The battles and rattles…" moaned the Sassafras.

"It's no business of ours," said the Elder. "It's a human concern. Small and petty."

"We've tuned it all out," said the Oak. "It is our only recourse as our roots are here and we cannot move to another, better neighborhood."

"Alas..." said the trees. "Alas. Alas."

Rufus whispered to Mary Ann. "I thought you said the trees were helpful to you before."

"They were," she said. "I suppose the ones in my neighborhood are less desensitized to local violence. You try. Perhaps you'll have better luck."

To the foliage, Rufus called, "Then, have any of you seen an unusually large crow recently? Perhaps that might be more worthy of your notice."

The Tumtum said, "The crows roost in us at night. They gather here and they hunt. They pluck insects from our branches and dine on small animals beside our roots."

"Yes, well, this particular crow we're looking for would give you serious branch strain and could eat a borogove whole. It's far bigger than a human. Have you seen anything like that today?"

"Oh dear ..." the Maple gasped, "your leaves! They are dying."

He frowned. "My what?"

The Maple said, "When leaves turn such a hue of red, they burn in momentary splendor but fade and fall too soon, too soon."

"Yet this is not the season," said the Elm. "Perhaps he has a rot ..."

"Underwatered..." suggested the Maple.

"Infestation..." said the Tumtum.

"There's rarely any coming back from that," said the Elm and shook its branches sadly.

"My leaves are fine, thank you. This is their usual color; I am not deciduous," Rufus said. "So, to get back to the point, none of you know of an incredibly large crow that might live near here in Tulgey Barrens?"

"What does it matter when the cycle of life is still turning? The details do not matter. The days do not matter. As today, the black clouds appear but are fleeting. The dark skies may loom but clear. The birds of any size move on to different climes. And your leaves will turn brown and fall and mulch the earth by the base of your trunk. And you will only be remembered for wasting time asking questions," said the Elder.

"So many questions," sighed the trees.

"All right, I'm out," Rufus said to Mary Ann, shaking his head. "I've got nothing."

Mary Ann understood completely. "Thank you for your time," she told the glen.

"Make good use of yours," said the trees.

As they moved further into the woods, Rufus was chuckling. "Rather glad I didn't chat with that group before I faced the Jabberwock, or I would have viewed our discussion as an ominous portend."

"You mean about your leaves dying? I have a feeling you'll weather the season just fine." Mary Ann grinned. "Besides, I quite love the color of your leaves."

"Ah, but infestation … rotting from the roots …" He shuddered. "Sounds dashed uncomfortable. They had me practically on the way to mulch."

"That thicket certainly was more apathetic than the trees near my father's cottage," Mary Ann admitted. "I got on with them rather well. But who knows? Maybe it has to do with quality of the soil or the hardness of the ground. I'm not an arborist." She scanned the forest before them. "Where do you think the best place is to find the closest murder?" Then she added quickly, "Er, flock. *Flock.*"

"Down by the Topsy River, I think," he said, pointing. "I can hear it ahead. The water draws other animals, and that makes it easier for them to hunt." He glanced to the sky. "But we need to be quick about it. It'll be dark soon and that gives our friends like the Bandersnatch the home advantage in the stalking department."

Mary Ann had never seen a Bandersnatch in person, but she had heard the stories of the wounded, innocent hikers missing significant chunks out of their legs as the heavy, low-to-the-ground creature struck hard, bit, ripped and teared. Since Mary Ann and Rufus had met, this was the second time Rufus had reminded her the Bandersnatches' home was Tulgey Barrens, and it was the second time the threat of their presence was well-worth remembering. Mary Ann noticed now that Rufus had brought along the Vorpal sword in its scabbard. Clearly, Bandersnatches were on his mind from the beginning.

The sun's angle cast long shadows now amongst the trees and the land grew rockier as they approached the riverbed. Looking up, Mary Ann could see some of the crows already perched to roost for the evening, normal-sized birds all of them, talking amongst themselves or grooming. She called to them, "Hello, up there! My name is Mary Ann Carpenter and this is Sir Rufus. My friend and I are looking into an incident for Queen Rosamund of Red Turvy. Before you turn in for the evening, we were wondering if any crow would be willing to chat with us briefly."

One crow flew down to perch on a nearby rock. Then another. "Perhaps," said the first crow. "What do you have to give us?"

"To give you?" Mary Ann admitted she hadn't anticipated this. In the past, she'd done quite well just getting people to talk to her, free of exchange. She considered it. She hadn't any birdseed, but she wasn't sure they'd want that, anyway. She wasn't exactly in the habit of carrying round bugs, small rodents, or suet in her pockets ... Then it struck her: *in her pocket...*

From the trousers of the training uniform she still wore, she pulled out a mechanical pencil, the shiny metal one that she'd taken from D.I. Tweedle when she'd questioned him. She hadn't meant to steal it; at the time, she'd only wanted his full attention, but... She held it up. "This?"

The crow's head tilted in consideration. Mary Ann saw the pencil's shine reflected in its bright black eyes. "That'll do," it said, taking the item in its beak, and setting it at its feet. "What do you want to know?"

"This may sound odd, but do you know of any unusually-large crows here in Turvy?"

"Large how? Gus is a rather strapping fellow. He's got an impressive wingspan, and you should just see his talons!" said the crow admiringly.

From up in the trees, a jaunty voice called, "Why, ahoy there, lovely human lady!" And Mary Ann looked up to see a sizable crow stretching and flexing his wings, tilting its talons this way and that in a dramatic fashion, bobbing his head. And once the tail feathers started getting worked into his routine, she realized this was getting terribly out of hand.

"Erm, thank you, Gus," she shouted to him. "You're a very handsome bird. But I'm rather looking for someone else."

An "Awwwww," echoed down from the tree. "You tease…"

"I'm looking for a very large crow, one of unnatural size, not simply in peak crow condition. Or possibly one who has a taste for Burgeonboosh cake?"

"The bird we're looking for has feathers the size of that tree," said Rufus, pointing to a nearby sapling. "That sound familiar to you?"

There was rustling in the trees and a shower of chatter:

"Nothing rings a bell."

"Not so as I've heard."

"Don't know if we can digest Burgeonboosh. Jerry got into a bit of Dwindleade once and he had hiccups for six weeks."

"Cake would be tasty. I enjoy it after a nice dead rat."

"You're absolutely certain it's not Gus?"

… And so forth.

The crow on the rocks said, "What you're describing sounds like Ole Inky. You know: from the fables?"

"Yes," agreed Mary Ann, "I've had something of an education on Ole Inky today. Have you ever seen a crow like that?"

"No," said the crow, with a vigorous shake of the head. "Never!"

Then a new thought popped into Mary Ann's mind. "What about a human man, about this tall?" She held her hand to a level a little taller than herself. "He's shaped like a…" She tried to think of how a crow might describe it, "shaped like a gazing ball and he has black feathers perched above his lip."

After much discussion, the murder's consensus was that no one had seen D.M. Tweedle.

In a final attempt to get some information — *any* useful information — Rufus asked, "Are there any other groups of crows you could recommend we speak with?"

"Well," mused the first crow. "There's Leonard's murder down the river, that way, south." It pointed with a wing. "And then Burt's murder east of there, by the hot springs. But it's getting late and I imagine they'd all be well in bed by the time you got there."

"Also," said the second crow, "it's never good to wake Leonard."

"Never …" said the rustle from above. "Never …"

"Tomorrow perhaps, then." Rufus bowed to the first bird. "Thank you for your help."

And it was the right time to part. The sun hung low now and Mary Ann guessed there was perhaps twenty minutes of daylight left for them to vacate the woods and make it to the Tweedles' cottage. Perhaps they could borrow a lantern from there.

"I love this job," Rufus said warmly as they trekked the way back. "You just never know what's going to crop up. Like that bird who was flirting with you?"

"Oh, he was not," Mary Ann said, trying not to relive it.

"Come now," Rufus grinned, "the head bobbing and the wings? And then the tail feathers?" He was laughing hard and was getting harder to understand. "When he did that little bob-and-weave maneuver?"

The image was too much. Mary Ann was laughing, too, now. "I'm sure it's very provocative in inner-crow circles."

"'Why, ahoyyyy there…'" Rufus said, managing a reasonable imitation of Gus, before he cracked himself up again.

And that got Mary Ann laughing even harder. "Now, really! This is a missing persons investigation. It's supposed to be serious business!" She was wiping tears from her eyes.

Rufus put an arm around her. "I feel reassured knowing that if things don't work out between us, you'll always have Gus."

She was getting a stitch in her side now. She elbowed him. "You're terrible…"

6

When they emerged from the woods at the Tweedles, they were able to borrow not just one but two lanterns from their household. They paused long enough to send Queen Rosamund a rocking-horsefly update on the investigation, and Rufus grabbed his travel bag, which he'd stowed at the cottage. Then they headed to the main road. Noticing the familiar upcoming path trailing off to the right that led to her father's cottage, Mary Ann said, "It was a full day, wasn't it? So much has transpired, I hardly can believe we were just at Cornelius Clashammer's this morning."

"Things do move quickly around here," Rufus said, "despite not being ahead of our time."

"I'll see you tomorrow, then," she told him. "I'll come to Carmine Manor after sun-up, and we can regroup."

Rufus eyed the nearing side path with surprise. "You're going to your father's cottage?"

"Yes, I thought I might." Truthfully, Mary Ann didn't fully care for the idea. She hadn't spent much time there since her father was murdered. And while the property was all technically hers now, she wasn't entirely sure how she felt about that. There were so many unhappy visions and memories trapped in its walls, in the russet stain on the floorboards of the workshop …Here at night, it felt like they might swirl all too close around her, creeping along the baseboards and lurking in every cobwebby corner. Still, she imagined she had to face it all again sometime and she supposed this evening was as good as any. She was so tired, perhaps she would fall asleep before their icy fingers could properly seize hold of her mind.

"Do you have any supplies there? Any food?" Rufus looked concerned in the lantern light. It cast dark shadows over the angles of his face. "Is the place in any condition for sleeping?"

"I…I don't know." Mary Ann had been thinking of it more as a roof over her head and a cot to lie in. She was so weary, all the more practical details seemed to fall by the wayside.

"Look — why don't you come to Carmine Manor for tonight?" he said. "We have guest rooms and there'll be supper. You can get your shopping done in Square Five in the morning, if you wish, and then stay at the cottage after that if you still care to."

It sounded so pleasant and reasonable, and he looked so very worried, she found herself easily persuaded.

Upon their arrival at Carmine Manor, their welcome was only slightly less dramatic than the day Sir Rufus returned fresh from slaying the Jabberwock, the difference being this time, he was in a far better mood. Much of the household had turned up to greet them—all the maids and footmen and cooks—but the most impressive of all was Lady Carmine. She was a vision in chartreuse and red, gliding from the sitting room to the entry hall at such rapid pace, it was like being set upon by a faerie queen.

"Rufus, you've returned!" She hardly let him put down the lantern and travel bag before she hugged him, then backed up to survey him properly, ultimately trying to tidy his hair. "Your father told me all about everything. The completion of your Jabberwock training? The special case you're working on for the Queen? The—" She turned to Mary Ann. "The fact that *you* were knighted today, my dear? Congratulations, Sir Mary Ann! I knew you had it in you!"

And the truth was, she *had* known. Lady Carmine had, in fact, been the very first person to suggest Cornelius Clashammer as Mary Ann's trainer. She was one of the first people to look past Mary Ann's housemaid's uniform (even while she was cleaning the bedchamber), and picture her in the role of a knight without any reservation. And as tears sprang to Mary Ann's eyes at this thought, Lady Carmine hugged her, too.

"Thank you, My Lady," Mary Ann managed finally, quite out of breath, and trying not to put tear stains on the woman's beautiful silk gown. For such a slim and statuesque woman, Rufus' mother was certainly not delicate with her affection.

"Mother, I invited Sir Mary Ann to be our guest for tonight," said Rufus, and Mary Ann found herself holding back a smile about how suddenly formal he sounded. "She plans to live in her father's cottage, but it likely needs some preparation before she does so. I imagine we have a free room for her?"

"Of course! Mrs. Cordingley?" Lady Carmine turned to the small, starched housekeeper who appeared at her side. "Prepare the yellow guest room for Sir Mary Ann, please."

"Yes, My Lady," said Mrs. Cordingley, and swept off, but not before fixing Mary Ann with a pinched sideways glance, one that crossed between bewilderment with displeasure. It was not that long ago that Mary Ann had shared the female staff's bedchamber with Mrs. Cordingley and much of the other cooking and cleaning entourage. In fact, there was a part of Mary Ann that half-expected she'd be assigned to sleep there this very night, relegated once more to her past position in the household through a sense of tradition and habit. This turn of events felt odd.

"We're soon to sit down to supper," Lady Carmine told the returned travelers, "so, I imagine you both would like to wash up and get changed. Then I look forward to hearing all about your recent adventures."

Washing up sounded very good, indeed. There was a grime of looking-glass travel, pollen and road dust upon Mary Ann that she longed to wash away. But she realized there was a small problem with that plan; mainly, because she'd nothing to get changed into. The sum of her wardrobe was the training clothes she wore on her back. She regretted now leaving the altered pink housemaid's dress back at Cornelius Clashammer's. That had lacked foresight.

To the maids, Lady Carmine asked, "Would one of you ladies care to show Sir Mary Ann up to her room?"

But it was Emmaline, the scullery maid, who volunteered before they could even make a peep. "Oh, I'd be right pleased to do so, My Lady! Your guest and I were bunkmates back in the day! Come along, Tamsin," for that was the alias Mary Ann had chosen when she first went to work at Carmine Manor.

They headed to the grand staircase. "But I suppose you don't answer to Tamsin these days, do you, since that's not your real name?" Emmaline's always-rosy cheeks flushed a deeper hue. "I'm afraid 'Sir Mary Ann' is going to be a bit of an adjustment for me. As much because of the 'Mary Ann' as the 'Sir.' Though calling girls 'Sir' feels a bit strange, too, doesn't it? Did they run out of titles for the girl knights or doesn't it matter, so long as you're good with a sword?"

Mary Ann had quite forgotten how much Emmaline could say in a single breath. "I'm not sure of the tradition," Mary Ann said. She wasn't even sure there were other female knights in Red Turvy. Rufus had never mentioned it either way.

Emmaline looked at Mary Ann's hands, empty now except for her graduation scroll. "Should I have Mr. Francis collect your travel cases or are your things being sent for?"

"No cases," said Mary Ann. "And none to arrive."

The scullery maid's brown eyes widened. "There's just you?"

"There's just me," said Mary Ann.

"My!" Emmaline started up the stairs, "you *do* travel light! I recall when you first came here, and you even had to borrow a nightdress. Weren't those the days? You were quite a source of interest for everyone then. Arriving out of the blue, vanishing all the time. Landing up on Jabberwock quests, helping Sir Rufus train, and getting into hot water with the Queen of Hearts. Did I hear right? Aren't you banned from Neath now?"

"I believe that's correct," said Mary Ann.

"I thought so!" Emmaline grinned like this was splendid news. "All right, this is it. This is you." She swung open the door to the yellow guest room, a beautiful space with sunshiny walls, a massive poster bed, seemingly endless fluffy pillows, and... Mrs. Cordingley, looking sour, turning down a blanket.

"Thank you, Mrs. Cordingley," said Mary Ann. "I appreciate your hospitality this evening."

"Sir Mary Ann," she intoned, inhospitably, and slipped past her, leaving the crisp smell of starch in the air.

"Oh, don't you worry about her," Emmaline said, as the door closed. "She'll come round. She's just a stickler for rules and I think she feels you've broken a few too many of them. You know, what with the lying, and all the time you've spent with Sir Rufus, and the fact you're not still a housemaid as is proper."

Mary Ann had a feeling it was something like that.

"Well," said Emmaline, "I'll leave you to your washing up. There should be washing-up water in the dry sink, and some lovely lavender soap and —" A thought creased Emmaline's brow. "How *are* you going to dress for dinner without any travel cases?"

"I suppose I thought I'd just wash up and wear this," Mary Ann said, indicating the grey tunic and trousers ensemble she was already in.

"Oh, Tamsin!" Emmaline's doe eyes filled with concern. "You can't wear your drawers to dine with the Baron and Baroness."

"Well, they're not drawers, they're—"

"You can borrow a dress from me. The one I wear to Unbirthdays. It's not fine enough for this household, really, but it'll be a sight better than you in your knickers."

"They're really not my kni—"

Emmaline ran to the door. "I'll be right back."

Mary Ann could hear her thunder away, down the hall, and up the back servant's staircase to the third floor. She'd hardly finished washing her face, when she heard the thunder resume in reverse, then a knock at the door. Emmaline burst in after the knock. "Here you go! It's my best!"

The dress was a colorful and dense floral print, with buttons up the bodice and two layers of sweet lace dripping from puffed sleeves.

Mary Ann held it up. Emmaline was tall and shapely compared to Mary Ann, and her taste was significantly more bright and lively than Mary Ann's was. Or at least, brighter and livelier than Mary Ann *thought hers would be*; she'd rarely had a need for garments that weren't uniforms, aside from the occasional nightdress, so she wasn't entirely certain what her taste was.

"Do you like it?" Emmaline asked, shifting from foot to foot excitedly.

"Very much. It is a beautiful dress," Mary Ann said sincerely. And it was. Both in the obvious Emmaline-ness of it all, as well as the thoughtful gesture to share it. "Thank you. I'll take good care of it and return it to you."

Emmaline moved to the exit. "Supper's in about twenty minutes. In particular, I hope you'll like the cheese tartlets; I made them! My own recipe! Cook's letting me debut a few of my own dishes these days. I'm not just a pot scrubber anymore, Tamsin; she said I've 'potential!'"

"I'm sure it will be wonderful." Mary Ann decided she would love it and tell the girl so, even if it gave her terrible indigestion.

"Oh, and there I go again…" Emmaline pressed a hand to her forehead, "calling you Tamsin." Her redness deepened. "I'm so sorry, Tam—uh, I mean, Sir Mary Ann. I mean no disrespect by it. I just—"

Mary Ann patted her arm. "For an old friend such as yourself, Emmaline, I think 'Tamsin' is perfectly fine."

"Oh, Mrs. Cordingley won't like that. Not that one bit."

"Even better," said Mary Ann.

Mary Ann came down to supper both looking and smelling like a day at the Red Turvy Royal Botanical Gardens and it made her heart happy. The dress was, indeed, a bit too big and certainly too long, so she'd rolled it up at the waist and tied the sash as tightly as possible, to avoid catching the hem in her boots, the only footwear she had. Lady Carmine was, of course, far too gracious to reveal what she might have been thinking about the ensemble, but Mary Ann noticed Sir Rufus raise an eyebrow before catching himself and putting on a neutral expression. And Lord Carmine didn't take notice at all, since Mary Ann was not a cheese tartlet.

Yes, it was a successful meal altogether, Mary Ann thought, as she and Rufus recounted their schooling at Clashammer's and their day trying to track down fabled, feathered fiends and the missing D.M. Tweedle.

Her thoughts were with Tweedle still, as she prepared for bed in the beautiful, big bedchamber that she had all to herself. If Damian Tweedle had indeed been plucked from his home by some enormous crow, was he — with his silver buttons and badge and glossy boots — simply some shiny object the bird coveted for its own? Or was he a tasty tidbit to quell an outsized hunger? If the latter, how long would it take for Tweedle to become said tidbit? Were they too late now? Or were they late before they even started?

Mary Ann thought these ideas would keep her from her rest, a swirl of concerns to path through in the space between consciousness and dream. But the bed was so lush and the bedding so soft and enveloping, and she was so very tired from the day, that she fell asleep before she'd rolled over even once, the trials of D.M. Tweedle somehow swiftly forgotten.

7

The noise was not the wake-up gong Mr. Springer rang each morning promptly at five. No, it was a rapid knocking, curt and persistent. Then it was the squeak of a door and a nasal voice, sharp and too-close, saying, "Sir Mary Ann! It is time to rise! You are wanted."

"Wanted?" Mary Ann murmured, prying her head from the most marvelous pillow she'd ever met. She didn't know bedding could have such an effect, and she couldn't imagine life outside of this bed when this pillow loved her so very much and only wanted her to be happy. "It's nice to be wanted," she breathed, as the pillow continued to whisper a feathery case for more sleep into her ear. "It makes *such* a frabjous change."

"Then we are both in agreement about the dubious need for your presence," said the voice sourly. "Wonderful. Yet nonetheless, Lady Carmine has requested it in the private family parlor for breakfast." Mary Ann heard water being poured. "Completely inappropriate for a random houseguest, I daresay. Some are simply far too flexible with the rules of society and etiquette in this household; though, out of respect, I shall not express whom." There was a clunk. "But here we are. Which means, Sir Mary Ann—or whoever you claim to be today—it is time to get up, get dressed, and meet with your hosts. I'll give you ten minutes to wash and put on some clothes and Mabel will bring you to the chamber."

Mabel was the parlor maid.

The footsteps started off across the wooden floorboards and then stopped. "Oh, and to avoid the flowered fright I saw you dining in last evening, I'm returning that dress to Emmaline, and the clothes you arrived in have been washed, dried and pressed. I've laid them on the chair. You should perhaps consider investing in a few new garments, if you plan to rejoin civilized society soon."

"Thank you, Mrs. Cordingley, for your care and attention to detail," said Mary Ann.

There was a noise, perhaps a sniff, then the door closed.

Mary Ann glanced at the clock on the fireplace mantel. It was half-seven. *My goodness,* she thought, swinging her feet to the floor. *When was the last time I slept until half-seven?* She couldn't recall. She'd no nightdress with her, so getting changed into the fresh clothes was quicker than normal, and the morning chill outside the glorious blankets encouraged that along. She washed, finger-combed and re-plaited her hair. And just as her feet slipped into her boots, Mabel knocked, calling to take her to the breakfast venue.

Mary Ann had never seen this room, as it had always been Mabel's territory to clean. It was decorated in traditional Turvian fashion, with cerulean blues, greens and reds, black and white checkerboard, and a series of family portraits. The wall was papered in a sculpted quatrefoil rose symbol, painted a metallic blue that reflected the morning light nicely. It was bordered at the top with an elaborate frieze of red roses and vines. Lord and Lady Carmine seemed dressed to enhance it. As Mary Ann laid eyes on the tasteful attire of her hosts this morning—neither of them wearing coarse grey training clothes —she wished she could have hung onto Emmaline's garden of flowers just a wee bit longer. She felt out of place, and she wondered if that hadn't been a point Mrs. Cordingley was hoping to make. She might have felt differently if Rufus were present, but for now, the Baron and his wife were the only family in the parlor.

Lord Carmine was slurping tea from a porcelain cup and reading the morning edition of *The Turvy Mirror*. "Ah, young lady, please have a seat. Martha, pour the girl a cup of tea, would you please?"

Mabel—for that was still her name—asked, "Do you drink tea? How do you take it?"

"Yes, please," said Mary Ann. "Just a bit of sugar, please." It was odd to have Mabel waiting on her, since not long ago, she and Mabel were colleagues. Worse, Mabel had been the one to spread rumors of Mary Ann's supposed calculating and inappropriate behavior with their young employer, before their whole murder mystery investigation side-job was revealed to the world. Being extra polite to Mabel was not likely to ease things in a better direction, since the girl already thought Mary Ann a social-climbing seductress, and her invitation here seemed more proof of that. But Mary Ann also felt the kindness couldn't hurt.

"Did you sleep well?" Lady Carmine asked, buttering a slice of toast with the delicacy of a painter putting detail on an oil masterpiece.

"Yes, Lady Carmine, frabjously so," Mary Ann said.

"I'm glad to hear it," and she patted Mary Ann's hand with her toast-free one. "Help yourself to anything on the table, dear. Rufus should be in soon. He's never much been one for early days."

Mary Ann smiled. "I'd a sense of that at Mr. Clashammer's. But he pushed through it well enough."

Lady Carmine looked pleased to hear this.

"Ruddy Pennwell!" exclaimed Lord Carmine. "I felt it in my bones and yet I didn't boot *his* all the way down the road the moment I laid eyes on him. Well, there won't be a second time. That I assure you."

"What's the trouble, dear?" asked Lady Carmine.

"Right here, second page!" Lord Carmine was folding the paper to the topic in question and jabbing a thick finger at it. "Mr. Pennwell does us dirty on the Tweedle case. Listen to this:

```
'After last months series of viscous serial
murders across Square Four, which left Red
Turvy shuttering in terror, the Baron
Sorrel, Lord Carmine certainly took his
time getting round to mounting any sort of
investigation. Somewhere out there, right
now, Detective Manager Dominic Tweadle's
mangled body could be lying in the nest of
a giant bird of pray whose not quite ready
for the leftovers yet. And Carmine's
guards, as led by his teenaged son and a
knight so new the ink's still wet on her
training certificate, show that nepotism in
Turvian aristocracy is alive and well, and
distracted by other more pressing
matters.' "
```

And that's where the photo of Mary Ann and Rufus kissing landed up.

"Oh, no," said Mary Ann. "I can explain. We were just so surprised about my being knighted and—"

Rufus could not have entered the room at a worse time. Or a better one. Mary Ann wasn't sure which. "Morning," he mumbled and uttered something else, possibly the word "tea," because he reached for the teapot, even as Mabel stood with a full cup at the ready.

Lord Carmine was certainly ready for him. "So, are you courting this girl or not, Rupert? We need to know, if we're going to deal with this *Mirror* nonsense."

The young man who was not Rupert regarded his father, foggily. "Eh?" Mabel just tucked the teacup straight into his hand.

"Since you blab everything to your mother, but I can't wring two civil words out of you myself, last night I asked your mum what the flappin' Jubjub was going on with you and this young lady. And she told me it was best if I talk to you. So, this is me talking to you."

"This'll teach me not to have a lie-in," muttered Rufus, taking a considerable draught of tea.

"You and Sir Madelyn here," said Lord Carmine, indicating their breakfast guest. "You start out stabbing Jabberwocks and solving murders together and now you're engaged, is that it?"

"Whoa, whoa there," said Rufus, waking up very fast now. "You went from courting to engaged in five seconds. What's happening?"

"We aren't engaged, My Lord," said Mary Ann.

"Ah, but I get it. Things like this happen all the time," said Lord Carmine. "Many a fine relationship has been built on a foundation of monster-slaying and amateur detective work. Why, all the great love stories of our time start out as a bit of convivial murder-solving, maybe a quick firedrake fileting. But you need to be more verbal to your family about these things! You can't go kissing in front of reporters without informing the family first that the mutual mystery and mayhem have ensnared you."

Rufus exhaled in frustration. "Father, ever since Mary Ann and I met, there's either been people trying to kill us, a whole knight school hanging round, or we're hiking through the forest looking for rampaging rooks and taken Tweedles. As far as courtships go, this has to have been one of the least romantic ones in Turvian history. Wanderlands history, perhaps! We've had no downtime whatsoever, and far less kissing than we deserve. So back off."

"Well, that sort of thing's unlikely to satisfy the readers of *The Mirror*," Lord Carmine said.

"And that is not our problem," said Rufus.

Mary Ann was trying very hard not to laugh.

Lady Carmine turned to her husband. "Oh, darling, I wouldn't worry about what Mr. Pennwell wrote. Everyone knows *The Turvy Mirror* is a horrible rag." She took a second slice of toast. "I mean, I spied at least four typos just in that one paragraph, not to mention the factual inaccuracies."

"Mother was originally a governess," Rufus told Mary Ann, *soto voce*. And suddenly Mary Ann had a much better understanding of the Carmine family dynamics.

Lord Carmine was across the room now and Lady Carmine craned her neck to see him. "Dear, what are you doing?"

He appeared to be rummaging about in the drawer of a table. "Penning a letter to the editor, to set this whole thing straight." He came away with pen, paper and ink.

The Baroness looked worried. "If you must, but I'm not sure what good it will do." And now Lord Carmine was headed for the door with his writing supplies. "Where are you going?"

"To the library for a dictionary. I need to check how to spell 'snollygoster' and 'prevaricator.'"

"I can help you with that, dear. S-n-o—"

But he was gone.

"So, er—" Lady Carmine's smile looked pained, "how did you sleep, Rufus?"

"Mostly on my side," he said, grabbing a scone and offering the plate to Mary Ann. "Also, better than I have in a while. Those cots of Clashammer's were little better than sleeping on the ground."

"Yes, it was nice to be in a real bed after all that time," agreed Mary Ann, thinking fondly once more of the best rest she'd ever gotten. "Your home is simply lovely, Lady Carmine. I was noticing the portraits there. How old was Sir Rufus in that one?"

The painting was of Rufus and another boy sitting in a settee outside. Rufus' deeply red hair was madder than usual and he hadn't quite grown into his facial features. The aura of attractiveness he projected now was not in evidence. The other boy, Mary Ann noticed, was ginger, too, but his hair was straight, orangey and plastered to his skull with a parting down the middle. He looked younger and stockier. He had a conventionally handsome face, very balanced features, and a little smile.

Lady Carmine assessed it. "Rufus is in his squire's gear there, so I'd say he was about 14."

Rufus turned to look at the painting. "Oh, that one's a horror. I wish you'd let me take it down and put something else up. Like a nice landscape. Anything easier to digest by. We eat here, after all."

"Oh, shush, you. It's a beautiful portrait," his mother said.

Mary Ann asked, "And who is the other boy?"

"That's Cliff," said Rufus flatly.

"Radcliff," corrected Lady Carmine, "Rufus' younger brother."

"I didn't know you had a brother," said Mary Ann.

Rufus popped in a bite of buttered scone. "Well, perhaps I don't."

"Rufus!" Lady Carmine's tone was uncharacteristically sharp.

"Be realistic, Mother. We haven't heard a peep from him in three years. We don't know what's happened to him. Whether he's alive, dead, carried off by a Boojum … Who's to say?"

"It *was* an unfortunate scene when he left," said Lady Carmine. "I wish it had all gone differently."

Rufus leaned back in his chair. "If it hadn't been that day, it would have been some other," he said.

Mary Ann set down her cup. "Do you mind telling me what happened?" And it got very quiet in the room. "If I've overstepped by asking, do say so. I meant no disrespect."

Lady Carmine said, "Radcliff was just 16 when he left us. It was the day Rufus was being knighted. It was a very big deal because being knighted at 18 is quite early. But Rufus had truly applied himself."

Rufus said, "Not having my guts strung across Tulgey Barrens was a powerful motivator."

"The way you talk sometimes!" Lady Carmine fixed him with a look, then turned back to Mary Ann. "With Rufus being knighted, I suppose Radcliff felt some pressure. He had always been competitive with Rufus, in the way little brothers are. Always following him around, wanting to do what Rufus did."

"Yes, but always too late," said Rufus. "Like, remember when he said he'd decided he wanted to be a knight? It was the very day I became a squire. And I remember Father telling him, 'Absolutely, if that's what you want. Train to be a knight.' But then when he learned that as a twelve-year-old, he'd still have to start as a page with the six-year-olds and pay his dues, he got cross about it and suddenly didn't want it anymore. He thought he was going to just jump into squiring right away."

"Oh, I don't know about that," Lady Carmine said, but her tone suggested he wasn't wrong. "It was on the day of Rufus' knighting ceremony, right before the event, that Radcliff told us he wanted to be the next heir to the Barony...That it was due him since Rufus got a knighthood and a prophecy. He said it was unfair that with all that, Rufus was also next in line to be Lord Carmine, and that there was nothing good left for Radcliff. He said if we would just agree to give him the Barony when the time came..." She shook her head. "He even had papers made up for us to sign to transfer the title upon my husband's death."

Mary Ann gasped. "I imagine that didn't go over well."

"Father hit the roof," said Rufus. "Literally. I mean he grabbed the papers on their clipboard from Cliff and just flung them as far as he could. And, you know, clipboards are fairly aerodynamic, so those papers in that clipboard ended up right on the roof by the tower. Stayed there for a good week like that, too, until the gardener got a ladder and fetched them down."

"Anyway," continued Lady Carmine, "you can imagine the argument that arose, and right as all the guests were arriving. Radcliff was shouting, 'Fine, I'll make my own future without your help, without anyone's help.' And that was it. He packed a trunk and left, right in the middle of Rufus' ceremony."

"Made as much noise as he could doing it, too," said Rufus. "Sending for a hired carriage, loading his things. All very... Cliff."

Lady Carmine said, "So it's been ... what, three-and-a-half years now? And we still haven't heard from him. And that's despite Lord Carmine putting feelers out for him with various connections."

"That carriage driver certainly wasn't talking," said Rufus. "I think Radcliff paid him off."

"My goodness, what a story," said Mary Ann, with a sigh. She'd often thought it would have been nice to have siblings to commiserate with about her own family situation. But she supposed there were no guarantees for harmony there, either.

The clock on the mantel chimed, and Mary Ann checked the time. "Eight. Well, if I'm going to do my shopping, I suppose I'd best be off." She didn't want to say it, but she planned to stop by her father's cottage first and see what she might sell, to create some workable funds for her shopping expedition. She was very tired of having less than the barest of essentials, and too many quick escapes meant repeatedly leaving behind the few possessions she had.

"I hope you know you're welcome to stay with us until you get your cottage settled," Lady Carmine said. "I know that's not an easy task."

"I appreciate your kind hospitality, My Lady. Yesterday was a very long day, and a good night's rest was just the thing. But I've imposed long enough, and I must find my own way."

Rufus said, "What time do you think you'll be done?"

"Ten, perhaps?"

"Fine. I'll meet you at your cottage at ten, then, and update you on where we are with the Tweedle issue."

"Perfect."

Mary Ann had not set foot in the cottage since she'd — well, "tricked," really *was* the right word, though she was loathe to fully apply it — *tricked* Rufus into helping her deliver a mirror from her father's workshop to Mr. Rabbit's home in Neath. This was back when Mary Ann was working as a full-time housemaid, part-time Jabberwock defense trainer for the Carmine family, and their interpersonal dynamics were very different then. She was glad she was seeing the little house today in the morning light and not the lantern glow of the previous evening. In day, the domicile drained of some of its burdened memories and heavy dread. In morning light, the wooden walls and floor looked dusty and washed out, uncleaned and unpolished, sapped of everything, possibly even the freshness of bad memory. It was like an eye that had cried so much, there was no more moisture left for tears.

Besides, she was on a mission today — a very practical mission—and practical missions had a nice way of keeping her going, the more practical, the better. So, she went through the pantry shelves, seeing what was there and what might be nice to have on hand. (Her father had some jarred and tinned foods, but it was hard to tell just how long any of it had been stored there.) He had some acceptable washing up things left, and an extra set of sheets.

With that assessed, she left the cottage for her father's workshop next door. She moved down the path, swung open the door and, to her surprise, what she noticed first was not that gorrible blood stain on the floor, the one that never quite scrubbed out. What she laid eyes on was an envelope, propped up on the workshop table, leaning against a wooden box. The envelope read "MARY ANN CARPENTER," in large capital letters.

She opened the envelope and withdrew a note. It read:

Dearest Miss Carpenter:

Our mutual friend Sir Rufus informed me that you would be pursuing vocational training in Thither for some time, but that you had offered me permission to select work from your father's remaining stock, as a form of thank you for past support. I trust, given Sir Rufus' reputation for forthright behavior, that this offer is correct.

As an avid collector of Rowan Carpenter's art, I was naturally honored to have been thought of by you in this way and at such a time. And it is as this avid collector, I was unable to resist the opportunity to choose a few small pieces from the items in this room that would enhance my current collection.

That said, after great consideration, I realize I am unable to accept them without some form of renumeration. Therefore, I have left you compensation for the items, estimated based on past purchases paid through Mr. Carpenter's business partner, J. Sanford Banks. I recognize it is possible the rates for Mr. Carpenter's work may have risen, as they are now limited in availability. So, I will leave it to you to assess whether the amount left in the box with this letter is adequate and add that I am open to further negotiation, as required.

Know that the pieces are now gracing my home, being cherished daily. I should love to have you over to tea when you find it convenient, so I may show them to you *in situ*. I hope that your career change brings you great joy and that this letter finds you well.

Your friend always,
Douglas Divot

PS: I have just discovered an amazing lavender Turvydale cheese that you simply must try. It is a game-changer at tea-time with a bit of fruit.

Mary Ann dabbed at her eyes with the sleeve of her shirt, feeling about six emotions at once, and still smiling at the note at the end about the cheese. Douglas Divot was a tove, a digging species native to Turvy, like a badger in appearance but with spiral horns and tail like a corkscrew. Douglas had been there for Mary Ann right after she witnessed her father's beheading, a time she'd particularly needed a kind word and a good confidant. And he was the one who introduced her to the Carmine family. He'd helped her bury her father. He'd helped her secure a job and a safe place to hide while Mary Ann sorted out the details of her father's murder. She would have done anything to repay Douglas Divot for his assistance during that painful time, and a bit of free furniture had seemed like only a start.

She set the letter aside and opened the box — a box, she noticed, her father had made himself. Douglas Divot had paid her for the furniture all right. She was uncertain at the total, but she had no intention of counting the money; it would be a betrayal of sorts to question it. All she knew was that in that box was more than sufficient funding for whatever Douglas Divot might have taken from the workshop. And she considered any imbalance that might remain through the items' increased rarity ripped up, set on fire, and ash to the wind, never to be spoken of again.

So, the possibilities of shopping at the Square Five market just got that much easier for Mary Ann Carpenter. She'd originally planned to tote a few pieces of her father's work with her, for sale or barter along the way. Now she was able to focus more directly on her shopping list and ways she could transform the cottage into a space that had fewer malevolent memories and a mite more Mary Ann-ness to it. It would be a good start.

She was on her way, money and list in hand, making the crossing from Square Four to Five. That's when she noticed a light coming from a shady treed area, right before the streams that marked the Four/Five crossing.

She paused and peered, as memories began swirling in her mind. That's right, that was the old castle she was fascinated with as a child. Things had grown up around it in the past decade, and it had been abandoned even back then. She had a sense it was result of some battle that even preceded the infamous Battle of Square Four. And the courtiers who lived there had fled, leaving nothing but architecture and atmosphere in their void. It was strange to see a light there after all this time, but then she wasn't seeing it now, was she? Perhaps it had been a trick of the morning sun, a quick reflection off a glass windowpane.

It hardly mattered. There were errands to run, and Mary Ann was greatly cheered by the idea of getting some long-needed supplies.

Square Five was at the height of its morning bustle. Mary Ann wished she'd gotten an earlier start to avoid all the noise and people, but it did add some energy to the experience. And Mary Ann was already energized by her prospects because, for the first time in her life, she was about to choose her own clothes. From age ten onward, Mary Ann's wardrobe had consisted of uniforms. Whether it was a housemaid's dress or even the training gear at Mr. Clashammer's, what Mary Ann put on her body was not of her own selection, and her liking or not liking it was irrelevant to the matter at hand; it simply *was*. Knighting, of course, came with its own general uniform. But for non-formal-knighting days, as it was for Sir Rufus, Mary Ann would be free to wear what she liked.

But what did she like? She had no idea. She knew the vibrant floral patterns and ruffles Emmaline preferred suited Emmaline to a T, but they seemed a bit overmuch on Mary Ann's smaller frame and less vociferous temperament. As to color, Mary Ann had been daily ensconced in pink or red, and even grey now felt very overdone. So, she chose a simple, everyday dress in a hunter green that seemed to coordinate well enough with her eyes. (It had not been lost on her that Rufus had an unspoken strategy of wearing pops of blue when the occasion presented itself, and that worked to good effect.) Perhaps she was still thinking of him as she selected another simple dress in a hydrangea shade, then a final selection — something for a special occasion — in a deep almost black burgundy. The gown was red enough to support her Turvian roots, of course, but far from the true red of her past maid's uniform. These items, with one pair of neutral dress shoes, stockings, undergarments, a proper nightdress, dressing gown and slippers completed her purchases at that shop. The proprietor was surprised she didn't want to have them tailored. The simple fact was she needed them now and there was no time.

She made a second stop at Knightwhere, a specialty shoppe "for the cavalier on-the-go." There she got two sets of tunics and trousers, one in red and one in cerulean, that she could mix-and-match. She picked up a cheap vanity set, some thread and needles, and toiletries at the chemist, and generally felt a renewed sense of hope. It had been so very long that she had been simply making do or borrowing things from people, she hardly knew how to handle it.

Lastly, she went to a general store and selected some dry goods — things that would make hearty meals but that would keep nicely. She a fetched a new bucket and a pot of zarlene oil, to put some warmth back into the wood of the cottage once it had a good cleaning. And there were other things she had her eye on, but there was a limit to how much one could carry by oneself during this trip. She vowed she would have to return when she was more settled. She had an idea that she might like fabric to make new curtains and bedding — something to freshen up the place. She also made note to pick up some of that Turvydale cheese for Douglas Divot on a future excursion. One when she was less pressed for time, so she could bring it by, show her gratitude, and they could catch up.

Mary Ann had not been long back at the cottage when Rufus knocked and poked his head in. "May I come in?"

"Oh, is it ten o'clock already?" She had no way of knowing. Her father had a clock—in fact, he'd made the casing for it— but it hadn't been wound and there was nothing to set it by. "I suppose my shopping trip took longer than I anticipated."

"Quite all right." Rufus eyed the pile of supplies. "Did you get all you need? That doesn't look like much for an entire household."

It had seemed like quite a lot to her, particularly as she was carrying it back across bridges and through woods. "I'm certainly in a better position now than I was," she said. "I'm afraid I didn't get very far in the cleaning, though."

"No worries. I'll help. And I can brief you on where we are with the Tweedle case." As he slung his jacket over a chair and started rolling up his sleeves, Mary Ann tried not to look at him with the surprise she felt. She had assumed, given his return home to the comfort of servants and lying-in, that the social gap between them might widen once more and they'd be back where they started. That the inequity of their situation which held her back in the beginning would ultimately make what seemed like a beautiful, treasured thing show itself for a fragile and far too optimistic idea. But he was off winding up the mantel clock, setting it to the time of his pocket watch. "There you are. At least, that's one thing solved. Where do the dry goods go?"

As they put things away, dusted and swept up, Rufus recounted news of the Tweedle incident. "Seems Detective Inspector Dorian Tweedle is as namblesiaed as he was yesterday. No memory of what happened, but he's been keeping himself busy polishing his rattle collection. So, I suppose some sense of self is still lurking in there, waiting for its resurgence. He asked the guards to fetch him a bottle of silver polish, I understand."

Mary Ann started on scrubbing the floor. "That does sound like our old D.I. Tweedle," she said.

"It's probably just as well he doesn't remember, with his brother gone," said Rufus, wiping down the cast-iron cooker. "The two were inseparable. I find it hard to see one without the other. It feels…wrong."

"And any news of Detective Major Damian Tweedle?" Mary Ann asked, looking up from her scrub brush.

"The other Square Four guards combed the area and gave it a nice parting, but…nothing. And our knights searched as best they could, even by lantern-light last night, then resumed this morning. As of when I left, Father hasn't heard anything new. I'm not holding out a lot of hope at this point. But Mother tells me I'm cynical."

"Then perhaps you won't be as shocked as I think you might be when I suggest the thing I'm about to say," said Mary Ann.

He peered at her around the half-wall between the kitchen and bedroom with interest. "See, that's one thing I love about you, Mary Ann. You keep me on my toes."

Mary Ann tried very hard not to get hung up on those words, though her heart was beating just a bit faster now. "Right then," she said, "hear me out on this: what if D.M. Tweedle was never taken by a crow?"

"All right...?"

"What if D.I. Tweedle is not suffering from 'namblesia' at all? What if he's pretending? And what if D.I. Tweedle is directly responsible for his brother's disappearance, and permanently?"

"Well, that's dark!" He paused, wet cloth in mid-air. "So, you're saying Dorian got sick of Damian to the point of murder? And buried him in the backyard or some such thing? Then staged the feather/crow/'namblesia' scenario for the postman to see?"

"That's exactly what I'm saying."

"Mary Ann Carpenter, you're terrifying." Rufus laughed, a tinge of admiration in his voice.

"I just keep thinking: they're always together, very insular. And they're always fighting. Plus, there was that resentment with Damian Tweedle being promoted over Dorian. The postman said there were rows over it specifically."

"It's certainly interesting," said Rufus, tapping his fingers together. "And I can't say your theory is without merit. But I will need to think about it further." He picked up the rag again. "In your scenario, the weapon of choice for this was...?"

Mary Ann rose and moved her bucket. "The missing rattle."

"The missing rattle," he murmured, nodding. "Terrifying! Absolutely disturbing, the way you think. Great gryphons, I am way in over my head with you, aren't I?"

At least he was still laughing about it.

In about an hour and a half, they'd gotten the cottage in pretty good shape. And as for the Tweedle case, Rufus sent a rocking-horsefly to the guards at the Tweedle residence, asking them to look for any area of recently dug up earth but to keep their goals from D.I. Tweedle. Rufus had additionally wanted to send a second rocking-horsefly to Lord Carmine, explaining Mary Ann's theory.

But Mary Ann urged caution. "I don't know if I'm right at all. And if I'm wrong, I don't want to openly accuse D.I. Tweedle of murder. Also, if he did dispose of his brother, there's no rule that says he would have done so on his own property. In fact, that seems quite unlikely. So, I'd rather not show our hand before absolutely necessary."

Rufus was so used to being able to take the direct route and just get things done, she could tell he was a little frustrated by these backchannel methods. But he agreed to try it her way.

He rolled down his sleeves again and put on the jacket. "In a quest to follow all lines of inquiry, I'm thinking this afternoon we go interview those crow families to the south and east."

"I'm for that," Mary Ann said.

"Hopefully one of them might have information on our supposed crow perpetrator. Or at least have laid eyes on D.M. Tweedle. That is, if Tweedle isn't pushing up the daisies in the back garden." From his coat pocket, he removed something wrapped in wax paper. It was a sandwich. "Want half?"

It was just past noon, and the morning truly had been hungry work. "Yes, please."

Munching roast beef, cheese and watercress, they headed to the main road. As they passed the junction that led to Square Five, Mary Ann was reminded of something. "You know, I saw lights there this morning."

"Where?"

"That old, abandoned castle or manor or whatever it is. I saw a light in one of the windows, as I was heading to the market. At least, I think I did."

"That's odd." Sandwich finished, he folded the wax paper from it and tucked it back in his pocket. "I hadn't heard anything about anyone moving in there. In fact, I can't imagine it's habitable."

"Is this still considered Carmine here?"

"I'm not sure where the boundaries are on this side of things," he said.

Mary Ann laughed. "Imagine having so much property you don't even know where it ends."

She shouldn't have said it. The moment it was out of her mouth, she knew she'd made a mistake.

"Well, it's not mine, is it?" He shot her a sharp look. "I've only been peripherally involved with the Barony. The Jabberwock business was quite enough to have on one's mind, I think."

"I'm sorry," she said quickly. "You're quite right. I misspoke. I—I shouldn't have—"

He put up a hand. "No, it's my fault; I shouldn't have snapped." He sighed. "And you're right. I really should know, shouldn't I? It makes me… I'm really not ungrateful for what I have, Mary Ann. And I know you think I am. Or that I'm out of touch, or too lofty or something. And sometimes I do forget how different our lives have been. I need to remember." The flush was dying down in his face, and now he just looked sad.

She took his hand. "I don't really believe you're ungrateful. And I do know you're trying. Sometimes I'm just acutely aware of how out of my element I am."

He nodded and squeezed her hand. "Well, if someone is living in the old Mulberry place, I would at least like to make Father aware of it. Do you mind a little detour?"

"Not at all."

And they headed down the road to the castle.

What hadn't been abundantly obvious in the early morning light was much clearer now, as there were workmen carrying boards and mixing mortar.

"Gentlemen," Rufus called to them, summoning a smile now. "This is Sir Mary Ann of Tulgey Barrens and I'm Sir Rufus of Carmine Manor. We're technically your neighbors. We just thought we'd stop by, introduce ourselves, and see what you all are up to here." Mary Ann found it amazing how he managed this, asking people straight to their face what they were doing. Even more amazing was that people were generally happy to tell him.

In this case, the people were two beavers and a frilled lizard.

"Not a neighbor of mine, Sir," said the frilled lizard, not unkindly, "as I live at Tulgey Lake myself. But we're preparing for the arrival of the Count. Getting the place in shape for him. Needs a bit of work, as you can see."

"Which Count?" Rufus asked.

"Lex, the Count Talionis," said one of the beavers. "He's originally from the realm of Erstwhile, but he plans to summer here in Turvy."

"Interesting," said Rufus. "I can't say I recognize the name."

"Oh, I'm sure you've heard it at one point or another, Sir. Count Talionis is the man who singlehandedly freed the forced labor from the Erstwhile mead mines."

Rufus frowned. "I didn't know there were mead mines in Erstwhile."

"That's because nobody's forced to work 'em these days," said the lizard, with a knowing nod.

"Count Talionis sailed the Molasses Sea in just two hours, breaking the Wanderlands' all-time record," said a beaver.

The other beaver said, "In his travels, the Count discovered a new form of chicken what lays square eggs."

"Those poor chickens," breathed Mary Ann.

"Perfect for stacking, you see," explained the beaver.

"And don't forget," added the lizard, "how Count Talionis rescued Princess Whosis from the clutches of some dangerous monster-something."

"Of course!" said Rufus. "*That* Count Talionis."

"But now, begging your pardon, Sirs, we'd best get back to work. Loads to do," said the first beaver.

"Understood," said Rufus. "A pleasure to have met you all."

And as they walked away, Mary Ann said, "You still have no idea who Count Talionis is, do you?"

"Nope," he grinned. "Curious thing, though. Off to the crows, then?"

"To the crows," she said.

8

Rufus said, "Now that I've had time to mull it over, there's one thing that bothers me about your latest Tweedle theory."

"Oh, yes?" Mary Ann was quite eager to hear this. Puzzling over the case was a wonderful way to distract themselves on their journey to interview the crows, and thus, get where they were going in better time. "Do tell."

"I believe the flaw in your thinking is this: you erroneously assume D.I. Tweedle to be mentally capable of engineering such a plot. You have given him too much credit for cunning. Moreover, it is D.M. Tweedle who is missing, yet he is a relative brainbox compared to his brother, and that is the reason he is the one who got promoted. Yet even Damian's quite lucky to be able to buckle his own boots and find his way out of the house in the morning. That is why your theory cannot stand."

"But if they're so incompetent, why did you father hire them?"

Rufus shrugged a shoulder. "It was never a drawback until Turvy actually started experiencing crime."

"I see," Mary Ann said.

"Otherwise, everything you mentioned fits together beautifully, and makes it worthy of further exploration. But the fact remains that you applied your quite impressive intellect to a situation that required the cognitive power of a Tweedle. And that is where it all goes pear-shaped."

"Now you mention it, you've a point there. I recognize my failure of logic in this case." Mary Ann was disappointed, but also somewhat relieved. Fratricide was an ugly thing, and she would have hated to think everyone had ignored and trivialized its potential warning signs all along. "You see, this is why I prefer keeping theories to myself a bit before setting them on the table. I'm not always right, so they need some time to marinade."

He nodded. "I can see the benefits of that. But no worries. We'll figure it out," and he squeezed her hand.

The group of crows to the south—Leonard's murder—were pleasant enough about questions, but the discussion ultimately revealed little new information. None of them knew of a massive crow in Turvy and none admitted to hitting the Burgeonboosh hard in recent days. No one had seen a human resembling D.M. Tweedle but all of them promised they would keep an eye out, as the crow flies.

So, Mary Ann and Rufus trekked east, looking for Burt's murder. They knew they were getting close when the mossy land began to bubble and they had to walk single-file down the path, to avoid sinking in the hot springs. (It ended up in their boots nonetheless.) Yet for all their effort, and sweat, and slog, the story remained the same. No Tweedle. No giant crow. And this time, a bit of croaky laughter about two grown humans believing Ole Inky was anything other than a faerie story.

The knights began their return trip with hot springs in their boots and less spring in their step than when they started. It was deflating.

"Maybe the postman didn't see what he saw," Mary Ann mused. They were heading back to Carmine Manor, to see if any new news about the Tweedle case had arrived in their absence. "Maybe it wasn't a giant feather at all. Maybe the postman just mistook something else for a feather because he's got birds on the brain."

"It did look like bird tracks," Rufus admitted.

"But did it really? Or did we just think so because the postman was already talking about crows? Could it have been the tracks of a wheelbarrow or some other cart? Marks from a dropped pile of wood? Or a carriage wheel on a muddy day?"

Rufus shook his head.

"Right then, I'm not going to think like a Mary Ann." To the forest she proclaimed: "I am going to think like a Tweedle!"

Rufus grinned. "Oh, I can't wait to see this."

"So, I am D.M. Tweedle. How d'ye do? And shake hands!" she said, trying to do the Tweedles' accent.

"How d'ye do?" Rufus took her hand, but it was far more of a clasp than a shake.

"Oh, come now! I'm D.M. Tweedle," she laughed. "You're not going to hold Damian Tweedle's hand like that, are you?"

"Erm, no." Rufus let her hand drop.

"So, I'm D.M. Tweedle and I've got this spiffing new rattle for the collection. I've carved out the perfect display space for it. I want to show it off a bit. I say, 'Look, D.I.—'"

"You'd likely call him Dorian."

"'Look, Dorian, at this splendiferous rattle that arrived for me today.'"

Rufus scratched the back of his head. "But his brother would know about it already, wouldn't he?"

Mary Ann frowned. "How so?"

"They were never apart. So, if Damian bought it, Dorian would have been with him. He'd know."

"All right," she nodded. "Maybe it doesn't arrive that day and maybe Dorian already knows about it. But we have this rattle. I love this rattle. It's our star piece, and there my brother is, being careless with it. Or claims it for his own."

"That scans," said Rufus.

"We fight."

"That also scans."

"And in my fury, I whack him one with the rattle. Hence the blood."

"Sure enough."

"But perhaps this time, for the first time, my brother gets really hurt."

"Alas, poor Dorian."

"He's knocked out cold, and he doesn't come to right away. I am overcome with guilt. I am also possibly concerned my brother will wake up, gain his strength back swiftly, and thrash me. So, I take the rattle—which is the weapon in an assault case now—and run off."

"And go where? Everyone knows him. It's been a full day, so someone would have come forward by now, reporting a free-roaming Tweedle on the run."

"Mpf," Mary Ann said.

"Exactly," Rufus said.

"And he wouldn't leave his brother injured without knowing whether he got help or not, would he?"

"Likely not," said Rufus. "See, that's the tricky bit. It always falls apart when it comes to the Tweedle in absentia."

Coincidentally, they were passing by the Tweedle cottage on the way back to Carmine Manor, when they heard a familiar voice call out: "Rufus! Melanie! Frabjous! You got my rocking-horsefly, then!"

Lord Carmine was hailing them from the Tweedle front porch.

"We didn't," said Rufus, as they joined him. "We were just on our way back to the Manor."

"Ah, blast it," grumbled Lord Carmine. "That bug got the directions buggered up then. I sent it to Sir Melanie's father's place, but who knows where it landed up."

"We weren't at Sir Melan — *Mary Ann's* — place for some hours," said Rufus. "We were interviewing crows across Square Four."

"What did we miss, My Lord?" Mary Ann asked.

"Only the very best news! D.M. Tweedle has been found alive!" Lord Carmine's bearded face was all relief and joy.

"Why, that *is* frabjous news!" Mary Ann certainly hadn't seen that coming.

"He's in there now," said the Baron, hooking a thumb to the cottage interior. "A very nice family of sheep found him in a field in Square Five early this morning, fast asleep. They were out for a bit of breakfast grazing and one of the lambs nearly nibbled the fellow's mustache. I let the Queen know."

Mary Ann rummaged around in her satchel and drew out a notepad and pencil. "I suppose we should debrief him, then."

Lord Carmine shifted uncomfortably. "I don't see why you can't interview him with his underpants on, Melinda. *Really.* I know you're new to the detective game, but save the aggressive tactics for the real criminals, eh?" He patted her shoulder in consolation. "Also, some things are best left to the imagination, and I'd be willing to bet D.M. Tweedle's nether-regions are one of them."

"Yes, My Lord," agreed Mary Ann heartily.

As they moved through the Tweedles' sitting room into the bedroom, Mary Ann noticed the still-empty spot in the curio cabinet. How it did nag! But in stark contrast, there in the bedchamber, an absence had been filled. Detective Inspector Dorian Tweedle occupied one cot, fully-dressed this time and polishing away on a selection of silver rattles. And now Detective Major Damian Tweedle was present and accounted for in the second bed, looking banged up and pitiable, ice pack slouched on his head like a funny cap.

Lord Carmine said, "D.M. Tweedle, this is Sir Marjorie Carpetbagger and you already know my boy, er, what's-his-name. They've been called in to assist with this incident, what with it being a Missing Persons case and you being missed. We would like to formally wrap-up this case, so please tell them everything you told me."

D.M. Tweedle cleared his throat. "Right-o, Sir and Sir... It was this week, on the day of Chooseday, which you might refer to as yesterday, my brother and work partner, D.I. Tweedle, and I had returned home for mastification of mid-day commestibles at approximately 12:17 P.M. We had not yet gotten into the domestic domicile when the sky come over very dark-like, and the wind picks up all windy, and my brother says, 'It seems like a storm is going to storm, don't it?' I was about to affirm this affirmably when I hear a great squawk and feel myself being grabbed most rough by the shoulders and my feet removed from bipedal contact with the ground! I see D.I. Tweedle below me, trying to grab on and pull me to earth by the regulation footwear. But despite his best of intendings, he lost his grip and tumbled backward, his noggin bouncing off the ground like a wooden croquet ball.

"So now I'm flying through the air, o'er fields and whatnot, all very fast, and I still don't quite know what got a hold of me, preciseably. I look up and all I sees is black feathers and great big talons. But I keeps my wits about me, you see." He tapped his temple at this. "So, I unhook me truncheon, and when we come in low enough over the ground, I whack the great feathery bugger with it. Well, he don't like this at all, do he? And I keep at it long enough that the monstrous fellow decides this midday snack is too spicy and ain't worth the spot o' trouble. So he drops me and scarpers, and it's as he's scarpering I can now fully see my menesis is a crow of the mightily out-sized corvid persuasion.

"Kicker is," he continued, "at this point, I've no idea where I am, and me leg feels a bit wibbly. I try walking on it, but I only wibble a few paces before it gives. So, I say to myself, 'Self, you get yourself a rocking-horsefly and send a message to Lord Carmine about the transpirations what transpired.' Only, not a single fly flies by in the time I'm there. And eventual-like, I fall asleep where I sits, until that little lamb tests me out as clover."

Mary Ann asked, "So it was a real crow?"

"As real as the mustache on my face," said Damian Tweedle. "And a thousand times the size."

"Ole Inky, then?" Rufus asked, and Mary Ann wasn't sure if he was being sarcastic.

But Tweedle answered sincerely. "Introductions weren't made in any formalish way, as such, Sir. What with my rushing through the air at high velocity during said constabular abductification."

"Any idea where you were headed?" Mary Ann asked.

"No itinerary was given, Sir. But I got some lovely views of Square Five and Six in the distance."

"And no one saw you during this time?"

"Well, I can't rightly say, can I? But I was largely over Tulgey Barrens and fields. Didn't spy anyone below, certainly, but it all happened so fast-like."

"And you're well then?" asked Mary Ann, feeling like his welfare had been neglected during her single-minded press for information.

"Well-enough, Sir, minus a bit of a bumpy landing, my wibbly leg, and I fell on my truncheon." He did have quite a goose egg on his head. And he threw back the blankets and pulled up the bottom of his nightshirt to reveal a large truncheon-shaped bruise on a rather hairy upper thigh. "Begging the lady's pardon," he said. His other lower leg, Mary Ann noticed, was bound up.

Lord Carmine caught her noting it. "The doctor said it seems all right, he likely has a mild sprain, but that it should be fine with rest and tight bandages."

"And you, D.I. Tweedle, how are you feeling?" Mary Ann asked, turning to the other man.

Dorian Tweedle put down his polishing cloth. "I have full sensory expression of the digital appendagees, miss, thank you for asking," he said, wiggling his fingers to prove it. "The trouble's in my remembery, you see, in that my head don't work."

"I'm sorry that it's not much improved from yesterday," said Mary Ann.

"I don't fancy I was using it much, anyways," he said.

"Right," said Lord Carmine, patting the bottom of the bed. "I shall check in on you boys tomorrow, to see how you're getting on."

It was as they were on their way out, that Mary Ann's eyes fell on the empty space in the cabinet again and, on impulse, she darted back into the bedroom. "One more thing! I notice in one of your collection cases, there seems to be a rattle missing, top center. I'm curious. What happened to it?"

D.M. Tweedle said, "Oh, that. It's not missing, Sir. It knows where it is."

"And where is that exactly?"

"Being fixed at the smithy's. *Someone* was a bit rough with it." Here his eyes darted to his roommate. "Involved it in a minor domestical dispute, and now it's off being repaired. Silver, you know. Soft metal. Happens more often than you'd think."

"Oh, I see," Mary Ann said. "I'd been concerned that perhaps someone had taken it."

"Just the smithy, miss," he said.

"Sir Mirabel?" This was Lord Carmine. "Are you ready to go?"

"Yes, My Lord! Coming!" And she waved goodbye to the Tweedles over her shoulder.

Lord Carmine was practically buoyant as they took the road that led to Carmine Manor. "Good news, eh? The best outcome possible, all round! Tweedle's back, and things can finally return to normal around here." At this, Lord Carmine turned to Rufus, "You and Sir Miranda here did a cracking job on the Queen's case, too. You've got that to be proud of."

"Her name is Mary Ann," Rufus said, clearly trying to moderate his tone with patience, but not doing the best job of it. "And we didn't find D.M. Tweedle at all. Full credit goes to an infant sheep. Not only that, but it sounds as if some giant crow is still out there somewhere, with potential to menace again."

"That's my biggest concern," agreed Mary Ann. "Who'll be next?"

"Yes, well …" The Baron seemed not to know where to go with this. He'd gotten started lavishing praise, and he couldn't turn the lavish off quite so easily. "Well … well done nonetheless, my boy! And … er, you, young lady! Frabjous effort!"

Rufus just shook his head. "Father, while I remember," he said, "have you ever heard of a Count Talionis?"

"Talionis…Talionis…" Lord Carmine seemed to be racking his brain, but Mary Ann wasn't certain any amount of stretching could get past the man's trouble recalling names. Lord Carmine was clearly trying to rack the rack-resistant here. "No, not in the least," he said finally.

"You know that abandoned property at the Four/Five junction?" Rufus asked.

"Yes. Lord Mayberry's old place."

"Mulberry, I think," said Rufus. "Anyway, Sir Mary Ann and I spied workers there this morning. Is that in Carmine?"

"No, our land ends at Caprice. Last I knew, the area with the manor on it was still Mayberry's. But I haven't chatted with him in some time. I understand he hasn't been well."

"Perhaps the land changed hands, then," Rufus said.

"I can look into it," said Lord Carmine. "Be nice to know if we were getting new neighbors."

"Speaking of neighbors …" Mary Ann began, grateful for the segue, "I was thinking just now, we might be able to get some information on our crow abductor from one of my neighbors, Mrs. Nightwing."

Rufus squinted. "That author the postman's a big fan of?"

She smiled. "The very one."

"A name like Nightwing, she'd make an excellent crow." He laughed.

"Raven," she said. And he stopped laughing. "But it's not her experience as a bird I'd like now. It's as a researcher. Are you up for a short stop on the way home?"

"Do we get to ask her why she's like a writing desk?"

"Please don't."

"I'll come anyway," Rufus said.

"I'm afraid I'll have to pass," Lord Carmine informed Mary Ann. "I've a few things I want to get done before dinner. But you young people go ahead. Have fun." And he gestured to them magnanimously.

"Understood, Lord Carmine," said Mary Ann. "Affairs of the Square must take precedence!" And she and Rufus tried not to snicker since neither of them meant to invite him in the first place.

9

As they stood at the roots of the pine tree, Rufus eyed the Dwindleade bottle Mary Ann drew from her bag with a forlorn expression. "Just when I thought I was done living life scaled down, we must dwindle another day."

"It's only proper manners," Mary Ann told him. "It's rude to peer into a person's nest at full-size and ask them questions. One must instead pop round at a genteel, non-predator scale like any decent neighbor would." She took one sip from the bottle and passed it to him quickly. And one *had* to be quick about it, because in half a tick, the world was growing up, and the girl was shrinking down.

The boy arrived among the tree roots only a moment behind her. He peered up the trunk now, which seemed to reach into the sky forever. "So, we climb?"

"We climb." And climb they did.

"My objection to being this size," mused Rufus, "is twofold." It had taken him about halfway up the tree before he'd become philosophical. "Point one, there are obstacles in every crack and crevice." This observation was courtesy of several rather large knotholes they'd had to navigate. "And point two, there is a challenge to our further survival in every winged thing." A bit of fiery breath from a dragonfly had prompted this particular note.

"I always find the change in perspective refreshing," confessed Mary Ann. "It makes me be more conscious of how I treat little things when I'm full-sized me again."

Rufus agreed there were lessons to be learned there, for certain.

Finally, they had reached the nest, and very good exercise it was to get there. They paused on Mrs. Nightwing's landing, getting their bearings, adjusting their attire and smoothing their hair before Mary Ann called the traditional greeting. "Knock-knock, Mrs. Nightwing! It's your neighbor Mary Ann Carpenter and I've brought a friend with me. Have you a moment for us?"

The door swung open, and Mary Ann was surprised to see Mr. Nightwing, a solid-looking bird with spectacles and a sense of heavy eyebrows, even though he hadn't any. He motioned for the visitors to come in, said, "A moment." Then he stuck his head out the doorway and shouted, "LENORE! GUESTS!" And with a wave of his wing to an overstuffed sofa: "Sit."

They sat.

It truly was only a moment before Lenore Nightwing came flying in, a squirrel's tail in her beak trailing out behind her like a scarf on a windy day. She landed in the sitting room with a light grace and removed the slightly bloodied tail before speaking. "My goodness, Mary Ann! How lovely to see you! Have I kept you waiting? Has Mr. Nightwing been chatting your ears off?"

"No to both," said Mary Ann. In the years Mary Ann knew them, Mr. Nightwing had said perhaps a total of ten words. She'd rather grown to think of him as an amiable avian mime.

To her husband, the raven lady said, "Roderick, I was thinking we could use this as a curtain valance in your study." Mrs. Nightwing was always scavenging bits of things from Tulgey Barrens to use around the nest, in unexpected ways. Many such trinkets were worked into the décor of the sitting room. Bits of bones and shells and oyster shoes, mirror, dice, and marbles. You never knew what you'd see.

Roderick nodded, took the tail from her and disappeared into another room.

"May I offer you some snacks?" And the lady held out a bowl of beetles that weren't very interested in remaining contained.

"Er, thank you, no," said Mary Ann, as Rufus blinked at the bowl mutely. "Mrs. Nightwing, I'd like to introduce you to my friend, Sir Rufus. We're working together on a case at the request of Queen Rosamund."

Rufus stood and bowed. "A pleasure to meet you, Mrs. Nightwing. I've heard many frabjous things about you. And your novels."

"Ah, dear boy, you flatter me," she said. And Mary Ann got the distinct impression she might be blushing under her feathers. "And yes, you two have been quite busy of late, haven't you? I saw *The Turvy Mirror.*"

"Oh, dear me," said Mary Ann, thinking instantly of the kissing photo from this morning. Her eyes darted to Rufus who seemed to be calculating how to respond.

But Mrs. Nightwing just went on: "The trauma poor D.M. Tweedle went through in the last day must be considerable. The story of his rescue in the evening edition of the *Mirror* was most intriguing."

Mary Ann gasped. "They already got that in the paper?"

"Pennwell certainly works fast," grumbled Rufus.

"It's a shame your search wasn't the thing to bring Mr. Tweedle home, though," said Mrs. Nightwing.

"We're just all very glad he's arrived back safely," said Mary Ann.

"And I hear you've been knighted." Mrs. Nightwing patted her arm affectionately. "Congratulations on that, as well! I'm very sorry I missed the ceremony."

"I'm afraid most everyone missed the ceremony. I almost missed it myself. It was rather impromptu for all parties involved," Mary Ann said.

"I'm guessing you're here because of the suspect in D.M. Tweedle's abduction," Lenore Nightwing said. "*I'm* not your suspect in that, am I? Crows and ravens are very different, you know. Same family and genus, difference species. And I, myself, am not fond of Burgeonboosh. Too crumbly and dry for my taste." She gave a disgusted shake of her head and ate a nice juicy beetle, as if to wash the terrible texture from her mouth. "I will, however, sit for a deposition, if need be. Though, I admit, I find the concept vaguely insulting. One tries to educate the populace but ..."

"Oh no!" said Mary Ann, "you're not a suspect at all! I never once imagined—"

But Rufus knew what to say. "Mary Ann suggested your research wisdom might be useful here, as we find ourselves trapped between seeking an individual crow with a Burgeonboosh problem or believing there's truth behind the legend of Ole Inky."

"I see," said Mrs. Nightwing, fascination now in her voice. "You want to know more about the folklore." And with that she got up and selected four books from a shelf on her wall. She set them on the table before them. "I take it from your tone, Sir Rufus, you personally question the validity of Ole Inky?"

"Mrs. Nightwing, my reservations are twofold," he began.

Oh, here he goes ... Mary Ann thought, and almost giggled.

"The first point being I've lived here all my life and I've never seen him. And the second, we've spoken to a lot of Turvians in the past two days about him, including three resident murders, and no one but the postman believed the Ole Inky hype. One would think a massive crow might be keen to meet his more diminutive relatives at some point, if such a creature were actually flapping about Tulgey Barrens."

"I understand your logic," Mrs. Nightwing said. "And ordinarily, I might agree. But the trouble with Turvian folklore is, half of what's in these books is still walking around out there some of the time. Like here ..." She flipped to an illustration. "Unicorn? Check!" She flipped to another page. "Gryphon?

Check!" Another flip. "Jabberwock?" She glanced pointedly at Rufus. "Extinct now, presumably." (Rufus shifted uncomfortably.) "But check! So who's to know if a ..." she flipped a page, "Snark or a ..." flip! "Boojum ..." (There was nothing on that page at all. The illustration was labeled but otherwise blank.) "... Or a massive mythic crow is right around the corner? One simply cannot be certain."

Rufus smiled. "You really should meet the Tweedles' postman. You two would get on like a nest afire."

She thumbed through the book to the Ole Inky section, which was quite swiftly done for a lady without any thumbs. She read: "'Ole Inky. Also sometimes called: Old Ink Pot, The Corvid Storm, The Taloned Terror, Bone-Muncher Blackie, and Steve. This black-winged beast of Turvian folklore is commonly described as taking the form of an enormous crow. It haunts the Turvian countryside with a focus on the marshes of the southern Topsy River and the Tulgey Barrens. Its great flapping wings are said to blot out the sun when it arrives, and it carries with it a rolling bank of storm clouds. Its caw is said to shatter glass."

"When we talked to them, the trees reported black clouds that day," said Rufus. "They spoke of a weather shift. No mention of a crow, though."

"D.M. Tweedle said they first thought it was a storm coming, as well," said Mary Ann. "And he reported hearing a crow cry, but the glass in the Tweedles' house wasn't shattered."

"Maybe Ole Inky's lost his touch," said Rufus.

"There's more," said Mrs. Nightwing. "The creature is said to be particularly vengeful about liars. It can tell by the scent on the wind when a liar is present. So, it scoops up local prevaricators like they were field mice, carrying them off to its roost in the Nobblybob, a massive tree that looks something like a banyan covered in boiled sweets. And it transforms those liars into a tidy snack. The Nobblybob is the only tree of its kind, is said to be so tall that its topmost branches reach to the roots of another land, and it grows on the Isle of Skewwhiff in the middle of the Topsy River."

Mary Ann leaned forward, eyes wide. "Where in the Topsy River?"

Mrs. Nightwing gave a croaky laugh. "You expect the latitude and longitude of Skewwhiff, do you, dear girl? The legend doesn't specify. Goodness, the Topsy River itself isn't there half the time! Once I flew by and it was a dirt road. Another time it was an extension of the Square Three railroad."

Mary Ann realized this was true, but when you were so focused on solving a puzzle, it didn't hurt to have the occasional reminder. Yes, the whole land changed quite regularly, like it got sick of itself and decided to try on a new look. Its residents had learned to cope well enough, of course, but Mary Ann had this sense that it was the constant uncertainty that had made them all a bit strange.

"Surely, you're not going to try to find the Nobblybob on the Isle of Skewwhiff, are you?" Mrs. Nightwing asked. "Even if it only pops up in our landscape for real once in a thousand revisions, there are a thousand ways I can think of that your time would be better spent."

"You're quite right, Mrs. Nightwing. It is a fool's journey. But I thank you so much for the information and for your time, as always. I'm proud and honored to have you as my neighbor and my friend." And Mary Ann rose to go.

The knights made it to the bottom of the pine tree again before Rufus said: "We are those fools, aren't we? The ones about to go on a journey?"

Mary Ann was rummaging in her bag for the Burgeonboosh cake. "Oh yes! I was thinking we could hire a boat first thing tomorrow morning."

"Fine," he said. "I can meet you at the Topsy Pier at nine, then."

"Make it eight," Mary Ann suggested. "I suspect finding a tree that doesn't exist on an island that isn't real will take a certain amount of time."

Rufus walked Mary Ann back to her father's cottage and lingered with her over a cup of tea and a little blissful quiet time before heading back to Carmine Manor for the evening. As they were parting, he asked, "Are you sure you'll be comfortable here? It won't be strange at all, after what's gone on? You're still more than welcome to stay as a guest of the Manor if you like. You do realize you're not required to tough it out here by yourself, when you have friends who care?"

She took his hands in hers and smiled up at him. "And you just happen to be one of those friends?"

"You should know the answer to that by now," he said chuckling. "Though I suppose I did once promise I'd spell it out for you."

"You did." And she knew it; she just enjoyed hearing it.

"I care very much, Mary Ann. So, if it were up to me, I wouldn't see you banished to a cottage at the edge of the Tulgey Barrens, to live surrounded by memories that … Well, I still don't know the bulk of them, I suppose. But the ones I do seem too dark and unfair for you to steep in, in solitude."

It was unnerving to hear the reservations she'd been trying so hard to ignore in her own head spoken aloud by anyone. It was also curious to think perhaps she wasn't wrong for feeling the unease she did about this place, this property that was now hers. It was like it opened up an old wound somewhere in her that could not and should not exist. Yet here she was, looking at it and wondering why it was bleeding.

"I'll be fine," she said, willing herself not to cry. Crying over such things was unnecessary and impractical. It was in the past, after all. So what if the cottage *was* the setting of an achingly lonely childhood, followed by a grisly murder? That wasn't the domicile's fault; it was good, solid shelter. It kept her from inconveniencing anyone. Why couldn't she just be grateful for that and move on? "I'm very lucky to have this place. It's just a small mental adjustment, I'm sure. I only need some time to create some better memories here."

"If you say so," he said, though he sounded unconvinced. "But please know, it *is* all right to need people sometimes."

"I do need you, Rufus," she said, though she knew that wasn't precisely what he'd meant. "I'm just down a bit of a rabbit hole in my mind about too many things I've believed; I need a chance to climb my way out." She put on a smile. "You, however … you've been nothing but lovely and thoughtful. I cherish our times together—I do, even if I don't say it. And there's no one I'd rather get banned from a whole realm with."

She thought it was funny, and that it might lighten the discomfort she was suddenly feeling in her chest and mind, but he didn't laugh. Instead, he sighed, kissed her on the forehead, and went to the door. "I'll see you tomorrow morning at the Topsy Pier," he said. Then his features gained a hopeful expression. "Any chance I could convince you to make it nine o'clock?"

"Oh, I don't know," she said. "That's one less hour for finding the unfindable…That's, what," she considered it, "over two days Thitherian time, completely wasted?"

He raised an eyebrow. "Did you just calculate that out?"

She smiled. "Maybe."

He grumbled. "Eight o'clock, then. But I'll be bringing a large canteen of tea."

As night fell over the cottage, the surrounding woods did seem to press upon its walls, the sounds of chirping insect and howling beast, cold comfort to a vivid imagination.

It was true, Mary Ann had never been completely alone in a domicile before. With every employer's home, there was always someone else present, whether residents or staff. And at night, she had always shared a room—and usually even a bed—with other servants, one of whom was Emmaline who snored almost as ferociously as the mystery snorer at Clashammer's. Impersonal as it had been, there was a presence with Mary Ann always, and perhaps that had been enough to keep her thoughts from rapidly folding in on themselves.

She told herself now she should be very glad the workshop had been the scene of her father's murder, and not the cottage itself. That that made things somewhat easier to handle. But then she pictured Rufus saying something sarcastic and entirely too incisive about it, like, "Oh, yes, what a marvelous consolation it is, not laying eyes on an indelible bloodstain from one's father's severed head every day. And solved so nicely by never opening the workshop door."

"Shut up, Rufus," she said, and pulled the blankets up over her own head.

But frankly, Rufus would have expressed the idea to her more gently.

10

Topsy Pier was busy at eight a.m., with Turvian commuters taking the ferry, a rowing crew getting their morning exercise, fishermen returning with early catches, and Mary Ann Carpenter having hired a spiffing red rowboat. The only thing that *wasn't* happening at eight o'clock in the morning at Topsy Pier was a certain red-headed knight, present and ready for riparian adventure. It was odd, frankly, because one thing Mary Ann knew about Rufus Carmine: he didn't make promises idly. Even so, she was starting to wonder if it really would be nine o'clock before their journey began; she supposed time would tell.

Time told at ten minutes after eight, when she spied the young man walking briskly down the dock, carrying a satchel, the promised canteen of tea, and a scowl on his freckled face. Suddenly she understood the minor delay; Mr. Pennwell from *The Turvy Mirror* was trailing after him.

"Sir Rufus, how do you feel about completely blowing the Tweedle case? When did you first learn you've got a thing for housemaids? How do you prioritize work and romance? What's your opinion on the Turvian crow situation?"

When they reached the rowboat's dock, Rufus whirled on him. "For the last time: SHOVE. OFF. PENNWELL." And it was Rufus' Jabberwock slayer tone — the one he used when he'd been patient too long and could now only be pushed so far. The reporter had no idea how lucky he was the Vorpal sword was back at Carmine Manor.

Pennwell responded by turning his beaming smile on Mary Ann. "Ah, Miss Carpenter! Or rather, I should say, Sir Mary Ann! Good morning!" He eyed the rowboat. "Off on a romantic cruise already this morning?"

Mary Ann said, "I've no comment for you, Mr. Pennwell. Not today, nor any day."

"No word on the giant crow situation?" he asked. "Is that a new tunic and leggings I see? Love the cerulean! Tell us the designer? What are your top ten favorite places for a secret rendezvous? Oh, and what's it like being engaged so far, you two? Say CHEESE!"

"What?!" The camera flash went off right at Mary Ann's most incredulity-filled moment.

"Oh, you're surprised we know about the engagement?" Pennwell did not miss a beat. "Yes, we found out, and in the funniest way, too. It's all in black-and-white, right here," and Pennwell pointed to the right breast pocket of his suit which was made of an article titled "Letter to the Editor."

"You might take that up with your Lord Carmine. He wrote in with *so* much to say about my lack of ethics and nerve for publishing photos of the happy engaged couple before you were prepared to go public. And I learned some new words this week, 'snollygoster' among them. Isn't that cracking good, 'snollygoster'? Now, usually, I just include my own bylines into my writing portfolio suit, but Carmine had so many pithy things to say about my treatment of your family that, well, this really *was* worth saving for posterity. Don't you think? Here one for you. Fresh off the press this morning." And he handed them a copy of the newspaper.

Rufus had folded it and was ready to throw it back at him, but Mary Ann snatched it from his hand. She didn't wish the day to begin with assault charges, because that would only delay them more. Also, she was curious to see what Lord Carmine had truly said.

"Come along, Rufus." She took his arm and guided him to the rowboat. "Things to do. Places to navigate. He's not worth it."

"Certainly right, he's not," growled Rufus, climbing down and then steadying the boat for Mary Ann.

The reporter waved. "Have a lovely day! Chat later!"

"Not if I can ruddy help it," muttered Rufus.

Mary Ann glared over her shoulder. "I hope it rains all over his paper suit."

They were quiet until they were both well out of earshot and absolutely certain Mr. Pennwell hadn't grabbed a rowboat of his own. Then they began swigging the tea and all bets were off.

"Father told him we were engaged!" shouted Rufus, waggling the Letter to the Editor in lieu of shaking his father. "Just right out there, bold-faced lied, told them we were engaged. I mean, I love you! You're mad and frabjous and I could want no one better! But that's our decision, isn't it? And we hadn't talked about that! We hadn't even gotten to do normal couple things like play charades, attend a concert, or have a row over something petty."

"Exactly!" said Mary Ann. "I mean, I love you, too, and I'd be absolutely honored, but people need to let us do these things in our own time. Everyone's in such a rush! This is just like the knighting. I wanted to be a knight. I wanted to have a nice little ceremony that I could look forward to, invite Mrs. Nightwing and Douglas Divot and Chester the Cat. That didn't seem like a lot to ask. But no! I was knighted on impulse with a flyswatter and now done is done. And it seems wrong to not be grateful for it. I should be grateful, shouldn't I? I mean, I was happy enough with it. And it's really about the end-result and not the process. But now there's this public engagement nobody asked us about! And the fun's been sucked out of that, too. I would like just one positive thing in my life to happen in a way that I can enjoy it."

"Understandable!" said Rufus. "And he wonders why we're not close!"

She frowned. "You and I?"

"No. Me and him!" said Rufus. "Wait: he and I? ... Father and me? ..." He waved it away. "Whatever. I'm so cross I've lost my grammar."

"Aw." She smoothed one of his curls.

"But this is a pattern with him," Rufus said. "Father doesn't mean to be problematic but he takes initiative in the worst ways, and it always seems to involve me." He picked up a set of oars now. "Like getting me very drunk and extracting my sense of humor to give to his sane brother. What kind of mind comes up with that?"

"Yes, how *is* your uncle?" For last she knew, he had been living locked in the tower of Carmine Manor, and that continued well after his presence was publicly exposed.

"He's still dressing like a banker and reading the stock reports," sighed Rufus. "For all the medical manipulations, nothing's changed. He is still sane and I am still down a portion of humor."

Mary Ann thought it a very good thing that Rufus was down a portion of humor. She hadn't known him at full humor capacity, but there were a few indications she wouldn't have liked him quite as much. For one, his relentless repertoire of riddles was ridiculous.

"I feel like I can't trust him anymore," said Rufus.

"Your uncle?"

"No, my father. I care about him, obviously, and I know he means well. But after all that's transpired, I cannot trust him."

Mary Ann was unsure what to say about grown children coping with their parents' foibles. Hers were foible-filled and one was dead and the other had disowned her.

Rufus asked, "Do you really feel like you were robbed of joy because of the speed knighting and this engagement business?" His tone was calmer now, concerned.

She forced herself to give a vague nod. After so many real feelings just spilling out of her this morning, she knew she couldn't let herself backslide into silence again. She felt somewhat lighter for it, and she wondered if that's how other people felt, just saying whatever they thought all the time. Feeling whatever they felt, shame-free. She'd have to reflect on that more later. It was odd.

"Maybe we can recapture a little of your lost joy, then," Rufus said. "I may have some ideas." And he turned his attention to rowing.

A lot had changed since the last time Mary Ann traced the course of the Topsy River. Her last foray there had been when her father's business partner, J. Sanford Banks, had been found dead on the banks of the Topsy, under mysterious circumstances.

Mary Ann realized it was a shame to taint the place now with such dark thoughts, since it was such a pretty morning, with the red river trailing lazily through green mossy lands, mushroom forests, busy office buildings, and massive cattails. In fact, here was a cat tail now, stripey and iridescent, hovering above their rowboat.

Rufus stared transfixed. "Whatever is happening?"

"Hello, Chester," Mary Ann said, but she didn't know why she'd bothered; it was no good without the ears. She waited.

One ear.

"Hello, Chester!" Then to Rufus, "Oh, curse it, I should have waited for the mouth."

The second ear. Then the mouth and the tiny pink nose. "Good morning, Mary Ann," said the cat, and the rest of him caught up. He levitated at the perfect pace of their boat, bobbing. "Adventuring early this morning?"

"Yes," she said, "and you?"

"Oh, just going with the flow," said the cat, rippling in the air. "This morning I've a wish for fish."

"May I introduce you to my friend Sir Rufus? I don't believe you've met."

"Ah, Sir Rufus, the Jabberwock slayer," said Chester. "A pleasure. The Jabberwock tried to flame-broil me once. Fortunately, they failed to account for my disappearing abilities. There is no love ... lost ... there ..." And he floated in a heart-shape before them. "What do you search for today?"

Rufus said, "You wouldn't happen to have seen a crow around here about the size of a carriage, would you?"

"Birds..." The cat sniffed. "I try never to tangle with birds larger than I am. There's a certain sense of degradation when the predator suddenly becomes the prey."

"Ah, well." Rufus took another sip from the tea canteen. "It was worth asking."

"We're searching for the Nobblybob Tree on the Isle of Skewwhiff," Mary Ann told the cat.

Chester smiled. "And you think Ole Inky is there, do you?"

"You mean the fabled bird on the imaginary island in the mythic nest? Can't say I'm holding out great hope for it, no. But we're determined to follow what leads we have. Have you ever seen the Nobblybob?"

"Well, I'll tell you what I think," said Chester. "I think that you will see what you expect to see. And you will also see what you do not expect to see. But you may not know what you have seen when you see it. You see?"

"Not in the least," said Mary Ann. But she was used to these sorts of conversations with Chester. You could ask him the time of day and he would say, "It depends on who watches the watch..."

"Well, it was frabjous chatting with you," said the cat. "And now, I must go see a man about a mullet... I wish you safe travels and answers to the questions you seek. Mary Ann, do give us a nice chin scratch before I go..."

He floated close and Mary Ann scratched him thoroughly about the chin, cheeks, and ears, with both her hands. He was very soft, and she thought it must be annoying being so irresistibly fluffy that everyone longed to touch your fur, whether you wanted it or not. Since she and Chester first met at the Duchess of Additch's house, Mary Ann had made a point to only pet him upon request. She thought that level of respect was, in part, what had solidified their friendship.

Chester turned to Rufus. "Mary Ann is one of the finest chin-scratchers in the Wanderlands…"

"I'll keep that in mind," said Rufus. "I'm considering a beard."

But the cat had faded away.

"How do you find something that doesn't exist?" Mary Ann asked, as she trained the binoculars Rufus had brought with him on the river ahead.

"Well, a hunting party from Hither recently went out questing for a Snark," said Rufus, while perusing the rest of this morning's *Turvy Mirror.*

"Oh? And how'd that go for them?"

"Snarkless," he said. "Also, one fellow completely vanished, presumed dead."

She shot him a look. "And how does that help, inform, or reassure us in this particular situation?"

"Doesn't." He shrugged and flipped a page. "Just conversation to pass the time." Then: "Oh, look! Count Talionis has officially moved into the old Mulberry Manor. Seems they were working on it much longer than we realized." He trailed a finger across the article. "Blah-blah…Earned his money in inter-Wanderlands trade … Blah-blah … Saved the daughter of a king somewhere from somesuch…Blah-blah… Fought parrot pirates …"

"Such an under-achiever," giggled Mary Ann.

"Wait, were they pirating parrots or the parrots themselves pirates?" He shook his head. "Doesn't say. Alas." He looked up. "What are you doing?"

Mary Ann had both oars and was turning the boat toward a rocky bank. "Hopefully saving us some time." With that, she started climbing out of the boat. "This is the furthest down the Topsy we've ever gone. And as the Nobblybob's supposed to be a giant tree, perhaps we could see it downstream if we just had the right perspective."

She withdrew the Dwindleade bottle from her satchel and tucked it in her trousers pocket. Then she grabbed the Burgeonboosh cake, unwrapped it, and took a bite.

Then she took *another.*

"Great gryphons," said Rufus.

Up, up, and even more up did Mary Ann shoot. It made her head spin and she struggled to keep her footing. Any shift there might be incredibly dangerous to the young man below, who she could no longer see through the treetops. But looking ahead, the entire realm of Turvy sprawled out before her. She spied a swarm of irrelephants, getting pollen from the dandleberry trees miles away. She could see it storming over in Yon. And she was able to take in every bend in the Topsy, until it emptied out straight into the sea, red against blue, creating a purple foam about the place like wine. There was no island. There was no Nobblybob. She had seen what didn't exist. She drank from the Dwindleade bottle and sank down, down, back down to the sandbank, deflated.

Rufus said, "Hopping hedgehogs, that was dramatic. I was suddenly very glad you believe in thinking about the little things around you. Your feet alone were bigger than sailing ships for a moment." He mopped his brow with a handkerchief. "Well, Captain Giganta? What say you?"

She shook her head. "Nothing. There's nothing there now, at least. The river has no island. There is no tree. I followed the Topsy clear to the sea. We're either unlucky in our timing or Ole Inky never was anything but a myth."

He nodded. "You didn't happen to notice that mound over there from the air, did you? I'd be curious to know what that looked like."

Mary Ann followed his pointing finger. On the other side of the river, a small distance inland, was a little spherical hill, of sorts, mossy green and lush with ferns. "No, the trees would have covered it," she said. "What is it?"

"I've been staring at it the past five minutes, because it's a weird level compared to the rest of the earth there, and that was the only reason I saw it at all," said Rufus. "It's quite perfectly round. What do you think it could be? Burial mound? Shed? A giant shelled-out egg?"

"I don't know. Rather hard to tell how large it is from here." And the longer she looked at it, the better she was able to pick out details. "There's something on the top of it. Metal, like a small spire."

"I don't see it."

"When the wind blows and the trees let the sun in, I just catch a dull shine here or there." They stood a moment in silence. "There!" She pointed.

Rufus didn't take much convincing. "All right, not certain how deep the water is here. We'll have to use the boat to get across," he said. And they climbed in and began to row.

Mary Ann had no idea what that place was, but there was something about it that made her need to find out. It was that need that drove her now. And it was that need that pushed them to row harder, and harder to get there.

And that was their mistake. Because this was Turvy. And the more you wanted to get somewhere, the less likely it would ever happen. They well-knew this from an early age, both of them. Why, Turvian children were born with this practically tattooed in their minds. But at one time or another, every Turvian had that funny moment they forgot themselves. They became a bit too excited, too eager, too unmindful and consequences were paid. Yes, in their curiosity, Mary Ann Carpenter and Rufus Carmine both completely forgot themselves and now the current was flowing against them. In a moment, the whole world around them was losing focus and they found themselves no longer on a boat on the Topsy River in Square Six or Seven or Eight. No, they were standing with wet feet in the fountain on the ground floor of the Royal Red Turvy Museum, and they were back to Square One, quite literally.

11

When one appears out of nowhere in the lobby fountain of a museum, one generally expects some questions. Questions like: "What are you doing, madam? This is not a public bath!" Or: "Do you require a docent, sir?" Or: "Is this performance art? I don't see a tip jar."

But today at the Royal Red Turvy Museum, these were unusual circumstances — and that was saying quite a lot for Turvy. So instead of questions, there was hubbub. And a hubbub that had nothing to do with two young people suddenly appearing in the middle of a fountain.

"What's happened?" asked Rufus, as he and Mary Ann emerged from the water. A crowd had gathered, and guards were blocking the entrance to the exhibits.

"There's been a break-in!" a turtle said.

Mary Ann asked, "Has anything been stolen?"

"People are saying something's happened to the First Looking-Glass."

Mary Ann gasped. The First Looking-Glass was a very important artifact in Turvian history. Contrary to the name's implications, it was not the first looking-glass ever made. But it *was* the first looking-glass that was able to reflect, not what was in the room, but other lands. It ultimately led to developing the mirror portal technology that Gilda Plaine had perfected in much more recent history. It dated back to the very first days of the Turvian renaissance and had been kept in the Red Royal Palace for a few hundred years before it was moved to the museum for public display.

Certainly, *something* important had just transpired here at the museum because now Queen Rosamund ran in, followed by her group of personal attendants, all working very hard to keep pace. The Queen had always been fond of a lesser-used method of getting from place-to-place in Turvy — sprinting at full-tilt, hoping to outrun the Turvian landscape before it had opportunity to change its mind. It was generally an effective strategy for Rosamund, but most people didn't relish arriving breathless, exhausted, and dripping with perspiration to every location they went. Queen Rosamund was in very good shape.

Spying Mary Ann and Rufus, the Queen said, "Why, you're here already? You arrived before I even rocking-horseflyed for you! Well done! Simon, horsefly them now then, please." An attendant, presumably Simon, began writing up the message to send to them, though it was not easy to run and write simultaneously. "Come along!" said the Queen, and she rushed through the guards' blockade into one of the display rooms. Mary Ann and Rufus came along.

Mary Ann had never been to the museum and she wished she had more time to focus on the objects there now. A quick glance revealed a fine collection of Turvian portraiture showcasing the back of historic figures' heads. She saw early Turvian weaponry, the first landscaping plans for Turvy's chessboard districting, and the original prophecy poem, *Jabberwocky*, as hand-written and illustrated by Sir Loral Clew. (She nudged Rufus at this, as she was amused to see the illustration looked absolutely nothing like him.) What she did not see was the First Looking-Glass. Instead, there was an empty place on the wall next to a sign that said what should have been there and wasn't.

JENN THORSON

"What kind of security was here when this occurred?" the Queen asked, pointing with her flyswatter to a nervous and sweaty museum manager.

"Well, Your Majesty, Eric Guardsman called off sick today with a case of the squillies, so we got a replacement guard for this room. He said his name was Nicholas Filch. He seemed a nice enough fellow; I'd no reason to suspect anything, certainly."

"And where is Mr. Filch now?" asked the Queen.

"Er," he dabbed at his beading forehead with his shirt cuff, "we're not exactly, sure, Your Majesty. He might have gone on break. But..." He offered a weak, long-toothed smile, "we've got people looking for him."

Rufus laughed. "Gone on break? Do you really believe that?"

"We've no proof it was Mr. Filch who took the Looking-Glass," said the manager, in a manner that suggested he was trying to convince himself, as much as everyone else.

Rufus said, "No specific proof that a fellow called Nick Filch, who vanished along with the First Looking-Glass and was the only one guarding this room today, isn't the one who took it? What security company did you hire him from? Pynchon, Pilfer and Steele?"

"I don't know that I like your tone, Sir," said the museum manager. "You can't judge a man by his name. Why, Eric Guardsman started out as a florist."

But Rufus wasn't finished. "Has it occurred to you that Nick Filch is a pseudonym and the fellow was having a joke at your expense?"

Judging by the manager's expression, it had not.

"That looking-glass was priceless," said the Queen to Mary Ann and Rufus. "I want this Nick Filch found."

"Yes, Your Majesty," they said.

Mary Ann added, "It would be helpful to have information about the service that sent Mr. Filch."

The manager nodded. "I can get that for you."

"And could you describe Mr. Filch for us?" Mary Ann's pencil was poised.

"Human. Stocky. Plump. Dark hair. Rather ordinary-looking fellow. Sloppy about his uniform, though," he said.

"Sloppy? How so?" Mary Ann wrote it down.

"It didn't fit him right. It was all a bit too tight and too bunchy. It looked uncomfortable."

"Did he have a beard? Mustache? Sideburns? Spectacles?" Mary Ann asked.

"He was clean-shaven, miss. No spectacles."

Mary Ann nodded and jotted that down, too.

It was at this point that another guard ran in. "Your Majesty, call off the search! It's been found! A gentleman found the First Looking-Glass outside! Follow me!"

At this, the whole group thundered outside, guards and all, no doubt leaving opportunity for a new wave of relic theft in the room. This mob of looky-loos converged with several other guards in the alley behind the museum. There were rubbish bins and unboxed crates, hungry stray animals, empty Dwindleade bottles and paper wrappings. And at their feet, propped against a brick wall like this week's bulk rubbish was the First Looking-Glass.

Mary Ann noted the mirrored glass was unharmed, but the wooden backing had been pried from the frame and was set to the side. "Why would someone do that?"

Rufus assessed it, hands in his pockets. "Maybe trying to remove the mirror from the frame, so it's less recognizable?"

"But that removes much of its historic value, as well," she said. "And you can't sell it like that, it wouldn't mean as much." Mary Ann knelt to examine the backing. Like the mirror, it was standard Tumtum wood. She replaced the panel in its slot. "Funny, it doesn't really fit very well now; it's a little loose. I think there was something between the mirror and the backing that's been removed. Something maybe a quarter of an inch thick?" She looked around the area for some wood or cardboard that fit the bill, but nothing was the precise size. She rose and turned to the guard. "How did you come to find this?"

The man removed his cap and kneaded it in his hands. "Well, miss, there was this fellow... a museum visitor I think, who was heading home when he saw it in the alley and he came to fetch us."

"Did you get his name?"

"No, miss. We told him to wait here while we went to fetch you, but he was gone when we returned."

"And what did he look like?" asked Mary Ann.

"Rather spherical gentleman. Nice red pinstriped suit."

Mary Ann raised an eyebrow. "Clean-shaven?"

"Oh no, Miss. A very luxurious mustache. Turned down at the ends."

"Interesting," said Mary Ann, exchanging a look with Rufus.

A little further investigation confirmed that the security agency had sent, not a Nicholas Filch, but one Mr. Artie Artwatcher, a local security professional of Square One. Mr. Artwatcher, it turned out, was found by Square One guards dazed and naked in a gazebo in Stalemate Park. He was taken into custody on public indecency charges but later freed once the statement on his assault and robbery was made. He did not see who assaulted him or relieved him of his clothes. Swelling at the back of the head indicated the assailant had hit him from behind.

"At least," began Queen Rosamund, as this latest news arrived by rocking-horsefly, "the First Looking-Glass is back in its rightful place. And that is what matters most. Thank you both for your help. And further, thank you for your assistance on the Tweedle missing persons incident. Will I be getting a formal summary report on that?"

"There are still a few loose ends we're looking to wrap up, Your Majesty," said Mary Ann, unaware until now that the job involved summary reports. "We're very grateful D.M. Tweedle is safely back with us, but we fear there's still a dangerous crow on the loose."

"Ah, yes, our feathered friend Ole Inky..." The Queen rested her chin contemplatively on the flyswatter. "I suppose if we only average one abduction-by-giant-crow every 400 years or so, we're doing well enough."

"We no longer think it's Ole Inky," said Rufus. "But we're still following some leads."

The Queen sighed. "All right, then. Do keep me posted. But for now, I must dash. I've got an Anthropomorphic Agriculture Awareness group I'm meeting with in an hour. They want to talk human rights for veg or some such thing." And dash she did. In fact, she fled the scene like a gazelle.

"Yes, Your Majesty," they said. But she was likely halfway back to the castle already.

Mary Ann and Rufus were not quite that energetic about returning home, especially since they'd landed up several squares from where they originally meant to be this day. ("I'm not going to get my deposit back on that rowboat, am I?" Mary Ann grumbled.) So, Rufus suggested they hire a carriage to drive them from Square One to Carmine Manor. "It will get us there in a more reasonable time and, if you're amenable to it, we can have a late lunch or early tea."

Mary Ann *was* growing rather hungry, so she agreed to the idea heartily.

They were clip-clopping past the railway station in Square Three when a figure emerged from the structure and stepped into the road — a familiar spherical figure wearing a red pinstriped suit, his face featuring a luxurious mustache that turned downward at the ends. He was also carrying a satchel. Mary Ann raised an eyebrow. "My goodness, is that—?!"

She didn't even need to finish her sentence. "It is!" said Rufus. He stuck his head out the window. "Please, driver, stop here a moment?"

And the carriage came to a halt.

"Why, D.I. Tweedle!" said Rufus from the carriage doorway. "What a surprise seeing you here. May we offer you a lift?"

"Sir Rufus! And Sir Mary Ann!" Tweedle looked from one to the other in surprise. And was that … a flash of concern? "How d'ye do? What a coincididdle it is, meeting like this! Very kind-like of you to offer me a ride, but I don't want to put you out none."

"No trouble whatsoever," said Rufus. "We can drop you off before we go to Carmine Manor. It's right along the way."

Tweedle considered it. "I suppose, then, my legs and I would be very greateable for it."

Rufus extended a hand to the fellow and helped him into the carriage. Then he explained the change of plans to the driver. With Tweedle taking Rufus' seat, the knight moved to sit next to Mary Ann. In a moment, they were jostling off on their way once more.

"Fancy seeing you out and about like this," said Rufus cheerfully.

"Did you have a nice train ride today?" Mary Ann asked.

"Pardon?" asked D.I. Tweedle.

"The train. You were coming from the train station," she said, "so I assumed…"

"Oh. Yes!" he said. "Very nice." His fingers drummed on the satchel in his lap. "See, with my rememberies being all dodgy, I had this sense I might have traveled by rail once. So, I thought the trip might jog something loose." He tapped his temple to emphasize the jogging.

"And did it?" Mary Ann asked.

"Not nohow," he said. "I fear I am doomed to cranial discombobulation for now and always."

"Did you go anywhere fun, at least?" Mary Ann asked. "I've never actually traveled by train myself."

"Not really, miss. I just done it for the train riding bit. I didn't get off anywheres. Only did me a round trip to see if anything joggled into my noggin."

"I see." Mary Ann hoped Rufus wouldn't call this out just yet as the whopping lie it was. But he remained silent and thoughtful, looking out the window.

Tweedle said, "Say, I hear you two are engaged for matrimonical unifications."

"I'm afraid that piece in the *Mirror* was a misprint," Mary Ann said.

"Lord Carmine's Letter to the Editor?" Tweedle blinked brown eyes under bushy eyebrows. "How'd that happen?"

"My father may have been over-passionate when he wrote it," said Rufus. "Nothing's been formalized."

"Ah, well, now that's a shame," said Tweedle. "You two seem like such a frabjous match. I wouldn't be too uffish about tying the knot, if I was you." And his voice sounded far away now, and oddly meditative. "You never knows when something could change for the poorly here in Turvy. You got to seize the opportuniblies when you have 'em."

"I suppose there's something to that," said Mary Ann.

"If something or other was to happen to either of you," said Tweedle slowly, "something like what happened to, say, Damian...Or a much worseable outcome..." He looked from one of his fellow passengers to the other and then shrugged, "well, then you wouldn't want to be wishing for what could have been but weren't. You'd want to best make your time together most countable while it counts, maybe even focus on being a pairing as a prioritree. Because you never know what lurks about the corner these days... or comes down from the sky with sharply claws. I'd take heed of that, if I was you."

"Sage advice," said Rufus, a quick concerned look to Mary Ann.

"We'll take it into consideration, D.I. Tweedle," she said.

The moment they dropped Tweedle off at his cottage and the door closed behind him, the carriage exploded with long-contained conversation.

"Hopping hedgehogs, I owe you an apology, Mary Ann," said Rufus. "I'd said the Tweedles weren't capable of your level

JENN THORSON

of twisted and devious thinking, but now I may have to recant. What was that all about?"

"He certainly fit the description of the man who 'found' the First Looking-Glass behind the museum. I mean, the mustache, the red pinstriped suit, the body type ... That can't be a coincidence."

"Indeed. Makes me wonder if he was in on it with whoever this 'Nick Filch' is."

A weird idea popped into Mary Ann's head now. "That couldn't be Damian, could it? Nick Filch?"

Rufus paused to think. "No facial hair. That's what the museum manager said. And the one thing you can guarantee about the Tweedle boys ... they're very mustache-proud."

"Valid point," said Mary Ann. She even recalled seeing tins of mustache conditioner and wax on the Tweedles' end table in their cottage. This image gave her a certain amount of relief, albeit not much.

Rufus went on, "But our friend Dorian didn't care to admit he was at the Royal Red Turvy Museum today in Square One. 'Just done it for the train-riding bit ...' Oh, really, Dorian? *Really?* Since when does any blasted Tweedle decide to go off and travel round by himself?"

Mary Ann always rather enjoyed seeing Rufus get worked up. Or, at least, she did these days, when it was no longer directed at *her* being sneaky and lying. She said, "And then that bit about us not waiting around to marry because something might happen to one of us and there might be regrets about time lost? That's what he said, didn't he?"

"That's what I heard," said Rufus. "I mean, he may have meant it in a perfectly kind way. Perhaps the 'namblesia's' made him introspective. But in a certain context, it does make one wonder. Was it a threat? Was it a warning? Did he really try to take his brother out with that crow?"

"I think we need to learn more about our friends the Tweedles," said Mary Ann.

"I think you might be right."

12

"Psst!" At Carmine Manor, Rufus was paying the carriage driver, when Mary Ann heard the sound. It reminded her of bubbly air escaping a fizzy drink when a cork was popped. "Psst!"

Mary Ann looked around for the sound's source but saw nothing. "Psst! Miss!" It was louder now, and Mary Ann determined it was coming from the shadows underneath the large tree next to the Manor. She drew closer and saw the person making the noise was a crow, standing in the dim light. "Are you one of those knights who came round Leonard's asking about Ole Inky?"

"Yes," she said. "I'm Mary Ann Carpenter. And you are?"

"Doesn't matter who I am," said the crow. "What matters is, I think I may have a line on your Big Bird."

Her heart fluttered. "You've seen Ole Inky?"

"In a way. What's it worth to you?"

Mary Ann rummaged around in her satchel. She had an inkling now what was considered an effective commodity in a crow payoff situation. She set down the pretty silver thimble from her traveling sewing kit. "It's yours, if the information is helpful."

The crow eyed it. "Sufficient," he said.

"Hallo, what's going on here?" asked Rufus, joining them.

Much to his surprise, Mary Ann shushed him. Then she said to the crow, "Do please go on."

The crow nodded. "Three days ago, I saw Evelyn was back in Turvy."

"Evelyn?"

"Originally part of Leonard's murder, but she hasn't been around the past few years. Word was she'd been on an archaeological mission in Yon."

"Crows do archaeology?" Rufus looked dumbfounded.

"Of course, we do! Excellent facility with languages? Acute memory? Appreciation for shiny objects? Many of us are naturals," said their visitor.

Mary Ann could picture it.

"Anyway, Evelyn was back but we only learned of it on accident. She seemed to be keeping a low profile, in the largest oak tree over by the Square Four/Five border. Not a regular roosting place for our families, I should add. I only learned of it because I was flying from our roost to Zugzwang Park in the Square Five market — always excellent snacking opportunities there, humans are quite generous during their food breaks after a good shopping deal. And at that little castle, I noticed some construction workers having a quick picnic."

"You mean at Mulberry Manor?" Mary Ann said.

The crow shrugged. "I don't know what you humans call it these days. Anyway, construction workers often have a certain amount of growing and shrinking foods with them to make it easier to do roofing, painting and whatnot. You know: to compensate for their sad inability to fly."

"Of course," said Mary Ann.

"Saves time with ladders, too, I understand. And that's when I saw Evelyn there, carrying off a parcel of Burgeonboosh from their supplies, straight up into the tree. Well, the workers were none too happy about it. They were trying to coax her down. But she wasn't having it. And when I swept in to say, 'Hello, Evelyn! Long time no see! How's the archaeology biz?', she pretended she didn't hear me and flew off, southbound. It seemed odd for her to be so fussed over the Burgeonboosh because, personally, I'd much prefer a ham sandwich with nice slab of meat to one of those starchy cakes that blow people up. I'd wager anyone in my murder would say the same. But she didn't go for the picnic at all. She was dead-set on what she took."

"Intriguing," said Mary Ann. "Now, this Evelyn, what's she like? Was she known to be, say, particularly violent?"

"I'd call her a free thinker," said the bird. "Not much for the flocking concept, bit of a rogue in that way. Very ambitious. Very smart. Always knew what she wanted."

"So, you don't think she'd attack someone, then?"

The crow pondered this. "I think it would depend entirely on who it was and why they needed attacking," said the crow. "Does any of that help you?"

"The thimble's yours," Mary Ann said sincerely.

"Frabjous!" And the bird started to pick up the payoff.

"But two questions before you go?" Mary Ann said.

The bird paused and tilted his head.

"Who was funding Evelyn's expedition in Yon?"

"Hm." The crow frowned at this. "That's a good one. Now you mention it, I don't actually know the school she was working for."

Mary Ann nodded. "And can crows even digest Burgeonboosh? There's been some debate."

"Oh, we can digest all sorts of things, miss," said the bird proudly, patting a wing to his gut. "Bugs, human food, live things, dead things, veg, seeds, nuts, garbage...They call us the Goats of the Air, they do!"

"Who does?" asked Rufus.

"Someone, probably," said the bird. "But the point isn't *can* we eat Burgeonboosh, but do we *want* to eat Burgeonboosh? And the answer is: certainly not when there are ham sandwiches about!"

Mary Ann nodded. She could understand the thought process. It was a busy day, and she was ready to make off with a sandwich herself. "Thank you for your help, sir. You've been invaluable!"

"And thank you for this fine, shiny…thingy. I shall treasure it always." With that, he grabbed the thimble in his beak and flew off.

"I didn't know a crow could also be a stool pigeon," chuckled Rufus, passing the plate of egg and cheese sandwiches to Mary Ann, and then helping himself to one. It wasn't ham, but it had potential. "And we're supposed to believe Tweedle's attacker's name is Evelyn?" He shook his head. "What do you think? Was that bird telling the truth, or having us on?"

Mary Ann saw there were two little meat pies on the tiered tray and seized one. "What would the motive in lying be?"

"Well, maybe that was the crow we're looking for and they wanted to pin Ole Inky on someone else, send us down a wrong path and waste our time."

"You think that black crow was a red herring?"

Rufus shrugged. "Or maybe they wanted to punish a crow who fell out with their murder. Or maybe it was just a quick way to earn a shiny thimble. It could be any number of reasons."

"I don't know," Mary Ann frowned, "I've told my share of fibs before, and that story felt rather genuine to me. The little details seemed right. Moreover, if Evelyn really is an archaeologist, that puts an intriguing spin on things. Things we should be able to verify."

"Well, I imagine someone in academia has to know her. We should be able to find out where she was working and on what, though I'm not certain where to start with that." Through a bite of egg, Rufus said, "It certainly would make a weird string of connections from this Evelyn to D.M. Tweedle, then D.I. Tweedle to the First Looking-Glass."

"Doesn't it, though? But in this scenario," said Mary Ann, "would Evelyn be working with D.I. Tweedle or against him?

Would she have taken Damian with Dorian's blessing, or as part of a revenge scheme of some sort? And, honestly, when has either Tweedle ever struck you as being interested in archaeology?"

"What D.I. Tweedle said to us in the carriage, about potentially dealing with a tragedy worse than what his brother experienced...Well, that makes me think he and Evelyn would have to be in on it together. Like he's in control and got Evelyn to attack Damian. So that would make Damian just an innocent victim in all this, wouldn't it?"

"Unless it was a set-up to make Damian Tweedle look like the innocent one and they're both in on it. Whatever 'it' is." Mary Ann forked in a bit of meat pie.

"Who's in on what?" asked Lord Carmine striding into the dining room and pulling up a chair. "Quite a late lunch, I see. Looks good."

"We are not prepared to talk about it yet, Father," said Rufus curtly.

"The case, he means," explained Mary Ann, "not lunch. The lunch is delicious."

Rufus said, "We'll present our final report once the information we've gathered has been properly affirmed and processed. Not before."

"Ah, I see someone is frosty today," said Lord Carmine, helping himself to a canapé. He turned to Mary Ann. "Have you noticed how moody this boy is? Ask an innocent question and I never know what I'm going to get. I cannot imagine, dear girl, why you even choose to bother with him." Lord Carmine said this with a smile in his eyes and good humor in his voice, but it was just one more example of his tendency toward questionable timing that Rufus had mentioned earlier. And she knew, as soon as it was out of his mouth, that Lord Carmine had unknowingly just brewed up a tempest at tea.

"Yes, I *am* having a few moods about some things, Father," said Rufus. "And would you like to know why?"

Lord Carmine started to shrug and say, well...Who knows what he planned to say? Because no matter what he thought up, it was already too little, too late.

"Do you think perhaps it was because Mary Ann and I learned this morning, courtesy of Mr. Pennwell and *The Turvy Mirror*, that we are formally and publicly engaged to be married? Do you think it could be that?"

"Oh." Lord Carmine was, coincidentally, pouring himself a cup of tea right now. He looked up reflectively, mid-pour. "I rather thought you'd be pleased about that."

"Pleased?"

"Certainly. You spend all your time together. You're quite obviously smitten. The fact that this young lady didn't go running for the hills the first time you started asking rhetorical questions and going pink and blotchy is a miraculous testament of her love and patience, as far as I'm concerned. Anyway, it was all going to happen eventually, wasn't it?"

"Well —" Rufus sputtered a moment. "That's not the point."

"No, the point is: young people who get themselves photographed kissing in newspapers have less input on these matters than young people who *do not* get themselves photographed kissing in newspapers. If you're not going to behave like you're completely indifferent to each other in public like the rest of decent Turvian society, the least you can do is be pretend-engaged for a while. I think I made the best of this situation for all concerned."

"Is that it?" Rufus scowled. "You think you've circumvented some sort of scandal?"

"If not forwards, backwards," Lord Carmine said. "Hard to say. Turvian timelines still jumble me up." He turned to Mary Ann. "You can manage to be pretend-engaged for a little bit, can't you, dear?" He patted her hand. "Or perhaps you could propose to Rufus, and that would move things along. He's digging his heels in now for spite, but I don't think he'd say no to you."

"Um, I'll … consider it," Mary Ann said, hoping that was non-committal enough, and trying not to meet Rufus' gaze.

"Good girl," Lord Carmine said, approvingly. "Now why did I first come in here?" He stroked his beard. "I hardly remember anymore."

"To be a bringer of merriment and sunshine?" muttered Rufus.

"No, that's not it … Ah!" He held up a finger. "Count!"

"One," Mary Ann obliged.

"Count… Tallywacker!" Lord Carmine continued.

"Talionis?" Rufus suggested wearily.

"Yes! There's the chap!" He clasped his hands together. "Lord Melbury's died and it seems his property's been passed to his only very distant remaining relative. I'm guessing that's the Count, then."

"Well, at least that's been solved," said Rufus.

"Sounds like he's quite a fellow, too. Rescued kittens from distress, and bags of damsels from being drowned, and… Also something about bands of pirates; I imagine their music was rummy and he fixed it for them or something. Anyway…" He rose. "I must be off."

"No comment," said Rufus.

Trying not to giggle, Mary Ann helped herself to a scone.

It was amazing what a few cups of tea and a nice beef and kidney pie could do for one's spirits. With a few hours left in the afternoon, Rufus and Mary Ann decided to make the most of them and see if anything new could be learned from the location this supposed Evelyn was last seen. Perhaps one of the workers or other local animals had spoken to her. Anything that might help them verify the information they'd gotten and understand her motivations more clearly.

"What if she's still nesting there?" Mary Ann asked as they journeyed down that familiar trail. Then a new thought popped into her head. "What if she was there when we stopped by

Mulberry Manor the other day and she thought our visit was related to her?"

"What if she did?" said Rufus. "You're worried about a real bird now?"

"I'm worried about a real bird with a bag of Burgeonboosh," she said. "One who carried off a whole Tweedle. Just because she's not mythic doesn't mean she's not a terror. Why are you not worried?"

"I'm not *not* worried. I'm *less* worried," he explained. "And I'm less worried because I feel like, at least, we could try to reason with a real bird. Mythic birds, who knows? Mythic birds have lengthy and dangerous reputations to uphold. Real birds with archaeology degrees, less so."

"I suppose that's sensible," she said and smiled up at him. "You certainly didn't inherit that from your father, did you?"

He winced. "I am so sorry you had to witness that at lunch. I swear, I let him bring out the worst in me, every time." He shook his head. "This is your opportunity, Mary Ann. Run. Run away now, run while you can. This is what you're getting yourself into. Marry me and you'll be dragged into mad schemes and never hear your name said correctly again." He laughed.

Mary Ann wound her arm around Rufus'. "I don't think he means to be so very... him," she said. "And he clearly does care. Maybe we can just pretend to be pretend-engaged for a while. Some people are engaged for years. We can pretend to be pretend-engaged for however long we like. No one needs to know."

"If you wish," he chuckled.

"And I understand your father can be frustrating. I'm not trying to excuse it. I'm sure it's even harder when you've been dealing with it all your life. It's just ... I would have given anything to have my father care so much about me for even one moment—even to fake-engage me to someone I loved. My mother, as well. You think you dislike the little quirks and foibles of the parents you know so well. But indifference ... the indifference is terrible ... And then knowing you're a burden, too, it becomes all that much worse." She wished she could take the words back as soon as she heard herself utter them. She was not sure why she kept bringing things to light that were likely so much better kept to herself, dark and buried forever. It couldn't help anything to put it out into the air, could it? If anything, it seemed to pain Rufus by hearing it, and that was certainly never her intent. So, now she settled for a distraction and, thankfully, one was readily available. "Oh look—we're here!"

The workers must have been done for the day because there was no sign of the fellows they'd run into before, and their working materials had been gathered into reasonable piles at one end of the yard.

"I assume that's the oak," Mary Ann said, indicating a stately tree at the property edge.

Rufus brought out the binoculars from his satchel and examined the oak from there. "Not seeing any movement in it. No nest, but I guess that would be unlikely, anyway. Wrong time of year, right? Let's get a closer look, though, shall we?"

With a careful eye on Mulberry Manor itself — they were trespassing, after all, and did not wish to face defensive caretakers—they ventured closer until they were at the base of the oak. Mary Ann found herself glancing around for careless Burgeonboosh wrappings, but that, of course, was a child's sort of thinking. That kind of evidence would have been entirely too easy and still proved nothing. Then she spied a beetle on the trunk of the oak. "Excuse me," she said, "could you please tell me if there's a crow living in this tree?"

"No reason to shout!" said the beetle in a voice Mary Ann could just make out. "You're giving me a migraine, you and your shouting!"

"Oh. I'm very sorry." Mary Ann lowered her voice to just above a whisper. "A crow ... does a crow live in this tree?"

"Do you think if a crow lived in this tree, I'd be out and about doing my errands right now? Not these days, she doesn't. And I'm well-happy to see the back of her, thank you!"

"Ah, so there *was* a crow living here, though! Do you know if her name was Evelyn, by any chance? And do you know where she might have shifted homes?"

"We weren't friends, in case you didn't catch that subtle implication earlier."

"Ah, yes, of course. One more question please?"

"Can hardly stop you," came the begrudging reply.

"What size was she when you saw her?"

The beetle looked at Mary Ann like she was very, very stupid. It was disappointingly evident even on such a small beetle-face. "Crow-sized, of course. Beetle-murdering crow-sized. And that's quite big enough for anyone, thank you very much."

"Yes, of course she was. Thank you again for your time."

As they moved away, Mary Ann asked Rufus, "Did you hear all that?"

"Just barely," he said. "So, our stool pigeon had one thing right; a solitary crow really was camped out in that tree. But if Evelyn was using the Burgeonboosh, she wasn't embiggening herself over here. It was more local to the attack."

"Which means it likely wasn't random, it was strategic. Which means—"

"Watch yourself," said Rufus, "you're going to—"

Mary Ann tripped over something and, as Rufus lent her a steadying arm, they looked to see what the troublemaker was.

She had stumbled into a bag of the contractor's tools. But it seemed that wasn't the specific thing that had caught her up. What she found was an elaborately-carved silver tube, a little over a foot long, with one end very smooth and sealed with a flourish. At her feet, was a separate bit of silver, the same diameter in one section, larger at the top, with a few knobs on it, and a series of rings with bells jingling off the perimeter. Mary Ann picked up the jangly bit and held it to the tube part. It could very well have screwed together if it had been made to do so. But there were no screw threads in either part.

"This isn't ... a rattle, is it?" Mary Ann jangled it about. It jingled merrily—too merrily for the situation's requirements, as far as she was concerned.

Rufus wrinkled his nose. "If so, it'd have to be a rattle for a baby giant."

"Just the sort of unique item a Tweedle or two might want in their collection?" Mary Ann suggested.

Rufus frowned at it. "Well, what's it doing here? The contractors had it? You don't think one of them, or even this Count Talionis fellow, is in on this?" Rufus looked reflexively toward the manor.

"I think it is here because Evelyn was here, and it just got gathered into the contractors' things upon end-of-day cleanup."

"Then the question is, what did Evelyn want with it? Not much, obviously, if it's been left behind. Not the archaeological treasure she was hoping for?"

Mary Ann peered into the tube. "You know, you could put something in here. If you wanted."

Rufus sized it up. "The same kind of thing you might put between a mirror and a mirror back?"

"Perhaps," she said.

"Curious," said Rufus.

"D.M. Tweedle did say he'd brought the rattle that was missing from their cabinet to the silversmith to be mended."

Rufus stuffed his hands in his pockets. "It does need mending. Now, at least."

"Where's the closest silversmith around here?" asked Mary Ann. "I'm afraid I've never had occasion to need one."

"Square Five market. That's the only one around that I know." He pulled out a pocket watch. "But it'd be closing before we got there, if we left now."

"I think tomorrow, bright and early, I might take a little trip to Square Five market," she said.

"How early?" His expression was wary.

She laughed and patted his arm. "Don't worry, it's not necessary for you to join me. I can handle this one on my own. I'd simply like to see if this was recently brought to and stolen from a certain silversmith and what condition it arrived in. Or perhaps it never made it there at all."

He nodded. "Sounds like a frabjous idea to me."

"I was thinking while I'm at the market, I might also pick up some cheese for Douglas Divot. I've been meaning to catch up with him, and things have been so busy since we returned from Thither, there's been no chance."

"A fine fellow. Please give him my regards."

"I shall." She tucked both pieces of the rattle into her bag, and they started back down the road, with Mary Ann jingling. "What are your next plans?"

"Oh, I get all the fun," he said. "I get to go home now and talk to my mother about our pretend-engagement and explain why I never mentioned it to her."

"I suspect, knowing your father, she's probably figured all that out by now."

He nodded. "I'd also like to see what I can wheedle from dear old Dad about the Tweedles' backgrounds. Possibly check his records, if he has any, which I doubt he does because… well, you've met him. You don't want to join me at all? We might be able to fit in dinner and that elusive game of charades we've been seeking?"

"Oh Rufus, I'm afraid I'm spent," she said, no lie being told. She loved the idea of a pleasant evening with him doing normal couples' things, and pretending their world was simple and carefree. But not this night. "There's too much on my mind for parlor games at the moment, and too much meat pie in my stomach from tea to even think about dinner. How about I just leave you to it, and you can tell me all about it tomorrow? In the meantime, may your Tweedle-wheedling go wonderfully well."

❧ ✿ ☙

Mary Ann spent her evening back at the cottage with a cup of herb tea, reading over her case notes. The part that bothered her most about this whole scenario to-date was the dubious, deep-driving duplicity of Damian and Dorian Tweedle.

When she'd suggested in the beginning that perhaps the whole thing had been Tweedle-engineered, and Rufus had teased her about it, she had indeed failed to take into account what she knew of the men. She'd been applying her own thought processes to it and that had clearly been the wrong approach. But now it seemed fairly obvious that none of that mattered, simply because they didn't know the Tweedles at all. This would mean their whole behavior up-to-date was an act. And that they'd been acting ever since they got their positions in Square Four, that whole month or so before Mary Ann even met them. Had their general ... Tweedleness ... been entirely designed to reduce everyone's expectations for them and give them greater leeway for some nefarious scheme? It was an unnerving thought. And a very long con, when you came down to it. It was a lot to absorb.

As the evening light dimmed, Mary Ann moved to the bedroom. And while she exchanged her day clothes for her nightdress, she considered how many other things there had been to absorb this day, many of which were on a personal level. Did it count, getting engaged, if neither party had done the asking and neither party had said yes, beyond a tacit agreement that the concept was wholly agreeable, if not the timing? Had Mary Ann really told Rufus she loved him, out loud and in person, with real words and feelings and things? She tried to think when she had ever told anyone in her life that she loved them. Or when anyone had said it to her...

No, no instance was coming to mind, though it may have happened when she was a toddler, and she knew no better. This was completely new territory, and it was as uncomfortable and awkward as it was thrilling. It was as if she were living someone else's life lately, someone who was much more flashy, flirty, and dramatic than she was. Someone who better knew what to do with the attentions, who conjured scandal, and kissed men in newspapers.

She was unbraiding and brushing her hair when she recalled how she'd also blurted out a bit too much about her family dynamics this day, too. What was it about Rufus Carmine that just made her want to tell him things? She'd gotten on very well for 18 years—20 years, if you counted two-and-a-half years in Thither, and she *did* count it — without telling anyone anything about her thoughts or feelings, likes or dislikes, pain, disappointments or ... or ... love. And now she felt like a leaky bucket spilling all her unpleasant business into the world. What did non-Mary Ann people do in such instances? What was the proper way to handle it? She'd no idea. But she must choose soon, that she was sure of. She either needed to just share and face the consequences of it or shut it up forever. Because these pangs of rethinking it were far too haunting in the dark of a Tulgey Barrens night.

13

It wasn't terribly hard to find the silversmith's shop along the main street of the Square Five market. The shop exterior was completely covered in broken silver cups and spoiled silver plates and bent silver flatware, silver buttons with no backing, silver hand-mirrors dented and squashed, silver jugs with cracked handles, silver platters, and silverfish. And, from the way the lady who gave Mary Ann directions to the place had described it, when the smithy needed supplies for his repairs, he just broke off a bit of his shop and melted it down.

A silver bell tinkled as Mary Ann entered. The shop was stacked with silver items, and a pleasant voice called out from somewhere in the thick of them: "Good morning! May I help you?"

"Yes, I hope so." Mary Ann stood on tiptoe, peering over the stacks in the direction of the voice but she still couldn't see anyone. "I've an item I wanted to ask some questions about."

"Brilliant, bring it here!" A figure emerged from behind the jumble of objects. It was a fox — a silver fox, to be quite specific—with a beautiful silver-blue face and striking orange eyes. His grey waistcoat hung open and his shirt sleeves were rolled up, ready for action. "What's the item?"

Mary Ann drew the two sections of rattle from her bag. "I was wondering if you could tell me about this broken rattle? I found it... well... in a rather unexpected place." It wasn't her best work in terms of lying, but it was early in the morning and she hadn't time to warm up yet. She thought the vagueness was a plus.

The silversmith turned the longest piece over in his hands. "Interesting," he said, looking over the exterior and peering inside. "Well, I've never seen one like it. That's for certain. Also, it's not broken and it's not silver."

"It's not?" This was news.

"I say it's not broken because the line between the top and the grip part of it seems to have been sawed cleanly off. With a metal saw specific to the task, I would suggest, since it's not jagged. As for the substance itself, I would need to test it, of course. But I'm likely to say it's gold that's been painted."

"Really?" Things were getting more interesting by the moment.

The fox scratched a nail against the surface. It left a little yellowish trail as silver flaked away. "See that? And if you look inside, you can see they didn't paint in there." He held it to an oil lamp, and Mary Ann could, indeed, see the metallic tone was different. "Also," he began examining the rattle head, "these rings and bells are not soldered to this piece, as they should be. Harder to tell under the paint, but it's a bit rough. It looks like it was some sort of glue and—oh dear!" A ring and bell came straight off in his hand. "I am sorry about that. But see? This cannot be a rattle. It would be a terrible thing to give to a baby. Never mind the size of it being wholly-inappropriate for a human child—or a young fox, for that matter. You know the first thing kits and kids do is put everything in their mouths? Well, a bit of sucking and chewing and the child would have eaten off the paint, choked on a bell, and be dead before you could say 'child endangerment laws.'"

Mary Ann frowned. "What are child endangerment laws?"

"Something I've heard they're trying in Thither. They're ahead of their time, you know."

She did know. "So, it's really not meant to be a rattle?"

"I daresay, only an idiot would have purchased this to use as a noisemaker for a child—or for anyone else, when it comes down to it. It just looks to me like someone's craft project gone wrong. Though why anyone would use a perfectly decent gold object to make a rattle is beyond me." The fox paused and said, "Let me get my magnifying glass. There's one more thing we can check." And he disappeared behind the stacks and came back with a visor with magnified lenses on it. It made his orange eyes look very large and acute. He turned the piece over several times, scratched a little at a spot under the top edge and said, "Ah there it is." He held it out for her to see. "Most gold —or silver pieces, for that matter—have a little hallmark on it. It indicates where they've been made and the quality of the gold or silver. This says ..." He squinted at it for a moment, then inhaled sharply. "Well, it's a four-leafed rose symbol! You know what that means, don't you?"

She thought she did, but she wanted to hear it from him. "Tell me."

"This was originally made for the King or Queen of Red Turvy! That's the Royal Rose. This was originally for the Royal Family!"

"My goodness," said Mary Ann. And it was here that she had to think very fast. She wished she had told him from the beginning that she was working for Queen Rosamund, but she hadn't wanted to involve the Queen in this matter yet. Now, it would seem like a too much of an unbelievable afterthought to say, "Ah, frabjous! I'm actually working for the Queen, she knighted me three days ago, so I'll just pop off to return this to her now."

Instead, she said, "And to think, all this time, this has been lying in a rubbish heap in the yard of an old, abandoned lot! Do you know the old Mulberry Manor in Square Four? It's been left to ruin for over a decade and this was in the rubbish pit. The things people do throw out, eh? A gift from the Queen one century, bog fodder the next." And while she was talking, she snatched up the piece the silversmith was not holding and put it in her bag. "Thank you so much for your help, sir," she continued, infusing extra warmth into her voice. "It was most illuminating! What I think I shall do next is approach the local historical society and see what they can tell me about the specific piece. Then perhaps have it restored to its original glory." And with that she shook the silversmith's paw with her right hand and slipped the jingly bit from his grasp with the left.

She jingled out of the shop, waving cheerfully over her shoulder and hot-footed it down the main street.

She paused long enough on her retreat to pick up two interesting cheeses for Douglas Divot, but the whole time she waited for the cow behind the counter to call her number, she was braced for guard whistles and shouts of, "There she is! There's the girl with the Queen's gold!" and so on.

It never did happen, of course. But as she was making her way back to Square Four, she had to admit, there *was* something to Rufus' technique of simply introducing yourself and telling people what you really wanted. Her back-door methods were effective in the long run, and she often felt she learned a bit more, but they always had the added element of "How the bloody Bandersnatch am I going to explain myself out of this?" And then, usually, the fleeing.

Originally, she'd been going to drop the cheese off directly at Douglas Divot's, but she was so filled with adrenaline from her silversmith escapade that she headed to Carmine Manor straight away.

The footman, who was a donkey, told Mary Ann that Rufus was up and breakfasting, but not ready to receive visitors, and would she wait in the guests' parlor? Which she did. But then Emmaline saw her sitting there, practically vibrating with the energy of new information to share, and she knew something was up. "Are you here for Sir Rufus, Tamsin? Congratulations on the engagement, by the way. Is this something about that case you're working on then? Oh, I'll just bring you up to the family parlor, he won't mind at all."

Well, Mary Ann didn't know if he minded at all, but he wasn't precisely coherent. His hair had clearly not yet been wet down and assembled into any sort of direction. He had not touched a razor. He was in a cobalt blue dressing gown. He was missing slippers and, it would appear, also the requisite nightshirt. Mary Ann got a sense of this noticeable absence and forced herself to focus on the task at hand, which had suddenly become rather more difficult. "Er, good morning, Rufus! Sorry to bother you this early, it's just the information I found out at the silversmith's is…well, it's really quite something."

He nodded and rubbed an eye. "I was up late…or early… research…I just…" He picked up his teacup and drained the whole thing, then poured another from the pot, not bothering with milk or sugar. "Sit. I'll catch up. Please resume."

So, Mary Ann sat and told him how the broken silver rattle wasn't a broken silver rattle at all. It was a gold, silver-painted item with bells glued on, bearing the hallmark of the Royal Red Turvian family, and it had been deliberately sawed into two. "But the best part is: now I know what it is!"

"And … ?" he managed.

"Picture this without all the bells jutting out." She pulled both pieces out of her bag and held them aloft, together, for his viewing.

He looked at it but didn't seem well-focused. "The jingling… It's so distracting…I don't know…Some kind of… club or flail?"

"Close!" she said, because she wanted to make him feel good about himself. "What we have here is Queen Rosamund's missing scepter!"

It still took him a second. "Oh, that? She misplaced that before we came back from Thither, didn't she? I got so used to the flyswatter, I completely forgot about that."

"Exactly," she said. "So, what we need to do is talk to the Tweedles. I want to see what they say when I ask them where they got it in the first place. Also, D.M. Tweedle said it was off being fixed at the silversmith's but the silversmith never saw it before. That was a lie."

"And, of course, it's not really silver," Rufus said. He was coming into his usual sharpness now. Still, he paused to pour himself a third cup of tea.

"So now we have the First Looking-Glass of Turvy and the scepter of the Red Turvian Queen, which have both been stolen, disassembled and left behind. Why?"

He had moved on to choosing foodstuffs now, so she knew they were making some headway. "Why, indeed? Which begs the question, does it stop at those two items? And if so, why? And if not, why not? What are they looking for?"

"Correct!"

"I think we can get to the matter, if we can find out what Evelyn was studying," said Rufus. "Her last dig. What was she working on? That might help us."

"You're right," said Mary Ann. "How do we find that out?"

He shrugged. "I'm afraid knight school and Turvian academia don't exactly share a career path."

"We'll stick a pin in it and come back to that, then. You mentioned you were doing research last night," Mary Ann said.

"Did I?" He seemed to have realized now what he was wearing — or, rather, not wearing — and he tugged at the dressing gown in an absent way.

"I can't help you, if you don't know, Rufus." Mary Ann grabbed a slice of toast. She hadn't had breakfast herself before she'd left the cottage, and she was rather fond of the bilberry jam at the Manor.

"Well, last night, I was just going through Father's papers, trying to find the Tweedles' original application and the letter of recommendation he'd requested before he hired them. I talked to him about it and, as far as I can tell, it's pretty much the only sort of records he keeps on these things."

"Anything interesting?"

"I'll show them to you. I have them downstairs, and you can decide for yourself. The tricky bit was finding them. Father knew he had them, but his filing system is…Well, it's what you would expect."

She munched toast merrily. "Not filed under T for Tweedle, then?"

"I found them stuffed in an old aquarium tank in a folder marked M."

"M?"

"For 'M-ploy.' His hiring folder, of course."

"Oh, dear heavens," she said. "Where's his sacking paperwork then?"

"Burlap bag in the corner. It was a long evening." He rose. "Help yourself to ... well, I see you already have, haven't you? Frabjous. So, I'm going to go put on something more suitable for the general public. And I shall be back with you shortly to tackle some Tweedles." He headed to the door.

"It is a lovely dressing gown, though," she called, with a giggle. "The color suits you."

"Good to know. I'll make sure I'm wearing it for the next time you pop round three hours early." He chuckled and padded from the room.

It didn't take Rufus terribly long to return to Mary Ann, looking much more kempt and alert, and significantly less nearly-naked. He arrived with papers in his hand and set them on the table. "Before we go, I thought you might like to see the Tweedles' application and the Letter of Recommendation for their positions. I'll be interested to hear your take on it." Mary Ann picked up the item on top, and it read as follows:

Dearest Sorrell, Lord Carmine:

Thank you for bringing to my attention the fact that two of my Guards, Detective Inspectors Damian and Dorian Tweedle, have applied for positions within your District of Carmine, Square Four, Red Turvy. Consider this the Letter of Recommendation you requested for their new Opportunity.

As Baron of your properties, you undoubtedly are already aware how finding good Guards in Turvy is not always an easy thing. In our land, too often, applicants are easily distracted, half-mad, bumbling, insufferable know-it-alls, with some peculiar quirk that makes it virtually impossible for them to do their job with any sort of efficiency.

The D.I.s Tweedle, however, _also_ have a unique way of expressing themselves. This has presented something of a learning curve for their colleagues and the community they serve, but it has not been entirely insurmountable. The benefit to having the D.I.s Tweedle on your staff is that they come as set, thereby offering some sense of great value when one compares their output to the amount of proper casework they might not get done individually.

When examining the Tweedle brothers as separate entities, I would suggest that D.I. Damian Tweedle is the stand-out, go-getter of the two, in that he has caused fewer mistrials when testifying in local cases and likes to go-get the post from the letterbox daily, which everyone in the main office really appreciates.

My recommendation to you regarding hiring the D.I.s Tweedle is to engage them swiftly and keep them close, as this means a significant Opportunity for their Continued Growth of Skills in a setting where we're not dealing with them here in Square Six. Particularly in Carmine, where the biggest crime was that dull masquerade ball your family threw last year, where no lobsters were invited to your Lobster Quadrille, the Tweedle boys should do all right enough. At least they are unlikely to cock up very much.

Best of luck with your new employees. We'll manage to get on without them here somehow.

Sincerely yours,

Barry, Lord Merlot

"And your father still employed them," Mary Ann said, shaking her head and setting the letter aside.

"You keep saying that. And I will keep answering: 'Yes, without hesitation.'"

She picked up the next paper. It was the Tweedles' application for the position. "One application for both of them?"

"Yep."

Other than that, it seemed fairly standard. Sure, whichever Tweedle had filled it out misspelled many words and made up a few of his own. But it had general address information, it said why they wanted the job ("To broaden our horizuns in a New Square"), and even tried to share a bit of their personal side. "Our hobbies lie in the arias of pugilizm, meat pie connaisewershippe, and we have the fynest rattle collecshun in Red Turvy, as feetured once in *Rattle Collecters Quarterley*."

Mary Ann put the application down. She noticed Rufus was looking at her expectantly, the small, widely-spaced blue eyes assessing her keenly. "Well?"

"Well, what?" Mary Ann said. "It seems fairly typical Tweedle."

"Exactly! You've struck it precisely. What *I* thought was interesting was that these pieces are consistent with how we used to perceive the Tweedles. Even Lord Merlot saw them as a bit goofy and ineffectual. So, if they're evil masterminds under it all, they've been planning whatever they're up to for ages. I mean, they worked for Lord Merlot for several years before coming here."

"I see! Yes, that *is* worth noting," said Mary Ann. "A very long con, indeed! How peculiar."

He nodded. "I'm not sure what to make of it." Papers in his hand, he moved to the parlor door. "But let's go interrogate some Tweedles, shall we?"

When they knocked at the Tweedle cottage, it was D.I. Dorian Tweedle who came to the door. He smiled broadly, or at least his mustache's width seemed to indicate so. "Why, Sir Rufus and Sir Mary Ann! To what do we owe this pleasurely social infestation?"

Mary Ann said, "We wanted to check to see how you were both feeling." On the way there, she and Rufus had agreed that she should be the one to introduce the subject of the "rattle." Given the delicacy of the situation, Rufus' tendency toward a more direct line of questioning didn't seem the right route to take. If the Tweedles were entwined in tweachewy — er, treachery—finesse was key.

"Please, come in and take a load off," said D.I. Tweedle, guiding them to the sitting room.

D.M. Tweedle was already seated in one of two armchairs. Mary Ann and Rufus took a settee to their left.

"How is the leg today, D.M. Tweedle?" Mary Ann asked.

"Oh, a mite better, miss, thank you muchly! Less wibbly by the day, it would seem."

"Frabjous! And D.I. Tweedle, you're looking chipper!"

"That's because my namblesia is gone, Sir Mary Ann. I remember everything I forgot. Like: this here fellow is my brother. And I'm a Guard for Lord Carmine. And my favorite color is blurple. And—"

"That is some wonderful news! So, this means you remember what happened the day your brother went missing?"

"Indeedly I do, Sir! We was coming home for some lunchtime foodliness, when the sky went darklike, and the wind got up its bluster and this giant crow came out of nowheres, and swept up my brother! I tried to pull him down by his bootstraps, but the crow was mighty strong on account of its largeness, and then it went and struck me on the head with something or other, and all went black. When I came to, I didn't remember nothing but a headache."

Mary Ann frowned. "The crow hit you on the head?"

"Yes, miss—er, Sir."

"While it was in front of you, trying to carry off your brother?"

"Yes, Sir. You express it so perfect, it's like you was there yourself!"

"Very kind of you," Mary Ann said. "Well, I'm certainly glad you're feeling better and I imagine you aren't keen to relive that gorrible day. In fact, I'm terribly sorry I brought it up. So, let us talk of happier things, shall we? Like this." She stood and went to their collection case. "Ever since I came here and saw your beautiful collection, I've been dying to know: however, did you get started on collecting rattles? It's an unusual hobby, isn't it?"

Well, Mary Ann had expected there might be some enthusiasm for the subject matter, but she'd no idea that she had opened a floodgate. D.I. Tweedle, who had not remembered anything about anything for the past three days, was now drawing on his complete history of rattledom. This ranged from the first rattle their dear departed parents gave them back in wee Tweedle infancy, and fond memories of trading rattles in their childhood clubhouse, to the different types, styles, materials and purposes of rattles, the rattle manufacturers and their unique stylistic variations, the highly-competitive rattle auctions he attended, and so forth. He recounted the brothers' brief offshoot into collecting rattlesnakes, which turned out to be an unfortunate detour on their collecting path, and shared how once they regained their proper focus, their extensive collection was even featured in *Rattle Collectors' Quarterly*, which had a circulation around the entire Wanderlands.

"It was a mighty honor," he explained.

For 45 minutes, Mary Ann Carpenter and Rufus Carmine learned about the wild, wide, wonderful world of rattles. And it was then and only then that D.I. Tweedle slowed down enough (and even his brother was nodding off in his chair at this point), that Mary Ann was able to get the subject back around to where she'd wanted it. "So where did you purchase the rattle that's off being mended?"

D.I. Tweedle frowned. "Being mended, Sir?"

"Oh, I think we found a hole in your remembery!" piped up D.M. Tweedle, waking up a bit now. "You pulled off one of the bells the day before the crow. I had to send it to the silversmith for re-belling. Remember?"

"Not nohow," D.I. Tweedle said.

"Contrariwise, you did."

"It was like as much your fault as mine, then. If it was. Which it ain't."

"If you can't remember whether it was or it ain't, how do you know it's not you who pulled the bell off?"

"Because I loved it so, and very much more than you. It was a rare rattle, you see, one I've never seen the likes of afore. Large and lovely, it was, with lots of big, beauteous bells. I wouldn't be rough with it. I would be gentle as a lamb, I would." D.I. Tweedle turned to Mary Ann. "We got it from the antique shop in Square Five. The proprietor, he knows my brother and me have an appreciableness of all finer things rattle-related. And he sent us a rocking-horsefly when he seed he had it in the shop. He's contacted us a time or two-ish, like as when he got in a Sterling Silver Jingler or a Mother o' Pearl Royal Rattler. That's connections!"

"Indeed!" said Mary Ann and rose.

The movement caused Rufus, who had glazed over a half an hour earlier, to blink rapidly and rise now.

"Well, thank you for the delightful chat," Mary Ann said. "I'm so glad you're both doing so much better. It must be such a relief to you to see your brother's memory restored, D.M. Tweedle. You two are so close, it had to be odd to be separated and alone here yesterday, while he was off riding the rails."

"Riding the rails?" said D.I. Tweedle. "Who was?"

"You was," said D.M. Tweedle.

"Not nohow."

"Contrariwise, you did. This is clearly just another sideboard of your namblesia."

Mary Ann took this as their cue to exit.

Mary Ann and Rufus waited until they were safely out of earshot until they let it all spill.

"So, there's another person involved!" Mary Ann felt like she was about to burst with energy. "Someone who hit D.I. Tweedle on the back of the head when he was trying to save his brother from Evelyn."

"I caught that, too!" said Rufus. "If Damian Tweedle was in the crow's talons as the crow was trying to fly off, what precisely came round and whacked him on the back of the head? Feathers certainly don't leave a lump."

"Someone working with Evelyn?"

"Perhaps our elusive Nicholas Filch? We still have no idea who that fellow is."

Mary Ann rubbed her chin. "I wonder if we could get that museum manager to describe Mr. Filch to a portrait artist. That might be helpful."

"I'll make a note to see if we can arrange that," said Rufus.

"Also, did you notice? D.I. Tweedle didn't know the rattle was broken," said Mary Ann.

"Well, he supposedly didn't remember he was riding the rails yesterday, either," said Rufus.

"True."

"Maybe he still does have a bit of 'namblesia,'" mused Rufus. "But great gryphons, we heard the entire history of rattle-making through the ages! How do you stand getting information this way all the time? That would push me right over the edge."

"It worked, though, didn't it? When people are relaxed, they tell you more things. I believed D.I. Tweedle when he talked about how he got the Queen's scepter. I got the distinct impression he really didn't know it wasn't a rattle," she said. "Still, I wish I'd known about the antique dealer when I was in Square Five this morning. I could have verified his story then. As it is, I've been carrying cheese about in my bag all morning to drop off to Douglas Divot and I still haven't gotten round to that."

"I tell you what: you go have a nice visit with Douglas Divot and divest yourself of cheese. I'll go to the Square Five market and talk to the antiques fellow."

"Would you?"

"Shouldn't take terribly long," he said. "I'll inquire at the dealer's and then, this afternoon, I really do need to meet with my squires. I've neglected their training rather badly, between the whole Turvy murders thing, and Thither, and now all this Tweedle trouble. But at six, please come to supper at the Manor tonight. We'll catch up on the case, of course, but I was thinking mostly we could have a pleasant evening together like a normal couple. Do the dinner-and-stroll-in-the-garden thing I hear other people get to enjoy when they're courting. I'll send the carriage round to pick you up. What do you think?"

Mary Ann kissed him.

He didn't fight this. Quite the contrary, he was a willing participant in the matter. Until he concluded the moment with, "Dear lady, please do control your impulses! Have you learned nothing? You didn't even check for newspaper men in the shrubberies."

She looked now. There weren't any. She laughed and swatted his arm.

14

Douglas Divot was delighted to see Mary Ann, and possibly even more delighted with the gift of cheese. The tove lived in an underground apartment under Tulgey Barrens' Wabe, a very green and soggy section of the land so, understandably, he didn't get a lot of visitors. Dwindleade was necessary to be comfortable in Douglas Divot's home, since it was constructed for a creature that was just two-and-a-half-feet tall. But that was the only requirement, for the place was beautifully furnished and very homey, and Mr. Divot was an excellent host.

First, he gave her a tour, showing her where the new items her father had crafted landed up in his domicile. There was a footstool he had cleverly repurposed as a side table, a picture frame he used to enhance a still-life painting of a cheese board, and a pretty corner shelf he employed to display favorite treasures. He poured Mary Ann tea now with skill and flair, and then sliced up a bit of the cheese she had brought him, to share.

"I'm so glad you've come back to Turvy," he said, his dark eyes glinting in his grey, black and white furry face. He nibbled the lavender Turvydale and sighed blissfully. "I understand it was quite the grand exit you made at the Queen of Hearts'

Unbirthday celebration. And I read you've not only been knighted, you've become engaged to Sir Rufus. Congratulations on both fronts, my dear friend!"

"Well, the engagement ..." Mary Ann's hands kneaded together. "Lord Carmine got a bit ahead of himself when he shared that with the *Mirror*."

"So not engaged?" His small round ear tilted.

"It's complicated. Things have just been moving a bit too quickly on all fronts for us recently. I've had no time to absorb it or breathe. And then there's this case we're working on."

"Oh, that Tweedle abduction, correct? Didn't they find him? How is he doing?"

"He's well enough. But he and his brother have been acting very strangely. Lying about little things, and not in a Tweedley way. I can't figure it out. It's like their whole Tweedleness was an act and they've been playing us for fools all along. Like they're far brighter than they've been letting on."

"Couldn't be a wild Deuce again, could it? I read how Dewey Hearts could shapeshift into whoever he wanted to look like, did the voices and everything."

"Dewey Hearts came to a very sticky end at the Queen's Unbirthday," Mary Ann said. "And as I understand it, of the remaining Deuces, two were already deceased and one is just terrible at impressions." She tried a bite of the cheese. It was a very strong flavor and not at all to her taste. She washed it away with some tea. "Do you know anything about the Tweedles?"

"They came from Square Six, didn't they?"

Mary Ann thought back to the Letter of Recommendation. "Yes, I believe so. I should check their former address on that paperwork Rufus has."

"I've never heard a bad word about them, besides their getting into regular squabbles. Their battles are legendary around here."

"Yes, I suppose they are," she said, and thought a moment. Douglas Divot had lived in Turvy all his life. He knew things. Perhaps this was an area where his knowledge could be of help. "If I wanted to study archaeology, where would I go?"

Douglas Divot blinked. "You just became a knight. You're quitting so soon? My! Things *have* been moving fast!"

She laughed. "I wasn't literally meaning me. I was just wondering."

"I'd say the Royal Red Turvy Academy in Square One would be the place to go. Who's studying archaeology?"

She explained to him about Evelyn, and the scepter and the First Looking-Glass. "It seems too much of a coincidence that two historic objects would be stolen and dismantled like that. Something was clearly in them that the perpetrators wanted, and I think one of those perpetrators is Evelyn. I just don't know what it could be."

"I suppose it depends on the objects' history. What do they have in common?"

"I know the mirror has a lengthy history and originally resided in the Red Royal Castle. I don't know how old the scepter is, other than Queen Rosamund was using it and it was made for the Red Royal family."

"Perhaps you should go and ask her," said Douglas Divot in a simple, no-nonsense way, like he was advising Mary Ann to bring an umbrella, it was going to rain.

"Why, perhaps I should." The very idea of just going to talk to the Queen to gather evidence would have seemed patently absurd even a week ago. But things had certainly changed a lot for Mary Ann Carpenter. "Thank you, Douglas. You know, I have always valued our chats. Talking with you always gets me thinking."

"Me, too," he said. "And I think I might crack open that second cheese you brought."

"Oh, for goodness sake, Mary Ann, you'd think you'd never worn a dress before," she scolded herself, as she was getting ready for dinner at Carmine Manor. After her time with Douglas Divot, she'd returned to the cottage to do a little laundry and plan out a list of next steps for their investigation.

With the wash drying on the line, she'd got down a few ideas like:

- Ask about Evelyn in the Archaeology Department of the Royal Red Turvy Academy

And:

- Ask Queen Rosamund about the scepter's origin

And:

- Arrange to get a witness portrait done of Nick Filch

And all those things could be done in Square One on the same day, so she felt that was a rather efficient use of her time. But try as she might, her eyes kept darting back to the clock on the mantel. And her brain kept trying to calculate backwards from six o'clock precisely how long it would take her to be dressed and presentable before the carriage came to pick her up. So, she never did get much further in her planning than those three to-dos. She just kept staring at them and the clock and her dresses hanging on the hook, and back again.

"You're ridiculous, you know. You only have two dinner-appropriate dresses to choose from and you only ever wear your hair the one way. This isn't complex," she said, quite sensibly.

The list ... the clock ... the dresses ... the list ...

"He's seen you every day for six months now, anyway," she said aloud. "In rain and unflattering training clothes and stolen housemaid's gear and Emmaline's borrowed gown. So, it's silly to put any weight on this. It's just the same old you in a new dress."

... The clock ... the dresses ... the list ... the clock ...

"Of course, the green one might be nice for this time of year..."

... The dresses ... the list ... the clock ...

"But the blue one would coordinate well with Carmine Manor's décor ..."

~152~

The dresses ... the list ... the clock ...

"Oh, fine! I'll get dressed!" And after trying them both on again, she settled on the hunter green gown. She contemplated doing something different with her hair, but she really wasn't sure what that would be. She could wear it down and loose, but that seemed ... overmuch. Too dramatic. Like she had gotten above herself or something. Or—worse—like she was trying to be one of those heroines in popular novels that roam about mist-filled moonlit gardens under romantically-mysterious circumstances, letting their hair fly all over the place like fragile madwomen.

"You're not one of them, you know," she scolded herself. "You're just Mary Ann Carpenter who looks like a chipmunk. And the only difference tonight is now you look like a chipmunk in a green dress." So, she unbound her plait, brushed her hair out, and plaited it up again. "There. At least you're a tidy chipmunk." And she concluded, as she always did when this matter arose, that that was the best she could hope for.

The carriage arrived at five minutes to six and the carriage driver, who was a young man about her age named Mr. Wheeler, seemed surprised she was waiting outside for him. "You could have waited inside, Sir Mary Ann. I would have knocked," he explained gently. And Mary Ann thought this was very good information to have, because she'd never had anyone call for her before, and she hadn't wanted to be a trouble to Mr. Wheeler.

She was oddly nervous as they clip-clopped up the drive. *I was just here this morning, entirely too early and completely uninvited (and with him inappropriately dressed, no less!), and I was fine. I had tea here yesterday, all was well. Gracious me, I worked here once, and I remained steadfast and unflustered then, too. Why am I being so silly?*

But telling yourself to not be asinine rarely improves the matter. She would just have to ride the silliness out and hope for the best.

They announced her when she entered Carmine Manor and it was Lady Carmine who came to greet her first, all smiles and soft, kind voice. She was wearing a marvelous violet gown that probably was just some everyday garment to her. But to Mary Ann, with the lady's graceful bearing, high cheekbones, and deep-red curls piled high, she looked so very tall and stately. Rufus clearly took after her side of the family, and it was interesting to see how the individual features all played out in varied ways on a man. And speaking of Rufus, he jogged down the stairs in a nice red coat and a blue waistcoat she hadn't seen before. He seemed to have put extra effort into taming his hair, and while she knew it wouldn't last, she smiled to think he'd worked at it.

"You look very pretty," he told her.

And before she could stop herself, she said, "As do you!"

She winced, but he just laughed. "Well, that's a first for me. Thank you." And he offered her his arm.

Dinner would be in about an hour, he explained, so they took to the parlor for drinks first. Mary Ann was given some wonderful concoction where squeezed lemons were transformed into smoother, sultrier versions of themselves with berries and a liqueur. She wondered if the berries and liqueur would improve her similarly. *One could hope.*

Mary Ann asked, "Did you get your squires squared away this afternoon?"

Rufus made a non-committal noise at this. "Russell's doing quite well with the training. I think in a year or so he'll make knight. Ruby is young—just came off her page training—but she's eager and shows promise. It's Horace that worries me. He's not applying himself. I think soon enough I'll have to ask the fellow if he's ever felt a deep and abiding passion for his family's milling business." He shook his head sadly. "And our friend Douglas Divot? How's he faring?"

Mary Ann recapped her discussion with the tove and shared her resulting three-point task-list for an upcoming trip to Square One. "What about the antique shop?" she asked.

"Everything D.I. Tweedle said was true, oddly enough. The only new interesting tidbit I learned was that the owner didn't remember how he got the 'rattle.' He said he just noticed it in his shop one day, and that's when he sent the rocking-horsefly to the Tweedles. I mean, it's true the shop was crammed to the rafters with various treasures, so I suppose it's possible to just not see what you have. But I've developed an alternate theory about that."

Lady Carmine, who was sitting on the edge of her seat and looking on with incisive, light blue eyes said, "That the person who stole it from the Queen quickly dressed it up as a rattle and stuck it in the shop to retrieve it later?"

Rufus blinked. "Why, yes, actually! Mother, would you care to join the investigative team?"

She let out a melodic laugh. "Oh, no. I just…" She blushed prettily and waved it all away. "Couldn't help myself. I have always liked a good puzzle. And speaking of puzzles…" Lady Carmine drew a small envelope from the table next to her chair and held it aloft. "We have been invited to a ball at Count Lex Talionis' home in two days."

Rufus put a hand to his head. "Two days?! Who does that? That's hardly much time to prepare. Or clear schedules. Or come up with a good lie."

Lady Carmine peered through a lorgnette and read: "It says here he wishes to introduce himself to his neighbors, and that it will be an 'evening to remember for the ages.'"

Rufus sniffed. "Well, I suppose it will be—for *him*—if no one shows up due to such short notice. It's incredibly rude."

"It promises drinks and dancing. I think we should go," said Lady Carmine, eyes bright. "Everywhere I go, I keep hearing all these marvelous things about Count Talionis. My curiosity is piqued. And I've been dying to know what the inside of Mulberry Manor looks like for simply ages."

Rufus let out a laborious sigh. "All right then. If you have your heart set on it, why not? We'll go," he said. "But I'll leave you to convince Father." He turned to Mary Ann. "Would you do me the honor of accompanying me or is your social calendar already booked?"

Mary Ann had not expected this. There was a part of her, from her housemaid years, that was so used to hearing others make event plans around her, that she hadn't imagined being actively included in this discussion. "Oh, I don't know, Rufus," she said now, as she began to realize the implications. "I'm afraid I've never been to a ball. And I'm embarrassed to say, I don't know how to dance." Mary Ann was increasingly understanding the skill sets she'd been relying on all her life were useless in the Carmines' world.

But Rufus was unbothered. "I can teach you. It's not that hard. You'll have it down in no time. If you can sword fight, you can dance."

Lady Carmine said, "I've attended a few balls that would have been improved by a bit of sword-fighting."

It was at this moment, Lord Carmine entered, holding a folded newspaper. And before he could utter a syllable, Lady Carmine said, "We are going to Count Talionis' ball, darling, in two days' time."

"Oh, are we? Fine. Look at this!" And he waved the paper at them.

"We can't read it if you're shaking it, dear," Lady Carmine said.

He held it still and pointed. It was another photo, this time of Rufus and Mary Ann in the rowboat from yesterday, headed down the Topsy River looking for the Nobblybob Tree. But it was the strangest thing, because the photo showed the two of them in a heated romantic embrace that had never, ever occurred. And both of them were clad in the most ridiculous pastoral costumes of extreme ruffles and lace. Ones neither of them would ever have selected, and certainly not for a day of slogging round a river searching for a giant crow. The caption read: "Sirs Rufus and Marianne working hard on the Tweadle abduction case."

"That was a business trip!" said Rufus. "We never sat for that photo."

"That's mad!" said Mary Ann. "It looks like us, but how can it be? That was not a romantic journey. And I do not own and would not wear that dress. I look like a sappy shepherdess spawned from a sentimental ten-year-old girl's art set." Mary Ann was starting to feel the drink taking effect and it was loosening her opinions. "You must believe us!"

"Now, now," said Lord Carmine, patting her shoulder. "No need to get your scabbard in a twist. That was as I suspected. What we have here is a photogaffe."

"Whatever is a photogaffe?" asked Mary Ann.

"New technology," he said. "When these slithy fellows at the *Mirror* don't have good stories, they make them up, using photogaffey equipment. It's a form of yellow journalism where the photos show embarrassing pictures of things that never happened. It's growing to be all too popular, and I won't stand for it used against the family. I simply won't have it."

Rufus sighed. "You're not going to write another Letter to the Editor, are you, Father?"

"I will not. Instead, I plan to have a word with Mr. Pennwell in person, along with the owner of *The Turvy Mirror*, and I will—"

"You won't," said Lady Carmine calmly.

Lord Carmine growled. "The deuce you say, Claret!"

"Not right away, certainly," she persisted. "And possibly not for some weeks. Not if that article there has even a kernel of truth to it."

"What article?"

And she pointed to a different column. The article on the opposite side had a headline that read: "AWARD-WHINING INVESTIGATIVE REPORTER ATACKED BY GIANT CROW!! OLDE INKY LIVES!"

Lord Carmine began frantically patting his pockets, presumably in search of his reading spectacles which were on the top of his head, when Lady Carmine took the paper from him, picked up her lorgnette and began to read aloud: "'Mr. Cyrus Pennwell, *The Turvy Mirror's* own senior investigative reporter, was brutally attacked this morning, suffering severe lacerations, water inhalation, and damp trousers. He was found on the banks of the Topsy River, by office workers from Topsy Turvian Doodads Incorporated, Limited, which operates sporadically in that location, Square Six, when it isn't appearing randomly in Square Ten as Notlob's Furniture Emporium. Mr. Pennwell indicated that he had been pursuing an important lead for the newspaper in a rented boat from Topsy Pier, when a giant crow came screeching out of the woods, capsizing his boat, and narrowly drowning him. He is recovering at home and working on a three-part personalized account of the incident that will be available exclusively in *The Turvy Mirror* beginning this Soonerday. Mr. Pennwell cautions anyone reading these very words to 'Stay away from the Topsy River and keep your eyes on the skies, Gentle Readers, for danger is in the air and it has a frumious heart and bitey beak.'"

"He can't be feeling that poorly, if he's got a three-parter in the works," grumbled Rufus.

"So, he rented a boat like we did," said Mary Ann. "You don't think he was trying to recreate what we were looking for that day?"

Rufus shrugged a shoulder. "Well, according to him, he found it, didn't he? Or, rather, it found him. Of course, he's also a liar, so …"

"Ole Inky's specialty," said Mary Ann. "Surprised Evelyn didn't carry him off."

15

When Mary Ann awoke the next morning back at her cottage, she had a deeper appreciation for the struggle Rufus generally experienced in waking up. It had been quite the evening at Carmine Manor, and it had extended far later than she had anticipated. The dinner was jovial and there was plenty to discuss. The Baron and Baroness treated her like she was very welcome and as if they'd known her forever. Lady Carmine was a delight and quietly brilliant in her way. And even Lord Carmine's many eccentricities were starting to grow on Mary Ann, to a degree. Of course, Lord Carmine did call Mary Ann "Millicent," "May-Belle" and once, "Megatha." (*Megatha?!*) But it bothered her less when she realized that he mostly called Rufus "my boy" or "son," and it occurred to her, it was a cover for not remembering Rufus' name half the time, either.

After dinner, they'd played a round of charades, which was enjoyable despite Mary Ann not having the background for a lot of the references; no one seemed to mind. And then, as Lady Carmine bid them goodnight for the evening, and Lord Carmine retired to the study to do whatever he did in there, Mary Ann and Rufus did, indeed, get that walk in the garden. Because of the evening dew, there were little frogs they had to avoid stepping on, and who cursed them out if they got too close, shaking their little frog fists. But there was something to be said for garden strolls. The fresh air, the quiet time alone, and briefly not having to focus on nefarious things, made a nice change. They looked at the evening sky and watched the stars and bats twinkling. No massive crow came out of the clouds to carry them off, so that was a surprising bonus. And once again, there were no newspaper men lurking in the topiaries, so that freed up their personal interactions in a rather pleasant way.

Even Mrs. Cordingley gave a nod as Mary Ann was about to depart for the night, and it was only perhaps two-thirds disdain this time, so Mary Ann considered the evening a great success.

But now morning had come, the green dress hung on the hook in Mary Ann's cottage, and Mary Ann herself felt distinctly off her game. She and Rufus had agreed to meet at Carmine Manor's stables at ten — the stables because the distance to Square One was a bit long to efficiently walk, when one added in their to-do list. And the later time was owing to their very late night. But getting dressed and moving was harder than Mary Ann expected, and half her brain was still busy rehashing conversations and lovely little moments from the previous evening. While satisfying to reflect on, there simply wasn't time to be moony when there were things to get done.

By the time she got to the stables, it really was ten o'clock, and Rufus was already there, saddling two horses. One was Goodspeed, Rufus' usual companion on these road trips and the other was a horse Mary Ann had not yet met. In the past, Mary Ann had ridden Lolly, a very sweet but elderly mare. Lolly was still present in one of the stables, she saw, but fast asleep dreaming sweet horsey dreams.

"Good morning!" she said to Rufus, kissing his cheek. "So, who's this then?"

"Sir Mary Ann Carpenter, I'd like to introduce you to Edgar, Lolly's grandson. He's agreed to take you on our journey today, since Lolly has retired from her chauffeuring career."

"Very pleased to meet you, Edgar!" said Mary Ann. "I look forward to getting to know you."

"And you, Sir! Sir Rufus has said some jolly good things about you."

"Oh, has he?" Mary Ann smiled at Rufus inquiringly.

But Rufus wasn't forthcoming. "You've got the job, Edgar, there's no need to butter her up." He laughed. "So, Carpenter, how do you want to approach this? Where to first?"

"Well, I think we should see the Queen first, so we have the fullest information in our minds when we visit the Archaeology Department. As for where we get ourselves a portrait artist, surely the Square One guards have needed them before in criminal incidents. There's got to be someone they use regularly."

"Actually," Edgar piped up, "my mother once worked for a mounted guard in Square One whose auntie was an artist they used for suspect sketches now and again. I can give you her name if you like?"

Rufus said, "Why, you're proving to be an invaluable part of our team already, Edgar. I knew you were the right man — er, horse — for this job."

"Right then!" said Mary Ann. "Let us be off to see the Queen!"

Mary Ann and Rufus had not expected that the Queen would be able to see them right away. And indeed, she didn't. They were led to a waiting room with a marble chessboard floor where many other humans, animals and, in one case, a large raucous turnip were seated. The turnip became all the more vocal, when the Queen, upon hearing that Mary Ann and Rufus had come to call, prioritized their visit over the others. "I've been waiting two days to speak to her! I'm starting to grow roots. But these two waltz in and the Queen agrees to see them already? Is that fair? Is that right? Humans over veg, is that how we do things here?"

"Do go boil yourself, sir," said Rufus, rising. "We are working a case for the Queen."

They'd hardly stepped through the door of the Royal Reception Room when Queen Rosamund was before them, close enough Mary Ann could smell her minty tea breath. "I assume you're here about that second crow attack that occurred yesterday. Any updates?"

Her sudden appearance and utter disregard of personal space were jarring. "Er, not specifically, Your Majesty," said Mary Ann. "Though I suppose, also, in a way, yes."

"What are you saying, child? Stand up straight, think before you speak, and start again."

Mary Ann looked to Rufus for help. Calmly, Rufus began, "What I think Sir Mary Ann was trying to express was, while we didn't come here specifically about the latest crow incident, we do have updates for you."

"Excellent," she said. "Because we simply cannot have a giant crow popping up and plucking people from rowboats every other day. It's a quality-of-life issue."

"Agreed, Your Majesty," said Sir Rufus. "But regarding the reason we did come...We have something we'd like to show you."

He motioned to Mary Ann and she drew the disassembled scepter from her satchel.

The Queen peered at it. "What is this? Some kind of noise-maker? Is it new technology designed to attract large crows? I understand they like shiny objects, don't they?"

"It's more like what it *was*, than what it *is*," said Mary Ann.

"My dear, you're just not making any sense at all today. You need a clean slate. Best go back to bed and start over is what I say."

Mary Ann tried again. "We believe it's your scepter that went missing from the Square Five market."

The Queen looked from Mary Ann to the metal parts before her and then to Rufus. Rufus nodded.

"No, no, it cannot be," she said. "You see, my scepter was gold and streamlined and was quite jingle-bell-free. You cannot have jingle bells on a scepter. Unless we're ringing in the new year that noise during affairs of state would undermine the dignity of the events. One cannot give a speech and not hear themselves for their own jingling. I'm afraid you're mistaken."

Mary Ann said, "We think someone either distracted you in the marketplace and took it from you or grabbed it when you set it down. Tell me, what happened when you learned you were missing the scepter?"

"Nothing much," she said. "Just the usual protocol."

"And what is that?"

"Well, the guards cordoned off both ends of the market street, scoured all the shops I was in along the way before I noticed it was gone, interrogated the owners, queued up anyone trying to leave the area, and searched them and all their belongings." She shrugged a shoulder. "Like I said, nothing much. Just a spot of bother."

"How many times exactly have you lost it before?" Rufus asked, frowning.

"Oh, not *lost*. Never *lost*, young man." She gave him a sour look. "I've *misplaced* it once…Well, twice…Once or twice…a month. It's fine, though, because we always find it eventually."

"And the guards always use the same process?" Mary Ann asked.

"Yes, of course. Not always at the Market, naturally. It might be in the castle, or going for a run, or at the theater. But our technique has worked, up until this last time," she said. "What are you two getting at with this impertinent line of questioning?"

Rufus said, "Because you lose — er, *misplace* — your scepter regularly enough, someone who was looking to steal it from you would expect your protocol. So, we believe they planned accordingly."

"They knew you and your guards would be looking all over for it," continued Mary Ann, "and they'd likely not have time to get it out of the area unnoticed. So, they chose to disguise it, hide it in plain sight, and then pick it up later when it was safer."

Rufus said, "That's why they glued some bells on it, slapped on a coat of paint, and disguised it as a large silver rattle. Then they stuck it in the antique shop until they could come back and retrieve it."

"But a rattle of all things?" said the Queen. "Why not a parasol handle? Or a unique croquet mallet? It's a rather odd and specific choice, isn't it?"

"We have some ideas about that," said Rufus, "but we're still working through the details."

The Queen said, "And I might add, it wasn't severed in two when I last saw it."

"Yes, well, we think the person who stole it wanted it, not for the scepter itself, but something inside the scepter," said Mary Ann. "And that's why we've come to you. We think this is related to the First Looking-Glass incident. What can you tell us about that scepter's history?"

"It's been with us for simply ages. It was gifted to my family at the establishment of Red Turvy."

"So as old as the mirror, then?"

"About that era, yes."

"And where has it been kept?"

"Here at the castle, as far as I know, and always under a glass dome when not in use. Many of us have used it over the centuries, though. It's a good size and a good weight, so it's been one of our most popular scepters. Second only to the scepter my great-great-great-great-grandmother preferred, called Billy, because she liked to club people with it when they weren't fast enough bringing her evening milk and biscuits. Now tell me: what have you come up with regarding our crow problem? Have you spoken to the latest victim?"

"That's on our list, Your Majesty," said Mary Ann, mentally putting it on their list. "Today, however, we're following up on a lead regarding the identity, motive, and location of that very crow. We're also hoping to get a witness portrait done of the impostor guard at the Royal Red Turvy Museum, to distribute widely across the realm."

"Then what are you waiting around here for? These are noble and important things that need to get done. Yet you two are here chatting with me like you don't need to track down giant crows or widely-distribute pictures of mirror burglars."

"Yes, Your Majesty," said Mary Ann.

"Consider us practically out the door, Your Majesty," Rufus said, with a bow.

16

The Archaeology Department at the Royal Red Turvy Academy was not what Mary Ann had expected. She had been picturing the realm's finest minds bent over carefully-arranged bones, fragments of pottery or intricate ancient artworks, using magnifying glasses and microscopes. What she saw were lots of long tables, a disarray of books and papers, and no one around to read them.

"Hello?" Mary Ann called, her voice echoing in the room. "Is anyone here?"

A shuffling sound came from a corner of the room and soon someone emerged from the door. It was a tove wearing so much grey tweed that blended so thoroughly with her fur, it rather gave the illusion that the tove was entirely naked. Only the subject's long tweed skirt allayed this initial impression. "Who are you?" the tove said. "You're not with the Dean's Office, are you? I told him specifically we were not ready to go public with the issue at this time."

"Er, no, Madam," said Mary Ann. "We're here on behalf of the Queen."

Her shiny grey eyes surveyed Mary Ann acutely. "Rosamund or the other one?"

"Rosamund," Mary Ann said.

The tove gave a curt nod. "That's all right then. Who are you and what do you want?"

"I'm Sir Mary Ann and this is Sir Rufus, and we're here to ask you about someone you may work with. A crow named Evelyn?"

"Ugh, have you found her, then? Actually, no, never mind," she waved a clawed hand, "I don't care about her. She can rot. In fact, she can't rot soon enough. Rot now, I say, and rot thoroughly. But more importantly, have you found the pages?" She peered up at them and tapped a foot.

Mary Ann exchanged a glance with Rufus. "I'm not sure to what you're referring?"

"The pages, the pages," she insisted, and folded her arms. "Didn't they communicate anything to you from the guard's office?"

Rufus said, "Er, perhaps you should start at the beginning. Or, in Turvian fashion, begin backwards and work toward the start."

"Great gryphons, it's impossible to get anything done in this realm, as no one knows how to properly communicate with anyone else! Whereas I pride myself on clarity in all things, others do not share the ability to elucidate with any sort of—" She sighed with the weight of her burdens. "Oh, very well! Evelyn Rookwood was a professor working out in the field for this college until two weeks ago, when she—Wait, what did you say your name was, young man?"

"Sir Rufus?" He said it with such a question tacked to the end, he sounded uncertain.

She leapt onto a chair, to get closer to his eye-level, and jabbed a clawed finger at him. "You're the fellow from the prophecy poems? The Jabberwock slayer?"

"Yes...?"

"Hm." She looked at him hard. "I hadn't pictured all the freckles. Interesting." She tapped the tips of her claws together with a clicking sound. "So, this should concern you as well, then, Jabberwock slayer."

He raised an eyebrow. "Because of the freckles?"

"Because of the prophecies," she said. "Evelyn Rookwood stole them."

"Stole them?"

At this, the tove let out a huff. "Important historic documents are in jeopardy, yet you numbskulls are just repeating everything in the form of a question. Yes, she stole them. Evelyn Rookwood uncovered a selection of previously unseen and unanalyzed documents written by Turvy's first and only effective prophet, Sir Loral Clew. We were preparing to authenticate them. If they proved to be real, they would be invaluable to our realm and especially to the subjects of them, such as yourself, Mister Slayer. Dr. Rookwood, however, took all the original parchments and flew the coop before we could get a look at anything. All the materials: gone."

"I see!" said Mary Ann. "And where did she discover these new prophecies?"

"The first of them was found wrapped in a large ball of wool—The First Wool produced after the founding of Turvy. It's displayed in Square Ten; that's White Turvy, if you were wondering. It got wet in a flooding incident at the White Turvian Museum of Textiles and Technology and needed to be unraveled and dried. It was as the curators were fixing the display, they found the parchment folded up within it. We got notified to come take a look, and regrettably I sent Evelyn. That was my first mistake. It appears that document pointed to a second manuscript page, one that was hidden in a previously undiscovered locket inside a Royal brooch."

"The White Queen's brooch?" asked Mary Ann, for the pin that Queen Crystal wore to keep her shawl on was a very well-known piece.

"Exactly," said the tove. "The clasp is notoriously always coming undone, so no one thought much of it when it disappeared. The pin went missing for a few hours one day and then turned up again."

Mary Ann said, "Then it might interest you to know that a scepter carried by Queen Rosamund was recently stolen and cracked open in the Square Five market about that time. And right here in Square One, just two days ago—"

"The First Looking-Glass was found dismantled in an alleyway, correct?" supplied the tove. "Yes, I suspected that incident was wrapped up in this."

Rufus raised a finger for attention. "Madam, if Evelyn is this serious scholar, why do you think she's keeping this information for herself? And why all the subterfuge? Wouldn't it be easier to simply explain to the Royal families or to the museum, 'Look, I have credible information that suggests there's lost documents written by Sir Loral Clew in this object. May I have a look?' I mean, it's relevant to the general interests of Turvy."

"Exactly!" said Mary Ann.

"Speaking only for myself," continued Rufus, "I appreciated knowing that the real gift of my 21st year was to battle a terrifying, fire-breathing behemoth. Without knowing that, I might never have become a knight. I might have become a barrister or a professional croquet player."

Mary Ann looked at him with surprise. "Really?"

"I know how to handle my flamingo," he said with a nod.

Mary Ann wasn't quite sure *what* to say to that.

Fortunately, she didn't have to, because the tove said, "That's something I've been pondering, as well. Evelyn's methods, I mean. Not your bird-wrangling capabilities."

"Was there anyone else working with Evelyn on this project?" Mary Ann asked.

"From our Academy, no," she said. "But I believe there was also someone called in from the Academy in White Turvy, as well."

"Any idea who it was?"

She shook her head, her twists of horn glistening in the light. "I'm afraid I didn't get a name."

"Speaking of names," began Rufus, "I don't believe we caught yours, Madam."

"Dr. Delphina Divot," she said, extending a hand.

"Divot?" Mary Ann blinked. "Any relation to Douglas Divot of Square Four?"

"Know him, do you? Second cousin, on my father's side," said Dr. Divot. "Bit of a strange fellow though, isn't he? Somewhat obsessive. All he talks about is cheese and hand-crafted furniture. One simply cannot pry him away from the food table at family get-togethers, for the cheese and artisanal furnishings. Embarrassing!"

"Er, well, he is quite passionate about his hobbies, but I've found he can be an excellent conversationalist on a number of other topics." Mary Ann wasn't comfortable leaving Douglas Divot's name spoken of in such a manner, undefended. "One last question before we go, though. Do you happen to have an address for Evelyn Rookwood?"

"I can dig it out for you, if you think it will help," she said. "I personally do not. That was the first place we checked after she failed to come back with the parchments we did know about. But I wish you both the best of luck. Bring those prophecies back to us, won't you? It may just be old paper to some, but depending on what they contain, it could mean the fate of the Wanderlands themselves."

The address they got for Evelyn Rookwood was none other than the old one they'd already checked out with Leonard's murder.

Rufus said, "So, we'll have to call on the Archaeology Department of the Royal White Turvy Academy to find out who they sent to deal with the wool and brooch situations." They were riding with Goodspeed and Edgar to their next destination. "*If,* that is, they'll talk to us. I know that we're supposed to be at peace right now, but there's still so many hard feelings about the war, even a decade later, I'm not sure we're going to get very far. If only we knew someone in White Turvy who could get the conversation started."

"*Welllll* ..." mumbled Mary Ann. She hadn't expected to say this one syllable aloud.

"*You* do?" Rufus gave her a sharp look. "Do you really?"

"No," Mary Ann lied.

"That was a suspiciously deep 'well,' then," he said. "You could soggy a whole museum's worth of artifacts in that 'well' of yours."

She exhaled. "I mean, yes, I do know of someone in White Turvy. She's a pawn for the White Queen."

"Mary Ann, that's frabjous! That'll make this so much easier." His smile was radiant.

"But if we're looking for someone to get the conversation started, the lady I know is likely the very last person we would ever want."

The smile vanished, and Mary Ann hated to see it go. "That took a turn quickly, I must say," Rufus said. "What's the problem? Did you work for her at some point?"

It was true that most of Mary Ann's former housemaid situations had resulted in dramatic and speedy exits. These were occasions where it was best that both former employer and employee never encounter each other again. Since Rufus was well-aware of this history, Mary Ann could understand why he'd assumed. But it was the history he was still unaware of that Mary Ann was reluctant to share now.

She decided that if they were to move forward seriously with any sort of non-pretend-engagement, it was probably best he knew, and sooner rather than later. It would hurt more later if things fell through. Though, she recognized, it would hurt now quite deeply enough, to the point she didn't know how she would handle it. She took a deep breath to brace herself. "The name of the White Turvian pawn I mentioned is Clarissa Snow. And she is my mother."

"Your mother?" This was the horse Goodspeed now, who liked to be a part of these conversations. "I thought your mother was dead!"

"As did I, actually," said Rufus.

"She may as well be," Mary Ann told them. "She left my father and me when I was very small. She went off and joined the White Turvian side as a pawn. She was born in White Turvy, you see. I don't remember her much as a child, and I've only spoken to her once as an adult. It was at Queen Valentina's Unbirthday party, in fact. She didn't recognize me —I mean, how could she? I was a toddler when last she laid eyes on me. And I didn't tell her who I was. I was serving as your mother's lady's maid, and she thought my name was Tamsin. Your mother talked to her quite a bit, though. They watched the croquet match together."

"I'd no idea this went on that day," said Rufus. "I had a feeling something was wrong. You were acting a bit strangely but... I'm sorry. It had to have been difficult, seeing her again."

"I know your father's feelings about the war, and the Battle of Square Four. And I heard him call White Turvians 'Alabastards,' once," she said. "I just figured this was something I should mention. That I'm half White Turvian. You know, should you need to call off our pretend-engagement before it's a real one."

"You think I would call off our pretend-engagement over this?" He looked gutted. Any time she spoke of her life from before, that was the expression he had, and it made her wish she'd kept her mouth quite shut.

"I wasn't entirely certain. This has all been rather too wonderful, you and I, and I keep expecting it to go wonky somehow. I've not had a lot of things that have made me this happy. I'm afraid I have a hard time trusting it."

"Well," he said, and it was another deep well, "nobody's calling off anything. I'm not quite sure how to convey to you that you really are not disposable or... what word did you use the other day? 'A burden.'" He frowned and shook his head. "I suppose that's just going to require some time. But ... I do appreciate your telling me. It's put quite a few things in perspective."

She was slightly concerned what perspective, exactly, he had gained from this. It was strange to have someone actively trying to understand her; it felt entirely too vulnerable. But at least she thought she could relax a bit more now the hardest part was over.

"Besides," he continued, "look at it this way, Mary Ann: now I know we don't have to invite your mother to the wedding. Think how cost-effective that is." He smiled, and it took her a second to realize he was trying to break the tension. "We'll figure out some other better way to get the name of that White Turvian archaeologist, no worries. If there's a well, there's a way. Now, let's go find ourselves that portrait artist."

17

Mary Ann and Rufus found the portrait artist, Flossie Tombow, at her home at the edge of Square One, in a quaint, flower-covered village, in a flower-covered cottage, in a brightly flower-covered dress. She was a petite, elderly lady with several enthusiastic hairpieces of curls layered upon her head, creating a striking effect, not only in the way they collectively made her two feet taller, but also because they neither matched each other nor the white hair that grew naturally from her head. Mary Ann felt it gave the impression that she'd stacked and balanced a selection of her favorite cats, though not a cat was to be seen in the Tombow residence.

What *was* in the Tombow residence was flowered furniture, flowered wallpaper, and hundreds of pencil portraits, hung gallery style, staring into the space with cold graphite eyes.

"You did all these for the Square One guards?" Mary Ann asked her, after explaining why she and Rufus had come.

"Oh yes, most of them," she said, surveying her work. "Once the case is solved, they let me have the pictures back, those nice boys! They're like my children."

"It's lovely you've developed that sort of relationship with the guards," Mary Ann said.

"Not the guards, dear, the drawings," she said, and laughed. "Imagine *people* being like *children!*" And she had a good titter over this. "Now see this one?" She indicated a portrait. "He was a highwayman. Stole the highway each night, just rolled it right up and carried it off, so no one knew how to get to work in the morning. And this one," she indicated a second piece, "she was a gold digger. Got caught digging for gold in the vault of the Royal Red Turvy Bank and Trust."

"Well, your work is excellent," Mary Ann told her, impressed with both the variety and the attention to detail. Though, admittedly, seeing it all at once with so many staring eyeballs made the hairs on her arms prickle. "I hope you will come with us to do a portrait based on the description of a witness of ours. As I said earlier, we'll pay you, and you'd be doing Red Turvy a great service."

"That depends…" And here she began to eye the visitors carefully. "You know, you both have quite interesting faces. And a face tells me quite a lot about a person." Her gaze settled on Mary Ann. "You, you're mostly all circles and ovals. The face, the eyes, the lips, the turned-up nose. But, ah, then there are those squares in that little overbite. That suggests variety and disruption. It lets the eye know not to get too comfortable here. Gives you extra character, I think."

Mary Ann had never thought the overbite gave her "character," but it was nice to hear.

The lady turned to Rufus. "And you, you're all triangles and diamonds, aren't you? Certainly not boring. But the eyes are quite widely set, which suggests an openness. And the hair's all circles, showing some softness, despite disarray. So yes, you'll be acceptable to work with—I'll do your job for you. I'll just get my supplies and my hat."

Mary Ann was never so glad to be geometrically acceptable. And as soon as Flossie Tombow grabbed her paper and pencils and topped her tower of wigs with a flowered hat (she had to toss it up there like a discus, for her arms were too short to reach), they were off to the museum.

It was halfway to the museum that Mary Ann thought of it. "Professor Goodnuff!" she exclaimed.

"Pardon?" said Flossie Tombow, who was riding with Mary Ann, sitting behind her, floral skirt hiked up to almost inappropriate levels and hair and hats jouncing with every hoof-fall. "Are you seeing things, girl?"

"No, I was just thinking, I know of someone who might be able to get information from the Royal White Turvy Academy's Archaeology Department. One of my neighbors, Professor Cyril Goodnuff is a Turvian zoologist. I would bet he'd know someone at that college."

"Oh, that's frabjous!" said Rufus. "Let's hire a rocking-horsefly and get a message to him immediately. Tell your neighbor that the Academy can send their information to Carmine Manor. At least, we can be sure there will be someone there to receive it."

Which is exactly what they did.

The manager of the Royal Red Turvy Museum seemed displeased to see them again. "Meaning no disrespect, Sirs, but I have nothing more to say about that day. It was a mar upon our fine institution and an embarrassment to my leadership, particularly. I'd prefer if we could put it all behind us and—"

"Absolutely," said Mary Ann. "We'd like nothing more."

The man looked relieved.

"*After* you give your description of the security guard, Nick Filch, to our portrait artist."

Flossie Tombow waggled the fingers of a lace-gloved hand.

ॐ ✿ ॐ

"Am I surprised, or am I not surprised?" Rufus asked, looking at the completed picture.

Mary Ann couldn't draw her eyes away. "I call it not surprised, but with a side of 'what the flappin' Jubjub?!'"

"Yes, that's it. That's it precisely it. You have summarized the essence of this moment quite explicitly."

"May I go now?" asked the manager.

"Yes, please, go, go…" said Mary Ann distractedly. "Thank you for your help."

If one were to describe the artwork they were looking at in the artist's own terms, the face before them was a circle. But it was a very familiar circle, for it was, in every respect, the circular face, circular nose, and circular eyes of none other than one of the Tweedle twins…

And there was not a mustache in sight.

Rufus let out a heavy, contemplative breath. "The lack of mustache is unsettling. It's like staring into a hairless upper lip void."

Mary Ann frowned. "So, are we to assume one of the Tweedles decided to pose as this Nick Filch, but didn't want to be recognized, so he shaved off his mustache?"

"So it would seem," said Rufus.

"But then someone shortly after the burglary saw a man in a red pinstripe suit point out the First Looking-Glass in the alley way. And that man had a downward-turned mustache."

"Which would be fine," continued Rufus, "if, that very same day, we hadn't also met D.I. Tweedle at the train station in a red pinstripe suit and downward-turned mustache."

Mary Ann said, "So was D.I. Tweedle wearing a false mustache to resemble his own normal mustache? Or was that D.M. Tweedle pretending to be Nick Filch?"

"And then also pretending to be his brother?!" Rufus' normally low, smooth voice cracked a bit here. "Or were they both here on the same day?"

"Dear me," sighed Mary Ann.

Rufus pushed on the bridge of his nose. "D.M. Tweedle had a wibbly leg, though, remember? He was recovering from his crow-napping. Would he have been gallivanting across three Squares all a-wibble?"

"But that's what he told us, didn't he?" said Mary Ann. "What if his leg weren't wibbly? What if it were an excuse?"

"He did have very real bruise on him in the shape of his truncheon. I don't think that was made-up."

"He did."

"I'm not sure what to believe anymore," said Rufus. At this, he turned to Flossie Tombow. "Well, one thing's for sure, madam, you're a very effective artist. You got to the crux of the subject matter with an eerie precision." And he paid her for her efforts.

As they were leaving the gallery, prepared to return the artist to her life of bouquets and piercing eyes, a museum worker ran in. "Sir Mary Ann and Sir Rufus? This rocking-horsefly just arrived for you. It's from the Queen!"

They thanked her and unfurled the message tied to its saddle. It read:

SIRS RUFUS AND MARY ANN:

COME TO SQUARE SIX, THE GREAT WALL, IMMEDIATELY.

I THINK IT'S ANOTHER ONE. SIT UP STRAIGHT IN THE SADDLE AND DON'T DAWDLE.

YOURS REGALLY,
QUEEN ROSAMUND

"This day just keeps getting better," sighed Rufus, rolling the message up and stuffing it in his bag.

Mary Ann asked the museum worker, "Can you see to it that Miss Tombow gets a carriage home? Thank you! We have to go."

18

The Great Wall was an archaeological remnant of the beginning of the separation of Red and White Turvy. It was not particularly Great in length, for most of it had either been knocked down or had fallen down over time. And it was not particularly Great in construction, for it had been built on the cheap and, thus, was poorly executed, with many bricks misaligned and very few of them level. It was not even Great in width, for each brick was just four inches deep. The most you could say for it was that it was quite high, and its height combined with its narrowness, and shoddy construction, made it a very peculiar choice for sitting atop and meditating. Yet sitting atop and meditating is precisely what one of Square Six's most infamous residents was commonly seen doing, day upon day, perched upon this wall, looking for all the world like a massive egg.

How he got up there without a ladder had always been a source of mystery to Mary Ann. As a child, Mary Ann had developed this theory that once the egg had climbed up there, he never left and that the ladder had simply rotted down around him. She had no idea whether this was true or not. It was just what her child-brain had rationalized.

Sometimes that was good enough.

But Humpty Dumpty — for that was the fellow's name — was not sitting and meditating on the wall at this moment. He was having a wheezing fit of panic, while all the Kings' men and horses tried to help him pull himself together again. It looked like it might take the lot of them, but most of the men were doctors to ease his anxiety attack, while some of them were knights who'd been called in to help get the fellow safely off the wall before it crumbled further. There was, at present, a single brick missing from the center of the wall, and large cracks had formed across the mortar radiating from that spot, an ominous presence for certain.

Rufus seemed to be on friendly terms with all the knights. "Hello, Sir Owen, Sir Erasmus, Sir Lillian…" He nodded to each one in turn. "What's gone on here?"

"If we can get him calm, you can ask him," said Sir Lillian, shaking her head. "He's in a dreadful state, though. I fear it's going to be a long evening."

"Indeed, it looks that way," said Rufus, surveying the scene. "By the way, Lillian, have you met Sir Mary Ann? She's —"

"Ah, there you are!" Queen Rosamund appeared, complete with flyswatter. Presumably, her real scepter was being mended and restored. "I need you two to come talk to this egg," she said.

"Is he an egg, though?" asked Mary Ann, quietly, for she'd always wanted to know. "Or is he just very *like* an egg?"

"Does it matter," asked Rufus, "as long as we get an eggsplanation of what's occurred?" He grinned. "Perhaps we should employ hard-boiled tactics with him."

Mary Ann winced. "Oh, I knew you wouldn't be able to resist. I knew it."

They approached Mr. Dumpty, though they could hear him wailing quite clearly from several paces away. "It's over, it's all over! Over so easy! One spends one's life on a wall, contemplating the meaning of all things, gaining true understanding of everything beyond the ken of regular, poorly-shaped people with their regular, poorly-shaped brains. And then a tragedy occurs, and one is shaken to one's very foundation and everything one thought one knew is dashed!"

"Has he cracked?" Rufus asked the physicians.

"Young man, we don't use ignorant terminology like that here," one of the doctors scolded. "This is an eggsistential crisis."

Mary Ann asked, "May we have a moment with him? We need to learn what he's witnessed. There's some idea it might be relevant to a case we're working on."

"You may try asking him questions if you like," said one doctor over Dumpty's wails. "It might distract him enough to get the panic to subside. But if it doesn't work, you'll have to go."

Mary Ann nodded and crouched beside the fellow. "Mr. Dumpty? It's a pleasure to finally get to meet you. My name's Mary Ann Carpenter. I recall hearing about you when I was a girl living in Tulgey Barrens. I'm quite a fan, you know."

"Woe, so near death was I! So near the ultimate destruct—" He looked at her with interest now and left off the amateur dramatics. "Fan, did you say?"

"Why, yes! Who wouldn't be a fan of an individual with so fine a shape? Such proud oval perfection? So soothing in its aesthetics?" She'd had to think quite fast with this one.

"Well, yes, my aesthetics *are* soothing, aren't they? It is good of you to acknowledge it," he said, adjusting his cravat. Or was it his belt? "Especially, given that you all have such irregular and unpleasant slopes and bends."

Rufus, Mary Ann noticed, had sucked in his lips so he wasn't compelled to say something.

"Are you one of the King's Men, Mary Ann Carpenter?" asked Mr. Dumpty.

"Yes, I am, sir," she said. "I'm—"

"You're nothing of the kind! You're a girl. The plaited hair gives it away."

"Well, I meant I'm a knight who serves the King and Queen, and—"

"Then you should have said it, straight away. I always say what I mean. Of course, I'm in charge of creating all the definitions of all the words in the realm. So whatever word I use, that is the perfect word for the occasion."

"You created the entire Turvian language?" Mary Ann wasn't sure she was able to keep the tone of disbelief from her voice on this one.

"It's a work in progress," Mr. Dumpty admitted. "But if you have a word that you particularly like, you may thank me for it." And he seemed to be waiting to hear it.

"I like the word 'witness' very much, thank you," said Mary Ann, struggling to get the interview back on track. "As in, 'Mr. Dumpty: I was hoping to get your witness account of what happened here today.' I see there's a brick missing from the wall. When did that happen?"

"That…" and he seemed to be having a hard time breathing again, "was the tragedy … I was met with … today … I looked mortality in the face … as he removed the stability … from my very life!"

"So you saw the face of the fellow who took the brick?" asked Mary Ann.

"When I use the word 'face,'" began Mr. Dumpty, "it means 'top of the head' …"

"So, you looked mortality on the top of the head," said Mary Ann, which she imagined was the view from his particular vantage point. "And what was mortality wearing?"

"Ah! … Fear … despair … a red helmet," he rasped.

Rufus raised an eyebrow. "Mortality likes hats, does he?"

"Indeed," said Mr. Dumpty. "The kind with the little propeller on top."

Mary Ann and Rufus exchanged glances. They happened to know of two such gentlemen who wore their red helmets fashioned with a little propeller on top. The helmets were regulation for Square Four guards. The propellers were not.

"So, mortality came round, just knocked a brick from your wall, and left?" asked Rufus.

"He did not. He chiseled all around the brick. The word 'chisel' here meaning, 'drew it out of the wall like a small drawer.' And then he set it on the ground there, retrieved some folded paper from it, and tucked that away in his bag." And Mr. Dumpty pointed to a small drawer that was sitting at the base of the wall. Interestingly, the drawer had a brick façade on the two opposite ends of it. "And I didn't catch your name, boy?"

"My name is Sir Rufus, Mr. Dumpty," said Rufus with a little bow.

"Ha!" shouted the egg-man. "If you were the least bit intelligent, the answer you'd have said was: 'You didn't catch it at all, because I did not throw it.'"

Rufus turned to Mary Ann looking weary. "Is there anything else we need here?"

"No, I think we're finished," said Mary Ann.

As they rejoined Goodspeed and Edgar, Dumpty shouted, "I daresay, you'd have thought of it yourself, if you were more egg-shaped and less … whatever *that* is!"

As they were taking the road to Carmine Manor, a carriage rode up with the words "All the King's Bricklayers" marked on the side.

"That's one crisis averted, anyway," said Mary Ann.

"Oh goody," said Rufus.

19

"What we really need," said Mary Ann, as they rode back to Square Four, "is to map things out. Which Tweedle was where and when. What can we verify, and what can we logically assume?"

Rufus said, "We also should—and this goes against my own personal desires in virtually every way—but we really should visit Mr. Pennwell at some point and hear what he has to say about his encounter with Evelyn. I doubt we can trust him, but we might be able to peel away the blatant exaggerations and self-aggrandizement from the inner onion of truth."

"As odious as he is, I agree." Mary Ann shook her head sadly. "The things you and I do for this realm."

"All right, then, my suggestion is this: we go back to Carmine Manor, take over the library tables, have a working supper and see what we can verify. You may not be surprised to learn we have quite a lot of books on Turvian prophecy poems in my household."

"I picture you being fed a steady diet of them from the moment you knew your alphabet," Mary Ann said.

"Admittedly, my study of them at the time was rather self-preservationist and not all-encompassing. But perhaps they might give us some insight into why Evelyn, and presumably one or both Tweedles, have been holding these newly-discovered prophecies back from the world."

"Can someone open the door, please?" came a gentle voice from the hall.

Rufus leapt up to open the heavy entrance to the library as Lady Carmine came in carrying a large chalkboard on legs.

"Great gryphons, Mother, what are you doing? You should have called me. I'd have fetched it." Rufus took it from her now and brought it the rest of the way into the room.

She dusted off her hands. There was chalk dust on her cheek and across the bosom of her dress. "Phew! I suppose I should have wiped it down first." She drew a handful of chalk and a chalkboard eraser from a pocket and plopped them onto the library table. "I imagine you remember this from our lessons?" Lady Carmine asked, smiling at her son.

"Yes, vividly," said Rufus. "Will I be building better memories with it now?"

"As before, that is up to you," she said, a twinkle in her eye. "I just thought given your various conundrums in this case, it might be useful, so you can see everything plotted out."

"Yes, very!" said Mary Ann. "Thank you very much, Lady Carmine!"

"You're quite welcome, my dear," she said, brushing chalk dust from her clothes. "I think it's frabjous the time and energy you're both putting into this case. I hope the Queen appreciates you."

Rufus said, "The Queen will appreciate it when there are no longer giant crows menacing her citizens and Turvian artifacts being dismantled."

"And have you made any progress?"

"Perhaps you could help us," Mary Ann said, sensing the Baroness' keen interest to be involved in some way. "This is where we are." And Mary Ann took a piece of chalk and rose.

"D.M. Tweedle, who wears his mustache turned up, went missing, crow-napped by Evelyn." Mary Ann wrote "D.M." and an upward arrow next to it. "D.I. Tweedle of the downward mustache got hit on the back of the head and lost his memory." She wrote "D.I." and drew a downward arrow. "D.M. Tweedle was found the next day, with a wibbly leg and a truncheon bruise and brought home. It initially looked like Evelyn needed to collect the Queen's scepter, as disguised as a rattle, from the Tweedles' rattle collection and the Tweedles put up a fight." Mary Ann drew a rough bird shape flying away. "She got D.M. Tweedle out of the way, whilst an accomplice whacked D.I. Tweedle over the head and fetched the scepter."

"I'm with you so far," said Lady Carmine.

"Then other relics started to be stolen and cracked open," continued Mary Ann. "Like the First Looking-Glass. There, temporary security guard Nick Filch took the mirror, dismantled it, and left it in an alleyway. Nick was described as a clean-shaven stocky fellow and the manager who hired him helped us generate a suspect portrait which looks exactly like one of the Tweedles, but without a mustache. A half-hour later, the looking-glass was found there in the alley. Guards were notified of its existence by a man in a red pinstripe suit with a downward-turned mustache."

Mary Ann went on: "We presumed this is D.I. Tweedle because we saw that very man emerge in a red pinstripe suit from the train station which is between here and Square One. He seemed to be returning home. The Tweedles do not normally spend their time apart, so this was peculiar, and D.I. Tweedle's behavior in itself was odd, to the point it even felt threatening. It is possible that this behavior was due to his head injury, but perhaps not."

"The next location of a historic relic being cracked-open was the Great Wall in Square Six. Mr. Humpty Dumpty witnessed a man in a red helmet with a propeller on it remove a secret drawer from the wall, with some papers in it. Both Tweedles wear these helmets. The witness did not see the person's face, just the top of his head because it's a very high wall, so no mustache identification was possible. And here we are."

"You forgot two things," said Rufus. "The First Wool and the White Queen's brooch. The wool started it all, as it became wet on accident, and that's when Evelyn Rookwood and one of White Turvy's archaeologists were called in by the museum to examine the first new prophecy. Then the White Queen's brooch disappeared briefly thereafter. But we didn't hear about it in good time, because it's White Turvy's jurisdiction. The identity of that thief remains a complete cipher. We do, however, know that someone from the Royal White Turvy Academy's Archaeology Department was on the case there, as well. But we do not know whom. Yet."

"Which reminds me," said Lady Carmine. "Sir Mary Ann, your friend Professor Goodnuff sent a rocking-horsefly confirming your request, and he has contacted the college for the information you seek. He'll let you know as soon as he hears."

"Thank you, Lady Carmine. That's excellent."

"So, based on what you're saying, you have two separate phases of problem here," said Lady Carmine. "In the initial incident, you indicate both Tweedles were victims of these scepter thieves, correct? One carried off, the other bludgeoned."

"Correct," said Rufus and Mary Ann.

"But in the next phase, one or both Tweedles are directly involved in the mischief. So, which is it? Either one or both are in on the plot. Or either one or both are not. You don't go from being attacked by crows and knocked out, to breaking in and pilfering antiquities in a mere day or two. Unless you were never actually attacked by crows or knocked out to begin with. Someone is lying."

"Exactly," said Mary Ann. "And that's our dilemma. The question is: which one, and why? I suppose we could arrest them both and start trying to rip off mustaches, but that isn't going to get us Evelyn, her accomplice in White Turvy, or the missing prophecies. It's only going to alert them to what we know so far."

"Based on what you're saying, I'd suggest it was D.I. Tweedle," said Lady Carmine. "He gets tangled up in something, he has his brother dragged off, and he steals his own 'rattle.' He shaves of his mustache to become this Nick Thievery fellow—

"Filch," said Rufus.

"—He whacks on a false mustache until his own can grow in again. He changes his clothes. Then he points out the looking-glass in the alleyway, so the museum gets it back. Then you see him on his travels home."

Mary Ann said, "So he'd pretend to be injured to keep up appearances with his brother?"

Rufus said, "Why not? How else does he explain why one of the precious pieces in their collection suddenly went missing?"

"There's only one problem with that," said Mary Ann. "I believe it was D.M. Tweedle who lied about the rattle being at the silversmith's when I asked about it back at the cottage. Why would he do that? The rattle was never sent there. And when D.I. Tweedle said he didn't know it was broken and being mended, D.M. Tweedle told him he was still having partial 'namblesia' and just didn't remember."

The room got very quiet.

"Maybe they hadn't agreed on a proper lie?" suggested Rufus.

"Well," Lady Carmine rose, "you've exceeded my depth of knowledge in this matter. I shall leave you both to it, then. Try not to stay up too late." She gave an affectionate ruffle of Rufus' hair, but mainly just put chalk dust in it. "Sir Mary Ann, the yellow guest room's been prepared for you. The carriage is also available to take you home whenever you like. Whichever you prefer."

"Thank you, My Lady. That's very kind." That Lady Carmine gave even two moments thought about Mary Ann's welfare and logistics warmed the heart.

Rufus, Mary Ann saw, had risen and was pulling books off the shelves. "<u>Turvian Prophecy Poems and Their Significance in Modern Red Turvy</u>... <u>Sir Loral Clew: Soothsaying for Fun and Prophet</u>... <u>Clew Little, Clew Late: A Critique of Prophecy Poems and Their Effect on Turvian Society</u>... <u>The Little Child's Big Book of Prophecy Poem History</u>..." He thumped these to the table. "That'll get us started."

"Started ..." Mary Ann sighed. She could see it was going to be a long night.

Mary Ann had not realized, prior to this evening, how very famous Sir Rufus was across Turvy. At least, in name and deed, if not in physical recognition. In all the books, his two prophecy poems appeared in full, with some accompanying analysis. And while Rufus' family likely owned the books because of this, thus skewing her data sample, it was still quite impressive due to their sheer scope and diversity.

But Sir Loral Clew had written prophecy poems on many non-Rufus subjects, as well. There was a rather long epic that Rufus mentioned came to pass recently, where a group of foreign men and one beaver went out on a quest for a Snark, and one fellow went missing, presumed dead. There were pieces on queens and kings and missing jam tarts. There were tales of lions and unicorns and a certain amount of cake. (Prophecies had an unexpected amount of baked goods in them in the Wanderlands, Mary Ann noticed.) There was even a rather dire prediction on Humpty Dumpty, causing Mary Ann to gain a better idea of why the ovoid man was so dramatic about his wall situation.

What she found particularly interesting, however, was the information about Sir Loral Clew himself. It seemed he was a knight to the first monarchs of Turvy, King Marbel and Queen Di, before it was split into the Red and White territories. Clew was assigned to protect Turvy's boundaries against the realm of Yon, a lush and luxurious land renowned for its unfathomable beauty. According to the history, the land was so enticing beyond Turvy's boundary, one of the knights in Clew's group got tired of just looking at it, crossed the border and deserted.

Well, everyone knows how when one person starts Yonning, everyone does it. And pretty soon all the knights but Clew had left their post and shifted to Yon. When the King presented Clew with a medal for his unique loyalty and asked what compelled the man to resist where no other could, to the King's surprise, Clew proclaimed it was neither loyalty nor bravery. He said war had exacerbated his madness to such a degree that he was overcome with precognitive abilities. He claimed he only held the border that day because he'd been too busy writing down the messages his madness dictated and that a life surrounded by staggering beauty had seemed petty by comparison.

The King said he wanted to see these prophecies. So, Clew rattled off a poem about the potential assault that one inexplicably spry old man named William threatened upon his son, and lo and behold, if the youth was not found crumpled at the bottom of the stairs two days later. Over time, Clew's poems grew more elaborate, with his prophecies extending far into the future and well across the Wanderlands. As his reputation grew, so did his mad behavior, and Clew could be found spilling out prophecies, stealing peoples' stockings off their washing lines for fun, and wearing mud hats. Naturally, he became a highly-valued advisor to King Marbel and Queen Di. Others tried imitating him, attempting different techniques to enhance their already mad tendencies, but no one else achieved verifiable prophecy — or successfully pulled off mud-hat fashion.

"It's interesting," Mary Ann said, finally breaking the silence, "some rather good information on Sir Loral Clew here, but I can't seem to find anything that says how many prophecies he made."

"I don't know that we know for sure," said Rufus. "He was at it for years, though."

Mary Ann grabbed a new book, opened it and wrinkled her nose. "Are you finding anything useful? Any reason why our Evelyn and the others might keep a collection of prophecies for themselves?"

"No. But I'm starting to think we've been viewing it too impractically." He looked up from his reading. "Maybe they plan to auction them to the highest bidder. Or perhaps they know who's in the prophecies and they want to use them for extortion. You know, like: 'You want to see what happens to you in the future, sir or madam? You'll have to pay for it.' That sort of thing."

Yawning, Mary Ann turned a page but realized she hadn't retained a word on it. "That's disappointing."

"People often are," said Rufus, yawning, too.

And the library fell silent once more.

Mary Ann wasn't sure what time she stopped reading, because the next thing she became aware of was the steam on her face. That was followed by the scent of something slightly sweet and lemony.

And a voice: "Tamsin?"

Mary Ann opened an eye. Just one. What she saw was a painted red rose on a light green background, very close to her eyeball.

"I thought you might like some tea," said the voice.

Mary Ann sat up. Her neck was stiff as a board. Her face had a ridge shaped like the edge of the table; she knew this, because it was noticeable to the touch, and it ached. There was a puddle of saliva on the tabletop next to a pretty porcelain cup filled with tea.

"There's crumpets and bread-and-butterflies, too," said Emmaline.

"Thank you," Mary Ann said feebly. Rufus, she noticed, was lolled back in his wing chair, looking for all the world like a memento mori photograph of himself.

Mary Ann rose, stiffly, and patted his shoulder. "Ahoy there. You. Dead man. It's morning."

The dead man opened his eyes, pale blue-grey in this light, and it didn't help to relieve the corpse impression much. "What time is it?" he asked. But he only got out "ime" and "is it" to any real volume.

"Seven a.m., Sir," Emmaline supplied, for she spoke Pre-Tea Rufus.

"Did we solve the Tweedle case?" he asked.

"No," Mary Ann said, rubbing her face and grabbing for her cup.

"Damnation." He stretched.

Mary Ann hadn't brought a change of clothes with her, since she hadn't expected to spend the night face-down on the Carmines' library table. But rather than go all the way back to the cottage, change, and return, she just washed up in the guest room and re-wore the clothes she had.

When she met up with Rufus in the Manor entryway, he was staring at the Jabberwock head that hung there, giving it the same narrow glare he usually gave it. "I swear," he said upon her approach, "as soon as I become Lord of this Manor, I am having the Royal Red Turvy Museum haul that head away. I mean, yes, I gave the creature every chance, and it made its choice. But why must I live with a souvenir of that dreadful, headful day?"

Mary Ann considered it a rather good day, simply because they'd both survived it. But she knew the issue was more complex than that. "You did your duty," she said. "You owe nothing else." And she hoped that reassured him. Especially since it was unlikely his more nuanced version of the event would be what the museum shared with its visitors. The prophecy poem version of the tale simply loomed too powerfully in the public mind.

She changed the subject as they moved to the door and glanced at the grandfather clock in the corner. "Do you think it's too early to call on Mr. Pennwell?"

"I think Mr. Pennwell can stuff it," said Rufus, and Mary Ann could see what sort of mood he woke up in. "He wants to insert himself into our case? Then he can ruddy well do it on our schedule. Besides, we have that ball at Count Talionis' place tonight."

"That's tonight?" Mary Ann moaned, having quite forgotten about it in all the hubbub. She'd always wanted to attend a ball, but now this felt like one more thing that was ill-timed and bound to be less pleasant for it.

"Yes, I'm hoping to get a quick nap in this afternoon so I'll be at all coherent for the thing. People expect coherency at these events — at least before the mushroom beer starts flowing. I also recall promising I'd teach a certain someone to dance." He looked at her with a little smile.

"At this moment, I'll take a nap over dance lessons," she said, hugging onto his arm. "No offense."

"None taken. At this moment, I'd agree."

Mary Ann was rather curious to see where Cyrus Pennwell lived. While Rufus theorized it was under a rock, and Mary Ann pictured him dug-in like a tick to the guesthouse of a wealthy, disreputable benefactor, neither idea proved to be true. It had been difficult to even get an address for the man, but eventually, Rufus was able to call in some favors, and they tracked him down to a flat above a pub in Square Five.

An elderly male rabbit with a pipe and spectacles answered the door. "Yes? May I help you?"

There was considerable noise coming from inside, the laughter of small children and the sound of little running feet.

Mary Ann said, "Oh, I'm very sorry. We're looking for Cyrus Pennwell, but we must have the wrong address."

"Oh no, miss, he's here!" said the rabbit. "Friends of his, are you? Do come in! You and the young man!" And the rabbit stood aside to let them pass.

Unfortunately, as Mary Ann stepped in, a small bunny in plum knickers darted past her.

The old rabbit gasped. "Oh, my whiskers! Bitsy! If one of you could just—"

Rufus caught Bitsy at the door—"Got 'em!"—and closed the door behind him with his boot.

"Well done, young man! Jolly good reflexes! That's the third time Bitsy's tried to dash today."

Rufus handed the bunny to the older man. It was hard to know where to stand; there must have been thirty rabbits of various ages running round. Rabbits singing, rabbits playing, rabbits pulling each other's ears and whiskers… Rabbits sewing quilts, rabbits practicing piano, and rabbits making tea, in the sunny pastel kitchen.

"Look, Mother, some friends have come to see Mimsy!" said the rabbit gentleman.

Mother, who was sitting in a rocking chair with four small rabbits in her lap said, "That's lovely, dear! Muffy, Puffy, put a second kettle on, would you? We have guests."

"Erm, I'm sorry," said Mary Ann. "There must be a misunderstanding. We're here to see Cyrus Pennwell? Investigative reporter for *The Turvy Mirror*?"

"Well, of course, miss," said the elder rabbit. "That's our Mimsy."

"Mimsy Pennwell?" asked Rufus, his expression somewhere between agape and a grin.

"Oh, no, sir. Cyrus Pennwell's his professional name, don't you know? Mimsy Flarfkin is his given name. He's had a very rough time of it the past two days due to that dreadful crow incident. But since you're here to check on him, I suppose you already know that. He's sleeping in the other room. Although, I wager, he won't be too tired for some nice visitors!" And with that, the elder rabbit knocked twice, then swung open the bedroom door.

There lay Cyrus Pennwell in a poster bed covered with a quilt featuring a carrot theme, propped up on lots of fluffy pillows, in a room of pastel yellow and green.

Rufus whispered to Mary Ann in a tone of wonder, "It's our Unbirthdays!"

"Mimsy, some lovely people have stopped by to see you," said the elder rabbit.

Mimsy—er, Cyrus Pennwell—sat up in bed, eyes filled with horror. He was wearing a sleeping cap and nightshirt that continued the carrot theme. "Father! I told you I didn't want to see anyone!"

"Well, these nice people have come all this way from…" The rabbit pushed up his spectacles. "Where did you say you were from?"

In a firm, official-sounding baritone, Rufus said, "We're investigating your son's assault incident on behalf of Queen Rosamund."

"Now isn't that nice? Justice being served and all that?" said the elder rabbit. "Well, I'll leave you to it. Muffy will have the tea ready in a mo.'" And he closed the door behind them. There was a long, awkward pause.

Rufus broke it. "Mr. Pennwell," Rufus clasped his hands before him and smiled. In a tone barely-disguising his delight, he asked, "Have you been a rabbit all this time?"

"Look, I was adopted," snapped Pennwell. "They didn't think they could have children, so they adopted me. Then, all of this…" he motioned in a general way, "…happened. But that is, frankly, none of your business and quite irrelevant."

"I wouldn't say it's *not* relevant…" said Mary Ann.

"And when does Cyrus Pennwell draw boundaries on what is or is not someone's business?" asked Rufus.

"All right," spat the man, "ha-ha, yes, so it's ironic, my family is fluffy and adorable, get it all out of your system. But it's not like we're close. I rarely even see them. Are you here to take my statement or not?"

"Oh, we'll take your statement," said Rufus. "But we want the truth. And I don't want to see one more photogaffe … not one more article on me, Sir Mary Ann here, or any member of my family with even so much as a whiff of scandal in your paper. Never again. Do you understand me?"

"Or what?" Pennwell's eyes were narrowed, his jaw set—a difficult look to pull off while wearing a veg-embroidered nightie.

"I think you know what," said Rufus, folding his arms.

"And if I tell all of Turvy that Sir Rufus Carmine, the Jabberwock slayer, tried to blackmail me?"

"Ah, but you won't." Rufus smiled. "Personally, Mr. Flarfkin, I think your family is quite charming, and I'm not certain you even deserve them. But you, sir, have chosen to build your whole personality on being an edgy, salacious, cutthroat, destructive parasite, with nary a single shred of carrot on view to the world. Your whole career banks on it. So, your continued silence on this matter? It's a chance I'm willing take."

Pennwell made a little growl-sigh and sank back into his pillows.

"So, now that's settled ..." Mary Ann pulled out a notebook and a pencil. She sat down in a celery green rocking chair with ruffled pillows shaped like lettuce heads, "tell us about your encounter with the crow."

Pennwell hadn't initially wanted to admit he'd been following Mary Ann's and Rufus' lead down the Topsy River, seeking the location of Ole Inky himself. But when the elder rabbit — who they learned was Mr. Radish Flarfkin—popped in with the tea things and some nibbles and asked whether Mimsy had ever told them the story of how he won first place in the Funny Bunny Fiction Contest down at the Briar Patch primary school, things moved along much easier.

"So where exactly did you encounter the crow?" asked Mary Ann.

"It was in south Square Six, I believe," he said. "I hadn't seen anything of interest the whole way down the river. But then I caught a flash of something shiny in the woods in an area I knew to be uninhabited. You know how crows like shiny things? So, I was docking the boat to check it out, when I heard this tremendous whooshing sound, and this massive crow appeared out of nowhere. I went paddling upstream as well as I could, but the crow was enormous — the size of a whole cottage. It kept cawing and flapping its wings... It made the waters even rougher, and, well, my boat capsized. I managed to get myself onto a rock and, from there, to shore. But it kept after me, flapping and cawing. So, I dashed further upstream, and somehow, I slipped in a bog. And that's where they found me, those workers from that Topsy Turvian Doodads factory that sometimes appears along the river. I had a twisted ankle, a wrecked knee and had inhaled an unfortunate amount of river water. No one saw the crow, though. I suppose by then it was long gone."

Mary Ann said, "So the crow didn't try to grab you and carry you off? Or even bite at you at all?"

"Clearly, I was too fast for it," he said, holding his head high, tassel on his sleep cap swinging.

Rufus raised an eyebrow. "Try again, Mr. Flarfkin."

Pennwell snarled, "Fine. No, I suppose it didn't try to grab me or bite me. It just chased me. But I tell you, the noise was chilling."

"Interesting," said Mary Ann.

"So, what — you don't think it was trying to harm me?" Pennwell surveyed them carefully.

Mary Ann rose. "I think we have all we need for now. Thank you, Mr. Pennwell."

"You think it's some sort of scam, do you? Something to scare me off?"

"Thank you for your time, Mr. Pennwell," said Rufus. "I hope we never need to speak of this day again."

"You think the encounter was leveraging the legend of Ole Inky as a distraction of some sort?"

They closed the bedroom door behind them.

20

Mary Ann said, "When Pennwell mentioned that shine in the woods, it reminded me. We saw the same thing, didn't we, in the woods right before we got sucked back to Square One that day?" They were moving through the Square Five market on the way back to the Manor.

"Ah, I'd wondered if you caught that, too!" said Rufus. "We'd been so busy, we never did get back to that spot, did we?"

"And I don't think Evelyn just appeared out of nowhere, like Pennwell said; I think she ate some Burgeonboosh and embigggened, so he finally noticed her. Which means she was already in the area when he came along. What is out there she didn't want him to see?"

"You know what we have to do, don't you?"

"No more rowboats, please," said Mary Ann.

He chuckled. "I was rather thinking we might invite the horses this time round. We can take the Baffle Bridge over the Topsy at Folly Junction."

Which is precisely what they did.

As they journeyed south through Square Six, Goodspeed had a lot of questions. "Is the terrain all going to be this full of tree roots? Had I known, I would have worn my other shoes.

How far south in Square Six is it? And what precisely are we looking for, Sir?"

Rufus let out an exasperated sigh. "To answer your questions in order…Yes, stop complaining … A ways yet, stop complaining … And we're looking for shed that isn't there."

"A shed that isn't there?" muttered the horse. "Sir Rufus, you and Sir Mary Ann do get involved in the most peculiar missions."

"Too true," said Rufus.

"I rather find this whole thing exhilarating," Edgar said. "Fresh air, new paths, a mystery…"

"Then you really are the right horse for this job," said Mary Ann. "My problem is, I'm having a hard time keeping myself distracted from wanting to get there and investigate that shed. If I'm not careful, I'll land us back at Square One again. Perhaps we distract ourselves with some singing?" Mary Ann was not a great singer, but quality didn't matter, so long as the mind was occupied.

"Or perhaps I give you something else to focus on," said Rufus, with a mysterious little smile.

"Oh, you know I'm not good at those riddles," she said. Rufus had a remarkable catalogue of riddles in his brain, and his joy of sharing them was almost equal to Mary Ann's dislike in having to unravel them. This was largely because half of them were vaguely unfair and most of them were terrible puns.

"No, I was just thinking," he said lightly, and his tone suggested she was in for something entertaining, "as we have that ball tonight, these dances have always been a social nightmare to navigate. With all the Red Turvian nobility invited, that means entirely too many unmarried daughters will be present. Since their options for courtship in Turvy are not endless, I have been the target of their attentions since I was about sixteen. Nothing to do with me, mind you. It's just some of the other unattached nobles are … well … For instance, the Viscount Frederick of Square Two got in the habit of walking backwards everywhere he goes. He thinks it's good luck. You can never tell if he's arriving or leaving, so his future spouse would probably have to make some concessions for that. Or Geoffrey of Square Three who's a lovely fellow, but the fact remains, he is a hamster. It takes a special kind of person to get betrothed to a man who lives in an underground manor of sawdust, pipes and tunnels. Things like that."

"You think you are popular because you are not a hamster," said Mary Ann.

"It's a factor people do tend to weigh, yes," he said, nodding. "However," he raised a finger, "it occurred to me that if I were truly and officially engaged to, oh...say...the maddest, most clever swordswoman in the realm—that's you, by the way —I could be spared these awkward social interactions from this evening onward. It would be a glorious relief to me—a service of mercy, really!"

"While I see your perspective," began Mary Ann, struggling to keep a straight face, "you forget we are already pretend-engaged, and that should work just as well to ward them off this evening. I'm certain they've all read your father's *Mirror* piece and have had their hopes of courting suitably dashed."

"Ah, but we'll be asked about the engagement, won't we? Everyone asks. And I'd prefer not to tell tales. A proper engagement would make this evening far more enjoyable. All transparent and above board. You'd be doing me the greatest favor. What do you think?"

She grinned. "Well, Sir Rufus, why don't you ask me and find out?"

"Perhaps I will," he said. And he cleared his throat. "Sir Mary Ann Carpenter, would you do me the honor of marrying me?"

"Goodness, Rufus, I don't know," she said. "I mean, I haven't met Geoffrey the Hamster yet. He sounds intriguing, and I do so love the smell of sawdust."

Goodspeed and Edgar both broke into whinnies of horse-laughter.

Rufus grinned. "If that would make you happiest, I'll put in a good word for you. That is how deeply I care. I would bow out to the better man—rodent—if it meant your joy."

"So, you're no longer ... what did your father call it?" She thought a moment. "'Digging your heels in out of spite?'"

"I'm out of spite, for now," he said. "Fresh out. It'll be a while before the next shipment comes in."

"Then yes," she said. "Absolutely, I'll marry you. If only to remove you from the ambitions of Turvy's young unattached nobility and free your conscience. They will be heartbroken, of course, but that is their burden to bear." And while she knew Rufus had been teasing, Mary Ann suspected there really *would* be a few disappointed young courtiers at the ball this evening. It was odd to think how their loss was her gain.

Meanwhile, Goodspeed and Edgar extended their congratulations.

"Engaged on horseback," Mary Ann mused. "Well, if that isn't the most 'you and I' thing there could be."

"A mite better than in the Letter to the Editor column, I thought," he said.

And Rufus was right. About the Letter to the Editor column, certainly, but more specifically, Mary Ann did, indeed, end up being quite pleasantly distracted for a good chunk of their journey. It was very surreal to think of herself as actually engaged, like she was this full, regular person and a real part of the active, visible world like everyone else. If one had talked to her back when she worked as a housemaid for Warren Rabbit, she would have said she didn't imagine she had a chance of marrying at all. But as no one *did* talk to her then, about that topic or any, she supposed that was part of the problem. Now the idea of marrying the man who'd become her closest friend, well, it really was a bit too good. It would all take some mental adjustment, but she was fully prepared to appreciate every moment while it lasted.

"I think it was right around here, wasn't it?" she heard Rufus say, and her attention was brought back to the scenery around her. They were operating on a different angle from their previous river cruise, but she could see the Topsy River on her right, as its pace began to grow with its rush to the sea.

She said, "As I recall, the shed was some distance from the shore. It should be somewhere to our left and—Ah! Up there!"

She could just make out a structure, covered in mushrooms and ferns. At the top, something metal offered a fleeting glint.

"Calm now. We don't want to get too enthused," said Rufus, dismounting from Goodspeed. "The land will smell our desperation." And he started whistling an old Turvian melody, which Mary Ann joined him in. It was in this way, on foot, they were able to sneak up on the shed.

"What if she's in there?" Mary Ann whispered.

But he took care of that by calling, "Evelyn Rookwood? Come out! It is time to talk."

Evelyn Rookwood did not come out.

"Wherever is the door?" Mary Ann asked, and they had to walk almost the full way around the little building to find it. It was angled and covered in the same moss and ferns as the rest of the mound. The only difference was, the rise had a doorknob.

Rufus, she noticed now, was not looking at the doorknob. He was looking at the metal object on the top of the mound. As the wind blew, it tinkled lightly in the breeze.

"Is that—?"

Oh, yes. It was an old, tarnished, silver rattle.

Mary Ann seized the doorknob and pulled.

Initially, in the change from outdoor light to sodhouse dark, it was hard to see. The room smelled of earth and damp and, disturbingly, other more human functions. She kicked something metal that skittered across the floor. As her eyes began to adjust, she could see something large and round in the corner. She heard now some muffled noise. Behind her, just outside the door, Rufus was digging in his bag. He came away with a box of matches, and lit one, applying it to a dry stick. He ducked in with it, and that illuminated the scene. There was a pewter plate and cup on the floor. In a corner was a stack of outdated, moldy issues of *Rattle Collectors' Quarterly*, as well as a set of dominoes and a rusted tin of marbles. There was a bucket of... Well, it certainly explained the smell. And before her was a very familiar-looking man, a no-longer-quite-as-spherical man in dirty underthings. His feet and hands were bound and his mouth was gagged. Mary Ann rushed to him, pulling the gag down, and discovered a second cloth wadded up within his mouth. She removed that and he exhaled and smacked his dry lips and tongue.

In addition to almost a week's worth of stubble, he had a mustache that turned upwards.

"Detective Major Damian Tweedle?" Mary Ann gasped.

"Thank the stars, you is you, Miss!" the man rasped. "And you, Sir Rufus! You would not believe the days I been having. Not nohow!"

"I think I would," she said. "But before we go any further… Please forgive me this." And she tugged on his mustache.

"OW! That there was assaultification of my personal facial region," he said.

"I had to be sure," she said.

"And after all I been through." Mary Ann untied him, and he rubbed his face.

"We should go," said Rufus, eyes darting toward the woods. "Now. Before Evelyn comes back. We'll take him to Carmine Manor and debrief him along the way."

"Not getting *my* briefs, you aren't! That's all they left me," he said, "and there's a lady present!"

Mary Ann and Rufus helped him to his feet. Mary Ann guided the Tweedle outside — his legs rubbery from recent disuse—while Rufus followed, swinging the door closed with a final thump.

"Help me get him up on Goodspeed," said Rufus to Mary Ann. And to the horse: "We've got one incoming passenger, my friend." It was with some effort, together, that the knights were able to maneuver Tweedle into the saddle. "Can you follow our lead?" Rufus asked the horse.

"Of course, Sir," said Goodspeed.

Mary Ann handed the man her canteen. D.M. Tweedle drank long and enthusiastically from it. "Ah, thank you, Miss.

That quenches to the inner-sides of my toes, it does." And she let him hold onto the canteen for the ride.

"Edgar, can you take us both?" asked Rufus.

"Certainly, Sir. I am strong as ... well, a horse, really, Sir," said Edgar.

So, Rufus climbed into the saddle followed by Mary Ann, who took the reins.

"That building was a clubhouse, wasn't it?" Mary Ann asked Tweedle as they rode off. "Your secret clubhouse when you were children."

"Indeedly, it was, Miss," said Damian. "But never did I expect to spend such extendiated time within it as I have of late."

She asked, "What happened, exactly? Evelyn carried you off and left you there?"

"Is Evelyn the name of the lady bird? Because she's the one what done it! Dorian and I was coming home for midday foodliness and she showed up. Filled the sky she did. Then I felt a pain in the back o' my noggin and all went black. When I waked up, I was in here, tied and gagged. She comes by now and again with commedibles, and water she gives me, and access to the bucket. But not often-like. Once a day, I'd say."

Rufus said, "What I don't understand is, if you're here, who's the D.M. Tweedle we've been talking to? Is it really some Deuce we don't know about, going round and stirring up trouble? See, that just makes me angry. It's been so... done. It's cliché at this point. Never redo a gag."

"Funny," said Mary Ann, "Douglas Divot had wondered that very same thing about the Deuce when I told him about our situation."

"Wait, there's another me, you say?" asked Damian Tweedle. "Beyond my brother Dorian, I mean? Who you'd never mistake for me, anyways, on account of the obvious handsomeness difference, in that I am so, and he ain't."

"At your home," began Rufus, "we have spoken directly with both a D.I. Dorian Tweedle and a D.M. Damian Tweedle. Simultaneously."

"Ah," said Damian. "Yeah. That'd like as be Dell."

"Dell?!" said Mary Ann.

"Yep. Dell Tweedle. Our other, other brother."

"There are three Tweedles?" said Mary Ann. "You're not twins, you're triplets?"

"Yeppers," said Damian, "but he and us don't get along with us like we and us do. He's too snooty for us since we growed, always putting on airs. Said we were idiots and such. So, we don't see him these days. Not for years and years. Not since our parents died. They was the glue."

"And let me guess," said Mary Ann. "Dell Tweedle is clean-shaven."

"Yes, Miss. He has always failed to appreciate the man-beauty that is a lush humdinger of a mustache."

"And he is an archaeologist."

"Nah," said D.M. Tweedle, "he don't study birds, like the postman do. He's one of them guys who digs in the ground for old stuff. Not even good stuff like interesting rattles or apples. Just old dead things and ancient paperwork. And that don't sound very smart to me."

"Dell ruddy Tweedle," murmured Rufus. "This has been one fun-fair of a day."

21

"Mother," said Rufus, ducking into the family sitting room, where Lady Carmine was reading, "we're going to need a guest room for tonight."

"Sir Mary Ann's welcome to the room she's been using, if that's acceptable," she said. "I rather expected that, since the ball starts at nine and runs to, what, five in the morning? I very much doubt, after so much dancing, she'd wish to travel all the way back h—"

"Not for Sir Mary Ann. Although," Rufus looked to Mary Ann there in the hall, who was nodding vigorously, "yes, we'll take the yellow room for Mary Ann, as well, but... We do have one more guest." And Rufus opened the door to reveal the dirty, half-naked, and somewhat thinner Damian Tweedle.

"Oh, my dear," Lady Carmine gasped. "Absolutely. Is he quite all right? I'll have Mrs. Cordingley arrange a bath and a meal and your father should have some clothes he can lend the poor man and—" Lady Carmine was already off the fainting sofa and across the room, pulling the bell for the housekeeper.

"No one's to know he's here," said Rufus. "No one is to say one word to anyone. I'll explain everything in a bit."

THE TROUBLE WITH TWEEDLE

"Yes, of course," she said. And Mary Ann liked that about Lady Carmine. She didn't ask a lot of questions when things got weird. "I'm assuming this is related to the rocking-horsefly that came for Sir Mary Ann from Professor Goodnuff?"

"What did it say, My Lady?" Mary Ann asked from the hall, though she suspected she knew.

Lady Carmine peered around the doorjamb. "He said the archaeologist working on the First Wool project was a Dell Tweedle." Her eyes were wide with meaning.

"Ding-ding-ding," said Mary Ann to Rufus.

"That rings hopeful," said Lady Carmine. "And I can't wait to hear all about it—but," her hands fluttered, "when you have time. I'll leave you to it."

"Thanks! Oh, and Mother," said Rufus, "one more thing. Mary Ann and I got engaged today. Like real-engaged this time, not Father's pushy fake-engaged for the newspapers. Just wanted to let you know. While I remembered. We've a lot going on. We'll be in the library."

❧ ✿ ☙

"What do we do? Do we just have Dell Tweedle arrested?" Mary Ann asked, leaning back in the library chair. "He's the primary suspect in the Looking-Glass theft. We could get him on that."

"We can and we should, but I'm not sure on the timing," said Rufus. "Evelyn's still out there and presumably she's the one with the prophecies."

"So, how do we lure Evelyn out into the open? She's going to discover Damian Tweedle's missing soon."

"I imagine the first thing she'll do once she learns Damian's not in the clubhouse is head to the Tweedles' cottage. She'll need to confer with Dell, or check for Damian, or both. But it's harder for Dell to pose as his brothers if they're both present and accounted for. I suppose how long he plans to keep up the charade depends a lot on how many prophecies are still out there."

"Should we go stalk the Tweedle residence? With a net?" Mary Ann laughed.

Rufus laughed, too.

Then they both stopped laughing. "Now you mention it..." began Rufus.

It was two nets. A large fishing net and a smaller butterfly net. Which one they'd use depended on whether they encountered regular or super-sized Evelyn.

Mary Ann and Rufus had walked to the Tweedle cottage along the grass, so there'd be no noise of their approach, and they slipped in amongst the shrubberies next to the side of the house. It was quiet enough that they could hear the home's residents in discussion.

"I thought I might wear the red jacket tonight with my pinstripe trousers," said one of them.

"I don't like the pinstripe trousers. Stripes and me don't go together. Not nohow."

"Well, contrariwise, you don't have to wear them."

"I do if you do, though."

"Who says we have to dress alike?"

"We always has, though, hasn't we? What is it with you of late? These ideas you have. Not dressing the same... Indeed!" The voice sounded disgusted. "The people have expectations. You want to make a good impressification on Count Tallyonion, don't you?"

Rufus and Mary Ann exchanged glances. The Tweedles were invited to the ball?

"Maybe I don't want to go to the ball," came the reply. "Maybe it don't seem worth my time."

"What better have you to do tonight? Besides, we represent Square Four. It's important-like for the community to see us in a socializable setting."

"If you *says* so."

"I *do* says so!"

"Did you find out if the King will be there?"

"I did. I have it on very good information from our postman's barber's cousin's milkman's sister, who works as a coach driver to the King himself, that him and Queen Rosamund have ordered a carriage to attend the ball tonight."

"Then that might make it an event worth my attendification."

"As I says to start with! Now where are you going?"

"Just out to the shed. I think I left my pocket watch out there."

Mary Ann and Rufus ducked low in the shrubbery as the door swung open. But the gentleman dressed as D.M. Tweedle did not go to the shed. Instead, he got the attention of a rocking-horsefly. He pulled a pencil and notepad from his coat pocket and wrote something down. Then he rolled it up and strapped it to the insect. "Take this to 29 Tweeholler Lane, Square Six. And don't dally." And off the rocking-horsefly started.

The door hadn't fully closed behind Dell Tweedle before Mary Ann was out of the bushes and running down the walk. She had the butterfly net and sprinted after that insect with all the leg power two-and-a-half years of accelerated knight training and a lifetime of housemaidery had given her. "I'm sorry about this," she said breathlessly and swung the net over the horsefly.

"Hey! What's the big idea?" it said. "I've been hired already!"

"Official business for the Queen," Mary Ann said and glanced at the cottage. The curtains were still closed, thankfully, and she could see Rufus peeping out from the shrubbery, a shock of red hair and a white-pink face, open mouthed and watching. She extracted the fly from the net and slipped the message from its tether.

It read:

KING'S A GO. MEET ME THERE.
YOU DISTRACT AT THE SIGNAL.

She rolled the message back up and fixed it into place. "All right then, off you go."

"Really?" The rocking-horsefly seemed surprised. "Suit yourself, lady." And it galloped away across the meadow air.

Mary Ann motioned Rufus to join her and, looking left and right, he emerged from the bushes, running. "Great gryphons! You don't give a man much warning, do you?"

"I just saw an opportunity and didn't want to waste it," she said. "But it was worth it. Let's go."

"We're leaving? Why? What happened?" They were almost to the main road now.

Mary Ann said, "There's no sense spending the afternoon in the shrubbery. I know where Evelyn is now."

"And that is?"

"The Tweedles' old family home in Square Six. I recognized the address from that job application you found."

"Well done!" he said. "We'll nab her right now, then."

"Not yet."

"What?" He stared at her. "Why?"

"I want her to show her hand, in front of everyone. And she will, because I know where she's going to be tonight."

Rufus frowned. "And where is that?"

"She's coming to the ball."

"Oh, frabjous. She's fond of a good quadrille, is she?"

"She's going to provide Dell Tweedle with a distraction."

"A distraction for what?"

"Something related to the King," said Mary Ann. "I'm guessing it's another relic they're after."

"All right then," said Rufus. "We know what we have to do."

"Stop her in her tracks before Tweedle gets to the King? Capture her, get her to confess, and solve the whole case?"

"Yes, that. But more immediately, you need to fetch your ballgown," he said. "And I need to teach you to dance in..." He opened his pocket watch and made a face. "...virtually no time at all."

They picked up the dark red gown and shoes from her cottage, as well as some overnight things and her toiletries. It was with some weary resignation that Rufus watched her stuff everything but the dress into an old flour sack. The dress she slung over her shoulder. "No travel bag. I should have expected it."

"I generally have nothing to put in one," she said, closing the door behind them. "This is a first."

Rufus said, "All right, we know there will be quadrilles, for there are always quadrilles at these events. Given we have limited time and are operating on limited sleep, I suggest we start there. We need six more people." And Rufus began rounding up individuals from all around the Manor and sending them on to the ballroom.

By the time he was done, he had Emmaline, Lord and Lady Carmine, Mr. Wheeler the carriage driver, Mabel the parlor maid, and Rufus's squire, Russell, all collected and deposited in the room. Rufus assigned his parents to be the Head Couple, since they already knew what they were doing and that freed him up to help Mary Ann.

Damian Tweedle had followed them in to observe. He was looking somewhat improved, having had a bath and a shave and he was wearing some extra clothes from one of the stable hands, as Lord Carmine's gear proved to be too short and snug. That along with a good lunch had restored him nicely. Rufus invited a bird into the mix—Mary Ann wasn't sure what the scientific name was, but she always thought of them as "gramophone-birds," a creature from Tulgey Barrens with a wide yellow bill that imitated orchestral music and could project it quite loudly into a room. Then they were ready to go.

A half hour later, Mary Ann was not entirely confident in the finer points of the various quadrille maneuvers or the multiple phases of the dance which, in her opinion, never seemed to end. It felt like an awful lot of slow pinwheeling and hand-holding with various people that were not always Rufus, and there was barely any vim and vigor to the steps at all. But she got through it with only some small errors, and Rufus assured her no one would think twice about them, particularly once the mushroom beer started flowing.

"I prefer sword-fighting, if I'm honest," she told him.

He said that he did, too. But as far as she could tell, Rufus was a skilled dancer who seemed to be having a rather frabjous time of it. She only hoped she could manage it passably so as not to publicly embarrass him.

There turned out to be enough time for a nap—and since the ball was set to run from nine o'clock and stretch long into the morning, Mary Ann was going to need it. But upon retiring to the yellow guest room, there seemed no way Mary Ann Carpenter could sleep. She kept picturing Evelyn and Dell Tweedle, and her brain crackled with various possible scenarios for the evening, which played over in her mind. Soon, she had an idea, though she wasn't entirely certain how she'd manage it. And after some quiet contemplation, she thought she finally was on to something. She ran down to the kitchen in search of Emmaline.

"Why, Tamsin, you should be getting dressed for the ball," she said. "Everyone else is getting ready right now. It's so exciting. Aren't you excited? I'd be so excited if it was me."

"Enthralled," Mary Ann told her. "And I'm on my way. But there's two things I need first."

And once again, the cook's assistant came through for Mary Ann in a pinch.

22

Mary Ann was not particularly comfortable in the gown, but under the circumstances, she didn't expect that she would be. She took a chance on her hair, wearing the greatest portion of it down, while plaiting the top and winding that into a bun. It was not in fashion, she knew, for ringlets were popular these days and Mary Ann's heavy, straight hair only held a wave at all because it spent its existence tightly plaited. But it made a change, and it seemed more elegant than her normal look. She evaluated herself once before the mirror, proclaimed it adequate, grabbed the little silk purse Emmaline had lent her and went down to the Manor's entrance.

Rufus was already waiting there, sporting a blue velvet coat, and from the surprised look on his face as she came down the stairs, she wasn't sure if she had miscalculated her style selection. He said, "Mary Ann! Your hair is…"

Her hand flew to the bun on top and she frowned. "Is… is it too much?"

"'Glorious' is the word springing to mind, actually."

"Oh," she felt her face grow hot. "Thank you very much."

"I don't think you'll need that, though," he said, pointing to the little silk purse dangling from her wrist. "They're not going to make you pay an entry fee."

She laughed. "You never know." And she was glad Lady Carmine's entrance distracted him from further discussion about it. "Oh, do look! Your mother is simply ethereal!" Lady Carmine was wearing a gauzy creation that seemed to have been made from a waterfall, all sheets of liquid translucence, sparkle and froth. On her pile of exquisite curls was a miniature ship that actually moved as if on waves, some wind-up creation by a genius in haberdashery. She could practically smell the sea salt around her. "You are most beautiful, Lady Carmine," Mary Ann told her sincerely.

"You are too kind, my dear." Lady Carmine patted her cheek, a tender gesture she'd seen her bestow on Rufus on occasion. It made her feel momentarily emotional in a way she couldn't allow herself to think about much.

As soon as Lord Carmine joined them, looking dashing enough but rather the usual in comparison to his wife, they headed to the carriage.

They were greeted at the front door of Count Talionis' home by a very familiar-looking beaver. Only instead of the work clothes Mary Ann and Rufus saw him in before, he was now wearing a black suit. In the entryway, Mulberry Manor's walls were swathed in golden draperies from ceiling to floor. And all around the room's perimeter were scented candles. There must have been hundreds of them, all flickering in the night. They lent a peculiar air of mystery to the place, a heavy, cloying smell, and a certain threat of fire hazard. The beaver directed them into the ballroom, which had received a similar decorative treatment as the front of the house. At one end of the room were tables laden with various fruits and cheeses and bottles of some clear liquid.

The beaver shouted: "The Baron and Baroness of Carmine! Sir Rufus Carmine and Sir Mary Ann Carpenter!"

Everyone looked their direction and Mary Ann looked back at a few familiar faces in the crowd, but many new ones, as well. Lady Carmine's ensemble certainly seemed to wow, and Mary Ann thought that distracted nicely from any fashion faux pas she might have committed herself. Hats with large flopping fish, she saw, were popular tonight, but there were wonderful creations with feathers and antlers and flowers, as well. The creativity and color were a joy to behold.

The second beaver came round with a tray of glasses. "May I offer you some wine? Made from Count Talionis' vineyard in Erstwhile. Nothing is like Erstwhile wine. It's prized for its clean, refreshing taste."

They were interested to try it.

"Well, it's...cold," said Lord Carmine after a speculative sip.

"Its bouquet is ..." Lady Carmine sniffed. "Airy and... er... uncomplicated."

Rufus said, "Its flavor is ... well, I suppose it *is* clean and refreshing. And Nothing is very comparable to it."

"I don't know much about wine, and perhaps they approach it differently in Erstwhile," said Mary Ann, "but I think this is water."

"Oh, it can't be," said Lord Carmine. "The taste buds of the people in Erstwhile must be different than ours. More nuanced."

Mary Ann looked to the other guests, to see their reactions, and many did seem to be eyeing their goblets in a perplexed way or holding the liquid up to the light. But most of them just shrugged, drained the beverage, and went back for seconds.

Clearly, curiosity had outweighed the event's short notice with this group, for it was fascinating to see the quantity and variety of people in attendance. Contrary to what she'd expected, the guest list seemed to include most everyone in Square Four, gentry and non-gentry alike, and from several surrounding Squares, as well. Mary Ann saw the postman and Mr. Dumpty. She recognized Harris March and Mr. Milliner. There was a large assortment of knights, off-duty. Mr. Pennwell showed up, wearing a different newspaper suit, this time with tails and carrying a walking stick. She noticed him look their way and then hobble off in another direction as swiftly as his injuries permitted. Rufus must have seen it, too, because he gave a happy little, "Ha."

Mary Ann saw two Tweedles had arrived, and she made a note to keep a careful eye on Dell. The strange thing was that their host was noticeably absent. "Is it common for the host of a ball to not greet his guests?" Mary Ann asked Rufus, for she wasn't certain about the protocol.

"It is odd," said Rufus. "But this whole thing is a bit odd, isn't it? The weird smell in here, the wine, the décor... It's all just a bit off somehow and I can't quite pin it down."

A group of musicians were setting up in a gallery balcony, and they were a little off, too. They were all dressed in the bright and silky clothes of some foreign land, likely Erstwhile, and their instruments were ones Mary Ann did not readily recognize. But Mary Ann was fairly certain one of them was the third contractor they'd met at the house—the frilled lizard — and she recognized another fellow from Neath who she thought did strolling minstrel work for jam tarts.

One of the beavers shouted, "King Garnet and Queen Rosamund!" and the band rushed to attention and played a few chords of fanfare. Mary Ann couldn't tell if they weren't very good, or if the instruments were supposed to sound like that. Mary Ann paid special attention to King Garnet. What precisely were Evelyn and Dell Tweedle hoping to purloin from this man's person? The crown was, of course, a likely candidate. But there was also a rather weighty livery collar, a bejeweled cloak clasp, an elaborate belt and shoe buckles. Any one of these could be hiding a prophecy poem folded into its construction.

A large golden clock at the far end of the room chimed half past nine.

"And now," shouted that same beaver, "the man of the hour, your humble host ... Beloved in his homeland, he has adventured far and wide, bringing prosperity and excitement to all who know him. He challenged the Dread Dragon of Doomsbladder, teaching it that fiend and friend stand just one letter apart. He withstood the siren song of the Middle Sea, drowning it out with an upper-deck dance party that frolicked till dawn. He trained under Cornelius Clashammer but eschewed knighthood because it is knowledge, not a title, that truly matters. I give you… Lex, Count Talionis!"

And a man emerged onto the ballroom balcony in gold and red silk robes as the band played. He seized a rope and swung off the gallery, down, down into the ballroom below, his descent triggering the release of a shower of butterflies and parrots from the curtains above. "Ahhh!" everyone said as winged things fluttered up into the rafters and perched on the stair rails.

As their host landed with a graceful thump against the ballroom floor, Mary Ann got a better look at him. He was a sturdy and stocky fellow, with even, handsome features on a pale face, and a very black beard and very black hair. It was hard to tell precisely how old he was; Mary Ann guessed he was still in his twenties, but maybe as old as 32. In a foreign accent she couldn't readily identify, he said, "Thank you all for joining me tonight, as I reclaim Mulberry Manor and return it to its former glory. I felt my arrival here in Square Four merited an introduction to all my new Turvian friends and neighbors. And what better way to get to know everyone than through a celebratory ball?"

The crowd cheered.

"Please partake of the refreshments. And I hope you are particularly enjoying the wine from my family's vineyards back in Erstwhile. Some history about our wine… Our grapes are rated for their unusual purity, which the unsophisticated may suggest lack inspiration. But in fact, the less you taste these splendid crystalline berries, the more rare and desirable they are." The crowd oohed at this. "At our vineyard, over the past two centuries, we've managed to selectively breed only the most flavorless Erstwhilian grapes, creating a wine that ferments into clean, pure nothingness in the mouth, refreshing to the last drop. This is an experience I am honored to bring to each of you this evening. But keep in mind, our vintage does have a kick. So, I will not be held responsible for how it affects your dancing tonight!" He laughed at this, and much of the crowd laughed, too.

But Rufus was not laughing. Rufus was staring at him with narrow eyes.

Mary Ann nudged him and whispered, "What is it? The Cornelius Clashammer comment? Perhaps he was a student before our time?"

Rufus made a non-committal noise. "That and—" He shook his head. "I don't know for sure. We'll see."

"Well, while you're seeing, I think we should warn the King about what might go down tonight," Mary Ann said. "Not the specifics, because I want Dell Tweedle to reveal himself. But I'd like the King to be prepared. How do we make that happen?"

"Follow me," he said. And he walked straight over to the King and Queen like they were old croquet chums. "King Garnet... Queen Rosamund..." began Rufus and bowed. "Sir Mary Ann has some critical information about this evening to share with you."

Mary Ann curtseyed. "King Garnet, I believe that tonight someone at this ball will attempt to steal something of value from you. Something with a long history of being in your family's possession since the beginning of Turvy. I don't know what it will be, whether it's the crown or your livery collar or something else, and I can't tell you when it's set to happen. But we are monitoring the situation to prevent it."

"Great gryphons!" the King said and turned to his wife. "That's jolly dramatic, isn't it?"

"It most certainly is, dear," she said.

Mary Ann said, "I believe, if all goes well, this will bring the crow case to a positive conclusion."

"Fascinating!" said the King. "Something intriguing to write in my diary tomorrow when this whole event is said and done."

"Indeed, Your Majesty! Thank you for your audience." With another round of bowing and curtseying, Mary Ann and Rufus left them.

She said, "That went rather more smoothly than I anticipated. That King Garnet is quite a good sport, isn't he?"

"Yes, you could do a lot worse for a monarch," Rufus said. "Now where's Dell Tweedle?"

Mary Ann scanned the room. "Oh, he's over by the fruit bowl, arguing with Dorian."

"That's all right, then. For now, anyway."

The quarter hour chimed, and one of the beavers shouted. "Fifteen minutes! In fifteen minutes, it will be time for our first dance: the Dodo Quadrille. All dancers, report to the dance floor. All those not dancing, please hop it to the perimeters. Thank you!"

And Mary Ann noticed an unusual number of dodos had filtered into the room, the beaver distributing them evenly amongst groups of seven dancers.

"Are you up for this, Carpenter?" Rufus asked.

"I'll test my memory from this afternoon," she said with a smile. "But I cannot promise it will be pretty."

The beaver grouped Mary Ann and Rufus with Lord and Lady Carmine, one dodo, the King and Queen, and Count Talionis himself.

Mary Ann thought it very odd that the Count did not have a particular companion for this ball. It made his partner, technically, the dodo in this figuration. The bird did seem to embrace the role, flirting with him rather enthusiastically.

"It is a pleasure to see you all," said Count Talionis, "and thank you for coming tonight to my humble little party."

The clock struck ten, and the music started. Initially, Mary Ann was not certain how the dodo entered into the formations of this dance, for she had only practiced a standard quadrille, all with human people and no additional frills. But as the dance went on, it seemed the role of the dodo was to induce some extra mayhem and merriment into the maneuvers, for the bird didn't really know where it was going and seemed aimed to make itself quite dizzy in the turning. So alternately, every dancer the dodo paired with in the coupling got thrown off a bit until it was passed on to the next one. This suited Mary

Ann's current dance style quite well because no matter what she did, she was bound to be more coordinated than this dodo. In the end, it left them all breathless.

They waited for the second piece in the dance to begin, the band giving them a little breather, and Count Talionis said to Mary Ann and Rufus, "I believe I have seen you both in the local papers, have I not? Survived a Jabberwock battle? Banned from Neath? A boat ride scandal? I confess, I was quite eager to meet you in person."

"And your reputation precedes you, Your Grace," said Rufus with a bow of the head. "It seems your name and deeds have been on the lips of everyone in Red Turvy for days now. Remarkable set of accomplishments you've achieved, based on what's on the wind."

"Especially for someone so young," Mary Ann said. Seeing Count Talionis more closely, Mary Ann had realized he was probably somewhat younger than she'd estimated. The enthusiastic mustache and whiskers had initially thrown her off, but there were no lines at all about the eyes, or the forehead. There was also something about his pallor that didn't seem quite right, and she couldn't put her finger on it. With his skin tone and the very dark hair, it gave her the vague impression that he was unwell.

"I have been gifted with a youthful countenance," said the Count, smiling. "But I assure you, I am older and far duller than I may appear at first."

Rufus gave a little exhale that Mary Ann wasn't sure was a laugh. But then he asked, "When did you study with Cornelius Clashammer?"

"Oh, it must be a decade ago now," said Talionis. "Wonderful fellow."

Mary Ann asked, "Did you find his accommodations in Thither surprising?"

"Not at all," he said. "I knew they would live up to his reputation, particularly in such a historic and elegant part of the city."

"But of course," said Mary Ann, and she purposefully avoided meeting Rufus' gaze.

But Rufus said, "I have a question for you that's been on my mind ever since I read your biography in *The Turvy Mirror*."

"How intriguing," Talionis said.

Mary Ann was intrigued, too, because she had no idea where Rufus was going with this.

He said, "Were the parrots pirates? Or were they pirating parrots?" Rufus smiled, and while his tone was playful like he was asking a riddle, the smile was not his usual one of good humor. This one contained an edge.

A slight crease formed between Talionis' eyebrows. Then he met the smile with one of his own, which appeared somewhat forced. "I am not sure to what you're referring. But all the parrots released here tonight are attending the ball of their own free will, I assure you." And he glanced to the musicians. "I do believe the second contredanse is about to start."

The topic of parrots was caged as the music picked up again.

By the third contredanse, the Count chatted with Lord and Lady Carmine, asking about their lineage, their life in Square Four, where their property lines were in respect to Mulberry Manor, and how they came to own Carmine in the first place. All of these were topics Lord Carmine was more than happy to discuss with enthusiasm.

By contredanse four, Talionis directed all his attentions to the King and Queen, praising them for the beautiful realm and civilized society they had built. Mary Ann watched him carefully, in particular, with the King, ensuring there was no tricky slight-of-hand, should the Count be some new and unforeseen party in the prophecy plot. But all the King's accessories remained in place, and finally, the dance was done.

Count Talionis offered a polite, "Until later," then moved on to mingle with the rest of his guests. After all this, Mary Ann was rather glad to be rid of the Count, because she wanted to talk about him behind his back.

"He never trained at Cornelius Clashammer's," said Mary Ann to Rufus in hushed tones. "You can't tell me he wouldn't have been surprised to learn Clashammer's school was designed to caterpillar-scale. And do you know what else? He's not as old as he's trying to project. He's about our age under that beard. Ten years ago at Clashammer's he'd have been ten or twelve at the most. He wasn't training to be any knight."

"He also doesn't remember what fantastic deeds he planted about himself in the papers. He's not running a particularly sophisticated operation," said Rufus.

"So, what is this all about? That's what I want to know," said Mary Ann.

"Cliff," said Rufus. "This is about Cliff."

Mary Ann blinked. "Beg your pardon?"

Lord and Lady Carmine had come over with fresh glasses of wine for themselves and a second glass each for Mary Ann and Rufus. Mary Ann was thirsty from all the dancing, so she did accept the beverage and drank it down, to no real effect besides hydration. Lord Carmine, however, looked flushed and jolly. "Well, this is some kind of all right, isn't it? I'm afraid the wine is starting to go to my head, but since it's a special occasion, I'll just have this one more. Isn't Count Ballywhosis a fascinating fellow? Very curious and such a good listener, too, eh? Wanted to know all about our family tree."

"He is on the tree. He is Cliff," said Rufus. "And a complete humbug."

"What?" Lord Carmine frowned over his glass. "The tree on which cliff?"

"My brother Cliff." At Lord Carmine's still-blank expression, Rufus sighed and clutched his hair. "Radcliff? Your other son?"

"Don't be absurd, boy! That fellow looks nothing like Radcliff." He slung his empty glass on the tray of a roving waiter. "Three years on, and you've clearly forgotten what your own brother looks like. Radcliff has ginger hair. About my shade. Count Talionis has black hair."

"He dyed it," said Rufus. "Squid ink or boot blacking. Something."

"And Radcliff was clean-shaven. Count Talionis has a grand and luxurious beard." Lord Carmine ran hands across his own grand and luxurious beard to emphasize the point.

"There's this thing called puberty," said Rufus. "There are also false beards."

"Furthermore," continued Lord Carmine, "he sounds nothing like Radcliff."

"His voice changed and he's doing some sort of foreign accent. Poorly."

Lord Carmine stuffed his hands in his pockets and rocked on his heels. "But Lord Melbury left this place to his last living relative. We're not related to the Melburys."

"Then Cliff is letting it for the summer from the one who owns it," said Rufus.

"I think Rufus may have a point, dear," said Lady Carmine gently. "It does seem quite mad, I know. And I cannot imagine what is going through his head. But his eyes are very like Radcliff's and there's something quite familiar in his mannerisms. The wine may be affecting your clarity on this particular issue."

"Poppycock! Why would he go to all the trouble, posing as this Count Tally-ho when he's been taking knight lessons and rescuing people from danger and whatnot? I mean, all that is quite impressive enough."

Rufus looked like he was getting a terrible headache. He turned to Mary Ann. "I think I know exactly what Cliff's goals are here. And if it's what I suspect, he's in it for the long game —one that may not end well for us." He eyed the man darkly from across the room, which was impressive considering his light eyes. "As far as I'm concerned, we should just conclude this charade here and now."

"Oh, but not yet!" Mary Ann said. "I don't want the ball to break up until Dell Tweedle and Evelyn have had their go at the King. I know you like to address issues efficiently, but let this unfold a bit longer, if you can bear it."

He groaned and she patted his arm. Reluctantly, he nodded. He turned to his parents. "Did you hear that? Say nothing that indicates we're on to him. Mary Ann and I will deal with it in our own time."

"Of course," said Lady Carmine.

"Fine with me, lad," said Lord Carmine, "because I still think you're talking out of your hat."

With a sigh, Rufus turned to Mary Ann. "What do you think the signal will be for Evelyn's grand distraction?"

Mary Ann said, "I don't know enough about how these balls work to know what the best opportunity would be."

Rufus considered it. "Could be anything. A new round of dancing? The breakfast gong? The first guest who kicks one of those ruddy candles over and sets us all ablaze?"

"A nice fire would warm the old place considerably," purred a familiar, dreamy voice. "I'd volunteer if it would liven things up a bit. The same old Quadrilles do get so dull. No amount of dodos can salvage them."

Mary Ann turned to see Chester the Cat, afloat at eye level and toying with one of the lit candles in a way that made one uneasy.

"How nice to see you, Chester," said Mary Ann. "Let me guess: you're a party crasher again this evening." He was rarely invited to events. But that did not prevent him from attending a great many of them.

"I couldn't help but investigate the handiwork of the Count's protracted public relations campaign," he said. "It's been all over Turvy. And I see most of our guests are greatly charmed by the Count and his fripperies. Not to mention, his rare ability to turn water into wine." The cat drew a goblet shape in the air with his candle. "But I have a feeling that you two might view the gentleman through more acute eyes. I do hope that you won't disappoint me."

"It's been suspicious from the start," Mary Ann confessed, "but Rufus has rather swiftly identified who Talionis really is and why he is here."

"It will all be exposed in due course," Rufus said.

"And why not burn it down now?" asked the cat in a hungry sort of way.

"We are only waiting for the proper moment," said Mary Ann. "As there are other issues converging here tonight that take precedence. A case we are trying to close."

"Oh!" The cat smiled, a wide, slowly creeping crescent. "I am glad to know, Mary Ann, that you have found yourself a sensible human companion. One who is, at least, sharper than the dull and bent knives we normally have here in the Wanderlands' drawer. Especially since I understand congratulations are in order?"

"It will be one event to which you are invited and most welcome," Mary Ann assured him.

"I shall be there with bells on," he told her and turned to Rufus. "Dear Mary Ann has not been over-loved in life, you know. But due to shared invisibility and our mutual time served with the Duchess, I have grown to think of her much like a littermate. In other words, I fully expect you'll do right by my human sister, won't you?" And Chester flipped the candle up in the air and caught it.

Rufus said, "I don't believe that should be in any doubt."

"Frabjous. Best keep it that way. For I will be keeping an eye on you." And the cat floated off, suddenly vanished except for one bright eye and a candle gliding across the room.

"I feel vaguely like I was just threatened," Rufus chuckled. "Tough crowd, your 'brother.'"

"A bit, to be honest." Mary Ann grinned. "He doesn't dislike you, though. He's just can be funny with people sometimes."

"We all have our moments," Rufus said, and Mary Ann was relieved he didn't seem to be taking it too personally.

The clock struck 11.

"Next up," announced one of the beavers, "The Teapot Quadrille."

"Oh no." Quickly, Rufus curled an arm around Mary Ann's waist and began leading her, not onto the dance floor, but to the side of the room with the observers. "We'll sit this one out. Trust me. This gets messy."

Now each dancer was being presented with a teacup, while one member of the lead couple was given a teapot filled with hot piping tea. As the couples spun and twirled, tea was poured into the cups, and upon shoes, and into large puddles on the floor, until everyone was quite soppy and smelling of bergamot. The second contradanse involved juggling sugar cubes, which went clattering and skittering across the floor like hailstones, only a few actually making it into the cups. And by the third movement, which added the cream to the situation, the whole scene had gone terribly wrong and no one was smiling anymore.

It required a break, as the beavers mopped and swept up the floor and towels were passed round for the guests.

"This suspense is killing me," Mary Ann said, noting the positions of Dell Tweedle and the King in her umpteeth visual sweep of the room.

"Suspense?" someone asked. "Sounds like it's right up my dark alley." And Mary Ann's heart leapt into her throat at the sight of the large black bird.

Only, it was not *that* large black bird, the black bird she'd been waiting for. This one had different shaped feathers and a thicker, more hooked beak. This bird was a normal large bird size and was wearing several necklaces of shiny baubles and a nice hat.

"Dear heavens!" Mary Ann pressed a hand against her chest, as if she could still her pounding heart from the pressure. "Mrs. Nightwing, you do know how to make an entrance."

Rufus, too, looked like he'd aged a few years in that moment.

"Sorry to have startled you," she said. "But isn't this a peculiar ball? Have you tried the wine? It seems virtually homeopathic in its wine-to-water ratio. And that Count Talionis is trying a bit too hard to ingratiate himself, if you ask me. His stories ... I feel like he needs his own personal fact-checker to just follow him round everywhere he goes."

Mary Ann didn't really want to get into details of Count Talionis at this moment. There were so many other things to focus on. "Well, the guests seem to be enjoying themselves," Mary Ann said noncommittally. As if to emphasize her point, a Red Knight (who was also a guinea pig) danced drunkenly past them to whatever music was currently playing in his head.

Rufus eyed him in wonder. "Sir Erasmus…" He shook his head. "That pig knows how to party."

"Is Mr. Nightwing with you?" Mary Ann asked the raven, mainly because she didn't want a recurrent jolt to the heart over a second large black bird sweeping into view.

"Oh no," the mystery novelist said. "As you know, Mr. Nightwing is not a particularly social animal. He is quite content at home reading the shipping reports in front of a nice fire, with a crunchy bowl of pillbugs and a nice berry-squash cocktail."

Another round of dancing was announced to begin in fifteen minutes — this time an Egg Quadrille, and all but Mr. Dumpty seemed to rejoice in it. It was here that Professor Cyril Goodnuff joined them at the room's perimeter. "Why, hello, neighbors!" He was clad in some sort of military jacket and hat that Mary Ann didn't recognize, instead of his usual mustard yellow safari gear. All the brass buttons and frills had been polished to a marvelous shine. From under an enormous grey mustache, he said, "Well, if it isn't the Yellow-Headed Mary Ann! Did you receive my rocking-horsefly about the information you wanted from the Royal White Turvy Academy?"

"I did, sir!" she said. "And thank you very much for all your trouble."

"Ah, it wasn't much trouble at all. I have some friends in Zoology, and they got me to the right contacts. Their response had me curious, though: Dell Tweedle. Is he any relation to those chaps over there?" And he indicated the present Tweedle brothers, one of whom seemed drunk and the other twitchy.

Mary Ann didn't know which lie to choose. She didn't want the professor going over there to chat to the Tweedles about it, but she also didn't want to deny the connection and then have to backtrack after some big reveal.

Thankfully, Rufus solved the dilemma with manners. "Hello, I don't believe we've met. I'm Sir Rufus, Sir Mary Ann's fiancé." Mary Ann found it highly peculiar hearing that term used aloud in reference to her, and she couldn't help but smile. He said, "It's so nice to finally meet you in person."

And that got the conversation flowing in another direction in no time. Discussion of their engagement reminded Professor Goodnuff about the fascinating mating habits of the Greater Turvian Plumwhistle, a bird that was part kazoo and part stonefruit. "What it does," said the professor, "is the male catches the attention of the female with a noise like—" The ballroom clock chimed midnight. "No, that's not it."

And before anyone knew what was happening, the room was filled with a great wooshing noise. A crow, bigger than a carriage, appeared flapping and screeching upon the minstrel gallery railing, causing that troupe to drop their instruments with plinks and plonks and run for the stairs.

"Get to the King!" Mary Ann shouted, and Rufus was off like a shot. Mary Ann had other things to take care of now. She had practiced this maneuver this afternoon for over an hour back at Carmine Manor and she only hoped it would work in the thick of the moment. She pulled the glass meat baster she'd borrowed from Emmaline from the bodice of her dress and opened the handbag. She removed the bottle of Dwindleade and poured it into the first empty wine glass she got her hands on, then pulled the baster's plunger, sucking up the liquid. She watched the bird's movements, its flaps, its caws. She waited. *Not now … Not now … Not now …*

Evelyn was making a great show of it, cawing enough to shake the crystal, feathers flying, candles flickering. As Mary Ann approached, Evelyn's great claws clapped down hard on the ballroom floor and she let out a mighty shriek, reeking of bird breath and Burgeonboosh.

Now! This was when Mary Ann let the liquid fly. Surprise filled Evelyn Rookwood's shiny black eyes as the Dwindleade flooded down her gullet. In a moment, her world began to change for the smaller and the monstrous magpie went from myth to mud. Mary Ann grabbed one of the curtains lining the wall—knocking over a series of candles that bystanders rushed to quench—revealing the ancient, musty, tattered wallpaper was still ever-present at Mulberry Manor. In one swift move, Mary Ann threw the fabric over the bird, scooped it up and knotted the drapery into a makeshift sack. She slung it over her shoulder to the sound of applause.

But Mary Ann barely heard it. She scanned for Rufus and spied him at the center of some action across the room. The King's belt was in Rufus' hand, and King Garnet was at his side looking defiantly out into the group before them. Dell Tweedle was being held by several knights, including Sir Erasmus, the drunk guinea pig who was now spoiling for a fight. Dell Tweedle's face wrinkled in fury, while Dorian Tweedle couldn't have looked more surprised.

The King was red-faced and shaking with anger. "Why, Damian Tweedle, I am absolutely ashamed of you! A representative of our fine Square Four guards, and this is how you behave! What are you involved in that would compel you to try to steal my belt? Not only is it property of the Royal family, but it held my coat closed so nicely." And King Garnet motioned to his now-open jacket, which revealed a very holey undershirt. Everyone stared. "What? It's my favorite one for dancing!" The King's eyes shifted to the crowd. "Stop looking at me like that."

But Dell Tweedle was not giving up on the sham so easily. "I ... I ... was not stealing your belt, Your Majesty! I was just seeing it had come undone and I aimed to assist you. I never expected the belt to, um, unravelate in my hands."

"Not nohow!" said Dorian Tweedle. "I saw you go on and grabbify it myself!"

"Contrariwise, you didn't!"

"Inversably, you lie!"

"My dear people," said Count Talionis, scowling, "could you all please take this ruddy ridiculousness outs—"

Mary Ann had approached the King, a squawking bag of bird over her shoulder. "Ah, but Your Majesty, this," she said, pointing to the apprehended man, "is not Detective Major Damian Tweedle! This is the Tweedles' brother ... Dell Tweedle!" And with that, Mary Ann reached up and pulled off Dell's fake moustache. It left a nice, painful red mark and some glue residue above his upper lip. As far as she was concerned, he deserved every bit of it.

The group gasped.

Mary Ann said, "The Tweedles are triplets, and Dell Tweedle is an archaeologist for the Royal White Turvy Academy. When the museum discovered a lost prophecy from Sir Loral Clew hidden in one of their displays, they called in Dr. Dell Tweedle to examine it. It revealed information about other prophecies that were hidden around Turvy. In this bag," and Mary Ann shook the bag, for Evelyn was trying to peck through the fabric, "is Evelyn Rookwood. Dr. Rookwood is an archaeologist from Red Turvy, who was called in to assist on this side of things. Together, Tweedle and Rookwood have been tracking down each antiquity hiding a lost prophecy. But, as you can see from tonight's example, some of these items are not easy to get to. They become easier to access when one poses as a friendly neighborhood guard like D.M. Damian Tweedle. And when that tactic won't work? A little fear and superstition is useful in the form of a legend like Ole Inky."

Mary Ann continued, "Evelyn used Burgeonboosh to make D.I. Tweedle and the postman believe the Ole Inky legend was true. She followed the legend by Tweedlenapping Damian and then hiding him deep in Square Six in a disused clubhouse that Dell Tweedle shared with his brothers as a child. This allowed Dell to be 'found' after a day and take Damian's place."

She took a deep breath. "But Dell Tweedle was there at the cottage that day his brother was captured. In fact, as Dorian Tweedle tried to save his brother from Evelyn, Dell whacked him over the head from behind, to make him let go. I don't think he meant for Dorian Tweedle to get temporary amnesia, but that was the result. And it inadvertently fit his plans. While Dorian was out cold, Dell was able to smuggle out a particular rattle from the Tweedle boys' collection. It was, in fact, the

Queen's scepter, that had been stolen and cleverly disguised by Dell days earlier, to sneak it out of the Square Five market without Queen Rosamund's guards catching him. He'd painted it silver, added bells to it, and stuffed it in the back of an antique shop."

"Oh, yes! I knew *all* about this part," said Queen Rosamund to the crowd, looking really pleased with herself.

Mary Ann turned to the thief. "Were you planning to buy it from the antique shop, Dell Tweedle, pretending to be one of your brothers? Or did the store owner contact them about this mysterious rattle before you could get to it?"

"I don't know what you're talking about," Dell Tweedle spat.

Queen Rosamund slapped him a few times with her flyswatter. "Confess, you weasel, confess!"

Mary Ann said, "Either way, the scepter landed in Dell Tweedle's and Evelyn Rookwood's hands. So, with a fake Damian Tweedle returned home, supposedly injured with a wibbly leg, and Dorian Tweedle with a terrible case of 'namblesia,' this opened up a new opportunity for Dell Tweedle to get the relics he needed. Dell posed as museum guard Nick Filch at the Royal Red Turvy Museum to get his hands on the First Looking-Glass. But as an archaeologist, once he got the prophecies from it, he couldn't bear to just leave it there in the alley. He had to make sure the First Looking-Glass was safe. That's why he basically ratted himself out, dressing as Dorian Tweedle, to reveal the location of the item he'd just stolen and dismantled. And it was easy enough to become Dorian. All he needed to do was change into a red pinstripe suit, whack on the fake mustache and comb it downward. And that's when Sir Rufus and I saw him returning home from the train station, pretending his head injury had given him wanderlust."

"And that's the part that had us stuck," said Rufus. "Because we though we knew the personalities of both Tweedle brothers rather well, but neither of them were acting like themselves. We were not expecting that both troublesome

Tweedles were the very same man, a third mustacheless Tweedle!"

"Exactly!" said Mary Ann. "We figured it out when Evelyn attacked Mr. Pennwell in south Square Six. He noticed a slight glint of metal on the roof of the clubhouse in which Damian Tweedle was hidden, and Pennwell was about to investigate. Rufus and I had seen that same shine once ourselves in that location, but we'd been diverted from investigating it in a timely way. The glint was caused by a rattle the boys had used as a sort of spire for their little playhouse decades ago. Well, Evelyn couldn't set Damian free until Dell was done impersonating him. So, she Burgeonbooshed herself into Ole Inky a second time and chased Pennwell off."

Rufus added, "When we heard Pennwell's story, we made a return trip to southern Square Six and found the clubhouse, complete with poor bound-and-gagged Damian Tweedle. He told us about Dell. Damian and Dorian had never gotten on with Dell, and so the brothers hadn't been in contact for years. Damian is now recovering in a safe place."

"And that leads us right here. Tonight," said Mary Ann. "Dell Tweedle learned the King would be here at the ball, and with so many Turvians invited here, including the Tweedles, it was the perfect opportunity to grab the relic they sought from the King. All they needed was one big, feathered distraction to snag it."

"And it was this," Rufus held up the King's belt. "A belt buckle that had been passed down through generations until it arrived in King Garnet's possession. It should also contain one of the lost prophecies of Sir Loral Clew. The question is: how do we open it?"

Rufus brought it to a table, turned the buckle over and fumbled with the back.

Dell Tweedle watched this over his shoulder for a moment, fidgeting, hands twitching, and finally said, "What are you doing? Not like that, you fool, you'll jam it. I'll do it; let me go." Mary Ann thought it was interesting how the Tweedleness of his speech patterns had vanished.

Sir Erasmus, who was the only knight who'd brought his sword to the ball, told Tweedle, "You make one wrong move, you do realize you'll be julienned vegetables, right, lad?"

"Yes, yes," sighed Dell Tweedle. He unscrewed a little knob on the side of the buckle's back, slid a tiny lever, and pushed what must have been a button, because a small door popped open, like a locket. Inside was a piece of yellowed parchment.

"This is a very old document. I should be handling it with gloves and tweezers," Dell Tweedle said. "I have some back at my office. I'll just fetch them." And he started to get up.

Rufus' hand, which clamped to his shoulder, and Sir Erasamus' sword at his throat suggested otherwise.

"Your job is done here, Tweedle," said Rufus. He snatched up a cloth napkin, picked up the belt buckle and turned it over, dropping the paper into the napkin. "This will be analyzed by a different expert."

"I could have a go at it," a hopeful voice suggested from the bag.

"Not you," said Rufus. He returned the belt to King Garnet and picked up the napkin with the prophecy in it.

"But what's it say?" said someone in the crowd.

"Open it!" said another.

"Don't we get to hear what it is?" shouted a third voice.

Rufus said, "Nobody's reading any prophecies here tonight."

The crowd groaned.

King Garnet turned to the knights covering Dell Tweedle: "Take him to my castle holding cells! The bird, as well."

"Awww ..." moaned the bird from the bag. "Say nothing, Delly. Tell them nothing. Hold strong."

"Hush up, you," said Sir Erasmus.

"Do you have any rope?" one of the knights asked Count Talionis. But before he could answer, ten party guests offered up their belts, sashes, and ties.

Once Tweedle's hands were bound, another knight took the bag from Mary Ann that held Evelyn. "You three have this under control?" Rufus asked them.

They assured him they'd be fine.

"Frabjous. Thank you," said Rufus. "Sir Mary Ann and I may have some things to wind up here."

And the prisoners and knights left the ballroom.

Count Talionis said, "Now that this absurd impromptu entertainment is done ..." His voice sounded annoyed. He turned to the King. "I am so glad you are all right, Your Majesty. Had I known, I should never have let these individuals into the ball."

And Mary Ann wasn't sure if he were referring to Dell Tweedle and Evelyn Rookwood or Sir Rufus and herself because he was gesturing to the latter.

The Queen said, "What I'd like to know is why they seemed to want to hide these prophecies at all. Wouldn't you think this would be an exciting discovery for our Turvian history?"

"We'd like to know that, as well, Your Majesty," Mary Ann said.

"Tomorrow," Rufus told the King and Queen, "we'll interrogate Dell Tweedle and Evelyn Rookwood and hopefully get some better insights into that. We need to find out what Evelyn did with the other documents."

Mary Ann said, "And we have a contact at the Royal Red Turvy Academy who should be able to assess the prophecy from your belt."

"Imagine," said the King, "carrying a prophecy around on my belly all this time! Perhaps it predicts the best time for meals."

"Can we get on with the ball now?" Count Talionis asked, a slight whine in his voice. He must have noticed it himself, because he cleared his throat and, with it, shifted more swash and buckle into his tone. "It's been such an exciting evening after all, there is much to celebrate!"

"Absolutely! We should celebrate! Shouldn't we, everyone?" asked Rufus, smiling. And this received only some mild cheering because everyone was still mostly in shock from the previous events. "We must get back to the party immediately because our host, Count Talionis, the renowned and brave adventurer, is feeling all sad about this shift in attention away from his ruddy event. Never mind that with all his supposed elite training, he did nothing to aid in the security of our King and Queen. *Or* to help subdue a monster in our midst!"

The crowd gasped. It was a level of blatant rudeness no one ever imagined coming from Sir Rufus Carmine.

Talionis had gone very red and said, "I was securing the perimeters and assuring the safety of the women and children."

"Only if the women and children were also cowering under a table," said Rufus with a grin.

Another collective gasp.

"How *dare* you speak to your betters this way!" hissed Count Talionis, but Mary Ann caught a quick flash of fear in his eyes. "You are quite welcome to leave, Sir!" And he pointed a finger dramatically to the door.

Rufus folded his arms. "So, you're still planning on perpetuating this charade, eh, Cliff? Don't you think the people who lived with you for 16 years, and who aren't fully daft or dullards, could figure out it's you under that terrible disguise?"

"Cliff? What is this Cliff?" He looked all around to his guests and shrugged. "I know no Cliff. Cliff is what?"

"You were never original, Radcliff Carmine," Rufus said. "And that's how I knew it was you. You never had a fresh idea for yourself in your life. You stole the idea of being a knight from me. You stole the idea of being a Lord from Father. And you stole the idea for this ball from <u>The Count of Outgrabing Wabe</u>, that cursed novel Mother assigned us to read for our childhood lessons."

Lady Carmine's eyes grew wide. "I thought it seemed familiar!"

Rufus nodded. "In it, a young man leaves his home where he's deeply abused, unappreciated and disinherited, and returns to wreak revenge on everyone in the guise of the Count of some mysterious distant land. He plots to ingratiate himself into society as the Count and then undermines his original family with the rest of the nobles. Ultimately, he sets them up for treason and they are beheaded by the King. As a reward for his honesty, the King gives him the family's property, restoring him to his supposed rightful place."

"What a dreadful book," said Lady Carmine. "Why did I make you read that?"

"But I don't *want* to behead anybody," said the King to his wife, who patted his arm.

And Count Talionis said, "You are sorely mistaken, Sir. I have never once heard of that bold and enthralling Red Turvian classic." He looked around at the crowd. "Will someone please do me the favor of escorting this gentleman out?"

Rufus continued, "If you hadn't copied the whole grand entrance scene, where the Count swings into the ball on a rope, giving everyone the birds, it might have taken me longer to catch on."

Mary Ann said, "But even so, one could tell something wasn't right. Your hair color doesn't match your complexion. Your butlers are also your building contractors. And serving water but claiming it's wine? That's very cheeky."

And a murmur went over the guests. "Am I not really drunk?" one of them asked.

"I'm on a budget!" shouted Cliff, his accent falling away in an instant. "And I can't help it if some of you fell for the wine. It's amazing what people will believe, in a quest to not look common. Anyway," he continued, "I wasn't going to have you all *beheaded*."

"That's generous," said Rufus, rolling his eyes.

"If it went that far," Cliff explained, "I planned to write to the King on your behalf and beg him to simply exile you — to White Turvy or something. You would have been all right. Slightly homeless, sure. But all right. You're resilient. You'd rally."

"Exile!" said Lord Carmine. "I am finding this all very disappointing. I'd send you to your room, young man, but I think you'd burn our house down."

"Clearly I've been a total failure as a parent," said Lady Carmine, wringing her hands. "And I'm not sure where I went so very wrong."

"Oh, you've been an adequate mother, Mother. But *I* would be a great future Baron," Cliff said, eyes sparkling. "And neither of you would give me a chance. Not one chance. Of course, I don't fully blame either of you. I blame him." And he glared at Rufus.

Rufus said, "It's my fault for coming first in the birth order?"

"You've always been so self-absorbed and greedy," Cliff said. "You don't need the title of Baron. You made knight. You got the prophecy. You're the famous Jabberwock slayer. And you even got the damsel," he surveyed Mary Ann here, "such as she is."

"Wow," said Mary Ann, suddenly glad she hadn't any real siblings. It was clearly not all it was cracked up to be.

"You apologize," said Rufus.

"I will not," said Cliff. "You've always had everything good just handed to you, and so easily. How much more could you possibly need? But you want the Barony, too."

"You do know that being Lord of Carmine comes with some judiciary duties, right?" Rufus asked. "It's not just running round, forgetting everyone's names and attending balls. You have to actually sit through local complaints, be fair, make decisions, and help people."

"I could do that! I was made for that."

"I don't think you can," said Rufus. "You've been stewing about this for three years and what do you have to show for it? A half-arsed party, a rented castle, a false beard, and a revenge plan from a novel no one really likes."

"My beard is not false," Cliff snapped.

Mary Ann said, "You're sweating, and we can see the glue."

"Curse it," he whispered.

"But despite all this," said Rufus, "you've done nothing legally wrong. Not yet, anyway. Humbuggery? Sure. Misguided and insulting? Those, too. A complete waste of everyone's time? Absolutely! But illegal? No. So, as far as I am concerned, we are done here. I am shut of you."

And Rufus and Mary Ann turned to leave, with Lord and Lady Carmine close behind them. Lady Carmine was weeping. Consequently, most guests were also starting to leave now, spirits deflated but bladders sloshingly full of not-wine.

"Pardon me, Sir Rufus?" Mr. Pennwell stepped forward, notepad in his hand. "About our agreement…"

"Our agreement is for my family. That still stands. But that one," and Rufus pointed to Radcliff, "is fair game. Have fun, Mr. Pennwell. Tell your readers all about 'Count Talionis' in only the way you know how."

"Oooh, thank you very much," he said. And Mary Ann hadn't seen him look so pleased with himself in several days.

Outside, Mr. Wheeler was bringing the carriage around, when Dorian Tweedle joined them on the front landing. "Um, Sir Rufus, sir?"

Rufus turned.

"Thank you for locatifying my brother Damian for me, Sir. You and Sir Mary Ann both. I'm most full-of-grates about it, and also a bit sorrowly in the way things shooken out."

"You're welcome," said Rufus. "He's staying at our house for tonight, but he'll be home with you in the morning."

"We're glad it worked out, as well, D.I. Tweedle" Mary Ann told him, giving him a little hug. "I'm sorry your family went through all that."

"But what I most wanted to say was, me and you both having a disappointish brother with false facial-hairs and interior motives, well, it does hurts a bit. But if you need someone to chin-wag about it sometimes, I'm here."

Mary Ann could tell Rufus was trying very hard to be stoic, very Jabberwock slayer about it, but he was having a hard time keeping that up. His eyes looked a little bit glossy, and he clapped Tweedle on the shoulder. "Come to tea at the Manor, day after tomorrow. We'll commiserate. I think we both need it."

Dorian Tweedle smiled and nodded.

23

"So, you had a meat baster tucked into your bodice during the whole of the ball?" Rufus asked over breakfast, which was technically lunch because they'd both slept until noon. Mary Ann had expected that the many events of the past 24 hours would have had her brain dancing a Dodo Quadrille of their own for the remainder of the wee hours. But the moment she climbed into the guest room bed, consciousness abandoned her.

"Not the *whole* ball," Mary Ann said. "It was out for all the dramatic bits."

"And Dwindleade in your handbag?"

"What else does one use to cut a Burgeonbooshed bird down to size?" She helped herself to a bread-and-butterfly.

"And you never mentioned this plan?" He gave an astonished smile over his forkful of egg.

"Why would I mention it? What if it didn't work? And besides, if you knew everything I was planning all the time, it wouldn't be as much fun, would it?"

He reflected on this. "Not by half."

"I think it's important to leave some surprises in a relationship," she said. "I plan to do it often. And sometimes that might involve kitchenalia in my bodice. You may as well get used to it. Besides, you did very well apprehending Dell Tweedle on your end of things. I'm just sorry I missed the bulk of it. It's been my experience that you're rather stirring when moved to swift action."

"I didn't realize you'd noticed." He snickered. "Then you'll love to hear that I already sent a rocking-horsefly today to Delphina Divot requesting a meeting to examine the new prophecy."

"I *am* glad to hear it! I was planning to suggest that very thing myself today."

"Also, I've pulled some strings to send some guards to the old Tweedle house in Square Six where you thought Evelyn and Dell Tweedle were staying. I'm having them search the place for the missing prophecies. Whatever they find, they'll bring here, and we'll take them all to Dr. Divot."

"Frabjous! Two possible things done before breakfast. Well done you! And here's me just lucky I was able to roust myself from my bed this morning." She glanced at the clock and corrected herself: "Afternoon, rather." She poured herself a second cup of tea. "Have you seen your mother? Should I go and speak to her? I feel like this Radcliff issue has hit her rather hard."

He nodded. "I spoke to her a bit myself before I went to bed this morning. But it might be nice if you spoke with her, as well. I suspect it might be different coming from you."

"Fair enough," she said. "I shall. And what exactly is to become of Radcliff?"

"Well, Pennwell's got him in his sights now, so that's one way to keep an eye on him for current and future shenanigans. I haven't really thought through the rest."

"And how do you feel about what transpired? Are *you* all right?" Mary Ann asked, for no one had asked and she imagined being fully-blamed for his brother's outrageous tactics in front of everyone in Red Turvy wasn't easy to hear. Or fair.

"I am not precisely all right, and I am angry," Rufus said. "And I would prefer not to talk about it right now over such a pleasant breakfast, after such a long, eventful yesterday."

Mary Ann could respect that. She nodded and went back to her tea.

After breakfast, Mary Ann looked all over the Manor for Lady Carmine but ultimately found her in the library, a location she probably should have checked sooner.

"<u>The Count of Outgrabing Wabe</u>," Mary Ann said, reading the title of the book in the Lady's hand. "I confess, I haven't read it."

"I cannot recommend it," said Lady Carmine. "Not anymore, certainly. I fear I am as ill-equipped as a governess as I am a mother." And she wiped away a tear, which Mary Ann could see was likely not the first of its kind this day. She was well-read and, well, red—and puffy, too.

"About that," said Mary Ann. "That's why I came to talk to you. Because I feel like now is probably the right time to tell you about my own mother."

"I recall some story about her being seamstress to the Red Queen, is that correct?" said Lady Carmine. "Or was that a fever dream from when I was under the weather?"

Mary Ann was a little embarrassed to think the Baroness retained that tale. "That was a lie, I'm afraid. All lies. And I am so sorry to have done it."

Lady Carmine offered a wan smile. "My sweet girl, there are no worries here; I knew it was a lie from the moment you began."

Mary Ann's jaw dropped on its hinges. "And you let me go on like that?"

"It was fairly obvious you needed the tale as much as I did that day," she said. "I was not certain at the time just why."

"All right, so you know that I am a liar." Mary Ann took a deep breath. "But perhaps you don't know that you have already met my mother. She is Clarissa Snow, a pawn of White Turvy. You met her at Queen Valentina's Unbirthday party. You watched a croquet match together."

It was clear from her expression that this, she did not already know. Mary Ann could see her trying to picture that day in her mind. "Oh yes. I know who you mean. I vaguely recall she'd talked about marrying an artist. An...oh, dear me!" Her hands flew to her face. "Rowan Carpenter! I wasn't even thinking of it associated with you, for you were 'Tamsin' at the time, weren't you? And there was something before we left for that match, wasn't there? Some very odd, uncomfortable exchange with you about..." The breath was short and sharp and inward now. "She said there was nothing detaining her when she moved to White Turvy. Just minor bumps in the road or some such thing."

"Yes," said Mary Ann. "She left when I was two years old, an inconsequential bump in her journey. Rufus is aware of who she is and what happened. I told him some days ago." Mary Ann slipped the book from the Baroness' hands. "But the point is, Lady Carmine, that you have been a better, kinder mother to me in the short time we've had together than I have ever had. Even as a housemaid, when there was no reason for it besides my being the hired help, you were gentle with me, understanding and interested. You saw me when many did not. We do the best we can with what we bring to our lives at a particular time. You have one son who, I think, turned out quite well in the long run, and he surely does love you. You have not failed. You didn't fail Rufus and you didn't fail me. And I imagine there are several former students of yours out there who would say the very same thing. This book—it is not a primer for success." And Mary Ann tossed it over her shoulder, half-expecting it, in true Wanderlands style, to flap about and make for an open window.

But either it couldn't manage it or maybe it wasn't in the mood, for at this moment, it just hit the floor and laid there, for all the world like a flat, uninspired, wholly-non-magical thing. Which everyone in Turvy knew, books never really were. Lady

Carmine must have expected grand things from the tome, too, for they both looked at it a moment and then they started laughing.

Mary Ann picked it up quickly and stuffed it back on the shelf, so whichever maid cleaned the library didn't have to refile it.

And when she rose, Lady Carmine hugged her, warm and loving and a bit bony. "Mary Ann, I am very much enjoying getting to know the real you. I'm grateful I've had the opportunity."

That was the only real magic Mary Ann could have wanted at this moment.

24

With Dell Tweedle safely in custody at King Garnet's and
Queen Rosamund's castle in Square One, the real Damian
Tweedle was free to return home to his cottage. He was feeling
much better now after some appropriate rest, a few good
meals, and a replenishment of his fluids, so Mary Ann and
Rufus walked him home. It wasn't specifically necessary, Mary
Ann knew, as D.M. Tweedle was quite strong enough to make
the journey himself now. But it felt right to keep him company
along the way, and it was nice to see the brothers reunite with
hugs and arm-punches.

"You actually thought Dell was me, did you?" Damian asked
Dorian.

Dorian said, "Oh, he did a very fine You, at times. I'll not
deny it. Better than you do You, intermittent-like, I'll wager."

Damian frowned. "How was he a better me than Me? I'm
the originationist of that act."

Dorian shrugged. "Just in a general sorta way, I'd say. More
likabler. Less yappish. Only, he's much more awfuler than you
are on the regular. So still I'd prefers you as You, over him
being Him. Maybe you could learns to replicate him acting like

You. And that would be the best of everything, what with you actually being You and not him."

It was about here that Mary Ann and Rufus decided things had been set to rights and left.

By the time they got back to Carmine Manor, they had two rocking-horseflies. One was from Dr. Delphina Divot, welcoming them to bring her any prophecy poems to analyze. And the other was from the guards in Square Six, who had combed the Tweedles' childhood home and did, indeed, find the documents Mary Ann and Rufus sought. They said they were sending a messenger with the parchments right away, as they were far too large, important and fragile to roll up and strap to even the most determined insect.

"And what do we do now?" asked Mary Ann, for she disliked being in stasis mode when there were still so many loose ends to wrap up. It made her fidgety.

"The only thing we can do right now; we wait. So," Rufus clapped his hands together, "what do you say to a quick game of croquet?"

"Hello, croquet?" She'd watched the Duchess play a few times, but she'd never gotten to play herself. It looked fun, and she thought it might channel some of the nervous energy she was feeling. She followed him from the room.

She had expected they'd go downstairs and outside to one of the lawns, but where they ended up was at the door to Rufus' bedchamber. She laughed. "Hold on now, Rufus. I know we're engaged and all, but is 'croquet' some euphemism I'm supposed to recognize?"

"I hadn't meant it to be," he said, laughing, too, and his face had reddened clear to the roots of his hair. "No, this is so frabjous—look…" And he strode through to the far end of the room and opened the double-doors to the balcony. From her previous housemaid's position, she'd known there was a balcony and possibly a sitting area out there; what she had not known was there was a mini croquet green. It was a lovely little place, with topiary trees, red roses climbing up the mossy brick walls and a staircase leading to the roof. The flamingos and hedgehogs seemed quite content out there, and the whole space was so idyllic, it seemed almost a shame to wrangle the creatures into a game.

Another thing Rufus had been truthful about was his potential as a croquet player. His flamingo seemed to understand him well, and his aim was precise. Mary Ann's own flamingo was all flapping wings and bending legs, so just trying to maneuver it into any sensible position was a challenge, let alone getting any accuracy on the swing. "I think you gave me a dodgy flamingo," she said, mostly kidding. But he swapped her his waterfowl for hers, and even then, in no time he and the new bird were three points up, while she gained nothing but a webbed foot in her face.

"It's because of your grip and your stance. You're stressing out your bird," he said.

"Well, I *am* stressed out," she told him. "How do I stand then?"

And he was trying to show her the right way to hold it, when the footman arrived at the balcony door announcing Mr. March.

Upon laying eyes on them, the messenger extended both his hands to them in delight. "Well, if it isn't the scroll people from before! Do you remember me? Your old friend Haigha?"

"Er, yes, Mr. March," said Mary Ann. "I hope you've been well."

"As well as water and as right as rain! Tanks for asking!"

Rufus, who normally liked a good pun, clearly wasn't in pun-appreciation mode. He cut to the chase: "You have some documents for us?"

"Do I?" The hare blinked.

"In your satchel, perhaps?" he prompted, pointing.

And the hare looked where Rufus indicated, like he'd never seen that messenger bag before. Curiously, he dug into it. "So I do!" And he withdrew a folder. "How clever of you to have thought of it!"

"Oh yes, such genius," muttered Rufus, freeing his flamingo in favor of the folder.

Mary Ann's heart began to pick up pace. What contents would this folder hold? She could feel the tension radiating off Rufus, as well. He moved inside and placed the folder on the bed, then opened it.

A quick read of the top document, and they shut the folder again.

"We definitely need to bring this to Dr. Divot," said Mary Ann.

"Double-quick," Rufus said.

"It appears what we have here are not, in fact, prophecy poems at all," began Dr. Delphina Divot, as she assessed the documents. She was using a tool in the shape of a large human finger to turn the pages so her claws would not damage them. "What it appears to be is Sir Loral Clew's confession."

That was precisely what Mary Ann had thought, from her quick glance at the first page in the folder.

Divot read aloud: "'I claimed it was my extreme madness that let me conjure the prophecies I shared. Because that is the society in which we live here in the Wanderlands: one of random change, mad coping, and blithe acceptance. I felt it was the best way I could spread the information I gained, which I began to recognize as important to our people.'

"'But I have not been entirely forthright.'

"'I play-acted the need to steal stockings off washing lines and mold the hats of mud. I did the things required to make my position as a grand lunatic more believable, so it allowed me continued acceptance in our society. I did this because I am a coward who is now, and has always been, sane. At least, I am sane by Turvian standards, which I now mistrust as being relative.'

"'The truth is: the prophecies I have shared are not gifts of the ultimate madness. I am no prognosticator. I am no prophet. I am not full of magic and ideas. I have been but a simple scribe.'

"'I believe my mind is connected, in some unfortunate way, to the Gamesmaster of our world, a very real creator and revisionist in some other universe who affects us all, causing our lives to be less buffeted and less random than we know. We have always attributed the fluid changes to our land, space, and time as simple idiosyncrasies—inexplicable random phenomena in the fabric of existence that we must patiently work around. And some of that may yet be true. But with every prophecy poem that came to pass, each piece transcribed by my pen into our world, I have seen us affected by this Gamesmaster. I believe we operate as an extension of his experience — sometimes delayed, sometimes distorted — all across the Wanderlands. He toys, rethinks and revises, and our scenery, too, shifts beneath our feet. I have seen it too many times.'

"'And now I must admit, over the years, I have copied down far more than poems, though poems are what I shared with the world. I also wrote down games, puzzles and mathematics equations, of which I have no personal understanding. I copied down mundane lists of tasks that were not mine to do, for endeavors in an existence I do not comprehend. I wrote down weather reports for places with names I did not know, and bits of letters of regard to people whom I had no personal connection.'

"'Taking these fragments into account over these years, I gained insight into the unique being who appears to be physically affecting our world. I believe it bears emphasis that many of these elements are not lofty things, ideas bigger than us, grand secrets of the universe with philosophical impact as one might expect from a grand Creator. They are quite everyday and usually very boring. How often I would have preferred being left to my own thoughts over feeling compelled to copy flashes of a diary entry about someone's elderly uncle's health problems. But this is our Gamesmaster and we must take the dull along with the dreamy.'

"'For what purpose this has happened, I do not fully ken. And it begs the question: what does this say of us, if we are the game pieces of a distant being who not only toys with our world, but pens diary entries and to-dos? Dare we ask the question aloud? This realization has caused me great emotional distress, and I have endured it silently for too many years.'

"'But now that I am no longer physically well—I have come down with a coughing disease—this becomes the time to share the full truth of my experience. I am sorry to have misled anyone with the information I have shared. Everything I brought to light was right and true as I know it. But I made a sin of omission for which I realize I must now pay. To King Marbel and Queen Di, I am sharing this letter along with all the notes I have taken, in my quest to make restitution for my personal failings, my weakness of character. I wish I had been stronger to share it all as it came to me. I hope our realms are strong enough to bear the results. — Sir Loral Clew.'"

"The other pages," Dr. Divot said, turning through several of the documents, "appear to be all his notes. And they're random snippets of ideas and lists and names, equations and wordplay, and weather and diary entries, just as he said."

"And this is what Evelyn Rookwood and Dell Tweedle were trying to keep from the public," said Mary Ann.

"It's certainly problematic," said Rufus. "It puts a rather different spin on, well, everything here, really."

Delphina Divot said, "We have gotten used to the disruption and madness of life here. But the idea of one Gamesmaster imprinting on our lives in this way—one with an everyday existence much as we have — is humbling." She set down the large page-turning finger on the table. "And I think that's why these pages were hidden so long."

"Who do you think hid them?" Mary Ann asked. "It couldn't have been Sir Loral Clew. He said he was giving the pages to the King and Queen."

"This is scribes' calligraphy at the bottom of some of these pages, giving locations of the next section of Clew's notes. I'd be willing to bet the Royal family of the time hid the information away, thinking some descendant of theirs might be able to better handle the situation, if the notes were found."

Rufus said, "So, basically, they were hoping to just kick it down the road and let someone else deal with it."

"Succinctly put, Sir," said Dr. Divot.

Mary Ann asked, "What exactly was the information hidden in the King's belt buckle?"

She flipped a few pages and came to one that had many creases and a few tears now. "'April 2, 1872: Went up to London at 2, and left my luggage at the Great Northern Hotel. Then to Onslow Square where I arranged to dine with Uncle Skeffington… who has had another attack of erysipelas, but seems in very good health and spirits.'"

"So… not prophecies about meals then," said Mary Ann.

"Er, no," said Dr. Divot.

"The King will be disappointed. What are the next steps?" Mary Ann asked. "From an archaeological perspective?"

"These pages all need to be authenticated," said the tove, "but based on what I'm seeing — the paper and the shades of inks used—they do seem to be consistent with the timeframe of the early formation of Turvy as an official realm. I suppose what is done from there is now up to you."

Rufus said, "It's up to King Garnet and Queen Rosamund, as far as I'm concerned. It's bigger than all of us. A lot bigger."

King Garnet and Queen Rosamund listened to the update from Mary Ann and Rufus with solemn faces and it was not more than a moment before they were all headed to the holding rooms — the Queen, far less than a moment, at a rather remarkable run — to address the issue before Dell Tweedle and Evelyn Rookwood.

It was in the lower level of the castle, a cool, grey stone space, with low ceilings and arched doors. By the time Mary Ann, Rufus and the King had gotten there, Rookwood and Tweedle had been moved to an interrogation room and the Queen was already down to business, and not the littlest bit out of breath.

"We are now in possession of all the documents you collected of Sir Loral Clew's," said Queen Rosamund. "An expert is currently examining them for authenticity. However, their contents have been reviewed. Now, we would like to hear why you withheld this information from the Crown."

"We were concerned about the content's impact on the realm, Your Majesty," said Dell Tweedle. "We believed the information to be highly controversial, if not openly inflammatory, and possible heresy."

"And is that not a decision that the King and I should make for the realm?"

Evelyn said, "We wanted to gather all the information first, and then present it to you, so you could make a full and most informed decision, Your Majesty."

"Er, yes. Absolutely our plan all along," said Tweedle.

The Queen said, "So rather than bring it our attention when the first piece of information was uncovered, you went on an independent campaign of thievery, kidnapping and destruction. You chose to gather all the pieces and then, possibly, share it with us afterwards? Including stealing my very own scepter and mugging the King?"

"Well," said Dell Tweedle, "when you put it that way it does sound a *bit* daft…" He tugged at the collar of his shirt.

"We were overcome by the importance of the information, Your Majesty," said Evelyn. "It was the archaeological and scholarly find of the century! We lost our minds over it. We felt we couldn't risk the chance that you would curtail our efforts. We needed to see all that there was, and we couldn't let anything stop us, not even you, and—"

Tweedle elbowed her. "*Ixnay on the onfessioncay.*"

"*Insanityay efenseday,*" she whispered.

"*Iay eakspay Igpay Urviantay uenthyflay,*" said Queen Rosamund firmly. "In fact, Pig Turvian was one of my A-levels. Besides, you cannot call an insanity defense here in Turvy or everyone in the entire realm would get off scot-free for every misdeed. That's no way to run a civilized society, even a mad one."

Mary Ann said, "So was the note in the belt buckle the last of it, or is there more out there?"

"We believe that marks the end of it," said Dell Tweedle. "But we didn't get to look at that last piece, did we? Because Sir Freckles McJabberwock-Stabby here confiscated the belt from us first." And he gave a haughty look to Rufus over the interrogation table.

"I have heard enough," said the Queen, rising. And when the Queen rose, everyone else rose with her. "You will hear more from me anon." She turned to the guards. "Take them back to their holding cells!"

"What do you plan to do about the Loral Clew information, Your Majesty?" Evelyn asked, as the guard seized her by the wings.

"That is for me to know and you to find out," she said.

"Meaning, she hasn't figured it out yet," said Tweedle.

"No talking! Another peep out of you, sir, and you'll be writing, 'I shall not backtalk the Queen' on a chalkboard one million times or until your trial date, whichever comes first."

25

"What *do* you think will happen to Dell and Evelyn?" Mary Ann asked finally, as she and Rufus arrived back at Carmine Manor's stable. It had been a long, quiet ride home, for there had been a lot to think about and even Goodspeed had known better than to break the weighty silence.

Mary Ann dismounted from Edgar, gave him a loving pat, and led him to his favorite stall.

"I don't know exactly," said Rufus, doing the same for Goodspeed, minus the pat. "It was poor judgement, certainly, and mad tactics, but not necessarily done for the worst reasons. I'm sure the King and Queen will give it the consideration it deserves."

"And the information?" said Mary Ann. "That we're all living some strange, evolving reflection of some person's ideas in an alternate realm that Sir Loral Clew happened to tap into ages ago?" She shook her head, as it was hard to wrap the brain around. Mere clairvoyance suddenly seemed so straightforward now. "If they let them out, those papers will be studied for centuries. Philosophies will be built around them. Religions, perhaps."

"Undoubtedly," said Rufus, unbuckling the saddle.

"And if the King and Queen don't choose to release the information, the Wanderlands will never know. Except for a handful of us who saw the pages." Mary Ann hung up the bridle.

"Do you wish you didn't know at all?" asked Rufus.

"I wish I could go over all the pages myself," she said. "Knowing but not reading it all with my own eyeballs seems somehow inadequate. It prevents me from absorbing the truth in any real fashion. I almost understand how Dell and Evelyn felt; once you know a part, you must know all. What about you? What are your thoughts?"

"The one thing that's consistent in Turvy is change," said Rufus. "Philosophically, I am not much bothered by it. A prophecy poem is a prophecy poem, and it must be handled either way. We are only trading one set of mad ideas for another. Ultimately, those will change, too, and then —" Someone had entered the stable. "Ah, Russell, is that you? Could you brush down Goodspeed and Edgar, please?"

But it was not the squire, Russell. It was Radcliff Carmine. His black beard had gone, though a little glue residue remained along one side of his jaw. His hair had been washed of whatever blackening had been used, and now it was a light orange with a vague smoky tint. He was not at all mysterious or formidable in the light of day. He was a stocky ginger boy with an attractive face, wearing a nice, if wrinkled, suit.

"What do you want?" Rufus eyed him. "I believe quite enough was said already."

"You had that reporter friend of yours write most terrible things about me in this morning's *Turvy Mirror*," he said. "Of course, I'm sure you already know that."

"He is no friend of mine. What Pennwell writes is of his own accord. And I haven't had time for the papers today. I've had other things to deal with."

Radcliff laughed. "Typical. You have not changed in three years. There is always some other thing that takes precedence, and it never does end."

"Admittedly, it has felt like that lately," said Rufus.

"Lately?" Radcliff let out a mirthless laugh. "What about knight training? Or lessons to learn? Or prophecy research? You've always been so self-consumed, you don't think how it affects others."

Rufus frowned. "So this really is all about you wanting more attention?"

Radcliff sniffed. "Hardly! It's about making you see what is actually due me."

"All right, then," said Rufus. "Perhaps I have not been listening properly. Perhaps I have not been fair. So, fine. Here's your chance. Make me understand." And he folded his arms and leaned against one of the stable doors.

Cliff seemed surprised by this, his clear oval face going blank for a moment. Then he took a deep breath. "Well, unlike you, I never got a plan. You had plan, from the very beginning. Those two prophecy poems laid it all out for you. Your occupation, your supposed heroism, your success. And then, being firstborn, that was all laid out for you, too. Who inherits the Barony? You do, the firstborn child! But nobody thinks about the younger son, do they? No plan for Radcliff! I was left to my own devices. I could have been a knight, too. I'd have been a great knight. But no one got me involved in it until I was too old to start."

"Father supported you when you said you wanted to be a knight. You just didn't want to be a page first."

"A twelve-year-old does not do a six-year-old's job. That's shameful," he said. "And I am the one speaking now. Do you plan to listen?"

Rufus waved a hand. "Continue."

"So, no knighthood for Cliff! Then I thought I'd try my hand at professional croquet…"

Mary Ann had a feeling she knew where he'd gotten that idea.

"… And I joined a youth croquet club. But did I get support for that? No! Mother only went to three of my matches, and Father didn't go at all."

"You were only in it for, what, four weeks," said Rufus. "Then you quit because you weren't getting enough greens time."

"That's not the point!" Cliff said. "The point is, when you were being knighted—early, no less, *of course!*—and then Father turned down my idea about being the next Lord Carmine, that is when I knew: I had to go where no one knew you were my brother. The only way to find success was to let people see me for myself."

Mary Ann asked, "So what did you do to support yourself for three years? Rufus said your family tried to find you but had no luck."

"I wasn't using my own name, you see," Cliff said with a smile and a wink.

"You weren't Lex Talionis all that time, were you?" asked Rufus.

"Oh no," he said. "I was Bolton Cracknabbitt."

Rufus frowned. "The croquet player for the Red Turvy Hog Hoopers?"

"I spelt it differently," Cliff said. "I added an extra 't'." He looked really pleased with himself over this innovation. "And as for supporting myself, I took jobs that I thought might suit my talents. I started out as a poet for hire. You know, to write love greetings and special announcements for people? But everyone wanted poems with rhyme and meter, and that cheap, popular tripe was simply not my artistic style. So, it ended up not being as lucrative as one might think."

"Imagine, less lucrative than that..." murmured Rufus.

"Then I decided to be a novelist. But it turns out—and you may not know this—it takes quite a long time to write a novel. Soon I was running out of the money I'd brought with me, and I had to take what position I could get. I became a hat salesman, a carriage driver, bookseller, flamingo wrangler, florist, hedgehog stylist, and a governor." He ticked off all these things on his fingers.

"Governor?" Mary Ann asked. "You got into politics?"

"No, I was a male governess for a week. Didn't suit me, though. Sticky and noisy. Plus, did you know? It's a twenty-four-hour job. Having personal time is very important to me."

"Ah," said Mary Ann.

He continued, "Well, it was throughout all this, it occurred to me what I really needed to do. And that's when I hatched the Count Talionis plan. But that was only part of it. I said to myself, 'Radcliff,' for it was an important discussion and I thought I should be formal, 'Radcliff, we must bide our time, and we'll just see who wins the final round: Rufus or the Jabberwock?' Because, no offense, dear brother, but if it were the Jabberwock, then the question of who'd inherit the Barony would suddenly become quite clear-cut and I could return home, and all rifts mended. But then, I read you'd triumphed against the Jabberwock, too—of course! another frabjous win for Sir Rufus!—so I had to go all-in on my Talionis plan, after all. And now we are here."

Rufus said, "You were hoping I'd snuff it by Jabberwock, so you could inherit the Barony?"

"Not 'hoping,'" he said, scratching at the glue still on his face. "Just… noting my viable options."

Rufus said, "You do realize this is not helping you build bridges here."

"I'm only being honest. That's what you wanted, isn't it?"

Rufus grumbled.

Mary Ann said, "And what if you did get to be the next Lord Carmine, Radcliff? What does that mean to you?"

"Why, what does it mean to anyone?" His eyes gained a wistful look. "Respect. Land. Connections. Support. A future. People looking to me for insight. It all comes with the title."

Mary Ann raised an eyebrow. "A position where people have to respect you, simply because that's the way things work?"

"Why not? Ask Rufus. That's what he got."

"That is not what Rufus got," said Mary Ann, and her voice came out a bit louder than expected. "Rufus was preparing for his prophecy since he was a small child. And trying hard to learn enough sword techniques so he would not be killed before he was 22. Did you know Rufus never thought he was going to survive? That he hadn't made any plans for his future at all, beyond that day? That he thought if only he prepared just a *little bit* harder, he *might* have a chance? That is what he was doing when you were feeling forgotten. Tell him, Rufus."

"Um, well … yes. That."

"Did you know that your father stole Rufus' sense of humor weeks before the Jabberwock battle? That he was trying to restore your sane uncle to proper madness? And that your brother spent the time leading up to that day humorless, deeply depressed, and going through the motions only because of a sense of duty to this realm? Tell him about that, too, Rufus."

"Er, well … that did occur, yes … Maybe I wouldn't put it in those words, but …"

"I am sorry for you, Radcliff, because yes, perhaps you did get lost in the shuffle a bit. Perhaps your family, no matter how well-meaning, could not give you all the time you required." She noticed the expression on the young man's face soften a bit. "It is a shame, because every child deserves that, and it sounds like you may have needed more than you got. But you also never learned that mastery of anything comes with a certain amount of effort; you seem to have missed that lesson, in particular.

"It is a pity that things transpired the way they did, and I do feel for you. It's a form of grief to carry that void forward and I understand it, because I've had to work through it myself, in some ways. But please realize: sometimes people also endure much quietly on their own, and it only looks easy and enviable on the outside. You feel your injustices profoundly, and that should not be discounted. But it's equally key to understand: yours is not the only pain. So, talk to your brother, Cliff. And maybe listen, as well." And Mary Ann left the stable.

Mary Ann's housemaid's sense of discretion suggested, having said far more than she ever intended, she should make herself scarce now, while the family hashed out the rest of the drama that evening. So it was a swift and silent exit back to the cottage for her.

She was just pondering the situation and simmering a simple soup when Rufus showed up at the door looking very grave. She said, "Oh dear. Things went that well with your brother, eh? Come in."

"Actually, I came because I was surprised to find you'd left. Is something wrong? I thought you'd stay for dinner."

"Ah, but I was not *invited* to dinner, was I?" she said with a grin. "But *you* are invited to dinner. Would you like some dinner? I've plenty of soup."

"All right," he said. "I'll set the table." And, as her bowls were in plain sight on the shelf, he began to do just that. "As for things with Radcliff, they are ..." He shrugged. "I don't know. Maybe a little better. After your verbal flogging, he didn't know which way was up. But we'll see where it turns from here. Am I wrong for not liking my own brother much? It feels wrong, but each time I speak with him, I'm reminded of it anew."

"Well, he's not shown you a great deal to love of late, I'm afraid."

"What's worse, I've inadvertently helped craft this monster. I *have* been self-centered and single-minded. He's not wrong about that. And now his resentment, grievance and sense of inequity have formed a Jabberwock all their own."

"I think, as usual, you are taking too much of a burden upon yourself. It's not up to you to slay everyone's monsters for them." Mary Ann spooned some soup into their bowls. "I'm afraid I only have water to offer you."

"Wine from Erstwhile? Who could refuse?"

She poured two glasses from a pitcher.

He said, "My parents are still trying to figure out how to handle the situation. But for now, Cliff is at Mulberry Manor and there he shall remain. Which is tolerable to him, mainly because he's let the castle for the month, and he wants his money's worth."

"So, it's a Cliff-hanger, then." Mary Ann smirked

"Har," he said, then pointed to the soup. "This is very good, by the way."

"I do all right," she said, and sampled it. He was correct; it wasn't a bad soup.

"And now I have a question for you," he said.

"Ah, but you can only propose once. No do overs. Sorry."

"A related question," he said. "When we get married, would you prefer to live here or at Carmine Manor?"

Mary Ann could only imagine what kind of facial expression she made at this. The idea that Sir Rufus Carmine, the future Baron, would agree to live in this remote and spare cottage with her seemed patently absurd. Great gryphons, even *she* had terrible mixed feelings about the place, she could hardly envision dragging him into that day-after-day. Even with its frustrations and foibles, Carmine Manor was a haven of roses and sunshine by comparison. Yet Rufus seemed quite sincere; she couldn't imagine what he was thinking. "I would never consider uprooting you from Carmine Manor. There is no question."

He nodded—"Fair enough."—and set down his spoon. "So, what if you had the option to come live at the Manor now? Tonight? Or tomorrow? The yellow guest room could just be yours. Or a different room, if you prefer. That way, all your dinner invitations would be implicit, since I'm apparently rubbish about remembering to ask."

Mary Ann laughed. "You do know most people don't just move their fiancées straight into their family home. Even if it is the yellow guest room. How is that going to go over?"

"Mother was the one who suggested it," said Rufus, with a one-shouldered shrug. "She's concerned about you out here in the woods with the Bandersnatches and Jubjubs; and *yes*, before you say it, this is despite your extensive knight training. She insists she would worry about me in the same fashion." He chuckled. "She also thinks it's ridiculous the amount of back-and-forth we've been doing between your place and ours throughout this case. And that is a valid point, I think."

"Your mother is worried about *me*." Mary Ann felt compelled to say it aloud.

"I suspect she's realized she gets a daughter out of this, which is something she's always wanted. And, therefore, I should warn you; if you do choose to move in with us now, be prepared for things like her checking on you. Or being concerned you're not getting enough rest. Or worried you'll need a heavier cloak. You might find it most intrusive." He smiled.

Mary Ann used a dinner napkin to dab at the cursed moisture that was suddenly pooling in her eyes. "Or I might love every moment of it," she murmured.

"Or that. She is very good at what she does," he said. "Despite Radcliff's views."

They finished supper, dealt with the dishes, and it took Mary Ann virtually no time to pack. "This is all highly irregular," she said at least once on their way there.

"'Highly irregular' usually means it's one of my better decisions," he told her. "I'd embrace it."

She embraced him instead.

But Rufus had apparently not been kidding about Lady Carmine's concern for her. When Mary Ann arrived, she was welcomed with such warmth and care, she needed to spend a half hour in the guest room by herself afterwards, just to let all the many complicated feelings about it run out of her eyes. It would be too hard to explain why such a good thing caused her to weep so, as she didn't quite understand it herself. But she imagined, like everything else, she would work through it all in due time.

26

It was the next day that Delphina Divot sent a rocking-horsefly to Carmine Manor confirming the legitimacy of the Sir Loral Clew papers; she determined they appeared to be the appropriate materials for the era and that the handwriting was comparable to Sir Loral Clew's. So, Rufus and Mary Ann prepared the horses and rode to Square One, to transfer the stack of information from the professor to the King and Queen.

Once they'd been announced, which took no time at all, King Garnet and Queen Rosamund saw them right away, and accepted the materials with all the gravity the situation required.

"Sir Mary Ann and Sir Rufus, I would like to thank you for your work on this issue for our realm," said Queen Rosamund, and Mary Ann noticed her restored scepter was in hand today, a big improvement over the flyswatter. "Your time, efforts, and self-sacrifice during this investigation have not gone unnoticed. You have done a great service for the Crown, your fellow citizens, and the good name of the Red Knights. Moving forward, I would like to employ you on additional specialized cases like this. You have proven you have an ability to unify and distill information across the Squares in a way that our regular Square guards cannot seem to achieve. Also, your tact and dedication, as always, has been greatly appreciated."

"Thank you, Your Majesty," they said.

"I do hope the situation with your brother, Sir Rufus, has been resolved as successfully?"

"Regrettably, that remains a work-in-progress, Your Majesty," Rufus said with an embarrassed smile.

"It was a jolly thrilling evening, though, wasn't it?" The King's face was lively and alight. "I haven't had that much excitement at a ball since the Earl of Idiom rolled his brand-new cannon into his Joyble Day party last year and shot it off simply because it was there. Blasted a hole clean through his own ballroom wall! It was extraordinary! A pity you young people missed it!"

The Queen rolled her eyes. "This ridiculous cannon story has become his gold standard for creative merry-making. Pay him no mind." She folded her hands neatly before her. "In less explosive news, you might perhaps like to know we are sentencing Dell Tweedle and Evelyn Rookwood with a failure to properly escalate their findings to this Court. We have also added various theft charges, abduction, and impersonating a Turvian cryptid."

The King said, "We're not entirely sure what the sentence for that last one will be, having just made it up. But going round pretending to be a giant fabled crow to scare the pudding out of everyone is really beyond the pale."

Rufus said, "Thank you for the update, Your Majesties."

"Indeed, thank you." Mary Ann said. "May I ask what will be done with the Sir Loral Clew information?" She recognized it was not really her place, but she had to at least inquire.

"We have been discussing this extensively the past day," said Queen Rosamund. "We will review everything, and then we shall open it up to the King and Queen of White Turvy. As some of the material was found on their land, this is a matter affecting us all. We wish to make the best decision for the realm as a whole."

"Very wise, Your Majesty," Mary Ann said.

"Of course, we will need you to sign this document stating you will not reveal the contents of the materials to anyone prior to any release."

A servant presented them with a scroll. It had large, beautifully-written letters at the top that began:

"I, hereby, will shut my gob..."

Another servant had a tray with quill and ink.

"Just there at the bottom," said the Queen. "Full names, please. Clear penmanship. And hold the pens properly!"

Mary Ann skimmed the document, peering around Rufus' shoulder, and then they signed: "Sir Rufus Clancy Carmine" and "Sir Mary Ann Carpenter" on the bottom, next to the date.

"Excellent!" said the Queen. "Well done! Now...You can do me one last favor before you go. Would one of you check and tell me if there's a very large, very angry turnip out there in the waiting area?"

Mary Ann moved to the door and ducked her head into the sitting room. The large, angry turnip — presumably the same one they'd met before, because how many large, angry turnips registering complaints to the Court could there be, really? — was, indeed, seated by the window, scowling at the world. Mary Ann returned. "Yes, Your Majesty. It's there."

"Thank you," Queen Rosamund said. "I'll be exiting through the back today, then. You are dismissed."

҂ ❀ ҂

One might think, after putting in so much horsepower, leg power and brainpower across the Red Turvian landscape while working on the Tweedle case, adventure-minded people such as Mary Ann Carpenter and Rufus Carmine would have found the sudden quiet to be a letdown. But for the next few days, at least, they both found it refreshing that the biggest mystery they had to solve was who to invite to their upcoming engagement party and what flavor cake they wanted. (Chocolate bilberry jam: it was the only valid decision, as far as they were concerned, and they thought it very nice it was one more thing they had in common.)

Lady Carmine forewarned Mary Ann that there would be a certain number of people attending this party that had been invited solely for polite society reasons, and she apologized that it was a regrettable fact of life at the Manor. But she also asked for a list of friends Mary Ann would like to include on the guest list. So, Mary Ann thought about it, and she wrote down the names of Emmaline, Douglas Divot, Chester the Cat, Professor Cyril Goodnuff and Mrs. and Mr. Nightwing, though she was fairly certain Mr. Nightwing would remain at home before the hearth.

Lady Carmine asked about Chester the Cat's current address and Mary Ann informed her he'd no permanent address at all these days, having grown tired of the Duchess of Additch long ago. She explained the best way to get an invitation to him was to fling the envelope upon the wind and let serendipity handle the rest. And that is exactly what Lady Carmine did. They received his affirmative RSVP a day later.

And now, Mary Ann's biggest concern was more of a traditional Turvian one. In Red Turvy, it was custom to exchange time pieces with your future spouse to clinch the arrangement, the happy symbol of giving your years to the one you loved. And while Mary Ann appreciated it metaphorically, it became more difficult on the practical end of things, when your betrothed already had a fine pocket watch he preferred, and she herself had a rather small budget.

Then she remembered the mantel clock with the casing her father had built, sitting above the fireplace at the cottage. Now *that* was a worthy gift of time! Surely, one of the last unissued pieces of Rowan Carpenter's woodworking held importance, and Rufus had kindly set the clock for her when she first moved there, so it held personal meaning, as well. It was easy enough to slip out early, well before breakfast, hike to the cottage and be back before no one was the wiser.

Mary Ann was returning from the successful mission and passing by Mulberry Manor, time quite literally on her hands, when a voice said, "Don't expect me, because I won't be there." Mary Ann turned to see Cliff, who was lurking in the shrubberies at the edge of the property. He was leaning against a tree in a dramatic-casual pose reminiscent of one of those brooding consumptive poets that were so popular these days. It didn't work well, though, when you were not very tall, but you were also hale and ginger. Lanky consumptiveness was integral to the pose's overall success, thought Mary Ann. When it came to that, Cliff didn't cut it.

"Good morning, Radcliff," she said. "And what it is you won't be there for?"

"Your engagement party to my brother. I saw you head to your cottage from my window. I wanted to catch you on your way back. I won't be attending. Consider this my RSVP."

He could have just posted it, Mary Ann thought with a weary, internal sigh, but told him, "I shall pass the word along." And she turned to go.

"Wait, who invited me? Was it Mother? I bet it was Mother, trying to mend fences. Well, I won't go back, you know. Tell her I won't go back without a proper, planned role within the family."

"It was your brother," Mary Ann said. For Rufus had debated it and decided it was the mature thing to do, despite his fervent hope that Cliff had other plans.

And it was just as she moved to leave this second time, that the most unexpected idea began to spark in her mind. "You know, seeing you here now, lounging amongst the shrubbery, it occurs to me: you already *have* a proper family role!" In this brief moment, the spark had become a flame! A flare! A blaze! And now her heart picked up its pace and the words couldn't come out fast enough. "One you were simply made for, only no one saw it because you kept trying to be industrious! But it's the one role all fine families tend to fill rather quickly, yet in yours, it has been uniquely lacking."

He looked intrigued. "And that is…?"

"The Family Eccentric Dabbler!" she said. "The Quirky Layabout!" And the revelation burned such fire in her brain, she couldn't believe she hadn't thought of it sooner. "The one family member with wild, random, and fleeting interests that never go anywhere, yet no one expects they should! These key individuals are highly-valued amongst the nobility because they make the rest of the family seem less dysfunctional and more productive by comparison. They're always in the news, they're considered whimsical, and they take the pressure off everyone else. In Neath, they're an absolute must in highborn families. They get yearly allowances to do just the sort of thing you've managed naturally!"

"You're having me on," he said, but his expression was unsure.

"Oh, no!" she persisted. "In Neath, they get together and call themselves the Lotus Club and they meet weekly in various cultural locales to discuss what they're not accomplishing. I'd check into it if I were you. There may even be a Turvian branch. Or, if there isn't, perhaps you could start one."

"Oh, come now! It's some kind of joke." Radcliff was looking at her very hard in this moment. "Rufus put you up to this, didn't he?" But the fire of hope seemed to be flickering in his eyes now, too.

The truth was, Mary Ann Carpenter had never been more sincere in her life. "The Duchess of Additch's nephew is the club's vice president—or at least he was before I left Neath. Look into it. Think about it. It might just be your calling." And with that, she turned on a heel and went back to the Manor.

It took a few weeks to arrange, but now that it was here, the engagement party seemed to be going swimmingly. The only drawback was that Mary Ann was not used to this amount of attention, and certainly not from so many people at once.

She was delighted to greet Chester and her former neighbors, of course. And it was lovely that Lady Carmine let

Emmaline set her duties aside this afternoon so she could join them all for the event. But so far, Mary Ann had received well-wishes from three dozen people she'd never met before, all of whom seemed to know her: Earls and Ladies, Counts and Countesses, cousins and aunts; it was an overwhelming mix of blood and bluebloods, which left Mary Ann disoriented and socially dizzied.

The cake, which was everything she and Rufus had hoped for, was not just consumed by this crowd, but absolutely demolished. It left the couple feeling fortunate they'd secured their slices before the whole thing vanished like a dream.

And, much to their relief, Mr. Radcliff Carmine was not in attendance at all — and not in theatrical protest, either. No, after confirming Mary Ann's information about his potential professional path and spending several weeks on his arrangements, Radcliff had shifted residence to Neath. For now, he had funding in his pocket, a community of likeminded individuals ready to embrace him, meetings every Chooseday, and shiny new career goals destined never to be met.

All told, Mary Ann and Rufus were both content with the day's overall outcome, and soon enough, the partygoers reached the timepiece exchange portion of the party's festivities.

Mary Ann had spent time polishing up the mantel clock for Rufus, and then wrapped it in some paper she'd decorated herself with drawings of little red roses and swords, because she thought it might make him smile. Rufus was kind enough to note the effort that went behind this, even though her drawing skills were far from frabjous. And he seemed to appreciate the clock, as well, which he planned to display on the mantel in his bedchamber.

Mary Ann received a much-needed pocket watch of her own, a beautiful timepiece, encrusted with pearl, a thoughtful nod to their first adventure together. It came on a chain so she could wear it as a necklace if she chose. And they were just working to set the time, which was a bit fiddly, when a rocking-horsefly whirled into the room, making a short stop mid-air and letting out a tiny neigh. It said, "Sir Rufus and Sir Mary Ann? Message for you!"

Upon the scroll it carried was the Royal Red Turvian seal. "What do you think, Mary Ann? Well-wishes from the Queen?" Rufus asked, removing the scroll.

"Open it and see," she said. The Queen was such a surprising sort of person, it wasn't out of the realm of possibility that she might congratulate two of her more successful knights on an upcoming marriage. While it wasn't completely unheard of that two Red Knights found love together, it wasn't an everyday occurrence, either. But then a second, less-happy thought popped into Mary Ann's mind. "You don't think they've made a final decision about sharing the Sir Loral Clew information, do you?"

And Mary Ann noticed Rufus tense. "I suppose we'll find out," he murmured.

But it was as he broke the seal and unrolled the scroll, they saw this was not a note of felicitations, and the missive was equally mum on Sir Loral Clew. It was a single question spanning the whole of the parchment. And it read:

"REMIND ME: WHAT DO YOU KNOW
ABOUT A GIRL CALLED ALICE?"

ABOUT THE AUTHOR

Jenn Thorson is a marketing writer by day and an author by night — so sort of like Batgirl, but with less crime fighting and more carpal tunnel. She lives in Pittsburgh, PA, with two curious cats, who are also locals and not from Cheshire. Her stories have been published in the *Humor Press*, the journal for the *Lewis Carroll Society of North America*, *The Timber Creek Review* and *Romantic Homes* magazine. She has written two books in *The Curious Case of Mary Ann* series, and her humorous sci-fi book trilogy is called *There Goes the Galaxy*. They are all available at Amazon.

IF YOU ENJOYED THIS BOOK...

The Trouble with Tweedle (The Curious Case of Mary Ann, Book 2) is an independently published novel. So if you enjoyed this book, the author would be delighted if you'd tell a friend about it.

Other ways to share *The Trouble with Tweedle* with your own mad crew are:

- Review the book on **Amazon.com**.

- "Like" the Jenn Thorson author page on **Facebook**, for regular book news and author updates at: **Facebook.com/jennthorsonauthor**

- Follow the author, Jenn Thorson, on **Twitter** at **Twitter.com/Jenn_Thorson** or Instagram at: **jenn_thorson_author**

- Visit **jennthorson.com** to check out news articles and goodies related to her books